A SECRET SHARED...

BY
MARION LENNOX

FLIRTING WITH THE DOC OF HER DREAMS

BY
JANICE LYNN

Marion Lennox was a country kid, a tomboy and a maths nerd, but whenever she went missing her family guessed she'd be up a gum tree reading romance novels. Climbing trees and dreaming of romance—what's not to love? But it wasn't until she was on maternity leave from her 'sensible' career, teaching statistics to undergraduates, that she finally tried to write one.

Marion's now had over one hundred romances accepted for publication. She's given up climbing trees—they got too high! She dreams her stories while she walks her dog or paddles her kayak or pokes around rock pools at low tide. It's a tough life, but she's more than ready for the challenge.

Janice Lynn has a Masters in Nursing from Vanderbilt University, and works as a nurse practitioner in a family practice. She lives in the southern United States with her husband, their four children, their Jack Russell—appropriately named Trouble—and a lot of unnamed dust bunnies that have moved in since she started her writing career.

To find out more about Janice and her writing visit www.janicelynn.com

A SECRET SHARED…

BY
MARION LENNOX

First published in Great Britain 2014
by Mills & Boon, an imprint of Harlequin (UK) Limited,
Eton House, 18-24 Paradise Road, Richmond, Surrey, TW9 1SR

© 2014 Marion Lennox

ISBN: 978-0-263-90787-2

Harlequin (UK) Limited's policy is to use papers that are natural,
renewable and recyclable products and made from wood grown in
sustainable forests. The logging and manufacturing processes conform
to the legal environmental regulations of the country of origin.

Printed and bound in Spain
by Blackprint CPI, Barcelona

Dear Reader

Right now my family is in the midst of restoring a fisherman's cottage that's protected by so many heritage restrictions it makes my eyes water. But when bureaucracy gets the better of me I head to our local ferry, which takes me over the treacherous Rip to the entrance to Port Phillip Bay and Melbourne beyond. Why? Well, my favourite cake shop is on the other side of the Rip—though the trip does make for expensive cake! But as well as cake I get to see dolphins. If I'm lucky they'll surf in the ferry's wake, leaping in and out of the water, joyously celebrating the fact that they can beat the boat twice over. They're smart, they're funny, and I defy anyone to watch them and not forget red tape and rotting roofing iron.

So it was with interest that I read of a dolphin sanctuary in the US where traumatised kids are offered time out, swimming with these gorgeous creatures as a type of therapy. *So what if...?* I thought as I watched the dolphins surfing alongside the boat. *What if...?* are my two favourite words. They send me off on another book almost as soon as I think them. *What if* my heroine finds a way to reach wounded kids with the same dolphins that make me smile? But *what if* she's hiding secrets? *What if* she's wounded too?

My hero is truly heroic—isn't he always? But in A SECRET SHARED... Jack needs all the help he can get to win his lady and to share the secrets that guard her heart.

The dolphins are just the guys to help him!

Marion

Dedication

To Ray and Deb, with thanks for making our dream a reality.

**Praise for
Marion Lennox:**

'Marion Lennox's RESCUE AT CRADLE LAKE is simply
magical, eliciting laughter and tears in equal measure. A keeper.'
—*RT Book Reviews*

'Best of 2010: a very rewarding read. The characters are believable,
the setting is real, and the writing is terrific.'
—*Dear Author* on
CHRISTMAS WITH HER BOSS

CHAPTER ONE

'You want to save your kid with mantra-chanting and dolphins that eat *our* fish, go ahead and waste your money. Dolphin Sanctuary plays you for a sucker, and you're walking right in.'

This was exactly what Dr Jack Kincaid didn't want to hear. He glanced at the white-faced child in his passenger seat and hoped Harry wasn't listening.

The little boy's face was blank and unresponsive, but then, it always was. Harry had hardly spoken since the car crash that had killed his parents.

'The sanctuary seems to be building a good reputation,' he said, which was all he could think of to say. He didn't want to be here but he needed petrol. The pump attendant, fat, grubby and obviously bored, had wandered out to have a word.

It was no wonder he looked bored. There'd be few cars along this road. Jack was three hundred miles from Perth, heading for one of the most remote parts of Australia. Dolphin Bay.

Dolphins. Healing. He thought of the hundreds of schmaltzy, New Age healing-type posters he'd seen in his lifetime and he felt ill.

What *was* he doing here?

'So your kid's crook?' the attendant asked, and Jack

flicked the remote. The car windows slid up soundlessly, ensuring Harry couldn't hear.

Harry didn't react. He didn't seem to notice he was being cut out of the conversation. He never seemed to notice.

'He was injured in a road accident a while back,' he said. The pump was snail slow and this guy was intent on an inquisition. He might as well accept it.

'You're his dad?'

'His uncle. His parents were killed.'

'Poor little tacker,' the man said. 'But why bring him to Dolphin Bay? What's the point? You're being conned, mate. Fishing used to be good round here, but not any more. New Age hippies have even got permission to feed them, encouraging them in from the wild.'

'How long have they been using them for healing?'

'Since that Doc Kate came. Before that it was just dolphin saving. The place's full of animal do-gooders and weirdos who think meditation's more useful than facing life straight on. If you want to know what I think, the only good dolphin's a dead dolphin. If they'd only let us shoot…'

But, praise be, the fuel tank was full. Jack produced his wallet with relief. 'Keep the change.' He wanted to be out of here, fast. 'Use it for fish bait.'

'Thanks, mate,' the man said. 'But if I were you I'd book into the motel and take the kid fishing. Much better than messing with hippies.'

That was so much what Jack was thinking that he had to agree. 'I'd go fishing in a heartbeat,' he admitted. 'But I don't have a choice.'

'You look like a man who knows his own mind. What's stopping you?'

'Women,' Jack said, before he could help himself. 'Isn't that what stops us all?'

* * *

Four-year-old Toby Linkler's death was sudden, heart-breaking—and a deep and abiding blessing.

One minute Kate was watching as Toby's mother, Amy, stood in the shallows, holding her little son close. Together they'd watched Hobble, the youngest of the trained dolphins, swim around them in circles. The little boy's face, gaunt from illness, racked from months of chemotherapy, was lit from within. He'd even chuckled.

And then, as Hobble ducked underneath and almost propelled Toby out of the water with a nudge under his backside, Toby's gaze suddenly turned inward.

Kate was four feet away and she moved fast, but by the time she reached him, the little boy was gone.

Toby's mother sobbed with shock and horror, but she didn't move. The dolphin's circles grew wider, as if standing guard. How much did the creature know? Kate wondered. This moment couldn't be intruded on and it wasn't, even by the dolphins.

'He's…he's gone,' Amy sobbed at last. 'Oh, Toby. The doctors said… They said he might…'

They had. More than one doctor had predicted seizures with the possibility of sudden death. Kate had studied Toby's notes as thoroughly as she read every patient's history. Four years old. Brain tumour. Incomplete excision twelve months ago. Chemotherapy had shown some shrinkage but eventually the growth had outstripped treatment. The last note on the history said: 'If tumour maintains its present growth rate, prognosis is weeks, not months. We suggest palliative care as required. Referral back to family doctor.'

But Amy hadn't taken Toby back to her family doctor. One of the other mums in the city hospital kids' cancer ward had told her about Dolphin Bay Sanctuary's therapy programme. Kate had had to squeeze to get them in.

Thank heaven she had, she thought now, and her thoughts were indeed a prayer. Toby had spent most of the last few days ensconced in a tiny wetsuit, floating with the dolphins that had entranced him. Kate had four dolphins she'd trusted with this frail little boy and in the end all four had been allowed to play with him. They *had* played too, making him laugh, nudging his failing little body as he'd floated on water-wings, tossing balls high in the air so they'd landed near him, retrieving them themselves if he hadn't been able to.

He'd still needed painkillers, of course, and anti-seizure medication and drugs to try and stop the massive build-up of calcium leeching from the growing tumour, but for six glorious days he'd been a little boy again. He'd experienced fun and laughter, things that had had nothing to do with the illness and surgery he'd endured and endured and endured. At night he'd slept curled up with Maisie, Kate's therapy dog. With his mum by his side, he'd seemed almost joyous.

Today he'd woken quieter, pale, and his breathing had been shallow. Kate had known time was running out. In a normal hospital she might have ordered blood tests, checked the cancer wasn't sending his calcium levels through the roof, maybe even sent him for another MRI to check how large the tumour had grown, but given his history there was little point. Toby's mother had made her choice and, weak as he'd been, Toby had been clear on the one thing he'd wanted.

'I want to swim with Hobble.'

He had, and as his mother had cradled him Toby had felt the rush of the dolphin's sleek, shining skin as he'd circled.

'He's my friend,' he'd whispered.

And now he was gone.

There was nothing to be done. There was no call for

heroics here, no desperate attempt at resuscitation. There was just the searing agony of a mother losing her child.

It was gut-wrenching. Unbearable. A void never to be filled.

But: 'I'm so glad,' Amy managed to whisper, as her racking sobs finally eased, as Kate stood waist deep in the water and gave her all the time she needed, and as Toby's body settled deeper into death. 'I'm so glad I brought him here. Oh, Kate, thank you.'

'Don't thank me,' Kate said, hugging her close and drawing her gently out of the water. 'Thank my dolphins.'

'Dr Kate's running late.' The pleasant-faced woman in Reception was welcoming, but apologetic. 'I'm sorry, Harry,' she said, and Jack felt a jolt of surprise. The woman was addressing his nephew instead of him. 'This is Maisie,' she told Harry, gesturing to a great bear of a golden-haired retriever snoozing under her desk. 'Maisie, this is Harry.' She prodded Maisie with her toe and Maisie looked up in polite enquiry. *Me? You mean me?*

'Maisie,' the receptionist said sternly, as one might chide a recalcitrant employee. 'Say hello to Harry.'

The dog rolled onto her back, stretched, sighed, then lumbered up, strode across the room, sat in front of Harry—and raised a paw.

Harry stared. The dog sat patiently, paw outstretched, until finally, tentatively, Harry took it. Jack noticed, with quiet surprise, that his nephew almost managed a smile. It wasn't quite, but it was close.

'Dr Kate is in the water, doing therapy,' the receptionist told Jack as dog and boy shook hand and paw for the second time. 'She should be finishing now. Would you like to pop down to the beach? Please don't disturb them but if you stay beyond the high-water mark you're welcome to watch.'

Jack would very much like to watch. Despite Harry's instant relaxation—he was now solemnly shaking the big dog's paw for the third time—Jack's guard was still sky high.

Why was he here? His home was in Sydney. Harry's home was in Sydney. What Harry needed was continued therapy for healing leg fractures and a decent child psychiatrist who'd finally crack his wall of traumatised silence.

But he'd found Harry some very good child psychiatrists, and none of them had made a dent in his misery. This was desperation. It had been his Aunt Helen's idea, not his, but she had been prepared to relinquish Harry into Jack's care if he agreed to bring him.

Was it worth the risk?

'Would you like to go to the beach or stay here with Maisie?' the receptionist was asking Harry, and Harry looked at Maisie and nodded. This was a miracle all on its own. He'd been limp since the car crash, simply doing what the adults around him ordered. Three months ago he'd been a normal seven-year-old, maybe a little cosseted, maybe a little intense, but secure and loved and happy. Now, without his parents, he was simply...lost.

'You're sure?' Jack asked, and of course there was no response. But Harry was kneeling on the floor with the dog and the dog was edging sideways. Jack could see what she was doing. There was a ball, three feet away, and Maisie was looking at it with more than a canine hint.

Jack nudged it close and Maisie grabbed it and dropped it at Harry's feet. Then she backed two feet away, crouching, quivering and staring straight at Harry with all the concentration a golden retriever could summon.

Harry stared at Maisie. Maisie stared at Harry. The whole room held its breath.

And then Harry very tentatively picked up the well-chewed ball—and tossed it about four feet.

Maisie pounced with dramatic flourish, reaching it before it hit the floor, but she wasn't content with a simple
retrieval. She whirled three times, tossed the ball upwards herself and caught it again—and then came back
and dropped it at Harry's feet again.

And, unbelievably, Harry giggled.

'I'll buy the dog,' Jack muttered, and the receptionist
grinned.

'She's not for sale. Kate values her above diamonds.
Go and watch her if you like. Harry and Maisie are safe
with me.'

They were. Jack watched the little boy a moment longer
and felt himself relax, which was something he didn't think
he'd done once, not since his brother had died. The dog
was taking care of Harry and the relief was immeasurable.

'Go,' the receptionist said gently, and her message was
unmistakeable. *It's better if you're not here. Let these two
bond.*

She was right. Harry didn't need him; since the accident he hadn't seemed to need anyone.

If one dog could make a difference...

He'd tried a puppy; he'd tried almost everything. But
now... Whatever this crazy dolphin-mantra place was, this
dog was breaking through.

Dr Jack Kincaid didn't need to be told again.

He went.

It was time to leave the water; time for the reality of death
to hit home. As wonderful as this place was, it was simply time out. Toby was dead. His mother now had to start
facing a world without him.

Kate's arm was around Amy's waist as they made their
way from the shallows. The world was waiting. Official-
dom would move in and there was nothing Kate could do
to protect Amy from it.

But at least she'd had this time. At least the week before Toby's death hadn't been filled with hospitals, drips, rush. Her dolphins had helped.

She turned for a moment as she reached the beach; they both did. Far out in the deep water, Hobble still seemed to be watching them. He was doing sweeping curves at the outer limits of the pool. At the far reaches of each curve he leaped from the water towards them, and then dived deep, again and again.

'Thank you,' Amy whispered toward him, and who knew if the dolphin could understand. But no matter what their level of understanding, the dolphins had helped ease one little boy's passing.

Kate had more patients waiting. She needed to move on, but what had just happened had eased the pain around her own heart a little as well.

Jack walked over the ridge of sandbank just as the two women turned to walk up the beach. Two women and a child. The women were dressed in plain blue stinger suits. The child was in a wetsuit.

The child was dead.

Jack Kincaid had been a doctor long enough to sense it even as he saw it. The child was cradled in the shorter woman's arms, the woman was sobbing, and every step they took spelled defeat.

What the...?

He broke into a run. If the child had gone underwater, it might not be too late. Why wasn't anyone doing CPR? Had they tried and failed? In children there was sometimes success when all hope was lost. He had his phone out, hitting the emergency quick-dial, thinking paramedics, oxygen, help...

'Don't phone.' The taller woman's voice was a curt command, urgent enough to make him pause. The other woman was sinking to her knees, still cradling the child. 'What the hell...?'

'It's okay.'

What sort of crazy was this? He reached them and he would have knelt by the child but the woman held him back.

'I'm Dr Kate,' she said. 'I'm so sorry you had to see this but, believe me, it's okay.'

'How can it be okay?'

'Toby's had cancer,' she said, softly so as not to break into the other woman's grief. She took his arm, drawing him away a little, giving woman and child space. 'He's had brain metastases. He was terminally ill. This afternoon he's been playing with the dolphins, he had a seizure and he died. There was nothing we could do.'

'Did you try?' Jack demanded, incredulous. A seizure... He thought of all the things that could be done in a major city hospital, the drugs that could stop a seizure, the re- suscitation equipment. 'Surely...'

'Amy wanted it this way,' Kate said. 'She has the right to make a choice on behalf of her son and I think it was a good one.' She hesitated and then glanced at her watch. 'You'll be Harry's guardian,' she said. 'I'm sorry I'm run- ning late but you understand...' She gestured to woman and child. 'Some things have to take precedence. Has Maisie settled your Harry?'

Maisie...the dog. She was depending on her dog to set- tle a new patient?

But, then, Maisie *had* settled Harry, better than ever he could have.

'Yes,' he conceded, dragging his eyes away from the distraught mother and child.

'I'm glad,' she said, and she smiled.

And in that moment time stood still. What the...?

He knew this woman! He knew her very well indeed.

Dr Catherine Heineman. They'd been students together. Tutorial partners. Friends.

He hadn't seen her since...since...

'You're...Doctor Kate?' His tone was incredulous.

'I'm Kate Martin,' the woman said simply. 'Dr Kate Martin.'

'You're Cathy.'

Her face lost its colour. She stared up at him and took an instinctive step backward.

'What nonsense is this?' He'd read the blurb for the dolphin sanctuary. The healing part of it was run by one Dr Kate Martin, this woman. According to the blurb she had qualifications in physiotherapy and counselling. Deeply suspicious, he'd checked, but the qualifications had been conferred by one of the most prestigious universities in New Zealand.

That didn't fit at all with what he was seeing here now, with what he knew. This woman was in her early thirties maybe. He'd last seen Cathy in her early twenties but it didn't stop him knowing her.

'You're Cathy,' he said again, and he saw her flinch.

'I can explain.'

She'd better. Counsellor with training in psychology? Physiotherapist? Had she abandoned her medical degree and retrained in another country? Under another name? Why? Had she been struck off the medical register?

He stared at her and saw shadows. She was five feet eight or so, and a bit too thin. At university he'd thought her attractive. Very attractive. Now she looked...gaunt? Her chestnut hair was tugged into a practical knot. Her blue all-in-one stinger suit was deeply unflattering. Her green eyes, which had flashed with laughter when he'd messed up a lab trial or someone had made a joke, didn't look like they did much laughing now.

Unregistered? Hiding? Why?

Drugs? Drug-taking was the most common reason for doctors being deregistered and instinctively his gaze fell to her arms, looking for track marks. The sleeves of her stinger suit were pulled up. Her forearms were clean, but she saw where his gaze went and stepped back as if he'd struck her.

'It's not what you think. I can explain.'

'You'd better.' If he'd dragged Harry all the way across the country to have him treated by an unregistered doctor...

'I can't now.' She closed her eyes for a millisecond, that was all, but when she opened them she seemed to have recovered. The look she gave him was direct and firm. 'I need to stay with Amy and Toby. Yes, I'm Cathy but I'm also Kate. I'd ask that you keep that to yourself until you hear my explanation.' She ran her fingers wearily through her hair and the formal knot gave a little, letting a couple of chestnut tendrils escape. It made her look younger, and somehow more vulnerable. 'Could you bring your nephew and Maisie down to the beach? Build a sandcastle. Give me some time. Please?'

And then she was gone, heading back to the woman and her child, stooping to help the mother lift the lifeless body of her son. Together they carried him up the beach and away.

Jack was left staring after her.

CHAPTER TWO

HE COULDN'T BELIEVE it. Kate Martin, physiotherapist and counsellor, medical director of Dolphin Bay Healing Resort, had transformed into Cathy Heineman who'd shared his undergraduate student life.

Cathy had been his friend, and in truth he wouldn't have minded if she'd been more than that. She'd been vibrant, fun and beautiful. But she'd also been a little aloof. She hadn't talked about her private life and she'd laughed off any advances. Friendship only, she'd decreed, though sometimes he'd wondered... When they'd stayed back late, working together, he'd thought there had been this attraction. Surely it had been mutual.

But it obviously hadn't been. In fourth year she'd turned up after the summer holidays sporting a wedding ring.

'Simon and I have been planning to wed since childhood,' she'd told him, and that was pretty much all she'd said. He'd never met her husband—no one had. Neither had the student cohort seen much of Cathy after that. She'd attended lectures but the old camaraderie had gone.

She hadn't even attended graduation. 'She requested her degrees be posted to her,' he'd heard. Someone had said she'd moved to Melbourne to do her internship and that was the last he'd heard of her.

And now... His head was spinning with questions,

but overriding everything else was the knowledge that he would not expose his nephew to treatment by anyone who was dishonest.

The Cathy he'd known had been brilliant.

The Cathy he'd just seen had been helping a dead child from the water. She was in a suspect place doing suspect things, and his nephew's welfare was at stake.

Get out of here now.

His phone rang. It'd be Helen, he thought. The road here had been almost completely lacking phone reception. There was only the faintest of signals now. Helen wouldn't have been able to ring him for hours. She'd be frantic.

'Where are you?' Her tone was accusatory.

'I'm at the dolphin sanctuary, of course.'

Helen's breath exhaled in a rush. 'You made it? Is it good? Oh, Jack, will it make a difference?'

'So far I've seen a dead child and a doctor who's not who she says she is,' he said bluntly. 'Helen, do you remember Cathy Heineman? She was a med student with Don and me. She faded from the social scene after fourth year. Remember?'

'The clever one you did your lab work with,' Helen said. Helen had five children under ten. She was still mourning her brother's death, but her mind was like a steel trap. She'd done dentistry while her brother, Arthur, had done medicine with Jack. Arthur and Jack had been mates, and in turn Helen had become best friends with Jack's sister, Beth. Arthur and Beth had married, bringing them even closer. They'd all been at university together and they knew each other's friends.

So she knew Cathy. Kate.

'The whisper was that the guy she married was possessive,' she said, turning obligingly thoughtful. 'He wouldn't let her out of his sight. No one saw much of her after her wedding and not at all after we graduated.'

'She's here. She's practising as a physiotherapist and counsellor. The whole place smells fishy.'

'Well, it is a dolphin sanctuary.'

'Helen...'

'Look, you promised to give it a go,' Helen said bluntly. 'Kate, Cathy, who gives a toss what she calls herself if it has a chance of working? You know I'd be there with him myself but I'd have had to bring the babies with me.'

She would. That was what this whole disaster was about. Helen was an earth mother, parent of five noisy, exuberant children, generous to a fault. She and her amiable husband had been more than ready to take their newly orphaned nephew into their expanding brood.

It had seemed the perfect solution. Helen was Harry's aunt, she loved him to bits, she was married and stable and able to take care of him.

Jack was Harry's uncle but he was single. He was a rising star in his chosen field of oncology, he had little intention of settling down, and there was no reason that he should take on his seven-year-old nephew.

Except...

Except that one wounded little boy had been failing to thrive within Helen's noisy throng. Harry had always been quiet and a little introspective, and the loss of his parents, plus the shocking injuries to his leg, had seen him withdraw into himself.

The last time Jack had gone to see him he'd refused to come out of the bedroom he'd been sharing with one of his cousins. Helen had shown him literature on this place. 'It can't do any harm,' she'd told him. 'I'll farm the three eldest out and the babies can come with us. Doug won't mind, will you, darling?' She'd smiled fondly at her long-suffering husband. 'We do what we must for each of our children and Harry's the same.'

Only Harry wasn't the same. Jack had watched him

that night, pushing his food from side to side on his plate, mentally absent from the noise and jostling about him, and he'd made a decision.

'Let me take care of him for a while. I'll take a few weeks off work. Maybe he'll be happier with me.'

Afterwards he hadn't been able to believe he'd said it. He knew nothing about children—zip. His current girlfriend, Annalise, had been appalled.'

'Well, don't expect me to help. Children and me... Darling, I'm a radiologist, not a childminder.

He was an oncologist, not a childminder either, but for the last two weeks he'd been doing his best.

But not getting through.

'But you will take him to this place,' Helen had decreed, flourishing the literature at him. 'I swear, Jack, it sounds just what he needs.'

'He needs time, not quackery.'

'If you don't take him, I will. Jack, I'll fight you for this. I should make the decisions. You're not capable of caring for him and I am.'

And there it was, out in the open. They were joint guardians. On the surface they had equal claims to guardianship, but Helen had the home, the experience, the love.

He should stand aside and leave her to it. Only Harry's desolation prevented it.

Taking him to the dolphin sanctuary had been a test, he thought. Helen—and others—wanted proof he was serious about this parenting role.

The problem was that he wasn't sure that he was serious about parenting himself, especially as he'd been sole carer for two weeks now and made not one dint in the little boy's misery.

Until this afternoon, when one bear of a dog had made Harry giggle.

'I'll find out about Cathy,' Helen offered, speaking

urgently now. 'I'll make enquiries. But unless it's really awful, you should still give the place a chance.'

'I told you, Helen, I've been here half an hour and already there's a child dead.'

'There must be a reason.'

'A brain tumour,' he conceded.

'They do palliative care work as well. You'd expect—'

'I'd expect resuscitation efforts on a four-year-old.'

'Give it more than half an hour,' Helen said urgently. 'It's taken me all the contacts we have and then some to get him into the place. Believe it or not, there's a queue months long. Don't you dare walk away.'

'And if it's dangerous?'

'You stay with him all the time. Bond. This is what you wanted, Jack. Now's the time to step up to the mark.'

And he knew it was.

Kate did what she could for Amy and for her little son. Amy's mother and sister had spent the last week here as well. Other arms enfolded the distraught mother, freeing Kate to leave her in their care. In the end she backed out unnoticed, as grandmother, mother and aunt collectively said goodbye to their little boy.

She put herself on autopilot for a while, filling in forms, phoning the coroner, clearing the way for funeral directors to fly Toby and his family directly back to Queensland, where they'd lived. She headed back to her bungalow and showered. Then she stood on her veranda and stared out to sea for a while, trying to get Toby's death in perspective. Impossible, but she had to try, just like she always did. Other children needed her. Somehow she'd learned to move on.

She'd learned to move on from a lot, she conceded, and part of that was her history. And her history included Jack Kincaid.

It had been such a shock to see him.

Jack. His name echoed over and over in Kate's head and she felt ill.

She couldn't be ill. Jack's nephew was her next client. Jack Kincaid was waiting for her to finish the formalities with Toby and his mother. Jack Kincaid had to be faced.

But maybe he wouldn't wait. She'd seen his horror when he'd realised Toby was dead; when he'd seen that she wasn't fighting to prolong his life.

She might have got Toby back, she conceded. If she'd tried CPR, had had oxygen on the beach, had fought with every medical skill she had, Toby might still be alive. He'd be unconscious, though. They all knew the tumour was massive and unresponsive to any more chemotherapy or radiation. If she'd fought he could have had maybe a week, maybe even longer, on oxygen, on life support, but his mother hadn't wanted that. No one had wanted it.

She hadn't had to flinch at the condemnation in Jack Kincaid's eyes. She had not one single regret over her care of Toby.

But what would she tell him? Jack had been a friend at medical school. If he was still here she needed to give him an explanation. What?

The truth? Did she trust him enough for that?

She might have no choice. It seemed Harry was Jack's nephew, Jack's sister's child. If she'd recognised the name she would never have accepted him as a client, but the booking had been done by a woman with a name as unfamiliar as all the names she so carefully vetted. Harry had been supposed to be coming with someone called Helen.

No matter. Chinks of her old life were bound to intrude sooner or later. She'd known that. It was just…she'd hoped it would be later.

She thought back to the Jack she'd known over ten years ago. He'd been acutely intelligent, intuitive and skilled. On top of that he'd been drop-dead gorgeous. Tall with dark hair and strong bone structure, always tanned, almost too good looking for his own good, and his dark eyes had always gleamed with mischief. Maturity had only added to his looks, she conceded, but it was the Jack of years ago she was thinking of now. If there had been pranks to be played, Jack had always been at the centre. If there had been a beautiful woman to be dated, Jack had been right there, too.

Early on they were allocated as partners in the science component of their course. They suited each other as study mates. Her seriousness didn't distract him, and his intelligence and humour pleased her. But his dating habits were legend. 'You should have a harem,' she told him. 'That way you wouldn't have to date one by one. You could have them all together.'

'I'd rather that than be stuck with one person for ever from sixteen,' he retorted. She finally told him of Simon's existence when he... When they... Well, late one night things got a little out of hand and she had to tell him the truth. That she had a boyfriend. That she'd had a boyfriend for years so she couldn't be attracted to Jack.

'Monogamy for life from sixteen?' he mocked. 'You must be out of your mind.'

Later, when his words proved true—for it seemed that she had indeed been out of her mind—she'd lie awake in the small hours and think about how different life could have been if she hadn't been a good girl. How it could have been if she'd been able to forget family obligations. If she'd given in to the attraction she'd surely felt.

Move on, she told herself harshly. The time for regrets was well and truly past. What she needed to focus on now was calming Jack down, persuading him to either let her treat his little nephew or tear up the contract and leave.

But whatever way he went, she had to gain his silence.

On impulse she headed indoors and hit the internet. Jack Kincaid.

Professor Jack Kincaid. Head of Oncology at Sydney Central. Research qualifications to make an academic's eyes water. Medical practice extraordinary. His early promise had been met and more; this man was seriously skilled, seriously qualified. More, as she flicked through the site she found links to patients' opinions of the man who'd treated them.

Seriously good. Seriously kind. Empathic. A workaholic by the look of it.

But he'd booked in here for two weeks. Two weeks of this man's time looked to be an incredible commitment.

Okay, she was impressed, but she was also scared. This wasn't a man to be deflected with weak excuses. It'd be the truth or nothing, if he decided to stay.

She headed back to work, and found herself almost hoping he'd decide to leave. That'd make her life a whole lot less complicated.

They had to wait for over an hour, and every minute brought fresh doubts.

He took Harry for a walk around the resort. There were a dozen bungalows built on the beachfront, with dolphins painted on their front doors. Wind chimes hung from their verandas and brightly coloured hammocks hung from the veranda rails.

Sand spits covered with stunted eucalypts reached out from both sides of the resort, the spits forming a secluded bay. A great sweep of netting enclosed half the cove. That'd be a pool for what the information sheet told him were the captive dolphins. These, according to his sheet, were either dolphins who'd been injured in some way or who'd been raised in some form of captivity and brought here in an attempt to rehabilitate them to the wild.

Some dolphins could never be rehabilitated, the sheet said, and these were the dolphins trained to interact with the resort's clients. Their injuries were so bad or they'd learned to be too dependent on humans to ever survive in the wild.

Jack and Harry wandered down to the beach again, hand in hand. Harry had fallen back into silence as he always did. For the last three months he'd simply done what he was told.

He still walked with a heavy limp—his left leg still needed to be braced. He stumped along and Jack's heart twisted for him.

One stupid moment of speed and carelessness. Metal on metal. Lives changed for ever.

There was a scattering of people on the beach, well away from the netted area where Toby had died. These must be more of the resort's clients, he thought, as this place was too far for tourists to come. There were gay little beach shelters scattered about for whoever wanted or needed shade. A couple of kids were in beach-tyred wheelchairs. A few kids were playing in the shallows. Parents were playing with them, talking among themselves.

He had no wish to join them. Did he have any intention of staying?

'Maisie,' Harry said, dragging his thoughts back from introspection, and he glanced back to where the little boy was looking and saw the big golden retriever bounding down the beach towards them. Carrying a ball. She raced straight up to them, dropped the ball at Harry's feet, then bounced backwards and beamed with a full-on canine beam.

'Toss it,' Jack suggested. Harry hesitated but Maisie was practically turning herself inside out with ball-need.

Finally Harry picked the ball up and threw it all of three feet.

The big dog pounced, but before bringing it back she raced towards the shore, dropped it into the shallows, quivered and then brought it back to them. Her message couldn't be clearer. *Throw it further. Throw it into the sea.*

'You throw it,' Harry whispered, and such a command was almost unheard of from Harry.

So Jack threw it, to the water's edge. The dog retrieved it with joy but this time she took it further into the shallows before bringing it back.

Once again her message was clear. 'Throw it even further.'

'She wants you to throw it deep,' Harry whispered, so Jack did. He hurled the ball out to where the waves were just breaking.

Maisie was on it like a bullet, streaking through the water, diving through the waves, reaching the ball…

But then not stopping.

The reason the waves were so shallow here, why the beach was so safe, was that the outer spits curved around, protecting the inner bay. At low tide the spits would be connected to the land but now, at high tide, the sand spits formed long, narrow islands. The island looked beautiful, sand washed and untouched, apart from a host of sandpipers searching for pippies or crabs or sand fleas—whatever sandpipers ate.

And now Maisie was headed for the spit island as well. She swam strongly until she reached it, then raced onto the sand, sending sandpipers scattering in alarm.

But then she turned and looked back at the beach. She looked at the water between herself and the shore.

She looked at Jack and Harry. She dropped her ball at her feet—and she shivered.

She was maybe fifty yards from them, through breast-deep water. She'd swum out with ease but her demeanour now was unmistakeable. *How have I got here? Uh-oh.*

'She's stuck,' Harry gasped, appalled.

'She can swim back.'

'She's scared.'

She couldn't be. Jack stared at the dog in exasperation. She'd swum through the shallow waves with ease. Of course she could get back.

He glanced along the beach, hoping someone official might appear, but it must be time to pack up. The few people left on the beach were two or three hundred yards away, gathering belongings, packing up the beach shelters, heading up through the sand tracks to the resort.

What was he supposed to do? Stand and yell, 'Help, the dog is stuck, save her'?

'Maisie,' he yelled, in what he hoped was his most authoritative voice. 'Come.'

The big dog quivered some more—and then as the last of the beachgoers disappeared over the sand dunes, she started to howl.

'Help her,' Harry said in horror. 'Jack, help her.'

And there was another first. Not once in three months had Harry called Jack by name. Not once had he asked for anything.

Jack, help her.

'She can swim back herself.'

'She's frightened,' Harry whispered. 'What if a big wave comes and washes her off?'

'Then she'll have to swim.'

'But she's scared.' And as if confirmation was necessary, Maisie's howls grew louder. She squatted on the sand and shivered, every inch of her proclaiming she was one terrified mutt, stranded on a desert island for ever, doomed to starve to death or drown on an incoming tide.

'Jack...' Harry whispered. 'Jack!'

And a man had to do what a man had to do.

'If I swim out and fetch her, promise you won't move from here,' Jack told his nephew, and Harry nodded.

'Hurry.'

Maisie was now crouching low, as if the sand was about to give way beneath her. Her howls had given way to whimpers. Loud whimpers.

'Promise out loud,' Jack demanded of Harry.

'I promise.'

The kid had talked. Even if he took him home now, the barrier of silence had been broken. Great, he thought grimly. Now all I have to do is rescue one stupid dog.

He hauled off his shoes, shirt and pants, thanking fate that he was wearing decent boxers. He hesitated for a moment, thinking he really didn't want to leave Harry on the beach, but Harry met his gaze head on.

'I promise,' he said again, and it was enough. The two words were a joy all by themselves. They were almost enough to make him turn to the water with enthusiasm, to plough into the shallows, to dive through the waves, to swim the twenty or so strokes it took him to reach the island spit.

Finally he hauled himself out of the water and headed for Maisie…who waited until he was less than six feet from her and then bounded to her feet, grabbed her ball, launched herself back into the water and headed for shore.

Jack was left standing on his island in his boxers, staring helplessly after her.

Maisie made it back with no effort at all. She bounded up the beach to Harry, dropped the ball at his feet and turned to stare out at Jack.

Her tail was whirring like a helicopter. Even from where he was Jack could sense the grin. This was a great dog con.

She walked over the sand hill and saw Jack in the water. She could see at a glance what had happened. Maisie the jokester dog. This trick almost always worked. Occasionally a parent reacted with anger but usually it was laughter, and Kate could see Jack's laughter from where she stood. He watched the dog paddle effortlessly through the shallows to the beach and she saw his shoulders shake.

She was smiling as well. So the humour remained.

She'd liked this man.

She'd also thought he was gorgeous—and he still was. He'd stripped to his boxers. He stood in the sunlight, the late afternoon rays glinting on his wet body. Even from here she could see the power of the man. He must work out at some time in his seriously impressive schedule, she thought. He looked ripped.

She watched as he headed back into the water, diving into the shallows, diving under, taking a few long, strong strokes before he caught a wave that took him all the way to shore.

Harry and Maisie were waiting, Maisie tail-wagging as if she'd pulled off the world's best joke, Harry looking worried.

Jack strode out of the water, lifted his small nephew and swung him in a big, wet circle.

'She fooled us,' he told Harry. 'Don't look so worried. The doggy fooled us both. Isn't she clever?'

Harry gave a tight little smile. His rigid body didn't unbend, however, and after a moment Jack put him down.

'This is a very strange place,' he told Harry. 'Do you know, I think it might even be fun. I'm not sure yet, but maybe we should give it a try.'

To be fooled by a dog was one thing. To be fooled by a woman you didn't trust was another. He set Harry down, looked up, and Cathy was there. Or Kate. Whichever, both of them were laughing.

'I'm sorry. Donna should have warned you. Maisie always tries that on.'

'Donna?' he said dangerously.

'Our receptionist. She's supposed to warn everyone. This is Maisie's favourite party trick to get adults into the water. Strangely, she never tries it on kids. Only adults. She's so clever.'

'Right,' Jack growled. To say he was feeling at a disadvantage was an understatement. He was dripping. He was in his boxers. On the other hand, Kate had obviously cleaned up after her time with Toby. She was wearing a soft blue skirt and white blouse. Her hair was neatly curled on top of her head. She looked fresh, professional…and deeply amused, but…

'Maisie saved herself,' Harry pronounced, and he was talking again. That was almost enough to make Jack forget about Kate. Almost. Her chuckle had him entranced.

Kate wasn't his type. She'd never really been his type, he conceded. Yes, there had been that initial attraction but he liked his women cool, sophisticated.

Kate was cute rather than classically beautiful, he thought. She had freckles. Lots of freckles.

She looked like the girl next door, he thought. So why was he looking at a pair of laughing eyes and thinking… thinking…

He didn't need to think in that direction. She'd always had secrets and he didn't like it. This woman had some hidden agenda and Harry's welfare was at stake. He needed to find out what was going on.

But Kate was no longer looking at him. She'd stooped to crouch before Harry.

'Hi,' she said. 'I'm Kate, Maisie's mother. I hear your uncle has brought you here to stay for a few days so you can meet Maisie and my friends, the dolphins.'

Harry was back to saying nothing. Kate, however, didn't

appear in the least bit disconcerted. She rose, headed over the sandhill and came back carrying a bucket. Of fish.

'I dumped these when I saw your uncle saving Maisie,' she said, returning to them. 'Wasn't he brave? But isn't Maisie clever to trick him? Jack, would you like to go and get dry while Harry and I feed the dolphins? Would you like a little time out?'

It was exactly what he'd like. He was feeling...exposed. He was bare chested, bare legged and a bit chilly now the sun was sinking low, but he still had reservations about this woman. He wasn't about to leave her alone with his nephew until he knew more.

Harry was still not speaking, but he was peering into the bucket. Fish!

'These are a snack for the wild dolphins,' Kate said, talking exclusively to Harry. 'We feed the dolphins in the healing pool, but every now and then we give our wild dolphins a treat. Some of the wild dolphins are ones we've treated here for injuries and let go, but most are just free dolphins who come to say hello. If we encourage them to stick around, when we have an injured dolphin who's better we can release him into a group of friends. Do you think that's a good idea?'

Harry nodded.

Jack had resolved not to trust this woman, but every ounce of Kate's attention was focussed on Harry. He thought, It doesn't matter if I trust or not, but if Harry trusts...

He had to stick with him. He wasn't going as far as letting this woman take over but something seemed to be working. He hauled his shirt over his still-damp torso and took Harry's hand.

Harry didn't respond. There was never a moment when those small fingers curled around his. He trusted no one.

'Where do you feed them?' he asked, and she motioned to where the net divided the free bay from the pool.

'At the boundary. I feed those in the pool and out so they see each other.'

'But the pool ones can't get out?' Harry asked, and once more Jack held his breath.

'The ones in the pool all have something wrong with them,' Kate said, starting to walk down to the water, leaving them to follow if they willed. And, of course, they willed. Harry was moving even before Jack led. 'If we let them out into the ocean they'll die. But we've made the pool enormous and we try and make them feel as free as we can.'

They reached the netted boundary. She walked into the water—she might look professional from the knees up but she had bare feet—and she lifted a fish out of the bucket. She slapped the surface a few times with the fish and she yelled.

'Grub's up. Come and get it.'

He was as fascinated as Harry. They stood on the shoreline and watched as far out a fin appeared and then another and another. And then there was a line of eight dolphins, surfing in on a wave to reach the shallows. They paused as a group in about two feet of water, and a couple reared back as if standing on tiptoe, watching.

And in the enclosure four more dolphins assembled and did the same, so Kate had a dozen dolphins at attention.

'Now, the trick is, one fish each,' she told Harry. 'And they're very tricky. Every time one gets a fish he pretends that he hasn't. So the ones who do the most jumping up and down and pleading are the ones who've had a fish. The others know I'm fair and if they wait their turn they'll get one.'

She lifted the fish—a fish Jack thought was a good breakfast size—and tossed it to the first wild dolphin. He caught it with dexterity. She then tossed a fish to each wild dolphin in turn. She was right, the ones who'd been fed became sneaky but Kate was sneakier still, and not one dolphin got more than his share.

'If we feed them too much they won't bother to hunt themselves,' she told Harry briskly, as she moved from the outer rim of the pool to the inner. 'And that'd never do. Now, would you like to give one of my tame guys a fish?'

Without waiting for an answer, she delved in the bucket, snagged a fish and held it up. 'This would make a good meal for me. Our dolphins get very well fed. Harry, if you'd like to meet my friends, the closest is Hobble. The next one is Bubbles. Then we have Smiley and Squirt. If you and your uncle decide to stay here for a while then you'll meet them close up. They like playing with a ball just as much as Maisie does.'

But it was enough. Harry closed up, as he'd closed up for months. Jack felt him withdraw, felt his small body clench with tension, felt his hand become rigid in his clasp.

Did Kate know how much progress he'd made in the last hour? he wondered.

'Maybe we need to stop...' he started, but Kate was there before him.

'Only if you want, of course,' she said cheerfully. 'You decide, but if you stay you'll have a nice little bedroom overlooking the sea. Some people who come here stay in bed the whole time and every now and then they peek through the curtains at the dolphins. That's all they want to do and it's why we call it a sanctuary. Everyone here is allowed to do exactly what they want to do. Now, I gather Donna has shown you your bungalow? It's the yellow one, and your bedroom is all yellow, too. If you want you can go there now. Dinner's in the dining room in half an hour but if you want to you can have it in your little house. There's a menu on the wall. We have everything from sausage rolls to pizza to great big hamburgers for your uncle. But you decide. Harry, I'm going to feed the rest of my dolphins now, but you can do whatever you want.'

It was exactly the right thing to say. Harry didn't move. The tension was still there but he'd been given an escape route. The pressure was off and if he wanted he could still stay and watch.

He didn't say a word but neither did he pull back, retreat, head for the safety of the cute little bungalow that was to be their home for the next two weeks.

Instead, he stood silent. His hand was still in Jack's, not responsive, not clinging but not pulling away either. They watched in silence as Kate waded into the pool and spoke to her four tame dolphins. She showed each of them a fish and asked them to spin three times and do a belly roll before she handed them—formally, it seemed—their supper.

Then she backed out of the water, waved to the dolphins and waved to them with the same cheer.

'See you later,' she said. 'Have a good night. Harry, the sausage rolls are great and the pizza's better. If you see me when you're peeking through your curtains tomorrow, can you give me a wave?'

And she was gone, clicking her fingers so Maisie fell in behind her. She was a formal, professional…doctor? A doctor with bare feet, an empty fish bucket and a bedraggled, soaking dog.

What sort of place had he landed himself in?

What sort of woman had Cathy…Kate…become?

He didn't know. All he knew was that the tension had once again gone out of his little nephew.

'I need to take a shower,' he told Harry. 'I'm all wet.'

He didn't expect an answer but it came. 'The dog made you wet,' Harry said.

He grinned. 'She certainly did. Would you like pizza?'

'Yes,' said Harry, and Jack knew that whatever Cathy/

Kate was, whatever she'd become, he needed to take a chance on this place.

He needed to take a chance on her.

CHAPTER THREE

HARRY RETREATED AGAIN into silence. Jack ordered via the cabin phone for them both—pizza and orange juice for Harry, a hamburger and beer for himself. A cheerful lass with a strong Canadian accent arrived at their bungalow fifteen minutes later, chatted happily to Jack and Harry, didn't seem to mind that Harry didn't respond, left their dinner and left them to the night.

They sat on their little balcony, a table between them, and watched the sun set over the ocean. They could see the dolphin pool from here. From time to time a dolphin broke the surface, the ripples spreading as if dispersing the tangerine rays of the setting sun. The gentle hush-hush of the breaking waves was all the sound there was.

No pressure, Jack thought. If Harry was at Helen's right now, the whole family would be pressuring him to eat. Even Helen's kids knew Harry didn't eat enough, so every time he took a bite was cause for family celebration.

Not here. Jack was taking a leaf out of Kate's book, backing off.

During the journey he'd insisted Harry eat, playing the heavy-handed uncle.

'I don't care if you don't want it, Harry, but you'll get sick if you don't eat. Six mouthfuls or you're not leaving the table.'

Now, at this place, it seemed less urgent. This seemed the time when they could both start again.

He ate his hamburger—extremely large, extremely good. He drank his beer and watched the sunset and didn't say a word, and as he finished his food a small hand snagged a piece of pizza. He didn't comment and when the lass came to collect the empty tray neither did she.

'Dr Kate says she might drop by later to have a chat,' she told Jack cheerfully. 'There are forms to fill in. Boring. She says there's no need to stay up if you don't want. It can wait until morning, but she'll drop by anyway.'

And Jack figured what this was about, too. Their formal appointment this afternoon had been missed. Kate would come—he'd expected it—but by forewarning them both, Harry would be reassured. If the little boy woke and heard voices he'd know what was happening. Harry needed no surprises, no shocks, no worries. He needed his world to stabilise again—if it ever could.

To lose both his parents in the one appalling moment... Jack could hardly imagine the black hole it had created. To be seven and to lose so much...

A shadow emerged from the trees, sniffing up the steps as the girl removed the tray and prepared to leave.

'Maisie,' the girl said. She smiled and turned to Harry. 'Harry, Maisie's very fussy,' she said. 'Every night she decides who she'd like to sleep with. It seems tonight she's chosen you. If you don't want her, I'll take her away with me now. She has her own bed with Dr Kate. We don't want her to be a bother.'

Harry didn't answer but it didn't trouble Maisie. The big dog proceeded ponderously up the steps and put his great head on Harry's knee. And sighed.

Her message couldn't be more clear. *No one in this world understands me. You're my only friend. Please let me stay.*

She put her paw up in silent entreaty. Harry cast a covert glance at Jack and then back at Maisie.

'C-can she stay?'

'Only if she sleeps on your bed,' Jack said sternly. 'I don't like dogs snoring on mine.'

'D-does she snore?'

'Sometimes,' the lass said cheerfully. 'Will I take her away?'

'N-no,' Harry managed, and the thing was settled. So half an hour later boy and dog were tucked up in bed. Harry's arms were firmly around Maisie's neck and Harry was fast asleep.

Helen had a dog. They'd also tried him out with a puppy but they'd got nowhere.

This dog, though, knew all the right moves. She knew just how to wriggle her way under a small boy's defences.

Like Kate was doing?

He'd walked into this place and felt deeply suspicious. What kind of a healing centre didn't try to save a child? Even if the explanation of terminal illness was true, why was no doctor in attendance? Kate was listed in the resort's advertising as being a physiotherapist and a counsellor. There was no mention of her being a medical doctor. Something must have gone horribly wrong with her career. He didn't trust her, and yet somehow he'd agreed to stay. By reaching out to Harry, she'd wriggled under his defences and he was left feeling more than a little vulnerable.

He didn't like it. Jack liked control. He had no kids himself. Now he had one small nephew who'd managed to touch his heart and leave him exposed. To charlatans? To a woman who called herself Kate but who wasn't.

'Jack?'

The voice was so soft he hardly heard it, but he'd been waiting.

Kate? Cathy.

The sun had sunk over the horizon; the merest hint of colour tinging the point where the sea disappeared towards Africa. The night was warm and still. No sound came from other bungalows. What sort of resort was this when by eight o'clock everyone seemed asleep?

'Hi,' Kate said, as she reached the steps. 'I have some forms for you to fill in, and some questions I need answered. Is now a good time?'

She was casually dressed, in jeans with a slouchy windcheater over the top. Her feet were still bare. The only hint of professionalism was the two thick envelopes she carried.

She'd let her hair out, he thought inconsequentially. It was curly and bouncy and touched her shoulders. Nice.

Um...don't go there. This is Harry's welfare, he told himself. Be professional.

'I need to throw you more questions than you throw at me,' he growled. 'What are you playing at?'

She was halfway up the veranda steps and she paused. 'You sound angry.'

'Why wouldn't I be angry? This is my sister's child. I'm responsible for him. You're not who you say you are. I don't want anyone messing with his welfare.'

'Do you think I could possibly hurt Harry?'

'I don't know what game you're playing...'

'No game,' she said stiffly. 'This place represents me exactly as I am. I'm Kate Martin, counsellor and physiotherapist.'

'You and I both know that's a lie.'

'It isn't a lie. I trained at university in Auckland. Years of study. My qualifications are real.'

'You're a doctor, or you were. Have you been struck off?'

'No,' she said flatly, defiantly. 'I haven't. But it's my choice whether I advertise my medical degree or not. With my counselling and physiotherapy qualifications, I don't need to add the medical stuff.'

'That makes no sense—and then there's the small issue of your name.'

'You're treating me like a criminal.'

'You're acting like one.'

'It's not a sin to change your name.'

'People don't change their names unless they're hiding.'

'So I'm hiding, but my reasons are personal and nothing to do with my professional ability. I ask you to accept that.'

'So if I ring the medical board and enquire…'

'I'd ask you not to do that.' Her face was pale but resolute. She stood halfway up the steps, holding onto the rail as if she needed it for support. 'I've taken a great deal of trouble to ensure there's no link between Cathy Heineman and Kate Martin. One phone call could destroy that. One phone call could mean I need to walk away from all I've worked for.'

'You mean the medical board—'

'Couldn't care less,' she snapped. 'I have my change of name recorded. Believe it or not, I'm still a registered doctor with no blemish against my name. I still accrue my professional training points and I keep my registration up to date. But the receptionist who receives notes of my continual professional training updates Kate Martin's file. I did the name change carefully with only a couple of trusted friends helping. I want no link.'

There were a couple of moments of silence. Intense silence. She was gazing straight up at him, unflinching. Defiant even. Still, she was pale.

One phone call could mean I need to walk away from all I've worked for…

This was personal, he thought. He shouldn't ask.

But this was Harry.

'Cathy…Kate,' he said at last. 'Harry's lost his parents. He has no one to protect him except me and his very bossy aunt. Helen demanded that I bring him here. I did so with reservations because alternative medicine makes me wary, and the first thing I saw was a dead child. That was followed by a doctor using an assumed name. Your defensiveness might be valid from your perspective but for Harry's sake I need an explanation.'

'You can't just let Maisie and the dolphins do their own work without probing into my past?'

'No,' he said flatly. 'Harry's too important for that.'

'You were my friend,' she said. 'You trusted me.'

'I trusted you not to break a test tube,' he said. 'And they were the university's test tubes. This is Harry.'

She bit her lip. Her gaze faltered for a moment. She stared down at her bare toes and then she raised her chin again. She met his gaze with that same defiance, but touched with the defiance was a hint of fear.

'I don't tell people.'

'No.'

'Can I trust you?'

'You can trust me not to tell anyone else. You can't trust me not to pick up Harry and walk away.'

'Fair enough.' She sighed and then seemed to come to a decision. 'There's wine in your refrigerator. I'm off duty. If I don't charge you mini-bar prices, will you pour me one? You can have a free beer as well.'

'Bribing as well?' he asked, but he smiled to soften the words and she managed a smile back.

'I'll do anything I need to stay hidden,' she said simply. 'Handing you access to your mini-bar is the least of it.'

She was settled in the deck chair on Jack's veranda. Jack had nearly finished his beer and she was halfway through a glass of wine.

She'd expected him to push, but he didn't. He seemed content to wait, giving her the time she needed.

And she needed time. Her story was simple and bleak and it was something that had happened to a woman called Cathy Heineman, not to her. She was Kate Martin and she'd moved on.

But Jack was still waiting. If he was to trust her, he had a right to know.

'You know I married,' she said.

'I did know that.'

'Fourth year. I was twenty-one. A kid.'

'We seemed pretty old and wise at the time.'

'We did, didn't we?' she said, and tried for a smile. 'But I was still a baby. Still living at home, the only child of elderly parents. Ruled by a loving despot. My father's health was precarious and my mother was terrified. Dad had two heart attacks while I was in my teens, and Mum's mantra was *Don't do anything to upset your father.*'

'So?'

'So that was the way it was,' she said. 'Simon was the son of Dad's best friend and business partner. Almost family. I was sixteen when we first dated. Simon was twenty four and the excitement our parents felt was amazing. The assumption from that first date was that we'd marry.'

'But you obviously liked the guy.'

'Oh, yes. But he was just…an extension of my family. He was older than me, good looking, powerful, and he fed my teenage ego no end. And suddenly I was in too far to get out. When I started university I started getting itchy feet, but by then Dad's health was failing even more. The pressure was on for us to marry before he died. Simon was pressuring me too, saying he was fond of my dad, we should do it. So I did.'

She said it almost defiantly, as if it was a thing that needed defending.

He stayed silent. There was more coming; he knew it.

'Only, of course, then I was a wife,' she said slowly. 'Before I'd been a girlfriend, almost a casual girlfriend as Simon had let me go my own way—as indeed he went his. He was training to take over our parents' business. He was an only child too, so we'd both inherit and the business—importing quality wine—was brilliant. Both families were wealthy, but Simon wanted more.'

'Is that why he married you?' Jack asked.

Kate stared into her wine glass for a long moment before she answered. Then: 'Yes,' she said. 'Of course it was, only I was too naïve to see it. All I saw was that he was a nice guy, and my father was desperate for the marriage. I think…maybe even then I was thinking if it doesn't work out, after Dad and Mum go I can divorce. I was only twenty one. I had my medical career to get off the ground. I didn't intend to have babies for years.'

'But?' he said gently, and she swirled her wine some more.

'But,' she said heavily. 'But.'

'If you don't want to tell me, I can get the picture.'

She glanced up at him then and managed a smile. 'So little, and you'll trust?'

'I assume you're running from him?'

'See, in his eyes I'm not Cathy or Kate,' she told him. 'Divorce or not, I'm his wife. I'm the other part of Simon's inheritance, and Simon doesn't give up possessions lightly.'

'I see.'

'You probably don't. The fights we had… First he wanted me to give up my medical studies. After we married he couldn't see the point. I fought him on that, you can't believe how much I fought, and I won but at a cost. And after that…every little thing meant a fight. If I defied him, heaven help me. He wanted total control. And then Dad died, Simon's father went into care with Alzheimer's

and the whole thing crashed.' She faltered. 'It seemed…
Simon gambled. No one knew. No one suspected. But he'd
mortgaged the business. He'd forged signatures so my half
as well as his was forfeit. I knew then why he'd married
me and I knew why he had to stay married. But after one
vicious fight too many I walked away, and then, after what
happened next, I ran.'

'Cathy—'

'I'm Kate,' she said fiercely. 'I'm Kate Martin. Cathy
Heineman is divorced and has disappeared because Simon
still thinks he owns her. Simon went to jail because he
signed contracts using my mother's name and mine. My
mother died in poverty because of him. His own parents
are penniless. Simon is a lying, thieving thug and I'm glad
my parents are dead because they never had to see…'

She caught herself. 'No. It's not necessary to tell you
all the gruesome facts. Just that I didn't take forgery and
theft lying down. It wasn't just me he robbed but I was the
one who sent him to jail. So Simon still hates me and he's
lethal. Ten years on, he's been in and out of jail and I'm
still afraid of him. His hatred is out of all context, off the
wall. So I'm Kate. I changed my name. I scraped together
enough from our assets to go overseas. I worked as a wait-
ress while I retrained as a physiotherapist. I did some psychology too—in some ways it helped with the stuff that
had happened to me. The university in Auckland was sup-
portive. My medical degree meant additional qualifications were fast-tracked and I qualified with my new name.

'Then I heard about this place. Even though it was back
in Australia, a dolphin sanctuary three hundred miles from
the nearest city seemed perfect. I can vet clients before taking bookings. If there's a familiar name I can say we're
full up, as we nearly always are. It's only because Harry
was booked in under his aunt's name that I missed you.'

'And your qualifications?' he asked. 'Why don't you advertise your medical degree?'

'I know Simon,' she said. 'He'll suspect I've changed my name. I wouldn't put it past him to check every doctor on the medical register, here and in New Zealand. You see,' she said simply, 'I'm still afraid of him.'

'No man has the right—'

'He has no rights,' she said flatly. 'But neither does he have reason. Somehow my lovely, smart divorce lawyer managed to scrape back enough money for me to retrain, but it took criminal charges to do it. Even though I didn't throw half the charges I could have at him, he's never forgiven me. But that's enough,' she said, moving on. 'That's all the explanation I can give, so accept it or not. I think I can help Harry. Today's reaction to Maisie says we can reach him. I believe swimming with the dolphins, one on one, will help him enormously but it's up to you. I won't push. Leave in the morning if you want—all I ask is that you keep my confidence. Will you do that?'

'Of course I will.'

Of course.

He thought back to the friend he'd had at university. Cathy had been a lovely, laughing girl whose humour had made lab work fun. She'd had her intense side but none of them had ever suspected she'd had such shadows.

Cathy was now Kate, he thought. She was a different woman, but underneath she must be the same.

Would he let her treat Harry? With her explanation, and after Harry's reaction to the events of today, it was a no-brainer.

'Let me show you Toby's notes,' she said, and he stilled.

'Toby…'

'You're Harry's guardian. I saw the way you reacted to Toby's death and I don't blame you. I need…for myself…to reassure you that everything that could be done was done.'

'It's not my business. There's no need—'

'There is a need,' she said. 'And I have Amy's permission. Her sister and her mum are here to help her take Toby back to Sydney. She's overwhelmed, but she still registered your shock on the beach. I told her you were a doctor. She said...' She swallowed, fighting for composure. 'She told me to do whatever I must to persuade you to let me help Harry. So here you are.' And she tugged a sheaf of medical notes and X-rays from the envelope and handed them over.

He glanced through them. There was no need for questions: they spoke for themselves. As an oncologist, Jack had treated brain tumours—of course he had. Even the sight of the first X-ray, before surgery, before chemotherapy, had him knowing the end had been inevitable. The surgery and chemotherapy had been acts of desperation, buying a little time but not much.

Resuscitation today would have been stupid and cruel. That this little boy had died where he had seemed little short of a miracle.

He stared at the films, at the notes, at the final letter from an oncologist he knew, saying take him home and love him, and he felt his chest tighten.

He'd so nearly intervened. If he'd come moments before...

'I wouldn't have let you interfere,' Kate said simply, watching his face. 'I'm in control here, and I don't make decisions lightly. I do what's best for each of my clients. I'll do what's best for Harry.'

'I believe you.' There was nothing else to say.

'And I promise I won't let Maisie trick you again,' she said, and the tension broke.

He gathered the notes and put them back into their envelope. It gave him time to collect himself, even drum up a smile. 'She's a smart dog.'

'I found her as a pup. Believe it or not, someone threw

her from a car. She was past the cute puppy stage so someone dumped her, scraggy and half-starved. I'd just accepted the job here and this place is a wildlife sanctuary,
no pets allowed. The powers that be had to be talked into
letting me keep her but they really wanted my combina-
tion of qualifications so they bent the rules. Now there's
not a soul who's not totally devoted to her. Sometimes I
think I'm not even needed. Maisie treats the kids for me.'

'As well as tricking parents.'

'She's discovered it makes kids laugh,' she said simply.
'What sort of gift is that?'

'Beyond price.'

She beamed, lighting up. Serious confidences over.
'Exactly. So you will stay?'

'I... Yes.'

'Excellent,' she said, and motioned to the second envelope. 'Let's get this done, then. Forms. Questions. I need
to know all about Harry, and all about you.'

'Me?'

'Are you Harry's legal guardian?'

'Yes.'

'Will he live with you full time when he leaves here?'

He hesitated. There was a huge question. It was one
he'd been asking himself over and over.

He was a bachelor, nicely confirmed. He was also an
oncologist and a busy one. He had a girlfriend but theirs
was long-term semi-commitment. Their lifestyle suited
them both.

He and Annalise were ambitious. Neither wanted to
be tied down—apartments in the same luxury block was
as close as either wanted to get. Annalise had her life and
he had his.

Where would Harry fit?

'Earth to Jack,' Kate said, and he realised he'd been
staring out over the sea for too long.

'I don't know,' he said at last. 'If you can cure him, maybe he can live with his Aunt Helen. She's a mother hen. She has five kids and would like more.'

'Define cure,' she said. 'What are you hoping for?'

'He's so withdrawn.'

'Some kids *are* withdrawn. Was he like that when his parents were alive?'

'He was quiet,' he conceded.

'You love him?'

'He's my nephew.'

'It doesn't necessarily follow that you love him.'

'I loved my sister,' he said inconsequentially, and she nodded.

'I'm sorry.'

'He's very like her.'

'Quiet.'

'Not so much quiet as observant. My sister noticed everything. So does...so did Harry.'

'But not now.'

'He doesn't say.'

'The original form we received said he was living with his aunt.'

'It's a good home.' Why did he suddenly feel like he was stuck on a pin, like an impaled butterfly? 'They have a huge house. Helen's great with kids, and so's her husband. Harry should be happy there.'

'But he's not.'

'He just...disappears. Shrinks. I can't explain it.'

'So you want me to make him outgoing and boisterous so he'll fit into a family of five kids. It won't happen,' she said bluntly. 'A family of five has their own pecking order, their own entrenched hierarchy. To put a wounded seven-year-old in their midst will never work.'

'He won't be wounded. If I can just get him talking...'

'He's lost his parents,' Kate said flatly. 'He'll always be wounded.'

This wasn't what he wanted to hear, but he stared out to sea some more and he knew it was the truth. Harry was never going to fit in with Helen's brood. So where did that leave him?

'Do you have a wife or partner?' Kate asked, not without sympathy.

'Um...yes. Girlfriend.' Maybe not partner. They weren't close enough for that.

'One who likes kids?'

'No. Not that I'm planning to palm him off—'

'I'm not saying you are. It's just that kids are hard work. Taking on a seven-year-old is huge. If you and...'

'Annalise,' he said, and he knew he sounded goaded but he couldn't help it. The sensation of being impaled was growing.

'Annalise,' she said. 'Nice name. If you and Annalise plan on having babies of your own it'll make things more complicated.'

'This isn't about me.'

'Of course it's about you. Harry's whole future seems to be about you.'

This wasn't what he wanted to hear. 'Look, can we get tomorrow over with first?'

'You're definitely staying tomorrow?'

'Yes.'

'But you haven't made your mind up about after that? Whether you're ready to be Harry's dad?'

'I'll be Harry's guardian.'

'That's not enough. Harry needs more and you know it. If Annalise isn't interested, you'll be Harry's mum and dad combined.'

'Will you leave it?' It was an explosion in the stillness of the night, startling him as well as the couple of bush turkeys scratching at the footings of the bungalow. 'It'll sort itself out as we go along.'

'Does Harry know where his future lies?'

'What do you mean?'

'I mean Harry's been in hospital and then at his Aunt Helen's with his five cousins and then travelling with you and now he's here. Does he have any idea where he's going to live; what his future life will be like?'

'What business—?'

'Is it of mine? Plenty. This isn't just a place where kids come to play with dolphins. The dolphins are background. What they do is help the kids relax so we can help them sort the problems surrounding them. We achieve therapeutic success because our environment is far less threatening than any normal medical setting. As well as that, the dolphins—and Maisie—actively remove barriers wounded kids put up around themselves. They forget to defend themselves. I'm willing to bet we can get Harry doing more with his legs tomorrow than he's done since the accident. As well as that, he'll be more receptive to talking. But, Jack, what Harry needs right now is certainty and that's up to you.'

She rose and laid the forms down on the table. 'These forms aren't just about you,' she said. 'They're about you and Harry. The mending team. The family. You need to work it out so that when Harry surfaces from grief and shock and manages to ask, you can give him the assurances he needs. Mind, it'd be better if you could give him those assurances now, but you have things to come to terms with as well. If you like, we'll organise you your own dolphin companion to help. Meanwhile, can you fill these forms in for me? I'll pick them up in the morning.'

She turned to go but then she hesitated, turning back.

'Jack, thank you for reassuring me about my name change,' she said softly. 'It means everything to me. And thank you also for entrusting Harry to my care. I will help. I promise.'

'I know you will.' Where had that come from? But he knew it was true. From total distrust, he now had faith.

Why? Because she told a good story? Because he'd known her as a student? Because she was forcing him to face something he'd been actively avoiding?

Or maybe it was none of those things. Maybe it was because she was standing in the moonlight in her faded jeans and windcheater and her bare feet, and she looked about fourteen, although he knew she was much older.

Maybe it was the freckles.

Maybe it was the smile. She was smiling now, quizzically, waiting for him to say goodnight and give her leave to go.

'Won't you have another drink?' he found himself saying.

She looked at him then, really looked, and he was reminded of the looks she'd given him when he'd been fooling round in the lab at med school, when time had been starting to run out and she'd reminded him they were there to work. And he remembered suddenly how much he'd wanted to ask her out, and how frustrated he'd been when she'd knocked back his advances.

But she wasn't thinking about the past. This was all about now. This was all about Harry.

'This is my job,' she told him gently. 'Jack, you're the parent of my client. I might have sand between my toes but here I'm every inch a professional. I had a glass of wine with you then because I needed to break that professionalism to gain your trust, but now we need to move forward. Besides,' she said gently, and she even managed a bit of a teasing grin, 'Annalise wouldn't like it. Goodnight, Jack.'

And she was gone, slipping silently into the shadows,

leaving him with the forms to be filled in, with the moonlight over the sea and with silence.

And with all the questions in the world racing through his head.

Inside Harry was asleep, curled up with a great lump of a trickster dog. He was seven years old and totally dependent on him.

Back at Sydney Central, Annalise would be expecting a call.

But it was Friday night. On Friday nights he and friends usually went out to Silence, a discreet and expensive supper club where great jazz was played, where excellent wines were served, where medics could unwind after the tensions of the week. And spend a lot of money.

Annalise would be there now, he thought, enjoying herself even without him. She'd be looking beautiful, tall, willowy, blonde, dressed simply but flawlessly. She'd be laughing, sparkling, the centre of attention. If he phoned her now she'd step out onto the balcony and watch the harbour lights while she talked sympathetically to him about what he was doing. Then she'd step back into his world.

How could he take Harry back there?

He was here to fix him and prepare him for entry into Helen's family. That had been his hope but now the plan seemed...flawed?

Why? Because a wounded and hunted doctor with bare feet and a freckled nose had told him it was flawed?

And why were those freckles superimposing themselves over Annalise's more glamorous image?

It was because he was tired, he told himself, and also because he was shocked. He thought back to the Cathy he'd known during med school—and he thought of how she'd changed after she'd married. She'd withdrawn into herself. They'd all noticed it but none of them had pushed to find out why.

They'd been kids. They'd been centred on passing final exams. The thought that any one of them could be in an abusive relationship had been so far out of their ken that it had been unthinkable.

Yet he'd thought of himself as her friend, and he'd never asked. He'd never pushed to know about this unknown husband. Maybe he'd even been a bit resentful that she'd clearly preferred someone else. Adolescent jealousy? How dumb was that?

But it was no use feeling guilty now, he told himself. As Cathy...Kate had said, from now on this was a professional relationship. He was here to cure Harry.

Cure?

Tonight Kate—and he would think of her as Kate, he conceded, because professionalism was the only way to face the next few days—had reminded him that Harry was still the same Harry he'd always been underneath his shock and grief and battering. She'd forced him to acknowledge that a quiet, shy little boy was always going to be quiet and shy and that maybe he'd never fit in with Helen's brood.

Which left him where?

He thought of his sister, Beth. She'd also been quiet and shy. She'd been his little sister and he'd loved her.

She'd want him to look after her little boy. Of course she would. But how?

He thought back to the supper club, to where he should be now and where he wanted to be again. Then he looked out to sea.

A burst of fluorescence broke the trail of silver moonlight over the water as a dolphin leaped high, curved and plunged into the depths again. It was no wonder people associated dolphins with magic, he thought. Here in the moonlight it was almost possible to believe they were right.

Which was nonsense. He had to stay practical.

The problem was that his problem had got past the practical. It was so immense it needed a little magic.

Kate had found peace here, he thought inconsequentially. She'd found a new life. She'd found a solution. Maybe...

Or maybe not. This place was a temporary refuge. The real world was waiting. He'd take Harry back and try and figure out a future.

As Kate had.

Why was he still thinking of her? Weren't his own problems paramount?

Maybe they were. He poured himself another beer but he didn't drink it. Instead, he stared at the sea, unconsciously willing another dolphin to break the surface.

It didn't. It seemed the magic was over for the night. It was time to head for bed, get rested ready for whatever tomorrow held.

It was time to stop thinking about a woman who'd changed her name from Cathy to Kate.

Kate walked back to her own little bungalow behind the administration building and prepared for bed. Today had been gut-wrenching. As much as she'd been prepared for Toby's death... No, nothing *ever* prepared you for a child's death. It had cut deep, and then, as she'd been still struggling to control her emotions, Jack Kincaid had walked back into her life.

Jack. Big, larger than life, smart, funny, nice. At med school she'd thought of him as one of her best friends, and after her marriage she'd struggled to withdraw from his friendship.

She shouldn't have had to withdraw but Simon's jealousy had been stretched to the limit coping with her desire to do medicine. For her to have an outside circle of friends had been something she'd had to sacrifice.

She should have walked away so much sooner. That first week of her marriage, on their honeymoon, Simon had left her at dinner to make a telephone call. A fellow diner had approached her and started chatting. Yes, it had been a come-on, yes, she had been dressed up to the nines, alone, female, and Simon's long telephone call had left her looking stranded.

But on his return Simon's reaction had been icy. He'd cut the guy dead, and for the rest of the night and the next day Kate had been 'punished'. Lesson: 'You want me to love you, then you're mine and mine alone. I'm in control.'

She should have walked. No, she should have run, but her parents would have been heartbroken and, besides, Simon had been lovely underneath—hadn't he? When he'd been happy he could make her happy. She'd just had to be careful.

How long until she'd been totally under his control? How long until she'd finally snapped out of it and realised how much of a victim she'd become?

It had taken a hysterical phone call from her mother— 'He's taken everything.' Bleak to the bottom of her soul, she'd gone to the police. Not just with evidence of fraud but with resolution as cold as ice.

Then...months in a women's refuge. Help from the wonderful women who ran these places. Help from the police—it seemed his family wasn't alone in the list of people Simon had cheated.

What had followed had been a name change and a move to New Zealand. A new life. Even a sort of peace, though trust in herself was still hard to come by.

And then today here was Jack, bringing memories of a time when she'd still been Cathy, when life had been fun, when the most important thing in the world hadn't been to hide.

Jack...

She'd always thought he was gorgeous, she reflected, but, of course, even in first year she'd already had Simon as her permanent boyfriend. She'd been able to watch from the sidelines and tease as he'd gone through his myriad girlfriends. Jack had treated life as one long game, though in his medicine that game had been used to effect. He'd never lost sight of his patients' needs, and his laughter had been used to make them smile.

He'd lost his sister now and his smile had faded but it was still there behind the grief. There was still Annalise in the background. He was struggling with his little nephew's needs, but he'd manage, he'd juggle, he'd call in favours, he'd get what he wanted.

Would he commit to Harry?

It couldn't matter to her, she decided. She'd do what she could for the time they were here and then see them leave. What was it they'd taught her in medical school all those years ago? Don't judge. Accept people for what they are, do what you can for them but in the end their choices are their own.

Don't…care?

Impossible.

She wouldn't mind if Maisie was here.

Maybe she should get another dog, she thought, now Maisie had taken it on herself to divide her loyalty between the kids she loved playing with during the day. But, then, a puppy would be adored by the kids as well, so she'd have two dogs out comforting kids. She wouldn't mind a bit of comfort herself.

'Wuss.' She'd said it out loud and it echoed in the quiet of the bungalow.

She thought back to those first few dreadful weeks of sleeping in the women's refuge. She'd lain in bed at night and she'd formed a mantra.

'I don't need anyone. I'm worth something in my own right and I can live alone.'

She'd been saying that to herself for years now and she believed it. Or she almost believed it.

Right now she'd like Maisie.

And, stupidly or not, right now she couldn't stop thinking of Jack.

CHAPTER FOUR

JACK WOKE TO a whump, whump, whump out in the living room. He opened one eye and peered out. Maisie was sitting at the front door, her big tail thumping with anticipation. She obviously wanted out.

Harry was standing beside her, looking worried.

He should get up and let her out, but after a moment's thought he decided against it. He closed his eyes again. Apart from the couple of outbursts yesterday when the excitement had been too much for him, Harry had retreated to silence, but here was another situation where silence might not work.

So he lay and waited while the thumping grew increasingly excited. Harry's indecision was practically vibrating through the bungalow.

And finally Harry cracked. Jack lay silent as he heard footsteps approach, as a small hand landed on his shoulder.

'Uncle Jack,' Harry said, and that was a breakthrough all by itself.

'Call me Jack,' Jack growled, still without opening his eyes. He'd already figured 'uncle' was a barrier. '*Harry, do what Auntie Helen tells you. Harry, go and play with your cousin Alice.*' Titles were a barrier he could do without.

'Jack,' Harry whispered, and Jack opened his eyes, but

sleepily, like there was all the time in the world and it was no big deal that Harry had called him by name.

'Morning,' he said. 'Is the sun up?'

'Everyone's up,' Harry whispered. 'Everyone's on the beach. Maisie wants to go. Should I let her out?'

'Is Kate on the beach?'

'Y-yes.'

'Then let her out but leave the door open so we can watch her. After breakfast we'll go down and see if Kate wants her. If not, we'll go down and bring her back.'

Brilliant. Kate knew what she was doing, leaving Maisie with him for the night. Left to his own devices, Harry would have stayed in bed, and there'd be no way he'd go to the beach unless propelled. But like yesterday, Maisie had done Kate's propelling for her.

Back in Sydney Jack had thought of this place disparagingly. It had seemed an alternative therapy of dubious repute. But right here, right now, it looked okay. This wasn't 'alternative'. This was working.

And Harry ate, not a huge amount but enough to keep Jack satisfied, and instead of needing encouragement at every mouthful Harry had obviously decided how much Jack would let him get away with and shovelled it in fast. Dog. Beach. Go.

Just as Harry gulped the last of his juice Kate arrived, Maisie loping along behind her. She was wearing her stinger suit again. Her hair was twisted into a knot on the top of her head, she had rock sandals on her feet and she looked about as far from a doctor as it was possible to get.

'I thought you might like swim gear,' she said cheerfully. The suits were probably the most unattractive garments in the planet but she held them out like they were gold. 'These mean you don't need to use sunscreen.'

'Are there stingers in the water?' Jack asked, and then

could have bitten his tongue. The last thing he wanted was to scare Harry.

But Kate was grinning. 'No. They're like school uniform, meant to make everyone here equal. Socialists R Us.' Then, at Harry's look of confusion, she stooped to talk only to him. Her body language was obvious. Her client was Harry. Jack was just a bystander.

'Later this morning I'd like to take you to meet the dolphins close up,' she told him. 'And dolphins don't like sunscreen. Kids like you go into their pool every day. If everyone had sunscreen on, it'd float off and stick to the dolphins. Then none of them would get a tan and we'd have a whole pod of pure white dolphins. Maybe they'd get freckles, just like me. So we all wear blue suits to stop dolphin freckles.'

Harry gazed at her in confusion. And then, very slowly, as if something was cracking inside, he managed a wavery smile.

'That's silly.'

'Yep, I'm always silly,' she admitted. 'But, seriously, dolphins don't like sunscreen; it's not good for them. Harry, I have two little girls I need to see before I can spend time with you. Dianne and Ross, our play therapists, are playing with a beachball down by the waves. You can join in, or you and your Uncle Jack can build a sandcastle or paddle or swim or do whatever you want.'

'He's Jack,' Harry whispered, and it was so low Jack could hardly hear. But he heard, for he was listening like it was the most important message he could hear. 'He likes us calling him Jack.'

'Of course,' Kate said, and finally that smile was directed at him. 'Okay, Jack and Harry, put your swimsuits on and go and have fun. And don't let Maisie fool you again—Jack.'

'No one's fooling anyone,' Jack said, and smiled back at her, and thought what the heck did he mean?

He didn't have a clue. All he knew was that he was off to build sandcastles.

On the beach Harry retreated again into silence. That was okay for Jack didn't need to do anything about it. Maisie had things under control. The big dog sat by Harry's side for a while, giving him time to get accustomed, and then suddenly she started digging. Harry looked astonished. Maisie dug some more, sand spraying everywhere, then sat on her haunches and looked at Harry. Harry looked back.

Maisie dug again, sand sprayed everywhere, then she sat on her haunches again and looked at Harry. Harry resisted.

Maisie dug even more, sand sprayed everywhere, then she sat on her haunches and looked at Harry some more.

Enough.

Harry dug.

Jack hadn't been aware he'd been holding his breath, but it came out now in a rush. He looked up and one of the therapists was giving him a discreet thumbs-up sign.

How had they persuaded Maisie to do that? Who knew? But he was profoundly grateful.

Pressure off, he sat back and watched the whole scene.

The play beach was distant from the enclosed dolphin pool and Jack could see why. In the distance he could see Kate with a couple and a child. Therapy? He couldn't tell; they were far enough away to ensure privacy.

The two therapists on the beach, Dianne and Ross, were working hard but they were like big kids. Dianne was a woman in her forties, Ross was practically a teenager but dressed in their standard-issue blue suits they seemed of an age. They mixed happily with kids and parents, gently encouraging kids to mix and play, but they didn't push.

They made it seem like the most natural thing in the world to join in and have fun.

But they didn't push Harry. He was left to his digging. There were a couple of other kids who stayed back, and that was okay, too. A couple of times the beach ball just 'happened' to fly in their direction and the therapists swooped to retrieve it, thanking the individual child as if they'd retrieved it themselves.

No pressure.

Jack looked around at this motley group of parents and children. Some were overtly injured, scarred, frail. Some must be emotionally injured for there were no outward signs of what was wrong, but he'd seen the application forms. The only kids here were those whose need was strong.

And for the first time since he'd had the phone call saying his sister was dead, he found himself feeling calm. Helen had been right: this was a good place for Harry to be.

He could relax. Someone else was doing the worrying for him.

Harry was digging his way to China.

The therapists were playing keepings off, swooping off along the beach with a ragtag of children following.

There was a stir just behind him, a cry. He turned and a woman was struggling to hold a child, a girl about twelve or thirteen.

She was arching back in her mother's arms, and her involuntary jerks told Jack she was in mid-convulsion.

Harry stared. 'Jack,' he breathed, and this, too, was amazing. Not only had he registered something was wrong, he was expecting Jack to do something about it.

Kate was in the water. The therapists were far down the beach, chasing children. With his medical training, Jack certainly needed to do something about it.

The child was only ten yards away and he reached her

fast, kneeling on the sand, automatically starting to check her airway as the woman with her tried to hold her still.

Toby's death yesterday was front and foremost in his mind. Another brain tumour? How many seriously ill children did Kate have here?

But it was no such thing. 'It's all right,' the woman managed. 'It's... Susie's epileptic. She won't take... I thought she'd taken but she hates...and she hates people seeing.'

'I'm a doctor,' Jack told her. 'Let me help.'

The kid was an almost-teen, Jack thought, automatically taking her from her mother's arms and shifting her sideways. As an oncologist he treated kids of this age, and he understood their trauma. Sometimes the side effects of their illness seemed more terrible to the kids than the illness itself. Hair loss. Hospitalisation and enforced distance from their peer group. Being seen as different. *Different*. A fate worse than death for a teenager.

'Put the beach towel down for me,' he told the woman, and once again got a shock as Harry moved to help. The girl was rigid, arching, breathing noisily and seemingly unaware of her surroundings. If she was indeed epileptic, though, all they needed to do was keep her safe until the convulsion passed.

He set her down, rolling her onto her side. Then checked his watch. Convulsions always seemed to last for ever. There was no need to worry if it didn't go past five minutes but, watching a kid convulse, it was very hard to register time.

'My husband's gone to make a phone call for work,' the woman sobbed. 'He's with the police; they're always calling him, even though he's supposed to be here, helping me care. And I don't know what to do. I never do. I hate these attacks. Don's better than me with coping. I can't... Should I call someone? Kate?'

But Jack had been here before, all too often. His little sister had been epileptic.... *Both* his parents had hated her attacks. Jack had learned to cope early, and his medical training had reinforced what he'd learned the hard way. The only thing Beth had hated more than her epileptic attacks had been people seeing her having them, and this kid would be no different. He glanced across at Kate and then along the beach to the therapists. Any call would make everyone on the beach aware of what was happening.

His body was blocking the view for the moment and no one else seemed to have noticed. If they could keep this private...

'I'm sure I can look after her,' he told Susie's mum. 'There's no problem. Harry, can you give me a hand to shift these two beach shelters so we can get some shade?'

It wasn't shade they needed. The beach was only pleasantly warm. But Harry was only too eager to help. They hauled two of the little shelters around so they made a V, the opening looking out to the water. It effectively blocked off anyone along the beach seeing, but it looked like he'd simply hauled two shelters together so two families could chat.

Then he settled beside her, checked her airway again, checked her pulse, kept watch. And as Harry looked unsure, he tugged him down so the little boy was on his knee.

'This looks a lot scarier than it is,' he told Harry, and as he talked, Susie's body lost some of its rigidity. Her mum was stroking her face, making sure her hair was out of her eyes, keeping watch as Jack was doing. The girl's eyes flickered open and registered her mum.

'I'm Dr Jack,' Jack told her, pretty sure she couldn't take it in yet, but he'd reassure her anyway. 'And no one can see.'

'What's wrong?' Harry breathed.

'It's called epilepsy,' Jack said, keeping his voice even and strong, knowing his presence would be reassuring the mother, if not the teen. 'But it's okay. Lots of people have it. When you watch television, do you ever notice that occasionally the picture goes fuzzy for a minute or you get funny lines? Only for a minute and then it goes back to normal.'

'Yes,' Harry said, cautiously.

'Well, that's what epilepsy is,' Jack said. 'It's like a little electronic signal in Susie's brain gets the wrong signals. It's called a tonic-clonic seizure. That's a long name for something that's usually very short. Susie's waking up now. She'll be back to being herself in no time.'

They sat on. Susie was gradually returning to normal. He watched as her eyes lost their dazed, faraway look, focussed, cringed.

'It's okay,' he said, as her focus returned. 'A momentary hiccup that no one saw.'

'Th-thank you.' Susie's mum was still close to tears, but Jack gave her a warning look. The last thing Susie needed now was emotion.

She was curling into herself, a fragile kid on the edge of womanhood. Her clinging stinger suit showed the faint budding of breasts. Her brown hair was tugged back into a glittery band, and if he wasn't mistaken she had a touch of make-up on under the sunscreen on her nose.

He remembered Beth at that age. It hurt to remember her.

'My sister had epilepsy,' he heard himself say and he hadn't meant to say it until it came out. 'Beth.'

'My...my Mum,' Harry whispered.

'That's right.'

'She never looked like Susie looked.'

'That's because she had control of her medication,' Jack

said. 'She never missed. Do you remember, Harry, that your mum took pills every breakfast-time?'

'She was old,' Susie managed. 'It'd be okay if…I was old.'

Jack winced. The thought of Beth as old was unthinkable but, then, at thirteen, even twenty probably seemed ancient.

'Beth had epilepsy from when she was a baby,' Jack said. 'It wasn't serious. The only time it was a problem was when she was a teenager and she thought the pills made her gain weight.'

And Susie stilled. Bingo, Jack thought, glancing at Susie's mum. Teenagers worrying about body image. Some things were perennial.

'She tried not taking her medication,' Jack said. 'That was a disaster. She had seizures at school and the kids saw her and that seemed to make things worse. Finally, though, she figured she might control her weight gain with exercise. She got her black belt for karate. After that no one messed with my sister, ever again, and she was beautiful.'

'But…what happened to her?' Susie seemed wide awake now, aware, even glancing at Harry. 'Is that…his…mum?'

'Beth was Harry's mum,' he agreed. 'She and Harry's dad were killed in a car accident. It had nothing to do with her epilepsy, though, Susie—a drunk driver crashed into the family car. Before that…she had a great life. She went to uni, had fun, met a gorgeous boy and married him, had Harry. Nothing stopped her.'

'I don't…I don't like karate,' Susie managed, and Jack had to suppress a smile. Harry's tragedy, Beth's death were taking a back seat to Susie's problems. Of course they were. Could any adolescent be different?

'Sports come in all shapes and sizes,' he told her. He glanced out at the sea. 'What about swimming? Do you like swimming with the dolphins?'

'Yeah, but...' She hesitated, licking her lips, and Jack knew she'd still be struggling with the feeling of coming out of the fog. Her mouth would be thick and dry, she needed fluids, then rest with quiet. But for some reason instinct told him he should go along with this conversation. 'I wanted to dance,' she whispered, and he knew he was right.

'So why don't you?'

'She had an episode at dance class last year,' her mum said. 'The girls...weren't very kind.'

'Ouch. Other girls can be horrid at your age,' Jack said bluntly. 'Beth used to complain about them, too. But she never let them stop her. Do you know that one person in every fifty is an epileptic? Two people in every hundred. So I'm willing to bet that some of the most famous dancers in the world are epileptic.'

'They can't be,' Susie breathed.

'Want to bet?' Jack demanded. 'Tell you what, if I'm wrong I'll let all the kids bury me up to my neck in sand and leave me there for an hour. But I bet I'm right. I have my computer here, and a printer. I'll look it up tonight and I'll have a list of dancers who have epilepsy sitting on your doorstep tomorrow.'

'You're...silly,' Susie managed.

'He is.' Harry beamed. Finally, here was something he agreed with. 'Jack's silly.'

'And I hope he's not bothering you.' It was Kate; of course it was Kate. How long had she been there, on the other side of the screens, listening and waiting for a chance to break in? He tugged back the screen and she was calmly sitting on the sand, with Maisie's head in her lap, as if this was where she sat all the time. 'Jack's an excellent doctor but he can be silly,' she told Susie, as if she'd been part of the conversation all along. But there was no mention of what had just happened. No fuss. 'I went to university with him,' she told Susie. 'So I should know.'

'He says I can still dance,' Susie faltered.

'Then make him prove it.'

'He says he will. I…hope.'

'Then, silly or not, if he says he will then he will,' Kate said, smiled down at Susie. 'You feeling okay now?'

'I… Yes.'

'Not too fuzzy-headed to swim with the dolphins this afternoon?'

'No!'

'Maybe a wee rest first?'

'Okay.'

'Great,' Kate said, and moved on, as if the whole episode was behind them.

'How did you know what happened?' Jack demanded, as Susie and her mum made their way back to the bungalows, walking hand in hand as if nothing had happened.

'I saw,' Kate said. 'I was about to come up but then you took over. Thank you.'

'You're welcome.' He hesitated. 'How many medical problems do you have in this place?'

'More now that I'm here,' she said. 'We don't advertise medical care, but now I'm here we don't turn away kids with conditions like Toby's. But Susie doesn't need medical care. She just needs…confidence.' She smiled down at Harry. 'And, Harry, your Jack might be silly but he did a great job looking after Susie. He said just the right thing. I'm grateful.'

What was there in that to make a man want to blush? Nothing. It was a simple compliment, nothing more. But Kate's smile transferred itself to him and he definitely wanted to blush. Or something.

That smile had stayed the same since the first time he'd met her.

That smile was really something.

'You want to meet the dolphins now?' Kate asked Harry, and the moment was broken. But not the sensation. Not the desire to see more of that smile.

Harry hesitated but Maisie had leaped to attention and her whole body quivered. She looked from Harry to Kate and back again, and her message couldn't be clearer.

There's fun this way. Come with me and play.

How did they train a dog to do this?

No matter, the message was irresistible. Harry put a tentative hand on Maisie's collar and it was like pressing a go button. Maisie headed off steadily along the beach with Kate, with Harry clinging behind.

Bemused, Jack was left to follow.

He walked slowly, watching Kate chat to his nephew. Down at the water two of the dolphins were playing with a ball, tossing it seemingly just for pleasure. The sun was glittering on the sea, the tiny waves were only knee high at most and sandpipers were once again searching for pippies along the shoreline. This was the most perfect place.

'You're welcome to join us but you don't have to come in with us, Jack,' Kate said, quite kindly. She'd slipped her hand into Harry's and to Jack's astonishment Harry didn't tug away. This was a child who'd hardly let himself be touched since his parents had died. 'We can have fun ourselves.'

'I'd like to come,' he said, thinking he did not want to be excluded from the fun his nephew could have with this woman.

Fun? He thought of the story she'd told him last night, of the pain she'd gone through, and he thought, here she was, dispensing fun.

'Then you need to know the rules,' Kate told him. 'Harry and I were discussing them while you dawdled.'

'I did not dawdle.' Astonishingly, she was laughing at him.

'You did so dawdle, didn't he, Harry?' She chuckled. 'But for the slowcoaches, here are the rules again. The main one is no touching.'

No touching? He'd been expecting touchy-feely stuff. Riding the dolphins? Maybe not, but close.

'Dolphins don't like being touched except on their terms,' she told him. 'All the dolphins in this pool were born wild. They're here because they've been injured, or orphaned, or somehow left so they can't survive in the open sea. But that doesn't mean they're pets. Some of them will nudge us. Hobble, for one, is a very pushy dolphin, but it's for him to decide, not us. But they do like playing. In the wild, dolphins surf. They seem to leap just for the joy of leaping when they're wild and free. But what's happened to them in the past means that they can't be free. Even though this pool is half the bay wide, it's not enough. They get bored so it's up to us to make them happy.'

And as she said it she walked into the water, lifted a beach ball floating in the shallows and tossed it far out.

It never hit the water. As it reached the peak of its arc a silver bullet streaked up from the surface. The dolphin's nose hit the ball square on, it rebounded, another silver bullet flashed from nowhere, the ball rebounded again—and landed in the shallows in front of Kate.

Harry had been standing behind Kate, open-mouthed with awe. Kate took a step back to stand beside him.

'This is our favourite game,' she said idly, and Jack couldn't tell whether she was talking to him, to Harry or to the dolphins. 'But it makes me tired.' She lifted the ball again and threw, with exactly the same results. 'My arm aches,' she said. 'I've been tossing it for ages. That might be all I can do today.'

'I will throw the ball,' Harry said.

'You'd have to throw it far out,' Kate said dubiously, looking out to where one of the dolphins was rearing out of the water as if checking to see if the ball was returning.

'I can.'

'If you think so,' Kate said, and stepped back still further.

She didn't pick up the ball for him, though. The ball was floating about six feet in front of the little boy, in the shallows. He'd have to wade forward.

For three months Harry had been totally passive. He'd done exactly what he was told. He'd submitted to everything with stoic indifference. His world had been shattered and he'd been totally, absolutely joyless.

Now, as the world seemed to hold its breath, something changed. The little boy's shoulders, for months slumped and defeated, seemed to square.

He looked out at the dolphins and as if on cue they both reared, skating backwards. *Come on*, their body language said. *What are you waiting for?*

And then they dived, so deep they disappeared, and that message was obvious, too. Time to start the game now.

And while Jack watched in awe, and Kate said nothing at all, Harry strode purposefully out into the waves, grabbed the ball and tossed it high out over the sea to the waiting dolphins.

There was nothing for Jack and Kate to do but stand and watch. The dolphins did the rest.

This must be a game they played over and over with withdrawn children, Jack thought. Harry was putty in their...flippers?

Harry threw the ball and they tossed it back to him, but as they did they gradually returned the ball a little further out. The waves were tiny and non-threatening. Harry found himself chest deep in the water before he knew it, but he was focussed only on the ball.

The next time he threw it, the dolphins flipped it back, but this time they flipped it over his head. He turned to grab it but before he could, a silver streak flew through the shallows, reached the ball before he did and flipped it back to where it had been landing before.

Harry lunged for it but the second dolphin reached it first, tossing it high again.

'It's mine,' Harry yelled, and grabbed for it, got it and tossed it out again. 'I got it, I got it,' he yelled, and he turned to Jack and Kate, his face alive with excitement. 'They tried to take it away from me but I got it.'

'Watch out, they're coming back,' Kate said, chuckling. 'They're champions at playing keepings off.'

The ball came back again and Harry pounced.

He was twisting on his injured leg, Jack realised. It had been badly broken. It still hurt to weight-bear so he usually tried not to use it. But Jack hadn't needed the physio's explanation to know where the problem lay—they all knew it. The only way Harry could get back the use of his leg was to use it.

He was using it now. It must be hurting, at least a little, but he was too entranced to notice.

'I can't believe this,' he murmured to Kate, while Harry was ball-chasing, out of earshot.

'It's our specialty,' she said, flashing him a look that was almost smug. 'None of your hospital physiotherapists have this—the means to make kids forget every single thing that's wrong with them. It's why this place is magic.'

'I don't believe in magic.' But maybe he did, he thought as he watched Harry pounce again. He thought of Susie, withdrawing into herself, desperately unhappy but still aching to play with the dolphins. He thought of Toby, his last days made happy. And he watched Harry.

It seemed like a miracle. Maybe he was even prepared to give magic a shot if it'd get Harry well again.

He was feeling disoriented, watching his nephew throw the ball, standing beside this woman in her crazy blue swimsuit.

He felt totally out of his depth.

Medicine. When all else was confusion, focus on medicine. It was a mantra that had served him well for years and he retreated to it now.

'His leg shouldn't be taking so long to heal,' he told Kate, trying to sound professional, two medical colleagues discussing a patient. Two medics in swimsuits. 'His femur was badly fractured but, even so, most kids with intramedullary nails are weight-bearing almost straight away. But we haven't been able to get him to use it.'

'He's had no reason to use it,' Kate said gently. 'It hurts and he's had enough hurting, losing his parents. Why put himself through more?'

He thought of the last physiotherapist Harry had seen—a young man not long out of training. He'd sat back and exclaimed in exasperation, 'Harry, you're not trying. I can't help you if you don't try.'

Harry's quadriceps were growing more and more wasted the less he used them, but that sort of reasoning got nowhere with him. Why should he try? It hurt and there was no point.

But now this woman had nailed it. She knew instinctively why Harry was like he was. They were in her hands, he thought, and his doubts were fading. Hers were competent hands. She knew what she was doing. He watched her subtly manoeuvre Harry, using the dolphins and the ball to have him bounce up and down, twist left and right. He threw and threw and the dolphins seemed to love every moment of it. Occasionally Harry winced and grimaced but he wasn't complaining. The dolphins—and Kate—seemed indeed to be magic. This was better than any medical intervention Jack could have thought of.

He'd love this back in Sydney. He thought of so many of his terminal cancer patients. How much joy this could give to families in distress.

He was willing to bet, even without his conversation, Kate would have got Susie back dancing.

He and Harry were blessed to have found this place.

Whoever Kate was, he thought, she was okay by him.

Finally Kate glanced at her watch and called a halt.

'It's almost lunchtime,' she told them. 'The dolphins need a break, even if we don't. Harry, later today you could do some leg exercises with Dianne in the swimming pool. She'll show you how to use a kick board so you can chase balls further. Then you can come back into the dolphin pool and see what the dolphins think of your new skills. Meanwhile, you can dig with Maisie or build sandcastles or have a nap or whatever you and Jack want to do. But now we're having hot dogs for lunch. Coming?' And she held out her hand.

Once again Jack found himself holding his breath. There was so much in those few short statements. *You could do some leg exercises in the swimming pool...* Using a kick board would be the best possible therapy for Harry—it would mean strengthening the quadriceps in the most natural way possible. The physios in Sydney had tried to get Harry to use one in the hospital therapy pool and Harry had refused, but here it had come out naturally, as if there could be no possible objection. Kate had moved straight onto hot dogs, and now she was holding out her hand as if she expected Harry to take it.

How did she do it? It wasn't only dolphins, Jack thought.

This woman created an aura of absolute trust. If he was Harry he'd put his hand in hers, he thought, and he wasn't in the least bit surprised when Harry did.

'I like hot dogs,' Harry said in satisfaction, and then turned to look out to sea.

'Bye, dolphins.'

'Bye, dolphins,' Jack repeated, and then added under his breath, 'And thanks.'

They ate in the friendly dining-cum-lounge room. This was no aseptic hospital cafeteria but a homey area with a couple of bustling, smiley women ladling food on the tables. Each of the small dining tables was set with home-like tableware and place mats made by kids before them. Windows overlooked the bay, toys were scattered on the veranda, and through the arch, big comfy lounge suites and a massive billiard table made you think it was worth hurrying lunch because the world was waiting.

Susie was there, with her mum. The mum smiled and waved as they entered, and even Susie gave a cautious, teenager-not-wanting-be-noticed half-smile. Jack wasn't tempted to join them. Act as if nothing has happened, Susie's half-smile said, and that was fine by him. They found a place by the window and settled in.

Harry had retreated into his customary silence but he sat calmly by Jack's side and ate his hot dog without prodding. And why wouldn't he? Jack thought, heading back to the serving table for his third. He hadn't even been throwing the ball and he was ravenous—as well as exhausted. How had tension made him so tired?

'They tell you that you're bringing the kids here to make them well,' a burly guy sitting opposite said. 'What they don't tell you is that you end up doing as much or more than the kids.'

'It wasn't me doing the exercises,' Jack said, but the guy

nodded toward the next table where a boy of about twelve was seated in a wheelchair, discussing the merits of which dolphin was fastest with a girl who looked like she'd been through chemotherapy.

'It takes it out of you just watching,' he said. 'I reckon every step our Sam takes, we take six. Your heart's in your mouth all the time. Wendy, the kid he's talking to…she's got some cancer called neuroblastoma and it's spread too far to fix. She's eleven, can you imagine what her folks are going through? But I saw her in the pool today, mucking round like she was just a normal kid and a happy one at that. Her folks were even laughing. Geez, we're pleased we found this place. Have another hot dog, mate.'

Jack did, and so did Harry. Then they retired to their bungalow for Kate's prescribed nap.

There was no protest from Harry. He was simply following rules and Jack thought, for a little boy whose world had been turned upside down, rules were good.

Harry slept. Jack did some highly satisfactory research on ballet dancers—it looked like he wouldn't be buried in sand after all—and then dozed.

Or sort of dozed. Images kept flitting through his mind.

Kate.

In less than a day he'd stopped thinking of her as Cathy. In less than a day he'd started thinking of her in a whole new way from how he'd considered her when she'd been his friend and lab partner back at university.

She was gorgeous.

She was hiding. The sensations of the morning faded and he was left with that one main thought.

She had to hide.

Jack Kincaid was a man who didn't do anger. Sure, there were things that annoyed him, but until Beth's death life had been pretty much how he'd anticipated. He'd had a great job, good friends, a beautiful girlfriend. He'd always known he was lucky. He'd appreciated his good luck, and he'd been making the most of it. In his work he'd seen how life knocked some people around but he'd never been knocked. What had he had to be angry about?

When Beth had died he'd been gutted. His perfect world had been knocked sideways but even then he hadn't been angry. Anger would have been better, he thought. Easier. Instead, he'd just felt empty.

Going back to work, taking his place in his perfect life again, that emptiness had remained. It was like there had been a gaping hole where his sister had been, where Harry's family had fitted.

And now, suddenly, for the first time, he felt anger, and it wasn't on behalf of his small nephew. It was for a kid called Cathy who'd been hauled from the life she loved and turned into the hunted. She hadn't needed to tell him how hard it must have been to run to New Zealand, to try and survive through a new university course, to cut herself off from every person she'd known in her past life. He could see it in the life lines on her face, in the shadows, in the way the laughter in her voice was edged with constant wariness.

This Simon had a lot to answer for, and Jack found himself staring out to sea and wishing he could face the bastard. Just once.

For Kate.

How corny was that? It was a caveman reaction, a testosterone-driven male protecting his own.

His own? Where had that come from? Kate was Harry's treating doctor—or treating physiotherapist and counsellor. He was here as Harry's guardian. There were professional boundaries that couldn't be crossed.

So why was he thinking of crossing them? He must have had too much sun, he decided, and on impulse he called Annalise.

'Jack!' Her voice was warm, but he could hear an edge of briskness, noises in the background that told him she was busy.

It was the weekend. She shouldn't be at work, but Annalise was often at work when she wasn't on duty. They both were. If you wanted to climb the career ladder, that's what you did.

'How's it going?' she asked. 'Dolphins, prayer flags and a bit of ear candling on the side?'

They'd laughed about this, both of them having the same reaction to alternate therapies. He was taking Harry here because Helen had insisted. He didn't believe in it.

But now, looking out over the bay, remembering the way Kate had stood back while Harry had turned again into a laughing, crowing little boy, thinking of Toby and of Susie, he thought he might well have been stupidly biased.

'It's early days yet,' he said cautiously. 'But I may have been wrong.'

'You're joking,' Annalise said. 'Are the dolphin mantras getting to you?'

'They're making Harry smile. I'm not asking for anything more right now.'

'Well, that's wonderful,' Annalise said briskly. 'If they can bring him out of his shell enough so he can come home and undertake real therapy then I'll even concede the uses of a little mantra-chanting. You're being marvellous, darling. Is there anything else? I really am busy.'

'Of course you are,' he said, and disconnected a moment later feeling strangely dissatisfied. Why? She'd said what they'd both been thinking. And brisk phone calls when they were working was what he was used to.

He hesitated and then phoned Helen. Any emotion he'd missed with Annalise was more than made up for by his Harry's paternal aunt.

He told her about the dolphins and she sobbed.

'Oh, Jack, that's wonderful. He laughed? He spoke? Tell me again what he said.' She wanted to know every detail and by the end of the call he found himself thinking maybe Harry should end up back with Helen. Five kids or not, there was no doubt Helen cared.

He'd argued hard with Helen to take over Harry's care. With memories of his quiet sister Beth, who'd spent her life engrossed in her karate and her science, happy with her boffin husband in her own little world, he'd seen Harry swamped by a world full of Helen's kids. But what sort of life could he give him as an alternative?

The question was too hard. Take one step at a time, he told himself.

'And I've been doing a bit of enquiring about Cathy Heineman,' Helen was saying, and her words pulled him back to the here and now like nothing else could. 'No one's heard of her for years. Everyone's astounded she's turned up there.'

Uh-oh. He'd forgotten he'd asked Helen about Kate.

'There's no need to make further enquiries,' he said, trying to sound as if it didn't much matter. And then he thought, Dammit, this was important, say it like it was. 'Helen, I talked to Kate—to Cathy—last night about the identity thing. It seems she's run from a violent marriage. She's changed her name. She doesn't want anyone to know.'

There was a moment's silence and then indignation. 'You could have told me that yesterday.'

'I didn't know yesterday.'

'Well, I hope I haven't blown her cover,' she said dubiously. 'I doubt it, though. How long ago was she married?'

'Several years.'

'There you go, then,' she said, relaxing. 'Old history. But I understand women who've faced abuse can't put it behind them. I don't think anyone I talked to yesterday would have taken it further. Most could hardly remember her, and no one seemed to know her husband.'

If you put Helen on a project she was like a terrier with a bone. How many people had she talked to?

'I wouldn't tell her I've been asking,' Helen said. 'You'll only make her fearful again, poor girl. And if she's helping Harry...from a selfish point of view I want all her attention on him. You keep them both safe, Jack Kincaid, and stay in touch. Give Harry a big kiss from me and tell him to get well fast.'

She disconnected, satisfied. Jack sat back and tried to feel satisfied as well.

He wasn't. He was disturbed.

Should he tell Kate that he might have blown her cover?

He thought of her smile, the way she'd laughed with Harry, her joy when her dolphins made Harry happy.

He'd be messing with that joy if he told her.

But if he didn't warn her...

He didn't have a choice, he decided. He had to. At least for the next couple of weeks he'd be here and could keep her safe.

Ha! That was the caveman in him. Neanderthal man, complete with club, protecting his woman.

But he looked out at the calm waters, at the peace of the bay, and he wondered how there could ever be threats here. Helen was right, Kate's marriage was history. Her husband would have long moved on. Telling her there might be the sniff of a threat would mar her peace for nothing.

I do need to tell her before I leave, he told himself. But I'm sure she's safe. Stop worrying. For now Helen's right. Let's just focus on Harry.

CHAPTER FIVE

LET'S JUST FOCUS on Harry.

That was all very well, Jack thought as the days wore on, but Kate was right there in his focus as well.

The more he saw her, the more entranced he became.

It wasn't that she was classically beautiful. Almost permanently dressed in a skin suit that flattered no one—a supermodel could hardly look good in skin-tight electric blue—with her often damp hair tugged back, her face devoid of make-up and her nose splodged with white zinc, she looked a world apart from the career-women in Jack's normal world.

Maybe that was the attraction—but surely the attraction was that she was so caring. The attraction was the way she made Harry smile—and the attraction was the way she smiled herself, her dimples, her freckles, her total and absolute focus on the child she was treating.

She loved her work, and she was good at it. Very good.

While Harry played with his dolphins he watched her discreetly manipulate play, so that Harry was forced to use his bad leg, so he was turning and twisting in a way he'd never do on land. The water took the weight from his legs so it wouldn't hurt as much, but still the unused muscles would be complaining. But because the dolphins were waiting for their new friend to join in with the next trick, Harry didn't notice.

In the normal physio sessions back at the hospital in Sydney, Harry hadn't tried. It had hurt and he'd wanted his mother. He'd been a ball of misery, and the more he'd curled into himself, the more the muscles had atrophied.

Here, under Kate's gentle guidance, he was stretching more than Jack had dared hope.

Kate couldn't be everywhere at once—she had a dozen small clients to treat—but the swimming pool physio sessions in the afternoon with the other trained staff were almost as effective. The physios back in Sydney had been good, Jack conceded, but they'd never had the enticement of 'If you can kick to the end of the pool, you and Hobble might be able to have a race tomorrow.'

'That's silly,' Harry had said, and once again Jack had caught his breath because this was Harry who was talking. Harry's tongue seemed to have atrophied as well, but now the muscles were tentatively in use again. 'I can't beat Hobble,' he said.

'He gets handicapped,' the physio told Harry.

'What's…what's handicapped?'

'We tell Hobble he has to zoom around the enclosure ten times while you use your board to kick from one side to the other. If he wins he gets a fish. If you win you get to feed all the dolphins a fish, so Hobble has to watch all his mates get one, too.'

Harry giggled, grabbed his foam kick board and started kicking. His wasted quadriceps meant he moved slowly but the up and down motion continued. With the dolphins used as a wonderful enticement to continue, Harry worked harder than Jack could believe was possible.

But as good as the support staff were, as successful as the physio programme was, it was Kate who did the most good. Harry and Kate had a one-on-one session each morning, supposedly playing with the dolphins, but there was a psychological component undercurrent running through it that stunned him.

The first time Harry 'beat' Hobble, Kate whooped with excitement. She fetched fish so Harry could solemnly feed all four dolphins. Harry giggled as Hobble took his fish and retreated to the far reaches of the pool—for all the world as if he was sulking at having to share. Kate chuckled, handed Harry the bucket of fish and said, oh, so casually: 'Oh, Harry, your mum and dad would be so proud of you.'

There was a moment's silence. The same sentence would have seen Harry shut down a week ago, but the dolphins were lined up for fish, Hobble was edging back and there was no corner to curl up in and withdraw.

Hobble sneaked in and knocked the bucket. A fish slipped out and Hobble had it. He reared back and Jack could have sworn he was laughing.

Harry smiled as well, but he still looked fearful. Kate had reminded him of things that were terrible.

'My mum and dad are dead,' he said.

And there was a breath-catcher, too. Harry had never referred to them, not once since the crash.

'That's right. They were killed in the accident where you broke your leg,' Kate said matter-of-factly. She took a fish and held it up. 'But I bet they're still proud of you. Some very wise people think that when parents die, part of them stays around for their kids. Not like they were, of course, but in the only way they can manage. It might be like the wind; when you feel a warm wind on your nose it's like a cuddle from your mum. Or the sunbeams. They could be your mum and dad smiling.

'Hobble, this is Splash's,' she said to Hobble, who was eyeing the fish she was holding, obviously wondering if another swoop would pay off. 'If you want to be the only one who eats fish then you have to beat Harry, and Harry's getting faster.' She tossed the fish to Splash and watched the dynamics as the two fishless dolphins shoved their way to the front. Jack thought she was abandoning the deep and meaningful—but no.

'But I'm guessing the accident must have been really frightening, Harry,' she said.

All attention was on the dolphins. When the psychologists had talked to Harry at the hospital all the attention had been on him and he'd refused to answer.

This time he answered. 'Yes,' said Harry.

'Was Jack there when you woke up at the hospital?'

'Yes. And my Aunty Helen. But I want my mum and dad.'

'I'd want my mum and dad, too,' Kate said, again matter-of-factly. 'More than anything in the world.'

'I want them to come and get me. Now.'

They didn't have pockets in these damned suits. What Jack needed right now was a man-sized handkerchief. Or six.

'What are you worried about most?' Kate probed gently, handing Harry a fish. 'Don't let Hobble or Splash get this one.'

That took concentration. Harry might forget the question, Jack thought, but it was a huge question and Harry didn't forget.

'I don't think Mum and Dad will come back,' Harry said at last, in a dreary little voice. 'They're dead.'

'Don't forget the sunbeams,' Kate said, and Harry looked up towards the sun and let his nose warm up a little.

'No,' he whispered, and Jack wanted a handkerchief again.

'So who do you think should care for you, now that your mum and dad can't look after you?'

There was a long silence. Harry took a couple of steps forward, gripped his fish, waited until the right dolphin edged close—and then put the fish in the waiting mouth just as Hobble swept forward to intercept.

Hobble missed out and Harry managed a quavery smile. The edge of the awful question had been taken away.

But it lay unanswered. Kate gave him all the time in the world, and finally he went back to it.

'My Auntie Helen will keep me,' he said at last. 'She said to Uncle Doug, '"One more kid doesn't make any difference. We'll scarcely notice."'

Jack drew in his breath. He remembered that conversation. Harry had still been in hospital. They'd all thought he was asleep.

'So your Auntie Helen and your Uncle Doug want you to live with them.'

'Yes.'

'Jack says they've given you a neat bedroom,' Kate said. They'd fed the dolphins the big fish but she had whitebait in the bottom of the bucket, tiny fish which could be eked out to extend a conversation. 'Is all your stuff there?'

'Mum and Dad aren't there.' He threw a tiny fish, hard, and the dolphins played a nudging game to get it.

'Your mum and dad aren't in your bedroom?'

'No. They're dead.'

'I can see that makes you feel angry,' Kate said, a nobrainer as he was hurling individual whitebait with force.

'They've left me with Aunty Helen.'

'You're with Jack now,' Kate pointed out.

'He doesn't want me. I heard my mum say that Jack and Annalise don't have time for kids. He'll go back to work. I want my mum and dad.'

Whoa. So much information, so much emotion, where there'd been nothing. He opened his mouth to say something but Kate shot him a warning glance. Don't mess with this, her glance said, and he subsided.

'You know, there's a whole lot of stuff you need to sort

out,' Kate said. 'There's a whole lot of stuff that Jack needs to sort out, too. Missing your mum and dad is the biggest thing. It must hurt and hurt and hurt. But Jack loved your mother very much. He's her brother. He must be missing her just as much as you are.'

'He's not,' Harry said. 'He's a grown-up.'

'Grown-ups cry,' Kate said. 'Only sometimes they do it on the inside where you can't see. Is it like that for you, Jack?'

'Yes.' There was nothing else to say to a question like that.

'I think you and Jack are hurting just as much as each other,' Kate said. 'But, Harry, you have a sore leg as well, which means you get more chocolate ice cream tonight than Jack. Uh-oh. We've run out of fish. Is it time to take a shower before lunch? I think it's fish and chips today.' She turned to the dolphins and waved her empty bucket. 'No more for you, guys, but we're having fish for lunch as well.'

And the session was over, just like that.

Jack was feeling winded. He turned to leave the water, but suddenly Harry was right by his side, and a small hand slid into his.

'Do you cry inside?' he asked.

'Yes, I do.'

Harry looked at him quietly and then nodded.

'I want some fish and chips.'

Why was she so...discombobulated by the sight of Jack? Why was he doing her head in?

He seemed to be everywhere and yet he was only doing the normal thing dads did with their kids. Playing on the sand. Splashing about in the shallows. Taking a little time out to do long laps of the pool while she played with Harry. That was the hardest—her attention had to be totally on Harry and it was, but there was a part of her allowing her peripheral vision to take in his long, lean body stroking lazily through the water.

He was struggling with Harry—she could see it—and that twisted her heart a bit, too. He wasn't Harry's dad but he was trying. Every time Harry fell over, literally or metaphorically, he was there to pick him up. The little boy was withdrawn, mostly unresponsive, but it didn't stop Jack from hugging him, laughing with him, teasing him, caring for him.

He was a high-flying, ambitious medic. He was taking two weeks to try and bond with Harry.

He was also helping with the other kids here, subtly but surely. The way he'd responded to Susie had been more than kind; it had been empathic and sensitive. Susie was already talking about dancing again. Jack had used the admin. equipment to print pictures of famous dancers and Susie had them pinned to her wall. Why that did her head in she didn't know, but somehow a chord was touched. And she loved what he was trying to do with Harry. She didn't quite understand how these two could manage at the end of their two weeks here but for now he was trying and she had to give the man credit.

She didn't, however, need to give the man attention. Unfortunately her hormones thought otherwise.

'It's just that they're out of practice,' she told herself crossly. 'Get over it. The man's here as a client and that's all. Remember it.'

It was hard to remember when he was on her doorstep. She was watching telly when she heard a tentative knock on her door. It was eight o'clock but she was never off duty here. She was the only doctor so in any medical emergency she was available.

This wasn't a medical emergency. Jack was on her front porch, looking worried.

'I know,' he said, as she answered the door. 'You're staff and I'm a client. I'm supposed to make an appointment to see you. But I couldn't go to sleep tonight without saying thank you.'

'What I do is my job,' she said gently.

He was wearing chinos, an open-necked, short-sleeved shirt and no shoes. How fast her clients became beach bums, she thought. The blue sun suits were practical but they were a great leveller. Clothes could be used as a defence and there were no defences here.

'I didn't want to bring him here,' he said, and she hesitated and then stepped out onto the veranda. It was a corny soap she'd been watching anyway. The fact that television soap characters had become a big part of her life was irrelevant.

'You thought we were a pack of crystal ball gazers.'

'Something like that. I was wrong. I just…needed to say it.'

'Thank you for admitting it.' She glanced back through the screen.

'I'm interrupting.'

'Of course you are. Natalie's ex-husband has been found in bed with Natalie's stepmother and Jake has just revealed a secret baby to his fiancée. Oh, and Brandon's been caught with his hand in the till to the tune of eight million dollars.'

He glanced through to the television and saw a hysterical blonde yelling at a guy in handcuffs. 'Um… Wow!'

'You think you have dramas,' she said, and grinned. 'I listen to personal dramas all day and watch soaps at night to get them into perspective.'

'Can I watch, too?' he asked, and it was so much what she hadn't expected to him to say that she took a step back.

'Sorry,' he said hastily. 'I didn't mean…'

But he did mean and she could see it. Most of the kids

here came with two parents, or a parent and support person. Jack was here alone.

She knew the need for adult companionship more than most.

'Harry?' she asked, but she knew already that this man wouldn't leave his nephew alone.

'He's asleep,' he said. 'The Fords have their teenage daughter with them, as well as Jacob of the injured spine. Misty Ford's currently sitting in my living room, playing computer games, with instructions to call me the moment Harry wakes.'

'You're paying her?'

'Of course.' He smiled. 'She's bored out of her mind and thinks this is an excellent plan.'

'So if I sent you back now, she'd be miffed.'

'I can go for a walk on the beach instead.'

She looked at him, this big, gentle man who seemed totally out of his depth with the future he was facing. He was asking for help, too, she thought. She should refer him to a session tomorrow. She did try to keep her professional life separate from her private.

But Jack had been a friend way back. A friend. How many of those did she have?

'Come in,' she said, swinging the screen door wide again. 'Welcome to the world where everyone else's problems fade into insignificance.'

So they watched a soap and then another one. Passion, drama, deception, intrigue, rage, tears, sex, all encapsulated in an hour and a half of hot television. When the second show came to an end Kate flicked off the telly and Jack felt winded.

'Whew.'

'What did I tell you?' she said, and grinned. 'Your problems are puny.'

'So I see,' he said, and smiled back, and she thought…
she thought…

Um, that sort of thinking wasn't appropriate. This man
was her client's uncle. Long ago he'd been a friend but
surely now all her thinking should be on a professional
basis.

But he was sprawled back on her settee. She'd provided
him with a beer. He looked relaxed and a bit sunburned—
she insisted on sun suits for the dolphins' sake but there
was no way she could force people to keep applying zinc
to their faces. He looked big and male and…gorgeous.

This man had been irresistible at uni, she thought. The
women had come running. She'd watched from the sidelines and understood why.

Now this man was sprawled in her living room. Asking for help?

He'd come to thank her. That was fine, but if there
was one thing she was good at it was reading undercurrents. The soapies had given him time out. He looked less
strained than when he'd arrived, but there were still lines
around his eyes that spoke of sleepless nights.

She had a sudden, irrational urge to reach out and
smooth…

Um, no. She'd invited him in, given him a beer and let
him watch soaps on her television. To take this further
would be crazy. He didn't want it, and neither did she. He
had a girlfriend, after all; and she did not do relationships.
One Simon in her life was enough for anyone.

'Want to tell me about it?' she asked.

He met her gaze head on. This was an honest man, she
thought suddenly. She could trust this man.

'I may have blown your cover,' he said, and, bang, there
went her trust.

'Like…how?'

'I hope I haven't,' he said seriously. 'But when I first

arrived, before I talked to you, I rang Helen about the discrepancies in your name. She did a bit of enquiring.'

'Oh,' she said in a small voice.

'I doubt it'll come to anything. It was simply a query as to what had happened to Cathy Heineman. I doubt any of the people she queried would have passed it on. Besides, your ex-husband would hardly be still trying to find you. Surely after all these years...'

'It'll be okay,' she said. 'Don't worry.'

But a shadow had flitted over her face as he'd said it. There was still fear. He felt like kicking himself. He shouldn't have told her. After all these years her fears must surely be unfounded but, still, he'd have done anything to stop that shadow of uncertainty.

'Cathy, I'm sorry.'

'It's Kate,' she said. 'But enough of the sorries. You did nothing I wouldn't have done in similar circumstances. Your first concern was Harry, and that's how it has to be. My private life is none of your concern. I only told you because...'

'Because once you were my friend?'

'Yes,' she said.

'I hope I still am.'

'Of course.' But something had changed, some indefinable thing. She looked totally vulnerable, he thought. She was wearing faded jeans and a sloppy windcheater, her curls were free, she'd been sighing and laughing over a soppy soap...and he'd scared her.

He wanted to tell her it was fine. He wanted to pull her into his arms and tell her he'd protect her, no matter what it took.

What sort of Neanderthal instinct was that? She'd kick him out. What he was feeling was not appropriate. Not!

He was here to talk about Harry and apologise for the chink he'd made in her defences. That's what he'd come to her for. He'd thought he'd talk to her for a few moments on the veranda, sort out the tangle his thoughts were in and then leave.

So even though the conversation had been delayed for a couple of hours, even though there was now this irrational emotion zinging around the room, he needed to say what he'd come for. He needed to tell her his decision.

'I need to prepare Harry to live with his Aunt Helen,' he said, and he wasn't prepared for the silence that followed.

She was professional. This should be a professional acceptance. Relative telling doctor the patient's future living arrangements.

'Because?' she asked at last.

'Because Helen loves him.'

'So do you.'

'Yes, but Helen has a warm, loving home environment. It might be a muddle but it's a loving muddle. He'll feel safe there.'

'He doesn't feel safe there now.'

'He doesn't feel safe anywhere, but he'll grow accustomed to it.'

'He loves you. I watch the way he is with you. He trusts you.'

'He trusts his Aunt Helen.'

'Who has five children of her own. Whereas you…'

'I don't have any.'

'You don't want any?'

'I don't have a family.'

'You have a girlfriend.'

'I do, but Annalise and I aren't parents.'

'You don't want to be parents?'

He sighed and raked his hair. Did he want to be a parent? He'd vaguely thought he would, but at some undefined time in the future. Not now. Not yet.

When Harry had been so appallingly orphaned, his own

world had turned upside down. He'd spent every spare moment with his nephew. He'd seen how unhappy Harry had been with Helen's brood. His reaction had been to take him himself, accepting the parenting role.

Somehow, though, these past few days had him looking past immediate need. Cathy...Kate...had shown him that Harry could be happy again, and the little boy's whole life stretched before him.

A life with a career-driven uncle?

'If you could make him happy enough to settle into Helen's brood...' he ventured.

'That'd let you off the hook. You could go back to being uncle on the side.'

'I did think I needed to keep him with me,' he said. 'But if he can be happy...'

'Jack, I can't perform miracles. He's a loner, as is, I suspect, his Uncle Jack. No matter how good my psychology is, I can't turn him into something he wasn't before the accident.'

'I can't look after him.'

'You mean you won't.'

'If I must, I will. Of course I will.'

'But not with your girlfriend,' she said, suddenly softening. Suddenly seeing what the problem was. 'Not with Annalise.'

'She won't.'

'This isn't my problem, Jack,' she said softly. 'I'm sorry but you alone need to work this out. You can send him back to his Aunt Helen—of course you can—even though we both know that's not what's best for him.' She hesitated. 'But, Jack, kids can survive what's not best for them. They're tougher and more resilient than you think. He'll work out strategies for making the space he needs. There are all sorts of people in this equation—Harry, you, Annalise, Helen, Helen's husband and kids, all the complex interactions that go into making a family. Harry's needs can't necessarily take precedence over everyone else's. You need to work on finding a solution that's best for everyone.'

Was that what he wanted to hear? That Harry would learn to compromise and survive? He thought of the lone little boy and things twisted. To have him so badly hurt, and then ask more of him…

But the alternative? A hard knot of grief was tightening inside his gut, giving him nowhere to go.

'It'd be easier not to have a family at all.' His words were an explosion, fury at the situation in which he found himself, grief at the loss of the sister he'd loved, and helplessness at Harry's ongoing loss. His words came out as a mess of tangled emotion.

Kate winced, then reached out and took his hands.

'No,' she said. 'Never that.'

And he felt a sweep of shame. This woman had no one. She'd walked—no, run—from her world. She was frightened of a bully of an ex-husband. She was giving her all to her little patients, but for herself she lived in a world of medicine and night-time television.

That he should whinge about too much family…

'Wow, Kate, I'm sorry…'

'Don't be sorry,' she told him. 'You don't have to be sorry with me.'

'Because I'm a client?'

'Something like that,' she admitted.

'No,' he said, strongly now, recovering sense. As well as his anger and frustration, he now felt like a king-sized rat. 'I don't feel in the least like a client. I believe I'm a friend. Kate, I've loaded too much on you tonight and I'm sorry. It won't happen again.'

'It's what I'm here for.'

'To be loaded? Who cares for the carer?'

'I'm fine.'

'With your dolphins and your soaps? I don't think you are.'

'Jack...'

'I'm here for you,' he said, suddenly and strongly. 'I won't let that bastard come near you.'

'You can't stop him.'

'He won't. It's old history.'

'Yes.' But he knew she didn't believe it. After all this time, he could still hear the fear. *What had that low-life done to her?*

'Kate?'

She didn't respond.

He still had her hands in his. He cared for this woman, he thought, and the sensation was a powerful one. She'd been his friend.

She was his friend.

More.

There were so many emotions in his head right now he didn't know what to do with them.

Kate was just here. She was his hold on reality, he thought. His hold...

The television has long been turned off. The night was totally still. There was only the soft wash of the breaking waves on the shore as a background to their breathing.

As a background to their emotion.

Things were changing around them. What? Jack didn't know. All he knew was that Kate's hands were in his. She was looking up at him and she was breathtakingly lovely. She was vulnerable... He'd made her vulnerable.

The emotional turmoil was building, building.

He couldn't bear it.

He kissed her.

One minute she was standing in front of Jack Kincaid, feeling angry, feeling betrayed about her own situation, feeling frustrated because this man wasn't seeing his little nephew's needs. The next she was being kissed. Solidly kissed. Ruthlessly kissed.

And she was kissing right back.

Why?

She had no idea.

Every particle of sense was telling her this was crazy. She should propel this man—this client—from her apartment and go back to being professional.

But she was over being professional. For this moment, for here and now, there wasn't a particle of room for it.

There was only room for Jack.

He was holding her hands, not tugging her close, just holding. She could pull away at any time. He wasn't pulling her into him.

He was simply kissing her. Their only connection was hands and mouth.

It was enough and more.

Warmth was flooding through her, and strength and need. The three emotions were warring and she had no space for anything else. Her mouth was under Jack's. He was kissing her almost as a question, but if it was a question, her whole body was answering.

The heat of this man. The strength. The sheer arrant masculinity.

She wasn't sure why she was being kissed. Anger? Frustration? Need? It didn't matter. All that mattered was that she wanted him.

She should break away but, quite simply, she couldn't. She didn't want to and she didn't see the need to try.

How long since she had been this close to a man? Maybe never, her body thought. Simon had demanded her, had taken her, but had never asked.

This man was asking and the question was indescribably erotic, indescribably delicious.

Her hands tugged away from his as if they had a life of their own. They sifted through his thatch of gorgeous hair, tugging him closer, closer, closer.

She wanted him.

She felt the response of her body and her response amazed her. Stunned her. But it didn't frighten her. For whatever reason, however this had happened, it felt right.

Her body was responding to his need with an aching desire of her own.

Maybe she'd always wanted this man. Maybe...maybe...

Maybe this wasn't the time for thinking maybes. She was instinctively pressing close, moulding her breasts to his chest, her body responding with a need that was so primeval she had no hope of fighting it. She was kissing and kissing, and she wanted more.

She needed more.

Her hands flicked the buttons of his shirt and went underneath, feeling the hard, hot strength of him, the broad expanse of chest, the size, the strength...

Jack...

But he was catching her hands.

He was pulling away.

No!

And in the fraction of a second that took her to think no, she regained her senses and so did he. He looked appalled.

He was appalled? To not be kissed for years and then have a man look at her as Jack was looking at her...

'That's the last time I ever watch soaps with you,' she managed, and heaven only knew how she managed it. She knew her voice was wobbling. Her whole insides seemed to be wobbling but somehow she said it and was inordinately proud that she'd managed it.

'Soaps must be...quite some aphrodisiac,' he said, and she was pleased that there was uncertainty in his voice, too. Though maybe not a wobble. This guy was testosterone on legs, and testosterone on legs did not wobble.

'Usually I watch them with Maisie,' she told him. 'Much safer. I...I think you should go home now.'

'Back to my bungalow.'

Did he think she'd meant back to Sydney? Did he think she'd meant he'd better leave the premises entirely because otherwise she might jump him?

'Back to your bungalow,' she agreed.

'Kate, I'm sorry.'

It needed only that. 'I'm not,' she snapped. 'It was a very nice kiss. Not quite so hot as Ronaldo on *Sunrise Babes* but, hey, a girl can only dream.'

He smiled, a tentative half-smile that did something to her insides that she didn't understand. And didn't trust.

'We should audition,' he said. 'Soaps R Us. Meanwhile, maybe we'd both best retreat to our own little worlds. It's much safer.'

'Much,' she said. 'Jack, from now on, consultations in my office, in work hours.'

'Of course.'

'Goodnight,' she said, and crossed to the door and tugged it open. Maisie was outside, sitting on the step. She looked vaguely astonished when she saw Jack inside. She walked forward, sniffed suspiciously and then climbed up on the settee where Jack had been sitting. Whatever child she'd been comforting tonight, clearly her job was done and she was coming home.

There were two seats in this sitting room. One for Kate. One for Maisie. No one else need apply.

'Goodnight,' Jack said, smiling at Maisie. He headed for the door, which Kate was holding open. He paused and touched her face, a feather touch with one strong finger.

'You're right, it was a very nice kiss,' he told her. 'We'd

surely give Ronaldo a run for his money. But not wise. We both have a heap of sorting out to do.'

'Speak for yourself,' she managed. 'I'm sorted.'

'Then why do you still look frightened?'

'I didn't until you came along,' she said. 'Now maybe I have cause. Back off, Jack, and leave me in my secluded world.'

'I will keep you safe,' he said, and he saw her flinch.

'Don't say that,' she said. 'That's what Simon said from the time I was sixteen. My parents kept me safe and then Simon did, on his terms. My wounded dolphins are safe, but they're locked in a pen. They're so damaged they could never survive in the wild. Even though that pen's as big as we can make it, they're still locked in. Here…I didn't feel locked in until you arrived. I felt like one of the wild dolphins, free to come and go of my own accord. That's how I want to stay, Jack. Thank you for the kiss. It was lovely, but as for safe… I've depended on myself for that for a very long time, and I'm not about to relinquish control now.'

Why had he kissed her?

He hadn't been able not to. She'd been right in front of him and every single part of him had wanted her. Every part of him had responded to her.

He'd felt this tug the first time he'd met her. She'd shrugged off his advances as unwanted but tonight she'd yielded. If he'd pushed… No, he wouldn't have needed to push. She had been his for the taking.

She was vulnerable. She was also his nephew's treating doctor, plus he was already committed. Semi-committed. More or less committed.

He didn't feel for Annalise what he felt for Kate.

But this was no ordinary situation. He was dependent on Kate to care for Harry, and somehow the professional side of him had surfaced. They needed to keep the doctor/patient relationship sacrosanct.

Except it wasn't. He'd gone to university with Kate. No court in the land would condemn…

Yes, but he'd condemn himself. That's why he'd managed to pull back. She was vulnerable, he needed her and the whole thing was unthinkable.

Except he was thinking. He was thinking so much his head hurt.

Thank God for babysitters. He needed a long walk. It was low tide, the moonlit beach beckoned and a man could walk for as long as he wanted. Until he found answers?

Were there any answers to be found? Who knew? All he could do was walk.

CHAPTER SIX

HARRY DID MORE healing in the next few days than he'd done in the three months since the accident.

Not just physically, Jack thought, although the physiotherapy sessions with the dolphins and in the pool were like gold. He was stretching his leg, he was moving his whole body, he was eating as if he'd been starved for three months—as indeed he almost had been because he'd lost all interest in food. In a week Jack could see a huge physical change.

The biggest difference, though, was in his mental wellbeing. He'd turned into a little boy again.

He had no worries here. This was a totally new environment and there was nothing to remind him of what he'd lost. He had Maisie, he had Kate and the rest of the awesome staff, and he had the dolphins. He tumbled out of bed every morning eager to see what the day would bring.

Eager to spend it with Jack.

Slight hiccup.

Had this been meant to turn into a bonding session between Jack and his nephew? Maybe it had. Jack had insisted on taking charge, even when it meant bringing him here. He might have realised it'd mean that every time something momentous happened, like when Wobble bounced the ball and Harry managed to catch it, or when

Kate released her hand under Harry's tummy and Harry managed to swim six whole strokes by himself without the kickboard, or when the bottom of the hole Harry and Maisie were digging high up on dry sand finally managed to ooze water, it was Jack he turned to.

Sometimes he'd give a tiny crow of delight. Most times he'd just catch Jack's gaze, make sure Jack was watching.

The same with Kate. She'd just catch his gaze, make sure he was watching.

Harry was bonding, hard and fast, with an uncle who wasn't sure where to take this.

Kate was judging that same uncle, waiting and watching to see where he'd take this.

It was up to him and it was overwhelming. Where was his nice, ordered world now?

Muddled.

Convoluted.

Tied up with Kate.

And there was another problem. The resort was small. Everywhere he went he seemed to see Kate. Her small patients adored her. Their parents thought she was awesome.

He thought she was awesome and the dilemma he found himself in kept growing larger.

She'd been his lab partner through medical school. He was starting to regret missed opportunities. Very much.

But he had a perfectly good relationship with Annalise. Didn't he?

No.

He'd always been on the outside, looking in, when it came to love. He never quite got it. He'd had relationships—of course he had—and they'd been fun and satisfying. But when Beth had come to him and told him she'd fallen head over heels in love, she'd glowed. His little sister had seemed transformed.

'It's hormones,' Annalise had said. 'That's all romantic

love is, your body responding biologically to the need to procreate. Once that surge is over, that's when the trouble starts. You need to put it aside, go into relationships with your head and not your heart.'

He'd agreed, not necessarily because he knew she was right but because he'd never had that surge of pure, focussed desire—which was what he was having now, every time he passed Kate in her perfectly appalling blue skin suit.

Why? One kiss did not a relationship make.

Annalise would laugh and tell him to get over it.

'When are you coming home?' she asked at the end of the first week. 'I didn't think you'd stick it this long.'

'It's doing Harry more good than I dreamed it could.'

'That's great,' she said warmly. 'But Helen wants to help as well. Maybe you could come home and Helen could take over. If Helen's going to care for him long term, wouldn't that be sensible?'

Yes, it would.

'Jack, if I helped you dig another hole we might be able to tunnel under.' Harry's request was almost a whisper as he disconnected from the call. It was as if Harry was still expecting the world to slap him down. 'We might be able to join up.'

Joining… Fathering a seven-year-old.

He'd volunteered to do this. He'd pushed Helen into stepping back. He hadn't realised until now how big a deal it was—or how much he wanted it.

'Excellent,' he said, and started to dig. Maisie helped— sort of.

'You're becoming champion diggers.' Two feet down, and intent on their digging, Jack hauled his head from the hole and found blue-suited Kate smiling at them. 'If you go far enough, you'll reach China.'

'I don't want to go to China.' Harry pulled back and

looked at her, anxious again. His anxiety was never far away. To say he was clinging was an understatement, yet when Jack thought of the silent waif of a week ago he was astounded at how far he'd come. 'I want to stay here.'

'This is a healing place,' Kate said, warmly but firmly. 'It's a place for you to get better. Most of the dolphins come here to heal, but when they're better they zoom off with their friends to where they belong. They come back to visit but they're free. It's the same for you.'

'Some dolphins stay,' Harry said stubbornly.

'Only the ones who are so badly wounded that they never get completely better, and that's sad. We all want to get better.'

'You stay here,' Harry said.

'Yes,' Kate said. 'Because it's my job to make people better so they can go home.'

'I don't have my home any more.'

Jack looked from Harry to Kate and back again. They were a pair, he thought suddenly. Two wounded creatures.

He couldn't do anything about Kate. Not yet. The *not yet* was an odd fragment of a thought, not fully formed. Maybe the *not yet* was a dumb notion that'd go away once the memory faded of an impulsive kiss.

But what came first, front and centre, was Harry staring bleakly up at Kate. Saying: *I don't have my home any more.*

It was time to make a stand.

'Yes, you do,' Jack said, and he reached out and hugged. Or tried to hug. The little boy froze as he normally did, but Jack kept his hold.

It's not only Harry making a decision, Jack thought. This is me. It's our future hanging on this moment.

He didn't have a clue what that future meant but somehow the last few days had changed things.

He loved this kid. This child was part of Beth.

He was part of him.

'We'll have a home,' he said, and still he held. 'Together.'

And finally, finally the child's body lost its rigidity. The tension seemed to seep out, slowly but surely. It was like a fight he'd been having for a very long time had suddenly been resolved.

'Will I live with you?' Harry whispered, in a voice that said he hardly dared to hope.

'Yes.'

'And with Annalise?'

'I don't know about Annalise.' He glanced up at Kate and she looked impassive. This decision was his, her body language said. It was nothing to do with her.

But somehow she'd made this moment possible. Somehow it had a whole lot to do with Kate.

She was beautiful, caring and...she was his friend.

Her body had fitted against his as if it was meant to be. He'd felt like he was coming home. The home he was offering to Harry?

That was a thought for the future, he told himself. What might or might not be between him and Kate was for sorting out when he and Harry had sorted themselves out.

'I don't know who else will live with us,' Jack said. 'But you and me, Harry...wherever we are, that's home.'

She had another client. Twelve-year-old Sam Harvey was waiting his turn in the dolphin pool. Another car accident victim, Sam had been more badly injured than Harry. He was paralysed from the waist down. He had three older brothers, all sports-crazed, and Sam couldn't see past the fact that he'd never be like his brothers.

His accident had been twelve months ago and he'd pretty much retired into a morose, sullen world where his parents couldn't reach him.

The dolphins were reaching him. His brothers had been left at home. His parents were here, giving him their total support. He'd been able to swim before the accident and the dolphins were pushing him to swim harder.

None of his older brothers were anything more than competent swimmers. Kate had found videos of paralympians, swimming for gold. Sam was booked in for a month but in only half that time he'd gained self-confidence and he had a goal.

He had a family who'd see that goal through, no matter what it took. It felt great.

And now Harry had a family, too. Jack.

The thought was just good, she decided as she watched Sam swim. Sam no longer took all her attention. The dolphins were taking on her role as mentor. They were playing a weird version of water polo where the dolphins kept shooting the ball just out of his reach so he had to swim for it. If he was too slow they zoomed in and took it back.

His parents were cheering from the sidelines. Sam's swimming was growing stronger every moment. Kate was cheering, too, but a part of her was distracted.

A part of her had stayed up the beach, by a two–foot-deep hole, by a man who'd just decided to be part of a family.

He rang Annalise that night. She heard him out in silence, and the silence extended after he finished.

'You do realise that's the end of us as a couple,' she said at last, and he'd known it was coming. He'd expected it to hurt, but to his surprise it didn't. There was sadness, but no regret.

Once upon a time a professor in medical school had said to his class, 'Make the decision and say it out loud. Then stand back and recognise how you feel. If it's the wrong decision your gut will tell you. Then be professional enough to change your mind.'

He wasn't changing his mind now.

He found himself thinking of Beth. She'd been studious, intent, totally committed to the work she loved. Her epilepsy had made her even more intent, finding an inner strength to achieve her goals. She'd had her work and her karate and she hadn't had time for boyfriends.

But at twenty two she'd reluctantly accompanied him to a student party. She'd met Arthur and she'd come home glowing.

Arthur had been a geek, a nerd, totally consumed with the need to discover new ways of keeping population water supplies unpolluted. That his shy sister had blossomed in this guy's presence had been unbelievable, but blossom she had. She'd adored him, and that flame had stayed bright until their untimely deaths.

But he didn't get it. He'd never felt like that, and there was regret but he felt no searing loss now knowing that what he and Annalise had had was over.

'I'm sorry.' There was nothing else to say.

'How will you manage your career?' She felt the same, he realised, and he wondered if she'd known it already. She'd never shared his concern for Harry; she'd made it clear from the start that it was his business.

'I don't know.'

'You'll need a bigger apartment.' She was masking disappointment with efficiency, and he was grateful. She'd been a friend for a long time and he didn't want to lose that friendship. 'I'll move back to mine at the weekend but you only have one spare room. You'll need a house with an en suite for a nanny. If you're coming back next week you should do some organisation now.'

'I'm not sure I'm coming back next week.'

'The Fraser International Symposium's the week after next,' she said, with horror. 'Jack, you're presenting. You need to be home for that.'

'I don't want to leave here yet. Harry's responding to treatment.'

'That's fantastic,' she said. 'But there are fine child psychologists here.'

'The dolphins are working.'

'You're kidding. Is this crystal-ball stuff rubbing off on you, too?'

'Of course it's not,' he said defensively, but he couldn't blame Annalise for her cynicism. He thought back to his scepticism of a week ago. How to explain?

'I've been trying to figure it out,' he told her, retreating into their common ground of medicine. 'I've done some reading. The thinking is that the dolphins somehow cause transfer of endorphins. Endorphins lift moods, ease tensions and therefore support receptive and learning abilities.'

'You're suggesting we buy every wounded kid a dolphin?' But she was caught. They'd had a good relationship, mostly based on their mutual passion for their careers. It eased what was happening now. She was open minded enough for her professional interest to be snagged.

'Not possible,' he said regretfully, thinking how amazing it'd be for Harry to have Hobble in his back-yard pool. 'Dolphins' brains seem as highly evolved as ours and they can't be held in captivity for our pleasure. Hobble, the dolphin Harry loves best, was caught in a net when he was young, cutting off the blood supply to his tail and leaving him permanently lopsided. He also lost his mother before he learned survival skills. Being here is the only way he can survive, but it's given Harry an enormous gift. It's a gift I can't bring home.'

'So you're risking your career, plus ditching a perfectly good girlfriend—'

'Anna...'

'It's okay,' she said briskly. 'I've never seen you as a

dolphin-loving daddy, and if I missed that then who knows what other levels of incompatibility we have? But I'm still fond of you, Jack, and I'm worried. This is your career.'

'But it's Harry's life.'

He was standing on the veranda of his bungalow. Out in the dolphin pool Kate was playing in the water with a kid called Sam. He'd been watching Sam's progress as well as Harry's. Kate was performing miracles with him, too.

Kate...

Break off with one woman, take up with another? What was he thinking?

'It's your life, too,' Annalise said sharply. 'Jack, be sensible. Think about it. If you change your mind...about us, I mean...'

'There'll always be Harry.'

'Then you're on your own,' she snapped, finally letting anger hold sway. She disconnected, and Jack gazed out over the water at Kate and thought about that bald sentence.

You're on your own.

Harry was inside, sleeping. Sam finished his session. His parents took him back up the beach and Wendy took his place. Wendy was eleven years old. She had neuroblastoma with metastases and she had only months to live.

Wendy greeted Kate with joy and Kate gave her a hug and swept her in large, splashy circles before the dolphins came to join them.

This place wasn't magic just because of the dolphins, Jack thought. There was this woman called Kate.

You're on your own.

He watched Kate some more. Things were changing inside him. What was it with these dolphins?

What was it with this woman?

You're on your own. He wasn't, he thought. He was here with a woman called Kate.

Theirs was a professional relationship. She was the doctor, he was the guardian of her patient.

He'd known her when they'd been students. They'd been friends before. Could he manage that again?

Friends.

He thought again of Beth, floating home after that long-ago party, blushing fiery red because of a boy called Arthur.

Why was he thinking of that blush now?

Why couldn't he stop watching a woman called Kate?

He worried her.

He messed with her equanimity.

'Everything was fine until he arrived,' she told Hobble. She was floating on her back in the dolphin pool. She spent almost all her time focussed on her small charges' needs, but at dusk, when kids and parents headed in for dinner, she floated on the water and let herself be still.

The dolphins didn't try to play with her. They never did. They seemed to sense that she had a need for healing almost as great as her small patients. Sometimes they swam in slow circles around her. Sometimes they simply let her be.

They were wounded, too. Each one of the dolphins in the enclosure had a backstory of tragedy. They put her own history into perspective.

Until Jack had arrived she'd thought she'd achieved peace. Why had he disturbed that peace?

Because he might have inadvertently told Simon where she was?

That was one reason but weirdly it was a minor one. The bigger one was the way he made her feel. He was an old friend, caring for his small nephew. A man faced with his life being turned upside down.

A man who had a gift of tuning in to troubled kids.

A man who just had to smile at her and who made her feel...

Like she was losing control again?

She would not lose control.

The only child of elderly parents, she'd been controlled since birth, not by aggression but by the power of too much loving.

She'd adored her parents but their pressure had been relentless. All their focus, all their adoration, had been on her. If she upset one, the other would gently blackmail her. 'You know your mother's not well.' Or...'You know your father has a weak heart...' And then, even more of a sledgehammer... 'It'd make us so happy and proud if you married Simon. We could die knowing you were safe.'

Safe. Ha! As a promise, it sucked.

Jack could keep her safe. He'd said so.

How could anyone keep anyone safe? By gentle or not-so-gentle control?

She wasn't making sense, she decided, but, then, when had emotions ever made sense? All she knew was that she'd had a lifetime of control and she wasn't going back. Jack Kincaid might make her knees turn to jelly, but that was no reason to forget resolutions forged by fire. He might want to keep her safe, but she'd learned to run and she'd continue to run. Or at least hold desire at bay.

Hold Jack at bay?

She was reading too much into a kiss, she thought. She was reading too much into how Jack looked at her.

But she knew she wasn't.

She'd organised a formal counselling session for Harry late that afternoon. Maisie was lying at Harry's feet, while, at Kate's request, Harry was drawing a picture of himself with Hobble.

Jack was leafing through a magazine, trying to fade

into the background. At first he'd felt he shouldn't be at these sessions, but Kate had insisted.

'Harry's had enough of being alone. He needs to know that every problem he has he can share with you.'

Jack was no longer arguing. The change in his nephew was amazing.

Harry finished his picture of Hobble but he'd only used a tiny part of the page. To Jack's surprise, the little boy drew a careful box around his picture of himself and the dolphin, then, underneath, he drew a table, and two figures sitting at the table.

And underneath the table a dog.

'That's you and Jack,' Kate said, and it wasn't a question.

'Yes,' Harry said. 'And our dog.'

'You and Jack would like a dog?'

'Yes.'

'And that's a picture of you and Hobble.'

'On our wall,' Harry said. 'So we'll remember it for ever and for ever.'

Then he paused, looked at his picture and added a box beside the table.

'Would you like to tell me what that is?' Kate asked.

'It's my ant farm.'

'You have an ant farm?'

'Yes.'

Kate looked a query at Jack but Jack gave an imperceptible shake of his head. This was news to him.

'So this is your house, where you live with Jack.'

'Yes,' Harry said, and he cast Jack a look that was half scared, half defiant.

The moment had come. There was no backing out now.

'That's right,' Jack said. 'You'll need to paint a bigger picture of you and Hobble for our real wall.'

'Yes,' Harry said, still a bit defiant, still suspicious.

'But it won't be the house where you lived with your mum and dad,' Jack said, because it seemed important to say it like it had to be. 'I work at the hospital and your house is too far away. We'll need to find a house just for us, somewhere closer.'

There was a long moment while Harry thought this through. Jack could see the conflicting emotion on his small face. He saw anguish, loss—and finally bleak acceptance.

'Will we find a new house?' he asked in a small voice.

'Yes.' A kid and a dog…a hospital apartment was no longer feasible. 'You can help choose it.'

That made him brighten a little.

'With my own bedroom? And a window with a tree?'

Harder, but manageable. 'Yes.'

'Will Annalise live with us?'

'No. Just you and me.' He looked dubiously at the picture. 'And a dog and an ant farm, though it might take a while before we can find a dog.'

'Can we find one like Maisie?'

Oh, hell, why not? He had a sudden flash of dog-sitters and big back yards and his social life going down the toilet, but there wasn't a lot of choice. 'Yes.'

'Why won't Annalise live with us?'

'She doesn't like dogs.'

It was obviously the right answer. 'All right,' Harry said, turning back to his picture. 'The dog can stay in my bedroom. And my ant farm.'

'Of course,' he said weakly, and Kate gave him an approving grin and went back to concentrating on Harry's picture.

Harry and Jack and Dog and ant farm?

Move over, Harry, he thought. I need counselling myself.

CHAPTER SEVEN

TELEVISION HAD FAILED her. This was a remote community, there were exactly three channels to choose from, and tonight, unless she wanted news of the day, hyenas feeding off dead zebras or a documentary about weight-loss programmes, she was lost.

Maisie was off doing her dog therapy with their latest patient arrival. Kate was on her own.

She wanted diversions but there weren't any. She couldn't stop thinking about Jack.

She'd listened to the commitments Jack had been making in the counselling session and she'd been astonishingly moved. He was losing his girlfriend, his apartment, his lifestyle.

Maybe he hadn't thought it through, but she'd watched his face as he'd said it and she knew that for now he believed in what he was promising.

Resolutions didn't always last. Don't believe in people, she told herself, almost fiercely. Once upon a time she'd believed in Simon.

Restless, she headed out to the beach. The tide was low, and the moon hung silver over the water. She could walk as far as she wanted.

She never went far. Like her injured dolphins, she wasn't leaving.

Why, tonight, was she suddenly thinking of leaving? Because a man called Jack had her...discombobulated. For discombobulated she certainly was. She needed to get herself in order, she told herself. Her day started at dawn. She needed to head for bed.

To sleep? Not possible.

She had to try. She'd been walking for an hour and she needed to be up at dawn.

She walked slowly across the sand hills, past the bungalows holding sleeping children and their parents.

She walked past Jack's veranda, keeping to the shadows in case he was outside.

He was outside, on the phone.

She had no right to stop and listen but there was no way her feet would obey her conscience. She stopped and she listened.

'Helen, what's happened to his ant farm?'

He was sitting on the cane settee with a beer. Harry must be asleep, she thought, and Jack was on speakerphone. Why not? It'd be easier to sit back and talk while gazing out at the moon.

He must have just come out, Kate thought, or he'd have seen her on the beach. The path up to the bungalows was heavily planted, with side paths to the individual accommodation. That was lucky. She didn't want him to see her.

Why? She hardly knew, and she certainly had no right to eavesdrop. But what was between them was starting to feel strange; uncharted territory. She should slink off into the shadows, but somehow she was caught. What Jack was saying would impinge on Harry's life, she told herself. Maybe she even had a duty to listen.

Ha! Yet she stayed where she was, unashamedly eavesdropping.

'What are you talking about?' Helen was demanding.

'An ant farm. I gather it's important to him. It's a tank

like a skinny goldfish bowl, full of ants. I used to have one when I was a kid. Did you take it to your place when we cleared up?'

'I can't remember seeing it. Hang on and I'll ask Doug.' There was a muffled conversation while Helen talked to someone in the background and when she came back on the line the news wasn't good. 'Doug says he wondered what that was. It was in Harry's room, a tank full of dirt. He binned it.'

Uh-oh. Kate had known Harry for little more than a week yet even she knew what was important.

This was important.

'Put Doug on,' Jack said, and she heard the tension in his voice. He must have also realised the enormity of this loss.

But Doug had a good memory. Jack pushed for details and Doug could describe size and shape.

'Right,' Jack said. 'I'll go on the internet and order a replacement. Can you set it up before we get home?'

'Where do I get ants?' It was Helen again, sounding horrified. 'Do you want us to go out to the garden and dig 'em up?'

'He'll know the difference between home ants and the ants he had,' Jack said. 'This is one kid you can't fool by swapping budgies.'

Kate smiled a little at that. How many kids had been spared trauma when their pet bird died by parents simply replacing them? But...ants?

'You're saying he can pick individual ants?' Doug demanded.

'He's his mother's son and I know my Beth,' Jack said simply, and then corrected himself bleakly. 'I knew my Beth. She'd know every characteristic of every ant. We may not be able to replace the exact ants but they'll be a certain breed. I'll grill him tomorrow and hopefully order them on the internet. I know we can't get it looking exactly the same but we can tell him the twins tipped it over and you've replaced the soil. His favourite ants might have got squashed. It's a compromise but it's the best we can do.'

'I don't believe this.' Helen came back on the phone. 'All this worry, and we're fretting about ants? And when are you coming home?'

'When the ant farm's ready.'

'So Harry's coming back here?'

'No,' Jack said, firmly and surely. 'Helen, your family is great. I know you and Doug love Harry to bits, but he's a kid who needs silence. He stays with me.'

'He'll get more than silence with you,' Helen snapped. 'He'll be totally isolated.'

'He won't be.'

'You work six days a week, twelve-hour days. What sort of life is that for a child?'

'I'll change things.'

'You need a wife. Annalise?'

'She's no longer in the picture and even if she was, I couldn't ask this of her. This is my call. Helen, I can organise my life. I can make things good for Harry. Trust me.'

'It's a child's life,' Helen said bleakly. 'It's a huge trust.'

'Don't I know it,' Jack said. 'I'll do what I have to do. Watch this space.'

He'd disconnected. Kate stood silent. She should back away, she thought. She had no right being here.

'You can come out now,' Jack said, and her world stilled.

There was nothing for it. She emerged from the shadows, feeling like a criminal.

'I'm sorry,' she said. 'I was coming up the path and didn't want to interrupt.'

'You want to help me choose ants?' he asked, as if she'd done nothing dishonourable at all.

'Jack, I didn't mean—'

'I knew you were there,' he said. 'Eavesdropping's only a crime when it's successful.'

'I had no right—'

'You have every right. You're transforming my nephew's life. You want to listen in on us twenty-four seven, it's fine by me. We need what you're doing, Kate. We need you.'

As a statement it took her breath away. Trust… He looked down at her and smiled, and if she'd had any more breath to spare she'd have lost it then.

That smile…

'Ants,' he said. 'Research. Glass of wine first or are you on call?'

'No wine,' she said, because with that smile she did not need alcohol.

'But you have time for ant-farming?' He shifted sideways on the settee and gestured to the laptop in front of him. 'Want to take a look? I know it's not *Sunrise Babes* but, hey, I bet what goes on in these closed, glass communities will make your eyes pop.'

And who could resist an invitation like that? She headed up the steps, still feeling shamefaced, but Jack had moved on.

'Gel?' He was staring at the screen. 'I thought you just used dirt. When did ants start needing gel? And it says you can't order queen ants on line. Quarantine between states? How did Harry get the first one? You're going to have to help me here, Kate. Tomorrow's counselling session has to be all about how he feels about his ant farm, and subtle questions as to technical detail on how he got the last one. And look at this! They shove the dead ones up the top and you're expected to remove them to prevent disease? They have to be kidding. Maybe that's why all mine died when

I was a kid. I think I need counselling. I'm an oncologist, not an ant funeral director. I think I'm in trouble.'

And then he glanced at her again and his smile faded.

'Maybe we're both in trouble,' he said softly, and she met his look for a long moment—and then flinched and went back to looking at a screen full of ants.

CHAPTER EIGHT

THEY SPENT A ridiculous hour researching ant farms. 'I can put it on my CV now,' Kate said proudly at the end of it. 'Doctor, physiotherapist, counsellor, dolphin expert and now ant-farm advisor.'

'Is there no end to your skills?' Jack demanded, and she grinned.

'Nope.'

'Do you take an active hand in caring for the dolphins?' he asked.

'We all do,' she said simply. 'This place runs with a team of committed professionals, and every one of us can turn their hand to anything. Even Bob, the groundsman, is expected to interact with the kids, and he loves it. We don't have a full-time vet—that's a gap—but we get on-line help. Usually injured dolphins don't come straight to us. They're found in more populated areas so the initial vet work is done there. They're brought to us to give them time and space to heal. There's not a lot of hands-on work to do for a healing dolphin. Dolphin heal pretty magically anyway.'

'What do you mean?'

'I mean if a shark took a chunk from your backside you'd be remembering it for the rest of your life, but for some amazing reason dolphins regenerate torn flesh. They arrive looking gruesome, yet as soon as we get them non-stressed, their regenerative power takes over. This place has released hundreds of dolphins, slightly scarred but ready to fish another day.'

'To the local fishermen's displeasure.'

'There is that,' she admitted ruefully. 'But when the founders of this place set it up they chose a place well away from any fishing harbour. We do get locals complaining that we're ruining their sport. Someone even shot a dolphin last year, but he got such appalling local press that he's not been heard of since. Gotta love a dolphin.'

He smiled, feeling the pride she so obviously had in this work. And for a stupid moment he felt...jealous?

Jealous of this slip of a girl, burying herself at the edge of nowhere, passionate about her patients and her dolphins but nothing else.

He thought of the life he lived back in Sydney. He was in charge of a large, modern cancer centre, but it was part of a huge teaching hospital. He spent so much of his time fighting for funding, organising support for patient care, dealing with the requirements to hold a large medical team on focus, that his contact with patients was becoming less and less.

This might be so much more rewarding.

'It's not all it looks,' Kate said, and he glanced at her sharply. She could guess his thoughts? She'd done psychology, he thought. Dangerous. He should stop thinking immediately.

'I need to fight for my patients, too,' she said. 'Every one of them has special needs, and those needs often can't be held in abeyance while they're here. I have two kids who are still on chemotherapy. I have to fight to get the drugs, fight to be given the knowledge how to administer them. If your Harry had come here with cancer, I'd have done my homework before he came. I'd have been onto his doctors, and I'd have pleaded with them to give me the resources to keep him safe.'

'You didn't have those resources with Toby Linkler.'

'He'd run out of options,' she said bleakly. 'If he'd stayed in Melbourne, if the family had wanted it, he might have been given another round of chemo, but the medical team who looked after him knew it was the end.'

'So this is partly a hospice.'

'It isn't,' she said hotly. 'Toby and his mother came here to heal, and that's what they did.'

'He died.'

'Yes, he did, but he didn't spend his last few days dying. He died with the sun on his face and dolphins swimming around and not a ventilator or IV line in sight. Jack, if anyone thought a last round of chemo was anything more than a forlorn hope, I'd have fought tooth and nail to get it for him. I've refused kids who need ongoing treatment if their doctors won't agree to let me administer it. I can't take kids sometimes because I don't have the skills to treat them.'

'You need me here long term,' he said, joking, and she looked at him in the moonlight and there was no answering smile.

'You're here to be treated,' she said simply. 'And then I'll let you go.'

'Me? Treated?'

'You're figuring yourself out. For instance, the importance of one ant farm, for you and for Harry.'

'I would have worked that out back in Sydney.'

'You might not have if you hadn't taken this time out.'

'So what about you?' he asked. 'When do you consider yourself healed?'

'I am healed.'

'Says the woman who spends her nights watching soaps.'

'I'm happy here, Jack,' she said, but she knew it sounded defensive. She knew she didn't sound like she meant it.

But she did mean it. The work she was doing was important. She was making a difference to people's lives. What else could she ask for?

Release from fear? A release from the knowledge that she was still hiding?

Release to start again, with someone like...someone like...

'You're doing an amazing job,' Jack said gently. 'Will you do it for ever?'

'Why wouldn't I?'

'Would they have trouble finding a replacement?'

'What are you suggesting? That I walk away? Why would I want to?'

'You might get tired of *Sunrise Babes*.'

'How could anyone tire of *Sunset Babes*?' she demanded in mock indignation. 'We have a divorce, a sex scene and at least one catastrophe a week. That's much more exciting than real life.'

'Would you like to go back to real life?'

His tone was gentle, and suddenly she stopped fighting to keep barriers in place. He was a friend, she thought suddenly. He'd been a friend when she'd been a student. Why shouldn't she say it like it was?

'I've been hiding for so many years I've lost count,' she said simply. 'I don't know any other way. This place makes me feel safe as nowhere else does. I'm like Hobble with his malformed tail. This is my home.'

'You don't have a malformed anything,' he said, even more gently.

'But when I hear a car arriving, I still flinch,' she said. 'How stupid is that? When I was at university in New Zealand every time I heard a door slam in the night I'd wake in terror. I'm worse than Hobble.'

'Just how badly did he treat you?'

She gazed at him for a long moment. She didn't talk

about her relationship with Simon. Talking about him brought back the fear, brought back the terror. But Jack was asking. Jack was her friend.

She tugged up the sleeve of her shirt, rolling it to the shoulder, and held out her arm for him to see.

They'd done a great job repairing her elbow. All that was left was a long incision scar. The scar was neat. The scars from the cigarette burns were not so neat.

Jack stared down at the scars for a very long time. She didn't say anything. She didn't have to.

'This isn't the extent of it?' he said at last, and her silence was answer enough.

He swore. The oath was almost under his breath but its savagery was so intense it frightened her.

'Don't,' she said. 'Please… It's over.'

'It's not if you're still terrified.' He reached out and grasped her arm before she could pull the sleeve down. No. He didn't grasp, she thought. He simply held. This wasn't a man who grasped.

'It's not over while that bastard walks the planet,' he said, quite lightly but the venom underneath was frightening all by itself. 'Did he go to jail for this?'

'He went to jail for fraud.'

'So you never had him face justice for abuse?'

'I… There was no need.' How to say she'd have never had the courage?

'There's no statute of limitations on abuse charges,' he said. 'I imagine you received decent medical treatment?'

She nodded, remembering lone visits to emergency departments over the years, trying to choose hospitals where she knew no one. Young doctors with shocked faces. Counsellors who'd told her to go to the police, to break free.

But it would have been his word against hers in a criminal court, and she hadn't had the courage to face him down. If there'd been outsiders who'd witnessed the beatings, if she'd been sure the charges would stick and she wouldn't have to face him afterwards, then maybe. But it would have killed her parents to know this about the man they'd thought was wonderful, and if the charges hadn't been proved, what then? Only when he'd robbed her mother had the cycle finally been broken.

Jack's expression had grown even more grim. 'Then we can still nail him,' he was saying. 'Put him back in jail. Kate, you need to face this head on.'

'No!'

'Why not?'

'I don't want to face him ever again. He made me feel... worthless.'

'While you're running you're still a victim.'

'I'm not running. I'm safe.'

'With your dolphins and your soaps.'

'Jack, don't. Please...' She hesitated, trying to get rid of the feeling she had every time she thought of her ex-husband. He still made her cringe. He still made her feel as if she'd been a coward and a fool, and she didn't want to go there.

'What about you?' she asked, in a desperate attempt to deflect the conversation, and she saw Jack's brows hike.

'What do you mean, what about me?'

'What are you running from?'

'Nothing.'

'So you're a normal heterosexual male in his mid-thirties who just broke up with his current girlfriend with apparently barely a touch of emotion.'

'I'm a seething mess of conflicted emotion inside.'

She smiled at that, but she was watching his face and saw that maybe he wasn't joking. But this man wasn't carrying a broken heart.

'Even at uni,' she said thoughtfully, 'you went out with the most beautiful women, the most popular, the women who were self-contained. The women who'd never cling. I saw you go through at least half a dozen girlfriends during med school and I can't remember any of them who seemed like they needed you. Or you needed them. And here you are, breaking up with Annalise and hiding your mess of conflicted emotion extraordinarily well.'

'That's 'cos I'm a guy.' But he seemed uneasy. 'You know guys don't show emotion.'

'There were lots of couples formed during med school,' she said, still thoughtful. 'Friends to lovers. It made sense, we got to know each other so well, but looking back…did you and I get on so well as lab partners because we knew the boundaries? I had Simon stopping me from getting close to anyone. You had your humour and your intellect and you used them as a shield.'

'Is this your psychology training talking?'

'Maybe it is,' she said, striving to keep it light. But it seemed to her that strain was starting to appear around Jack's eyes. Her faint suspicion that he had his own ghosts was starting to crystallise into full-blown surety.

'So tell me about your mum and dad,' she said lightly. 'Were they a happy-ever-after story?'

'This is hardly appropriate.'

'It's not, is it?' she agreed. 'It's just that you now know all about me and I know nothing about you. Except I know your parents were wealthy. The other med students used to talk about your dad with awe. He was a QC, wasn't he? And you had a little sister called Beth who I know you adored. You want to fill in the gaps?'

'No.'

'Why not? Are you running from shadows, too?'

'No!'

She didn't talk back. She simply hiked her eyebrows in a mock mirror image of his own gesture, folded her hands, looked out to sea—and waited.

* * *

What was going on? One minute he was probing about her past, pushing her to do something, being proactive. He was playing the male role, the protector, acting as he would have if it'd been Beth in the role of the abused.

Suddenly she'd turned the tables.

She was no longer pushing. She was simply...waiting.

She was an extraordinarily restful woman, he thought, and then he reconsidered. No, she was just extraordinary.

But she was asking him to reveal personal stuff. He didn't do personal stuff.

Was that why it didn't hurt that Annalise had agreed to move from their apartment with minimal fuss? Was that why he always chose girlfriends who saw him as a useful accessory rather than the love of their life?

Did he see them the same way?

He'd barely thought about it until now. But maybe he had, he acknowledged. Maybe he'd thought about it and blocked it out.

He remembered how he'd felt when Beth had met her Arthur.

She'd come home glowing, she'd wafted round in a mist of happiness, and he remembered being...fearful. That she'd left herself exposed.

She'd married, Harry had arrived and for the first time then she'd revealed to him how frightening it was.

'If anything happened to them, I'd die,' she'd told Jack simply. 'Arthur and now Harry...I love them so much, they're my whole heart.'

'How can you do this?' he'd asked. It had been a rare moment of truth between the siblings. Normally they'd avoided talking about their home life. 'How can you expose yourself to what Mum and Dad put up with?'

'Because it's worth the risk,' she'd said simply, and

smiled down at her sleeping baby. 'Oh, Jack, I hope you find that out for yourself.'

And then Beth herself had died and every single one of his fears had crystallised. He'd stood at the graveside and felt empty. Dead himself. Annalise had stood beside him but he hadn't held her hand and she hadn't tried to take it. They'd respected each other's space.

Kate was still waiting. She was still watching the sea, giving him space. She was a woman who'd seen it all.

Why not tell her?

'My parents…overdid the love thing,' he said, keeping his voice neutral. After what Kate had been through, this was no big deal. Poor little rich boy? What was he on about?

'How can you overdo love?' Kate asked, and then hesitated. 'No, that's a dumb question. My parents manipulated me through love. Simon swore he loved me. Love has weird guises.'

'Theirs was passion,' he said, suddenly grim. 'They married in a storm of passion—a two-week courtship and then off to Gretna Green, for heaven's sake, because my mother thought that was the most romantic place on earth to be married. Only it rained and the hotel had lumpy mattresses so they fought at the top of their lungs, they broke up, and then they came together again and headed for another romantic "wedding" in the Seychelles. And that was the entire foundation of their marriage. My father was a lawyer at the top of his game. My mother was an interior designer, a good one. Both of them had enormous professional respect.

'Both of them used their marriage to rid themselves of stress, to shout, to fight, to break up, to passionately come together again. Beth and I were the catalysts for a lot of the conflict. Our parents were either in a passionate clinch like hot young lovers, not able to keep their hands off each other, even in front of us, or they were hurling things at each other. Their fights were vicious and real, and Beth and I were in the middle.'

'Tough.'

'You said it,' he admitted grimly. 'I hated it. Beth was four years younger than me, she was epileptic, stress brought on attacks and I seemed to spend my childhood protecting her. Maybe I did too good a job. Maybe that's why she was able to fall so passionately in love with Arthur.'

'That marriage worked?'

'It seemed to,' he admitted. 'But it was a huge risk. Love leaves you wide open—and now she's dead.'

'Would she still be dead if she hadn't made the decision to love?'

He closed his eyes. 'I know. Her death was random. One drunk driver late at night, ice on the road... But she knew the risks. When Harry was born, she made me swear I'd look after him. As if she knew...'

'Every good parent thinks about worst-case scenarios,' she said simply. 'They talk it through, do the asking, then get on with their lives. But you...maybe love cost you your childhood, and here you are, losing again through love. Maybe you're the one who's scarred.'

'I'm not scarred.'

'I think you are,' she said gently. 'Almost as badly as Harry.'

'Kate—'

'Use this time,' she said urgently, rising. 'Jack, this is time out for both you and Harry. You have so much to think about. If you're uncomfortable talking to me, then think about using Louise—she's a competent psychotherapist.'

'I don't need a psychotherapist!' It was an angry snap, but Kate didn't flinch.

'This is a healing place,' she said softly. 'Yes, we do

have kids who come here when they're dying but even in dying, the family can find a kind of peace. If you give in to that peace, that acceptance, we can help you for the rest of your life.'

'It's Harry who needs help.'

'Via you. Harry needs you. Are you prepared to open yourself up to him? To anyone?'

'I've just organised his ant farm. How much more do I need to do?'

'I think you know how much,' she said softly, and then, as if she couldn't help herself, she raised her hand and traced the contours of his cheekbones. 'You're a good man, Jack Kincaid, but you do need help.'

'Says the woman in hiding.'

'Jack…'

He caught her hand in his, and he held. The night was still between them. Underneath the veranda a tiny rock wallaby was snuffling through the bushes. Trusting. Here in this retreat, there was no threat.

So why did Jack suddenly feel that there was a threat? Why did he feel exposed?

Because of what this woman had said?

Because of what this woman was?

But right now his emotions were changing. Needs were changing. They'd been talking of the past, of things that had threatened them both.

Right now was…now.

And right now he wanted to kiss her. It was as simple as that. The conversation faded. Reservations faded. He looked down into her face and he thought what a gift had been in front of him all those years ago. He'd accepted her statement that she'd had a boyfriend. He hadn't explored past it.

Maybe he hadn't wanted to explore past it. Maybe he was running as scared as Kate was.

'"Physician, heal thyself"?' he said, striving for light-ness—and failing. 'Maybe...it should read, "Physician, heal each other."'

'Jack...'

'Maybe we could try,' he said softly.

He kissed her then, a gentle, questioning kiss that he didn't understand. He'd kissed her before, with passion. Tonight passion had taken a back seat. This was a kiss of questions, an asking if things were possible, a kiss that asked where they could take things from here.

She kissed him back and he felt the same uncertainty in her. The same need?

The kiss went on for a very long time. They simply held, warmth flooding through, questions being asked and answered, a future tentatively opening before them. It felt right, he thought as he held her close and felt the sheer wonder of her. It felt like the beginning of some-thing...amazing.

She felt right. She...fitted. It didn't make any kind of sense, but all he knew was that she was right for him.

But when they finally pulled apart, when finally the kiss ended, as all kisses eventually had to, she backed away in the moonlight and her look was troubled.

'What?' he said, and touched her lips with his finger. 'What, my love?'

'I'm not your love.'

'No, but—'

'Neither am I an answer to your problems.'

There was a moment's silence. The trouble deepened. She was withdrawing, her armour slipping back. It was imaginary armour but he could almost see it.

'I don't know what you mean.' He reached to hold her again but she shook her head.

'No. Jack, I love...' She touched her lips. 'No, I mean I like you kissing me. I like you touching me. Our friendship goes back a long way and you know how isolated I've been. Maybe my reaction to you is a response to that isolation. Maybe it's not. But you and Annalise—'

'It's over.'

'That's right, it's over,' she said, sounding still more troubled. 'And isn't that the problem?'

'I don't know what you mean.'

'You must see it,' she said. She was struggling to sound calm, as if she was trying to figure things out as she said them. 'Jack, you have a child to care for. Your girlfriend's ditched you. You're facing a future as a lone parent and it scares you. And now you're kissing me.'

'This has nothing to do with—'

'I think it has.' She closed her eyes, and when she opened them she'd withdrawn still further. 'Jack, my parents needed me for physical care and their love for me was bound up with that. My dad was sixty when I was born and Mum was over forty. My birth almost killed Mum, and Dad already had heart problems. My needs came a poor second to their health, to their needs. My job was to make them feel secure, make them proud, not rock the boat. And then Simon came along and I fell in love with him but he needed me for my money. He needed me to play the subservient wife. Even when I was struggling to escape from Simon I was still trying to protect my parents. I don't know whether you can understand this, but I don't want to be…needed…again.'

'Kate, I would never…'

'Ask me to take a share in raising Harry?'

'This was only our second kiss!'

'I know.' She managed a rueful smile. 'I'm looking at an egg and seeing a dinosaur. Talk about forward catastrophising. But when you hold me I feel…like it could be the beginning.'

'That makes two of us. Kate, I think I could love you.'

'That's what you say,' she said gently. 'But how can I trust in such a word? It'd fit really neatly for you, wouldn't it? You need a family for Harry. Harry already likes me and he loves Maisie. Replace Annalise with good ol' Kate and your problems are solved.'

Whoa. How had they got here? A kiss and she was projecting forward to marriage, parenthood, delegation of responsibility? This was nuts. But as he looked at her he felt a jolt of recognition in what she was saying.

She was gorgeous. She was an old friend. She was the answer to his problems, wrapped up in one very desirable package.

Maybe subconsciously she was right.

'Get your house in order,' she said softly. 'Do what you need to do to make you and Harry into a family. Then think of expanding.'

'I'm not kissing you because I want a family!' It was an explosion and she smiled faintly, almost teasingly.

'But are you kissing me because you don't want a family?'

'That's unfair.'

'Unfair or not, I'm taking no chances.' She rose, putting physical distance between them. 'I'm your nephew's treating doctor,' she said. 'Kissing you is unprofessional, crossing boundaries that shouldn't be crossed. I need to put those boundaries back into place.'

'We both know that's nonsense.'

'We both know it makes sense. Jack, this needs to stop.'

He rose, too, anger building. She'd built this into something it wasn't. She was insinuating he was manipulating. He wouldn't.

A tiny voice in the back of his head said he might. It would be so easy to give Harry a loving, caring Kate.

Her phone rang.

She'd laid it on the wicker table. All the tension in the

room seemed to turn and focus on that table, and maybe that was a relief. How had they reached this point? Kissing had never meant this much before, Jack thought. How had it escalated so fast?

How much easier to focus on a telephone than on the tension zinging between them.

Kate flicked it open. 'It's Alan,' the voice said, audible in the stillness, and Jack recognised it as one of the parents. Wendy's father. The eleven-year-old with the neuroblastoma.

And Kate switched into medical mode, just like that.

'How can I help?'

'Wendy's vomiting,' he said. 'She's getting distressed. Would you—?'

'I'll be there in two minutes.' She disconnected and turned to Jack.

'Harry will be okay,' she said, and he realised she'd turned back into the professional she was. Personal interaction was over. 'You and Harry will make a great family,' she told him. 'You have the skills to help him. Talk to me again if you need to—that's what I'm here for—but between you and me, we're done. I need to fetch my bag and take care of Wendy. Goodnight, Jack. Give Harry a hug for me.'

And he'd been dismissed. She'd finished with one client and she was moving on to another.

CHAPTER NINE

THE NEXT FEW days went well, as far as Harry was concerned. Every day he woke up brighter, more voluble, embracing life again. He had his reassurance from Jack, and even more than the dolphin therapy it seemed to make a difference. He turned to Jack over and over—'Jack, watch me. Jack, can we do this? Jack, get up, Hobble's waiting. Jack, I don't like spaghetti.'

It seemed Jack had turned into a parent, just like that. It left Jack feeling confounded, maybe even trapped, but as he saw the difference it was making to Harry he could only feel relief.

He couldn't want it any other way, but still there was the sensation of walls closing around him. It seemed he was a family, like it or not.

A single parent.

'You'll manage,' Kate said to him on the third or fourth day after that last kiss, and he wondered if his face was so revealing.

'Of course I will.'

'Even without a woman,' she said, and chuckled. He watched her head back to the dolphin pool and felt—on top of everything else—a gut-wrenching sense of loss.

If he'd done things differently he might...

What? Have Kate for a wife? Have a mother for Harry? Bind Kate to the solution he had to find?

It wasn't fair. He accepted that. What was between them had escalated far too fast, and he understood her fear. But he watched her with her little patients, he saw the care and the kindness, he heard her laughter, he watched her tease, cajole, empathise, and he wondered why he hadn't seen this all those years ago.

Was it because he'd never thought of wanting a permanent partner—a partner in the real sense of the word? Was it because he'd never wanted anyone to share his life?

And he was honest enough now to accept that he couldn't differentiate his needs. Yes, Kate was seeming more and more desirable, but he knew Harry was in the equation, too, and he couldn't lay that on her.

Maybe in the future...

Ha. In the future he'd be in Sydney and she'd still be here. She was treating him with professional distance now. How could putting the width of Australia between them make anything different?

'Jack, watch me. Jack, I can swim eighteen whole strokes before Kate has to put her hand under my tummy. Jack, Hobble pushed my tummy up even before Kate reached me.'

Woman and dolphins were an amazing medical team, he thought as he made admiring noises and tried not to make eye contact with Kate—because making eye contact with Kate seemed to make things harder. More convoluted. More needy. He tried to focus on his nephew's achievements and they were indeed awesome.

Someone should write up what she was achieving in the medical journals, he thought, but then he thought of the shadows in Kate's past and he knew such a thing was impossible.

Besides, there weren't enough dolphins in the world to do what Hobble and his mates were achieving. He'd been truly lucky to find this place.

To find Kate?

And it always seemed to come back to Kate. She was racing Harry now—or pretending to race him. They each had a cork kickboard and they were kicking to the side of the pool.

Hobble was zooming between them, creating a wake, heading Kate off so she had to change direction just as she got a lead. Harry was laughing so hard he was almost forgetting to kick—but kick he was, with his injured leg, putting aside pain as unimportant.

This was miracle territory. Hobble and his mates were miracle-makers.

So was Kate, but she was a woman alone and he needed to respect that.

At two the next morning he woke to a knock on the bungalow door. It was such a light knock he might have dreamed it, but years of medicine had given him a knack of sleeping lightly. He was out of bed even before the knocking stopped.

He flung the door wide and Kate was in front of him. She was wearing her customary jeans and a windcheater, and her curls had been tugged back into a loose knot. She looked as if she'd woken in a hurry and rushed out.

Her feet were bare. He looked at her in the moonlight and thought...he thought he'd better not go there.

'Jack, could you help me?' she said, and emotion and desire took a back seat as he switched to medicine. The professional side of him was awake and alert and ready to act.

'Of course.' No hesitation. After all she'd done for Harry, whatever this woman asked of him, she had it.

'It's Wendy,' she said. 'You know she has neuroblastoma. It started in the adrenal glands but she presented late. Her parents put tiredness and weight loss down to puberty. They were busy, they have three other kids and they just didn't notice. So it's already metastasised, with spread into the abdomen and the liver. She's been through twelve months of intensive treatment, with chemo and radiation targeting each tumour, but she's run out of options.'

'So what's happening now?' Two weeks ago he would have asked what a child with such a diagnosis was doing in a place like this, but that had been before he'd got to know Kate and her miracle-workers. All he needed was a medical status update.

'She's vomiting. She had an episode four nights back—that was when you and I...' She paused, and her colour mounted a bit but she had herself under control in an instant. 'I got things under control then, but tonight she's vomiting again and she's worse. I've given her promethazine and set up an IV line for fluids but she's not settling. Jack, I'm out of options. If you can't help I need to get a chopper in and transfer her to Perth.'

'Is that what her parents want?'

'They're desperate for her to stay here,' she said simply. 'After twelve months of hospitals and intensive treatment, she's had enough. She came in three weeks ago, traumatised and almost as withdrawn as Harry after months of coping with frightened adults, but here she's turned into a kid again. She's loving it, and we're fighting to have her stay as long as we can. But I can't stop her vomiting. Jack, you're an oncologist. I hate asking—you're here as a client as well—but if you would take a look...'

'Of course I will.' There was no hesitation. But then he glanced back toward Harry's bedroom. Problem. He was a single dad. He wasn't free to leave.

But once again Kate was ahead of him.

'I've woken Louise,' she said. 'If you agree to help, she'll be here in two minutes to take over Harry duty. She's great at this sleep business. She'll be on your sofa, snoozing as if we hadn't even woken her, two minutes after she gets here, but she'll hear the slightest sound from Harry. It's a splinter skill she's proud of. Let her show it off.'

And there was nothing else to say.

'Give me ten seconds to haul on jeans and T-shirt,' he told her. 'Kate, I make no promises. There's every chance Wendy will need to be evacuated to get decent symptom control but I'll see what I can do.'

She'd known Jack was good back in med. school. It took all of five minutes of watching him with Wendy and that knowledge was confirmed. He had the empathy and he had the skills to match.

Wendy was exhausted and sick and frightened. Her parents were terrified.

It took a whole thirty seconds with Jack to calm them down.

'Hi,' he said, as she showed him into the little cabin, into Wendy's bedroom where her parents were standing by the bed, looking like deer trapped in headlights. 'Hey, Wendy, Dr Kate tells me you can't stop being sick. Is it okay with you if I see if I can help? Dr Kate's good—she and I went to university together so I know she's about the best doctor around—but while she specialised in family medicine I specialised in caring for people who have cancer. People like you, Wendy. That means right now I have skills that might help.'

He was talking straight to Wendy. It was the right thing to do. Wendy's parents straightened a little, and she could see the sliver of hope lessening their despair. Courtesy of Jack.

'How long since you've been sick?' Jack asked.

'Five...about five minutes,' her mum said haltingly, and Jack gave her a smile that said, excellent, he obviously had another professional on side. And the sliver of hope intensified.

'That's good. This awful retching usually goes in about twenty-minute cycles so we have a window of time to get this sorted. Let's see what we can do before the next one hits. Wendy, I might not be able to stop the next couple of vomits but I should be able to stop them after that. Is it okay with you if I try? Can I take a look at your tummy?'

'Yes,' Wendy quavered.

'You must be tired of doctors,' he said. 'But I have one advantage. I have very warm hands.'

'Wh-why are they warm?'

'I have hot blood,' he said smugly. 'I've trained it. Some people can touch their foreheads with their toes. I can warm up my hands on command. Want to feel?'

'Yes,' Wendy said, and Kate almost gasped. Ten minutes ago the atmosphere in this room had been one of despair. Now not only was there hope, there was a touch of fascination. A blood-warming specialist...

Jack was moving fast, with light banter, as he lifted Wendy's pyjama top. His hands probed gently. Kate knew what he'd be feeling—an enlarged liver in her distended tummy, a hard, appalling mass of unmovable tumour.

'I don't suppose you have an X-ray machine lying around here someplace?' he asked Kate, as if it didn't matter too much.

But it did matter. If he could diagnose what was going on...

'Yes,' she said. 'Basic films are all I can organise, though. MRIs are out of our league.'

'Basic films are good,' Jack said fine. 'In the main building?'

'Yes.'

'If I wrap you up nice and warm and carry you, will you try very hard not to be sick on me?' Jack said to Wendy. 'If you're going to be sick, call out and I'll give you to your dad to carry. If I'm not mistaken, you had spaghetti for tea and I have my favourite T-shirt on. If you're sick on it I'll look like I'm covered in spaghetti graffiti. I'm cool but not that cool.'

And unbelievably, incredibly, Wendy giggled. 'You're silly,' she managed. 'Everyone says...everyone says you're silly.'

'Yes, but I'm silly and clean,' Jack said, grinning back at her. 'Okay, my lady, let's get you X-rayed. Ready, set, go.'

Kate hadn't bothered with taking X-rays. No matter what they showed she was beyond her level of expertise, but what she saw confirmed what she expected. A complete bowel blockage. That meant evacuation. There was no way she could cope with this here.

But Jack took the X-rays and as they went into her little side office to check them he didn't even suggest evacuation. 'Right,' he snapped. 'What medications do you have? Dexamethasone? Morphine? Sedatives?'

'Yes, but I don't have the skill—'

'I do,' he said. 'This isn't a huge blockage. I'm thinking steroid can reduce the swelling and clear it.'

'But if it doesn't work...'

'It has just as much chance of working here as in Perth. Kate, I'm looking at this mass of tumour and thinking no surgeon's going to operate. One blockage will be followed by another. But if I can get the swelling down we may well buy some time.' He put a hand on her shoulder. 'You know there's no easy answer, Kate, in fact there's no answer at all, but there is a way forward. If we use steroid to ease the swelling and unblock the bowel then she may well have a few good weeks. When things catch up with her, the steroid will be discontinued. Death will be fast. But right now this is a no-brainer in terms of treatment.'

'And you can do this here?'

'Yes,' he said—and she believed him.

Trust was such a nebulous thing. She'd sworn not to trust but as she looked up at his face, as she felt the strength of his hand on her shoulder, she felt trust sweep over her. Stupid or not, she trusted this man.

And not just as a doctor.

She nodded. He gave her a smile that said he understood the mix of emotions swirling in her head and for some reason she trusted that, too.

And then it was time to face Wendy. Her parents had taken her back to their cabin. She'd just copped another bout of retching and was limp in her dad's arms but she was still awake and aware. Her mum was sitting to the side, looking as ill as her daughter.

The little girl looked beyond exhaustion but Jack still talked directly to her. 'Wendy, what Dr Kate and I can see in the X-rays is lots of fluid. That's why your tummy feels so hard. It tells me you have a blockage in your tummy so the food you've been eating can't move through. So you have a choice. The doctors who looked after you before you came here could look after you again—Dr Kate says we can organise a helicopter to take you to Perth—but Dr Kate tells me you'd like to stay here. If that's what you want, then you need to trust me to care for you. Is that okay?'

And he didn't need to go further. Kate had told him that Wendy's parents had been warned of potential problems like this before they'd come here. Spelling those problems out now would terrify their daughter. He could take them outside and talk, but Wendy had had a year of medical procedures and lots of bad news. She'd have figured by now what doctors taking her parents outside meant.

So now Jack was treating Wendy as the decision-maker, and Kate could feel the family's trust in him grow stronger. Trust…it seemed to be growing by the moment.

'What can you do?' Wendy's father growled, and Kate could see the big man trying not to cry.

'Stop the vomiting,' Jack said promptly. 'Dr Kate tells me we have steroid here, and morphine.'

'I like morphine,' Wendy murmured, and Kate felt ill at the thought of the mass of the procedures and illness this little girl had endured to make her say such a thing. No child this age should even know what morphine was. But Jack was smiling. He was good, this man. He was exuding confidence, and it was making everyone relax.

'I'll bet you do, and for good reason because it's good at making you feel better. I'll give you steroid, too. That'll make the swelling in your tummy go down, and the vomiting will stop. Wendy, if it's okay with you, I'll give you something now to make you go to sleep. That'll make your tummy relax while we slip in the drugs that'll make the swelling go down. If you and me and your tummy all cooperate, I think you might be back in the pool with Hobble by tomorrow.'

'You're kidding.' Wendy's father's words were an explosion of disbelief. Minutes earlier they'd been facing evacuation to Perth with no promise of any real improvement at the end of it. Now they were being promised...dolphins?

'I'm not joking.' Jack met his disbelief head on. 'I would never joke about Wendy's tummy.' Then, as the man veered between distrust and hope, he put a hand on his shoulder. 'I'm an oncologist,' he said. 'Treating problems like Wendy's is what I do. I can see what's wrong on the X-rays and I know how to fix it.' He glanced again Wendy, and the look Wendy returned was that of a kid older than her years. Be honest, Kate pleaded silently, and he was.

'This isn't a long-term cure,' he said. 'Wendy, you know you still have cancer. But I can make you better for now. What do you say, Wendy? Will you let me make you feel better?'

'Yes,' Wendy whispered, and because she was a polite child she added a rider. 'Yes, please.'

* * *

It sounded easy but it wasn't easy. Even sedated, the involuntary retching continued. The steroid took time to work, and there was a real risk of dehydration and exhaustion simply making her body shut down.

But she wasn't ready to die yet. If they were lucky, Kate thought as the night wore on, blockage wouldn't be the cause of death. She could have a few good weeks courtesy of the steroid, and if the fates were kind she could simply drift peacefully away.

That was what Jack was fighting for. Time, but more than time—a chance for her parents to be able to say goodbye to their daughter without the gut-wrenching awfulness of watching their daughter's distress.

Kate stayed as Jack administered dexamethasone subcutaneously. She didn't doubt him. His skill as he injected the steroid was matched only by his gentleness. He gave haloperidol for the nausea and she watched with him until the retching stopped, until the little girl's body finally relaxed into sleep, until the steroid had a chance to start working.

Even then he wouldn't leave. She would have taken over—it was simply a matter of keeping the little girl's airway clear, keeping the obs up—but when she offered, Jack shook his head.

'I'm physician in charge,' he growled. 'If Louise is happy to care for Harry...'

'She is.'

'Then you have patients to treat in the morning and I don't. Go to bed, Kate, and leave Wendy to me.'

She didn't want to leave.

There was no need for her to stay. Wendy was asleep. Her parents were asleep, too, on the armchairs just through the door, but she knew the slightest noise would rouse them.

They slept, however, because they trusted Jack to take care of their daughter.

She could do the same.

But...but...

She didn't want to leave...him?

'Bed,' he said gently, and he raised a hand and ran his finger lightly down her cheek. It was a feather touch, the slightest of caresses that should have meant nothing but in truth meant everything.

'Jack, thank you...'

'It's my job.'

'You came here to be treated yourself.'

'I brought Harry for treatment.'

'Treatment here is for the whole family,' she said. 'That's what you and Harry are. A family.'

'And what about you, Kate?' he asked softly. 'Where's a family for you?' And then he smiled, that warm, endearing smile that made her heart do back flips.

'That's not a question to be answered tonight,' he said. 'Tonight's for sleeping. But in the morning...next month... next year... You're too precious a person to stay alone. I won't let that bastard scar you for ever. But go to sleep, my Kate. Let's worry about tomorrow tomorrow.'

She left and Jack was left with the sleeping Wendy. The night stretched on. Every now and then Wendy stirred and Jack checked, making sure her breathing was secure, keeping her safe.

Why? It was a question he asked himself often as an oncologist. Many of his patients were facing inevitable death. Why prolong it?

Because life was good.

He'd always believed it—sort of—but tonight that belief was suddenly intensified. Why?

Because he'd touched Kate's face? Because he'd seen

the change in her expression that said she trusted him, and there was hope in that look.

So many factors were coming into play. He had the long night to think about them, and think about them he did.

The unhappiness of his parents' marriage, pushing him to turn into himself.

The loss of his little sister.

Harry's dependence.

A man could lose hope, he thought, but as he watched the gentle rise and fall of Wendy's chest, he knew that the opposite was true.

Hope was all there was, he thought.

And trust.

Kate trusted him. For some reason the thought was almost overwhelming. It was a gift beyond measure.

Not to be taken lightly.

Not to be rushed.

The night wore on. As the first rays of a breaking dawn showed through the curtains, Wendy's sleep settled. The tension on her face faded. He felt her tummy and listened and heard unmistakeable bowel sounds.

Things were moving. The steroid was starting to do its job.

She'd have time.

How much time?

Did it matter? he thought. A day, a month, a year, a lifetime. He'd take everything he could get and make it good.

Was this about him or Wendy?

Both of them, he thought, tucking the bedclothes back around the little girl's body. Right now he felt almost a part of her.

'Any man's death diminishes me, because I am involved with mankind.'

Donne's words... He'd heard them, he'd even said them

to himself as he'd fought for patient after patient over the years, but now they seemed clearer.

He was fighting for Wendy. He was involved.

He was involved with Harry in a way that couldn't be undone.

He wanted to be involved with Kate.

And isolation? The desire to stand apart so he couldn't be hurt? Where was that now?

Dissolved, he thought, or maybe it had never existed. Maybe it was something he could never achieve because Beth had always been there, and then Harry, and his patients like Wendy.

And Kate...

He wasn't sure where to take this.

'But I will try,' he told the sleeping Wendy. 'For your sake. For all our sakes. Life's too short and too precious. For now let's get out there and play with some dolphins. Let's let ourselves love. Let's give everything we have.'

Wendy stirred again but this time it wasn't a movement of discomfort. It was just a child stirring in normal sleep.

'You stay well,' he told her. 'For as long as you have. Let's grab life with both hands, Wendy, girl. While we can.'

CHAPTER TEN

WENDY RECOVERED, AND something had healed inside Kate as well. For some crazy reason she felt she'd recovered with her.

But maybe this recovery was just like Wendy's, she told herself. Wendy's cure was short term. She was splashing in the dolphin pool, lying in a rubber ring, being pushed around the pool by the dolphins, weak but happy. She seemed to be soaking up every moment of this respite, and maybe that was because it *was* a respite. They all knew her cancer was waiting in the wings, pushed back for now but still there.

Maybe Kate's distrust was still there as well, but some time during the night of Wendy's illness she'd put it aside.

Jack was here now. She was trusting him.

She was loving him?

There was a question.

To all the world he was simply another parent. After the night with Wendy he'd reverted to being Harry's guardian, Harry's carer, Harry's playmate. But things had changed with him, too, she thought. He'd relaxed in his relationship with Harry. He no longer seemed reserved. Harry was turning into a normal little boy. He was still quiet but maybe he'd always be quiet. He was gaining in confidence, the strain had gone from his eyes and he seemed confident of his world again.

'I read on the internet about tame dolphins,' he told Kate at the end of a session where he'd pushed his injured leg to the limit, so much so that Kate had called a halt and made him slow down. 'It says it's really cruel to keep them in enclosures.'

'There are people who think that,' Kate said gravely. They were sitting in the shallows, watching Hobble and his mates toss balls to each other. 'They're the ones who say we should let nature take its course. We could open the gates now, Hobble and his mates would be free—but the experts tell us that with their background and their injuries they'd be dead within weeks. There are people who say that's better than them being in captivity. I don't know. What do you think?'

She was talking to Harry as she would to an adult. Jack sat in the shallows beside them and listened. This was what Harry wouldn't get if he went to live with Helen, he thought. Helen treated her kids as kids. Helen and Doug had brought them up on baby talk. Beth and Arthur had explained scientific theories to Harry before he could talk back.

'I don't want them to die,' Harry said cautiously. 'But the internet said it's wrong for humans to treat them as play things.'

He was seven years old. Jack blinked. This kid astonished him more and more.

As did Kate. He waited for her to say it was silly. After all this was a defence of everything she worked for, but instead she gazed out at the dolphins and took her time to answer.

'I've thought about that,' she said at last. 'A lot. I studied this place carefully before I came to work here. I'm not sure whether my decision is right but here's the premise I'm working on.'

Premise... It was a big word for a seven-year-old but

Harry didn't blink. He knew the word. He was a scientist at seven.

And Jack felt a sudden swell of pride that had nothing to do with the fact that this was his nephew and Beth's son and he was his guardian. It was everything to do with Harry as a person.

It'd be a privilege to raise this kid, he thought, and then he caught Kate's glaze. She smiled and he thought, She knows what I'm thinking.

Drat, he didn't do emotion.

He was doing emotion now.

'My thinking is that these dolphins have been saved,' Kate said. 'It's very hard to see an injured or orphaned dolphin and not help it. The argument for and against saving them is hard, and I and the people who work here don't have control over it. All we do is take rescued dolphins and care for them. And caring for them means not letting them get bored. We've given them a ginormous enclosure but that's not enough. In the wild these guys would surf and catch fish and swim for miles. So we figure they need toys. That's what you are. A toy.'

'A toy?' Harry asked, fascinated.

'Exactly.' She beamed. 'You may think you're lucky getting to play with the dolphins but think of it from the dolphins' point of view. Every day we give them a different set of toys to play with. One of them's called Harry.'

Harry thought about it. He thought about it deeply, his small face a picture of concentration.

Kate said nothing.

She really was the most restful of women, Jack thought. She really was...

Um, no. Not yet. There was no way he could rush what was becoming blindingly obvious.

This was too precious to rush.

'So it's like giving Hobble a toy train,' Harry said—

cautiously. 'Only instead of a toy train you're giving him a Harry.'

'Exactly,' Kate said, and beamed some more. 'We cover you up with a blue skin suit so you can't damage the dolphins with sunscreen. We give you the rules and we let the dolphins play with you. And they know that every blue-wrapped gift is different. They figure it out. Watch how they treat Sam and his swimming—they know he's strong in the upper body, they know he loves to swim. See how they react to Susie jumping up and down. They seem to jump, too. Watch how they nudge Wendy round the pool in her water ring. They never frighten her. Watch how they tease you, every day trying to make you swim faster. I don't think it's cruel to let them play with you, Harry. I think they love it.'

'But they're still stuck.'

'They are still stuck,' she agreed. 'They've all been permanently injured in some way and there's nothing we can do to fix that. So they're stuck like Sam's stuck in his wheelchair, but there are so many ways they can still have fun, just like Sam still has fun.'

Silence. Harry considered some more, and finally his grave little face cracked into a smile.

'I think they need their toy called Harry again,' he said, and chuckled and tossed a ball out onto the water, whooped as dolphins leapt to catch it and headed out into the water to join them.

Leaving Kate and Jack together.

They sat in more silence for a while. They were watching Harry and the dolphins, only they weren't just watching. There were so many undercurrents...so many things waiting to be said.

'That pretty much describes you,' Jack said at last, feeling he was walking on eggshells. But he wanted to get close to this woman. It was so important…

'What does?'

'Injured and stuck.'

'I'm not…' But she faltered and looked away.

Time to probe, he thought. Dared he?

'What would happen if the gates opened and you were free?' he asked, feeling like this was eggshell territory.

'I'd be terrified,' she admitted. 'I've been there. This suits me.'

'For ever?'

'For as long as I can stay hidden.'

'When a dolphin's cured, you do open the gates.'

'Yes, but—'

'But you don't think you'll ever be cured?'

'Maybe not. You think I'm a coward?'

'I don't think anything of the kind, but I do think you could use help. Like you're helping everyone else.'

'I'm happy as I am.'

He motioned out to Hobble. 'So if he had the choice—fix his scarring and join his mates out to sea or stay here for ever—what do you think he'd choose?'

'It's a big world out there.'

'And dangerous. But for him to swim for miles, catch his own fish, do his own thing…'

'I'm doing good here,' she snapped.

'Yes, you are, but the boundaries are still there and they worry you.'

'I have enough to keep me occupied.'

'What about me?' he asked into the stillness. 'I'm on the outside, Kate.'

'I don't know what you mean.'

'I mean I think I'm falling in love with you.'

She drew in her breath and stared out to sea for a while. Refusing to look at him. 'You just want a mother for Harry.'

'That's not true, and you know it.'

'It has to be true, Jack. I'm not in the market for a relationship.'

'Neither am I,' he said softly. 'But, Kate, the way I feel about you...I've never felt this way before. I've been running scared, too. My parents' relationship left me soured, thinking isolation was the way to go. That's how it's been all my life, holding myself contained. I never took a risk like you took with Simon. All my girlfriends have been just that—friends. I don't think I've ever hurt anyone. The women I've dated have all valued their independence as well. But you... Suddenly that independence doesn't seem so important. In fact, it seems crazy to want it. Loving you might entail risks but wouldn't the risks be worth it?'

She did turn to face him then, her eyes troubled. 'Jack, don't.'

'Why not?' he asked gently. 'Why not say it like it is?'

'Because it's too...pat,' she retorted. 'I can't believe it. Independent Jack Kincaid, having his pick of beautiful women, never committing, then suddenly landed with his orphaned nephew. I know you've fallen in love with Harry. I also know how much Harry will change your life—unless you find someone else to share the loving. Who else but Kate? Kate, who's been blackmailed all her life to love, whether she wants it or not.'

There was silence at that. He didn't know where to take it. How to change a woman's faith in the world? How to even begin?

The problem was that no matter how attracted he was to her, Harry was in the equation as well. The vision of a home with Harry and Kate was a thousand times more appealing than a home with just Harry.

A thousand times easier? Kate would make Harry a great mother. She understood him. Was part of his subconscious wanting that?

'See,' Kate said bleakly. 'You can't deny it.'

'I think I can,' he told her. 'Kate, I should have fought for you years ago. You're the most beautiful, the bravest, the best...'

'But you didn't,' she threw back at him. 'Because you didn't have Harry.'

'No,' he admitted. 'And Harry's changed me. I hardly understand what that change is all about either. I agree I'm struggling. But what I feel for you...'

'Needs to be tempered with sense. What you're struggling with is a good dose of panic at being a single dad.'

'I don't think I am,' he said, looking out at Harry. 'I want to do this.'

'Then do it,' she said. 'And in a year or so come back and see me—if you still want to.'

'You'll still be in your enclosure?'

'Leave it,' she said roughly, rising to her feet. 'Let it be, Jack. I'm happy here and it's taken all my life to get this happy. Please don't mess with it.'

'I won't,' he said, and he didn't rise to stand by her. He let her be, even if it nearly killed him. 'It's your call, Kate. You're right, my life is being turned upside down. All I know is what I feel. How can I trust that? I'm not sure I can, but I need to try. Let me know if you do, too.'

'I'm fine as I am,' Kate said.

'I'm sure you are,' Jack said. 'But I'm also sure you'd like to be free. But the way you're feeling...asking you to love me might be asking you to go from one enclosure to another and I'd never do that to you. Just know that if you ever want it, Harry and I will be waiting for you. Waiting to be free together.'

* * *

There was a lot there for a woman to think about—
almost too much. Luckily the rest of the day's sessions
were straightforward. The dolphins did their stuff, the
kids didn't push injured limbs too far, the day was gorgeous, the mums and the dads were happy—all was right
in her world.

Except Jack loved her.

What was wrong with that?

It scared her witless. It made her want to run.

Why?

Because a part of her—a really big part—said giving
in to love left her exposed, as she'd been for most of her
life. Love was gossamer chains that, when tugged against,
became spiked steel.

Maybe she was being stupid, she conceded. She was
comparing the love Jack was offering to the suffocating
love of her parents—and to what Simon called love, the
love of greed and cruelty.

But still...it was too much of a coincidence, she told herself, and she knew it was true. Jack had been left to care for
his injured nephew. She'd formed a bond with Harry. Jack
knew, or at least he must guess, how much she'd love to
care for such a child as her own, and Jack needed that commitment. Because if she committed, he wouldn't have to.

Her parents had loved her because they'd needed her.
Simon had 'loved' her because he'd wanted control and
money. And here was Jack, who needed a mother for his
child.

But it was more than that. She could trust Jack.

How? She didn't know, but there was somehow a deep
sense that seemed to be working by instinct, that watched
him up the beach now as he dug holes with his nephew, that
said here was a man she could trust with her life.

But there was another part of her, the part that had been

on the run for years, the part that had been battered and broken by a dreadful marriage, and that part said she was a fool. Had she learned nothing?

If Jack had come to her without Harry then…

No. Not even then. Trust had to be absolute, and how could she ever leave herself vulnerable?

She wanted to head somewhere and weep.

She wanted to lay it all out in front of Jack and let him tell her it was nonsense.

Instead, she bounced in the water and cheered on her little clients, and as she worked with each of them she thought of the shocking paths that had brought each of them here. Life was cruel. Random.

You had to protect yourself, she thought, and suddenly Maisie was lunging down the beach, through the shallows to reach her like, beaching herself on her mistress like she'd found her very own island. She was landed with an armful of soaking golden retriever. Maisie wriggled and licked and dripped and Kate thought this was the kind of treatment Maisie reserved for her very neediest of patients.

So why her? Why now?

Because she needed her. She hugged back and if she sniffed back a tear it was hidden in the fur of soaked dog. Finally she pulled away, and smiled and looked back to where Matilda Everingham was using her one good arm to try and keep a ball out of Hobble's reach.

Matilda was recovering from a car accident. This place was helping her recover.

Like it was helping *her* recover.

'And you can't recover by jumping from the frying pan straight back into the fire,' she told herself, and glanced again at the man and the boy on the beach. 'They need you but so does everyone else here. I won't let love blackmail me into anything.'

Yet…Harry was earnestly telling something to his

uncle. Jack laughed and hugged his little nephew and the sight did something to her insides.

She could be part of it.

Yeah. And she'd be left keeping the home fires burning, taking over Jack's domestic responsibilities, and Jack would go back to the life he knew. *She could not trust.*

'And that's the end of it,' she said, turning back to Matilda and trying to edge aside her soggy dog. 'Thanks for the hugs, Maisie, but stick around. I just might need more of them.'

So much for taking things slowly. He'd scared her witless. She thought he was wanting a mother for Harry.

Maybe he did. Maybe her doubts were justified. He spent the next couple of days trying to give her space, while he tried to sort out his own thoughts.

A couple of days didn't help. Or maybe they did. Every time he saw her he became more and more sure that what he was feeling had nothing to do with Harry.

His thoughts kept drifting back to the night of that student party all those years ago, when Beth had floated home after meeting Arthur. His normally quiet, reserved little sister had been glowing.

'I can't tell you... I can't explain... All I know is that he's the one. If I'm wrong I'll break my heart but he seems to feel it, too. Oh, Jack, I don't believe in them but I seem to be in the middle of a miracle.'

Her joy had left him confused and concerned. What was she letting herself in for? How had it happened? Maybe if Arthur had looked like the next James Bond he'd have understood, but Arthur had been a bespectacled, mild-mannered man who'd looked at his sister as if he'd been granted his own miracle.

And now he was looking at Kate and feeling exactly the same.

But it wasn't reciprocated. Kate was running scared, and with reason.

So what to do?

In the end he decided he simply didn't know, but one thing was sure, nothing could happen here. He was the guardian of one of Kate's patients. She was treating him with professional detachment and he had to accept that. Pushing boundaries would not only be unfair on Kate, it could very well jeopardise Harry's recovery.

So wait.

Until when?

He didn't know. He and Harry were only booked here for another couple of days.

Still, he had to wait.

Waiting was easier said than done, but he did have things to do to fill in the time.

He was thinking of his life in Sydney as it had been. On call twenty-four seven. Living and breathing for his career.

He was thinking of his life as it now had to be, if he was to fit a small boy into it. No, he thought as he worked through priorities. He didn't need to fit Harry into his life. His life and Harry's had to merge. Two lives, equal priorities.

With Kate…three?

He couldn't ask her. Not yet. He got it, he thought. She'd been controlled for so long that for him to assume the control was his had been…cruel. He didn't know how to fix it. He only knew, for now, he needed to focus on Harry.

So for now his focus was total.

He had a life to reorganise. He had a family to make, including Kate or not.

CHAPTER ELEVEN

SATURDAY. LATE MORNING. Harry was Kate's last client before lunch. Up until two days ago Jack had joined them in the water, but for the last couple of days he'd pleaded a need to get work done. But it wasn't true. He'd done everything he needed to get his life after Dolphin Bay sorted. For now he had time to sit on the beach and watch a vibrant, loving woman encourage his nephew to do things no one could have imagined him doing two weeks ago.

She was a miracle-worker. Harry's bad leg kicked now with full extension. What's more, almost the whole time in the water he chatted. He'd never be the most voluble of kids, but he answered questions and he asked his own.

'Tell Hobble what you want him to do,' Kate told him, and the little boy considered the dolphin and set him a challenge.

'I want you to swim all the way round the pool before I get to the edge,' he decreed, and Jack grinned at the little boy's school teacherly tone. Also the task he'd set him. The pool was vast in circumference and they were fifteen yards from the edge. But Harry started swimming, and Kate whistled. Hobble zoomed round the pool like lightning, Harry splashed in a frenzy to the side of the pool and they arrived together. Harry surfaced nose to nose with the dolphin, crowing with delight. 'I almost beat you.'

'I don't believe it.'

He'd been so entranced an entire battalion could have sneaked up behind him. It wasn't a battalion. It was scarier. His sister-in-law was standing on the sandhill behind him. Helen.

Helen wasn't looking at him. She was staring out at Harry.

'Oh, my,' she murmured. 'Oh, Jack, look.'

'He's good, isn't he?' As astounded as he was by her visit, his pride rang out clear and true. 'Two weeks and he's a new man.'

But Helen was already running down the sand, calling out to the pair in the water. 'Harry. Harry, it's Aunty Helen. Oh, Harry...'

Jack watched as Harry froze. Kate was beside him. She put her hand on his shoulder and bent and said something, and Harry's shoulders braced. Who knew what Kate had said but whatever it was it seemed to have worked. Kate took his hand and together they waded from the water. Harry was promptly enveloped in a giant aunt-hug. Then Maisie bounded along the beach. Of course she did. Visitors and Maisie not on hand to welcome them was an unheard-of phenomenon. Aunt, kid and dog became one gigantic cuddle.

Jack grinned, but then he thought, Why is she here? To take Harry home?

The hug was separating into its component parts. Helen took Harry's hand, whether he willed it or not, and led him up the beach. Jack saw Kate hesitate and he sent her his very best pleading look. She hesitated a bit longer, eyeing the group unenthusiastically, then gave a rueful smile and a shrug and came.

He was a stronger man with Kate behind him, he thought. Or should that be in front?

'Hey,' Helen said, releasing Harry for a moment to give Jack a hug. 'You're a magician.'

'It's Kate who's the magician,' Jack said mildly. 'Kate, this is Harry's aunt, Helen.'

'So you're the hunted wife,' Helen said, and Jack winced. How many people had Helen told?

'I'm Harry's counsellor and physiotherapist,' Kate said, carefully calm. 'Harry, I'll leave you to your family re-union.'

But Helen stopped her leaving. 'Is Harry ready to go home?' she asked. 'What he's doing with his legs...that's fantastic. And Jack says he's talking. He's healed?'

'We've been talking of going home, haven't we, Harry?' Kate said, and the little boy nodded. Mutely. He wasn't sure what was going on and he wasn't prepared to com-mit himself.

'We have two more full days,' Jack said.

'I'd rather take him home earlier if it's possible,' Helen told him, briskly efficient. 'Doug's looking after the chil-dren for the weekend but he needs to be back at work on Monday. If we could take Harry tomorrow, that would be splendid. Jack, when you were dubious about this place you told me your airfares from Perth are flexible. Annalise has told me you two are splitting up. I've thought about it and I've decided it'd be best if we go home together, giv-ing Harry time to adjust to me.'

What followed was silence. A very long silence. Kate stayed still and watchful. Helen was smiling, expecting assent to her plans. Harry stood mute, staring down at the sand. Into the stillness Maisie crept, pressing firmly against Harry. It was as if she sensed she was needed.

Kate took a couple of steps back but she didn't leave them. Jack was looking...tense. His look had been a plea for her to stay. Why?

This was none of her business. She should go—but she was riveted to where she stood.

'It would be good if we could fly home together,' Jack said at last, choosing his words with care. 'It's great of you to offer, Helen, but I've promised Harry we're staying until Tuesday. I don't break promises.' He hesitated. 'And he probably doesn't need time to adjust to you. He'll be living with me.'

'Well, that's dumb,' Helen said. 'That's why I'm here. I know you're being sentimental but sentimentality doesn't come into it. It's crazy to think you can fit childcare around your career. Harry'll fit into my tribe so easily we'll hardly notice. You know we can love him, Jack, and you know you can't.'

Harry studied the sand some more. Kate found she was holding her breath. Could she breathe? She seemed to have forgotten how.

Jack looked at Helen for a long moment and then he looked at down at his small nephew. He stepped forward and swung Harry up into his arms. And held.

'I thought we'd agreed, Helen,' he said, quite lightly. 'Harry's a bit of a loner. He likes quiet and having his own space. He and I get on together. You have your five kids. I have Harry. We can organise things around my career.'

'But Annalise said...' Helen started.

'What did Annalise say?' Once again, he spoke lightly but behind his words Kate sensed steel.

'That you can't manage him together. She's not prepared to take him on. She says it's breaking up your relationship.'

They shouldn't be having this discussion in front of Harry, Kate thought, but Jack had the little boy in his arms and he wasn't letting go.

'Our relationship,' Jack said, just as lightly but still with that undercurrent of steel, 'has already broken up.'

'Only because of the child.'

Harry had pretty much gone limp. His head was burrowed into Jack's shoulder. She should take him away, Kate thought, but then she decided it wouldn't work. Words had been said that couldn't be unsaid. Harry was bright. He'd have taken in everything. This was all about his future and he was entitled to stay.

'You're on call all the time,' Helen was saying. 'Your career is brilliant but life-consuming. Tell us how that fits with childcare. Even a nanny won't give you the sort of commitment that fits in with your career. You need to find a nice domestic wife and you've never looked like finding one of those.'

A nice domestic wife…

Kate thought again that she'd been right to back away from the magnetic appeal of Jack Kincaid. *Come into my parlour, said the spider to the fly…* What he'd offered had been a sweet and sticky trap. It was another form of the loving she'd been used to—with his needs and manipulation behind it.

But…

'No,' Jack said, deeply and evenly, and she blinked. So did Helen. The word was a resounding negative, a blunt statement, loud and strong, echoing over the sand hills and out to sea.

'What do you mean, no?' Helen said waspishly. 'What are you intending to do? School and after-hours crèche at the hospital? What if he's ill? You're Head of Oncology, Jack, have some sense. I won't let you neglect him.'

'I have no intention of neglecting him. I've quit at Sydney Central.'

'What…?'

'Harry's not the only one who's been doing some healing here,' he told Helen. 'Dr Kate's good. She's been telling I can't rely on anyone to do what I need to do myself.'

And Kate blinked. What was happening? Instead of

reacting angrily to her rejection, he'd changed his course? Surely not.

'Okay, maybe I could find someone,' Jack said, and was she imagining it or did he glance at her? 'As you say, a nice domestic wife. I have no idea how to find one but I dare say I could try. But this isn't anyone's responsibility but mine. Helen, these last two weeks have been time out for me, too, and I've figured a few important things out for myself. First and foremost is that I love Harry. He's my nephew as well as yours. I loved his mum and dad to bits and I love him.'

Wow. That was a biggie for a guy to say. Kate watched the stillness of the little boy's body and knew he was taking in every word.

'Secondly, my work's important,' Jack went on. 'But as I said, these last couple of weeks have been an eye-opener. I've been watching Dr Kate and seeing the amazing work she's doing. I've fought my way through medical circles to be top in my field in oncology. Nothing's been more important than my work, but Kate's shown me that there are different types of important. So, yes, I still want to work in my field but I'm going back to basics.

'I've rung Sydney Central and resigned as Head of Oncology. I've applied for a hands-on position, working at grass-roots level at a town further down the coast. Nothing's firm yet but I'm hoping it comes off. It's a large town rather than a city. There's a need for an oncologist but only one who treats patients directly, and that need's not vast. I'm thinking I can work from nine to four on weekdays. It'll be a huge cut in income, a huge cut in status but it means with the help of a decent housekeeper who's prepared to step in in an emergency, Harry and I can look after each other.'

'But you can't!' Helen was staring at him in stupefaction. 'A rural doctor...you! Jack, what about your research? Even I know how important it is.'

'I can still do that,' Jack said evenly. 'But not as much. As Harry gets older I may be able to pick up the threads of my academic career, but right now that's not what I'm interested in. I'll take care of Harry, and nothing else comes before that.

'It's not like I'm stepping away from my career,' he told her, quite gently because her shock was genuine and she loved Harry, too. 'But there's a community without an oncologist. I treated a kid here the other night...well, you don't need to know the details but it made me realise that grass-roots medicine is still what it's all about. I can treat a community. I can stop many, many cancer sufferers having to go to the city for treatment, and Harry and I can get a life in the process.'

He hugged Harry a bit tighter. 'And there's a beach there too and, amazingly, a dolphin sanctuary,' he added. 'Not like this, it's not a treatment centre, but I figure maybe Harry and I can volunteer to clean pools or something. We're pretty much committed to dolphins now, aren't we, mate?'

And Harry tugged back and looked at his uncle. His face was inches from his. The look that passed between man and boy made something inside Kate twist as it had never twisted before.

'We'll live near dolphins?' Harry whispered.

'Yes.'

'Near a beach?'

'Right near a beach if we can manage it. You'll need to help me hunt for a house.'

She was crying. Stupid, helpless tears were slipping down her face and there wasn't a thing she could do about it.

She'd suspected this man of trying to manipulate her

to solve his problems. She might have known he'd do no such thing.

And then she thought…she thought… *He didn't want her to make the problem go away.*

What was happening in her head? Her thoughts were a confused jumble, but through the weird mist she could see a flicker of light. Hope?

Maybe…just maybe he'd like her to join him while they solved problems together.

The thought was huge.

She stood numb while Helen probed Jack's new information, decided she was pleased and hugged Jack and Harry. This family was sorting itself out, she thought. She had a happy ending here. She sniffed and backed off a little. She had more clients waiting.

What was between her and Jack…well, it'd have to wait.

It might not be anything, she conceded. He might indeed have been considering her as the answer to his problems, and then when she'd knocked him back he'd been forced to find another solution.

Maybe he'd talk to her about it. She hoped…

She desperately hoped, she conceded, but now wasn't the time or the place. She was the treating medic. She'd done all she could.

Jack and Harry were still enveloped in Helen's weepy hug. Leave them to it, she told herself, but it took sheer, physical effort to turn away. To turn again into Dr Kate, moving from one client to another.

She did it, though. She sniffed and wished skin suits came with pockets for handkerchiefs. She needed to head for her bungalow before she saw the next client.

She forced herself to turn away, she took two steps… but suddenly Helen broke away from the group hug. She reached her and put a hand on her shoulder and she had to stop and turn.

'Kate,' Helen said. 'C-Cathy?'

She'd met this woman before, a long time ago. Helen had been one of the university crowd, studying pharmacy before dropping out to start a family. She looked at her now and saw the echoes of a wild child who'd seemingly settled contentedly into motherhood. But Helen was looking worried. Was she about to appeal to her to support her?

'This is between you and Jack and Harry,' she said gently. 'I'll leave you to it.'

'It's fine. I mean...I don't really know if it's fine but he's prepared to try...I have to support him,' Helen said. 'But there's something else. I was feeling bad, and then when Doug said I should fly over I thought I should, not just to see Harry but to see you, to see you face to face.'

'Why?'

'Because I think I've blown your cover,' she said bluntly. 'When Jack first got here he asked me about you and I made some enquiries. Then the next day he rang again and told me not to ask around. He said you've been battered and were hiding. So I hoped nothing would come of the enquiries I'd made. But the night before last we got a phone call. From your Simon. He wanted to know all about you. Only he already knows too much. Someone's passed on the stuff I was asking about. He knows where you are, and...well, he sounded vicious. He said he couldn't afford to fly but he'd drive and he'd get here even if it took three days, and he'd make you face up to what you've done. I'm so sorry, Cathy. After all you've done for us...I'm so sorry, but...he's coming.'

'Here?' Kate said, stupidly.

'He made such threats,' Helen said, and her voice told them more than any words could just how terrible those threats had been. 'Doug said we should call the police but I thought...he's driving and it takes three days, so I'd fly. I thought, I'll take Harry home, get him out of here.

Then you can phone the police, or leave, or do whatever you have to. Either way, you still have twenty-four hours before he's here.'

CHAPTER TWELVE

SHE'D BEEN FREE for years. Or maybe she hadn't.

The last time she'd seen him Simon had been in court, where she'd outlined the deceits and dishonesty with which he'd destroyed her family and his own. After that she'd had phone calls and emails full of a hate so great it had made her run. She'd changed her name, she'd changed her life, but she knew Simon. She knew wherever she went, his hate would follow.

His hate was bringing him here.

She stared at Helen and she felt like the sand was shifting under her feet.

Simon. Coming here.

She remembered his response when she'd told him she was divorcing him. 'Once my wife, always my wife,' he'd said, and there'd been pure venom behind the words. Venom that had made her skin crawl.

Always my wife... The words made her feel ill.

She'd have to run.

'Kate?' It was Jack. He'd put Harry gently aside, ushering him into Helen's care, and was there beside her. 'There's no need to look like that. We have time to plan to face him. And I *will* be beside you.'

Simon. Coming here.

It was like her world had been knocked off its axis. The

fears of years of abuse hadn't gone. She'd buried them but here they were, bursting from deep, dark recesses, making her feel like a kid again, like she had the first time she'd felt his fist.

'Kate.' Jack's hands were on her shoulders. 'Don't look like that. It's okay. This is no threat. You're not alone. You're surrounded by friends.' His hands held her with more strength, forcing her to look at him. 'I will be beside you,' he said again. 'I swear.'

And somehow her terror faltered. Somehow her world steadied.

Why?

Less than a week ago when he'd said he'd keep her safe she'd responded with fear. She hadn't wanted anyone to keep her safe. She hadn't trusted. And she'd had enough of hiding. To stay behind someone…to depend on them for her safety…

But somehow, some way, the promise Jack was making had changed. She reran it in her head, and the terror retreated still further.

I will be beside you.

Those weren't the words of a man who wanted to control her, she thought wildly. Her thoughts were all over the place but they were no longer centred on her ex-husband. They were veering around. They were starting to centre on Jack.

I will be beside you.

Those weren't the words of a man who wanted to manipulate her.

Jack.

They were all watching her—Helen with fear, Harry with worry, Jack with quiet empathy. Empathy. Where had that word come from? Why was it front and centre? Was it because he'd just told Helen what he planned for his life, and those plans didn't include her? Or...they didn't need to include her.

But she could...she might...

What if...?

'Together we'll confront the bastard,' Jack said, quite mildly as it was no big deal at all. 'You have enough medical evidence to put him away all over again. It'll just take courage.'

And there it was again. Jack was offering to help, to stand beside her but not protect her. To stand with her.

It'll just take courage.

She looked around her, at the gorgeous beach, the dolphins, the kids she was helping. Where was her terror taking her? She'd run from this? She'd let Simon drive her from this?

And then she turned and looked at Jack again. His gaze met hers, steady, grave and true. He was giving her space, she thought. He was offering her...something, but her future was hers to decide.

He'd decided his future. He'd planned it without her. He was talking on Harry's care and he was asking no one to share it with him.

But she might... She could...

Her mind was a mass of whirling thoughts, but it was still centring on Jack.

'I don't know where to start,' she faltered, and Jack smiled.

'If you're ready, you can start right now.'

'Ready?'

'To accept help. If you're ready to give statements, Susie's dad is a cop. High ranking. He doesn't look powerful in his sunsuit but he is. A word from us and Simon can be stopped before he even reaches here. If you're prepared to give statements...'

Then he paused. He let her thoughts take her where

she willed. No pressure, his silence said. The future was hers to choose.

So many thoughts…

What had Jack said all those nights ago when he'd seen the scar on her arm? *There's no statute of limitations on assault charges.* She thought of the litany of assaults she'd had at Simon's hands. She thought of the medical evidence she could show.

It took courage. It was easier to run.

'If you say the word, I will be beside you.' He said it again gently, and the terror had receded enough for her to hear the vow behind the words. It was as if a blanket had been put around her, a fleece of strength and comfort.

And love?

And she thought again of what Jack was prepared to do. Stand aside from his career. Give up his home, his friends, the world he knew, so he could take on the care of one small boy.

She thought, wildly, that if he could, maybe she could too.

'It'd have to work both ways,' she whispered, and she thought he wouldn't hear, but he did. His eyes warmed, gleamed, and his gaze caressed her.

'That could be arranged,' he said, and he smiled, and Helen stared at them both.

'What are you two on about?'

'Decisions,' Jack said. 'Holding each other up. The whole being greater than its parts.'

'You're not making sense. Shall I call the police?'

But Kate didn't want the police. Not yet. Not when such an important sensation was swirling…

Hope…

She shook her head. 'I… Not yet. There's time.'

'There is,' Jack said, his eyes still on hers. His smile

was a little quizzical, like he hoped he'd guessed right but he wasn't sure.

But she was sure. Or she was as sure as she could be.

She looked around her once again, at the beach, at her dolphins, at this place of healing. Jack would stand by her while she defended herself, she knew. He'd fight for her right to stay here.

But he was moving to another life. Her mind had been whirling but his smile was settling her. Showing her true north.

'You will be free,' he said, gently, lovingly? 'We'll get details of every injury. We'll outline the steps you've taken to run from him. We'll also have Helen outline the threats he made to her. Given his history, his past convictions, we can see him in jail for a very long time.'

'G-good.'

'There's no need to run. You can do whatever you want.'

Whatever she wanted?

She wanted Jack. She knew it then, surely and truly.

She loved this man with all her heart. She looked at him and she knew. All she needed now was the courage to say it. To ask?

She must. Jack had asked her once to share his life. Now that he was walking away from her life, could he want her still?

To ask seemed almost outrageous but she watched his face and she knew he wouldn't ask himself. She'd accused him of wanting a mother for Harry. She'd thrown it back at him. But now...

'I'd like to be with you,' she said.

'Be...'

'If you'll have me.' She hesitated. Was she misreading his touch, the way he was looking at her? She hoped not. With all her heart, she hoped not.

'I figure,' she said gently, 'that we both fight for control.

I've been fighting for control for so long that it's going to be hard, but if…if you'd like us somehow to merge… If you could consider something like…joint control… If we could face Simon down together… And maybe…maybe if we could make a home for Harry together?'

There was a gasp from Helen. Harry was staring, open-mouthed, trying to figure out what was going on. Even Maisie seemed stunned, but it didn't matter. All that mattered was the way Jack was looking at her.

'Kate…'

'Not if you don't want,' she said, hurriedly now, scared that she'd gone too far, read too much into what had happened between them. 'I mean…in this new life…this new town you're going to…there'll be women there. You can get a housekeeper. Find someone else. Build a life. Move on.'

'So I could.' He sounded dazed.

'So, you see, you don't need me. It's just, if there's a position vacant…if I'd fit… You see, even if I don't run, I don't have to stay here. This is a place of healing. I believe…somehow I seem to have healed. Somehow a doctor called Jack has worked his magic. But I don't depend on you, Jack. I can go anywhere. It's like the sea gates have been opened. I'm free.'

'So you are.'

'So you don't have to have me… I mean, if you do want to be alone…'

'Kate, shut up,' he said, sounding strained. 'Give me a moment to get things straight.'

So she shut up. She was having trouble getting things straight herself.

There was a long silence. Then… 'Harry?' Jack asked.

'Yep?' Harry seemed entranced. Puzzled but entranced.

'Your Aunt Helen hasn't met Hobble, or the rest of the team. How about you and Maisie go and introduce them?'

'I want to listen,' Helen said, and then she grinned and

held up her hands as if in surrender. 'Fine,' she said. 'I have not the faintest clue what's going on, or maybe I do but I'm too gobsmacked to say anything. Harry, dolphins.'

'You want to give them some fish?'

'Yes,' Helen said. 'But, Jack…do you need anything before I go? For instance, I could lend you an engagement ring…'

'Helen…'

She threw up her hands again. 'Okay, just offering. Just loving this. I came over feeling sick. Now I feel…'

'Better?' Harry asked, anxious now. 'If you're sick, this place makes you better.'

'Well, you and Jack would know.' She grinned, a beautific grin that almost split her face. She took her nephew by the hand and she clicked her fingers for the dog. Where Helen ordered, dog would follow.

Maisie considered her, then dived into Harry's pile of belongings and grabbed a ball. And headed deliberately to the water.

'Uh-oh,' Kate said. 'Should we warn her?'

'Let's not,' Jack said, and tugged her closer. 'Kate.'

'Y-yes?' She was scared to breathe. How could she make so many assumptions? She'd thrown herself at him. Why? Because she was free?

It didn't matter if he didn't want her, she told herself— but she knew that it did.

It mattered so much…

'Kate, I'm trying to think this through,' he said. 'Bear with me if I falter. Let me think out loud.'

'Okay.' This was hopeful, she thought. Sort of.

'It seems to me,' he said, still holding her close, 'that somehow you seem to be taking control of your life. That's great. But in the next breath you're making an offer that takes my breath away. But I need to be honest. Kate, love, if you stay with me, there will be times that I try to be in control. I will get bossy. But, Kate, I'd like you to get bossy back. The way I see it, we'd be headed for something like flexible sea gates. Maybe we can go in and out together.'

'Oh, Jack...'

'But, Kate, this is fast.' He wasn't losing contact. The warmth and strength of him was flooding into her, making her feel...extraordinary. 'Love, even while I've been planning Harry's and my future, a future without you, more than I wanted anything in the world I've wanted you. That holds true now. But I won't hold you. I'm prepared to risk losing you if you want time to make up your mind. No strings attached. Just...loving each other until you decide...how free you want to be.'

'I don't want to be...that free,' she managed.

'But what about Harry? He's my responsibility. Not yours.'

'But if I want that responsibility? If I want the privilege of loving him?'

His hold on her tightened. She could feel his heartbeat under hers. She could feel the power of him. She could feel the love.

She held him back, and things were said in that moment with no words said. Vows were made in total silence.

Life shifted. The sea gates, locked for so long, creaked slowly open, and Jack was there, waiting for her to swim free with him.

'You'd want me?' he asked.

'More than anything in the world.'

'You'd leave here?'

'There are rehab. places for kids everywhere, and if there aren't I can set them up. Someone else can take over my place here. Some other doctor who needs healing.'

'You no longer need healing?'

'I think,' she said unsteadily, 'that all I have is a void

in my heart that needs filling. And I might…I just might be looking at a guy who could fill it.'

He smiled. He smiled and he smiled, and then he dropped to the sand.

On bended knee.

'I'm not sure if this is the time or the place,' he said. 'You need rose petals and champagne.'

'I don't need anything but you.'

She was smiling down at him. Smiling as much as he was. She was dizzy with smiling. Dizzy with…love?

This was all about Jack and the rest of her life.

'Then will you marry me?' Jack asked, and the world stilled.

She thought… Marriage. Jack. The feeling flooding through her… Who could describe it? Euphoria was too small a word.

'Is it too soon?' he said, mistaking her silence for hesitation. 'Kate, I can wait. I'll wait as long as I must. I'll do whatever I must to win you. To love you. But if you'll marry me I swear I'll not confine you. I swear I'll keep you free. All I'll do is love you, for as long as we both shall live.'

Silence. He needed her to answer, she thought desperately. She needed to get her voice in order, her thoughts in order. Somehow she made a massive effort.

'Jack, I've never had a family,' she said, softly and lovingly. 'Not really. I'm not sure how to start, but if you wouldn't mind taking on a raw beginner… You and me and Harry, and Maisie and whoever else comes along. Family. I'll do my best. I'll love you with all my heart and if that's not enough I'll love you some more. So, yes, Jack Kincaid, I'll marry you.'

She dropped to her knees to join him on the sand. He cupped her face in his hands, and looked at her, caressing her with his eyes.

'I will love you for ever,' he told her. 'I should have loved you and married you years ago but I'll make up for it. I have no idea how to be a husband, how to be a father, but I'll learn. The only requirement I know is love, and I have that in spades.'

'You, too?' She could barely speak. 'The way I feel…'

But she couldn't go on. He'd tilted her chin to kiss her. His mouth met hers. She felt his warmth, his strength and his love. His kiss was tender, loving, perfect, and it was the sealing of vows that were as yet unsaid but were already stronger than chains.

She kissed him back. His hand tugged her close and she surrendered to the kiss. She surrendered to this man but it was okay, it was fine, because he was surrendering, too.

She kissed him back. She loved him and held him and the kiss could have lasted forever, but finally, eventually, they became aware of laughter and applause around them.

They broke apart and patients, parents and staff were clustered around, smiling and smiling, ready to share in their joy.

Everyone but Helen.

Out on the sandbank Helen cut a lone figure, dripping wet, gesticulating hysterically as Maisie swam serenely back to shore.

Kate choked on laughter. She stood with Jack's arm around her while Maisie bounded up the beach to drop the ball at her feet.

'Oh, Maisie,' she faltered. 'How could you do that to Helen? Not when she's come all this way to warn me.'

'It'll be fine,' Jack said grandly, hugging her closer with one arm and waving to the beach in general with the other. 'Helen is family, and forgiveness come with the territory. I'm thinking family might take some getting used to, but we're about to start.' And he kissed her again. 'We might rescue Helen first, but we're about to start right now.'

* * *

Six months later... A coastal town south of Sydney. Sunday morning. They were down at the dolphin enclosure, watching Harry swim.

This was a different place from the dolphin sanctuary that had played such a huge part in their lives. This was simply an enclosure where injured dolphins were rehabilitated. Dolphins needing long-term care were sent somewhere like Dolphin Bay, but these were short-termers. They were wild dolphins, recovering from shark bites or encounters with fishing nets.

Jack and Kate had wed back at Dolphin Bay. It had seemed the only place. Helen had grumbled about needing to bring all her kids to the other side of the country but once her kids saw Dolphin Bay all grumbles were put aside.

The ceremony had been magic, on the beach at sunset. Kate had worn a simple dress, soft silk, floaty, beautiful. She'd worn frangipani in her hair, and nothing on her feet.

Harry and Maisie had been joint ring-bearers. Harry had carried the ring while Maisie had stood by his side, solemn and true, as if she'd understood the significance of the occasion. The fact that seagulls had intruded right after the ring ceremony and had needed to be chased was immaterial. Kate had been wed. A dog's duty was done.

Helen and Doug had beamed. The staff of Dolphin Bay had beamed as well. A new doctor had arrived the week before. Isabelle was a burnt-out surgeon. She'd arrived tentative, not sure if this could work, but after a week there was already colour in her cheeks, smiles, dolphin magic.

As for Simon, he was now nothing but a shadow from a forgotten past, safely back in prison for the foreseeable future.

Susie's father had done wonders, even finding outstanding charges that had nothing to do with Kate. 'And we'll have a watertight intervention order to protect you when he finally gets out,' Susie's dad had told them. 'Forget him.'

So they had. They'd moved on to happiness.

The staff of Dolphin Bay had given them a beach umbrella dotted with dolphins as a wedding gift. They were sitting under it now, while Harry lapped the pool. These dolphins in their new home weren't tame, but they seemed to lap with him.

'It's magic,' Kate whispered. 'We're so lucky.'

'Lucky indeed.' Jack held his wife's hand and thought of the last few months. The house they'd found, a beautiful cottage just back from the beach. His job, satisfying in a way he'd never dreamed. The new rehab centre Kate was setting up. Harry's school, where he was blossoming.

And this place...this dolphin sanctuary... They had such plans.

Because he'd spent his life so focussed on his career, Jack was financially secure. His money and Kate's skills had secured them seats on the board and already they had plans in place for expansion. Kate had visions of a bigger pool attached to a smaller hospital pool. She dreamed of an educational centre where kids could learn about the needs of wild dolphins.

She had hopes that one day kids might also come here to heal, just as they did at Dolphin Bay.

This was okay, Jack thought. Actually, this was more than okay. This was pretty much perfect.

'I don't want anything more in life than what I have right now,' he said, and he kissed his wife on the nose. And then, because who could resist, he kissed her on the lips.

She pushed him away, but just a little so she could still watch Harry. She was standing lifeguard, as all parents did. To Harry, the word 'Kate' was synonymous with 'Mum'. He loved Kate and she loved him right back. His parents would always be a part of his life, a loving memory, the foundations of his future, but he had his Jack and his Kate and he was as happy as a kid could be.

Actually, he had an extra lifeguard as well. Maisie was standing guard on the sidelines. She wasn't allowed in the dolphin pool but everyone knew that one hint of trouble she'd be in there. Harry was hers.

'So you don't want anything else?' Kate asked, as they watched, and Jack thought about it.

'A beer,' he conceded. 'In a while. But that's pretty much it.'

'That's a shame,' she told him. 'Because I have something for you.'

'What?'

And in answer she took his hand. She was wearing a bikini. Her stomach was smooth and flat, yet when she held his hand over it and pressed down he felt...he felt...

'You really want nothing else?' she asked.

He closed his eyes, and when he opened them he'd come to a decision.

'Harry,' he called. 'Time to come out.'

'Aw...'

'No arguments,' he called. 'Out, now.'

So Harry reluctantly emerged. Maisie met him, boy and dog hugged—they'd been separated for a whole fifteen minutes!—and then he turned to Jack.

'Why did I have to get out?' he demanded.

'Because lifesaving duties have been suspended,' Jack told him. 'Harry, could you pour yourself a drink and go sit in the shade with Maisie?'

'Why?'

'Because there's something I need to do,' he told him. 'Our Kate has just given me a gift, something so priceless I can scarcely take it in. I love you, mate, but right now I need to devote all my time to telling Kate I love her. So you concentrate on your soda and your dog while I take our Kate into my arms and tell her I love her for ever.'

'Can I help?' Harry asked.

'Join the queue,' Jack said. 'But don't rush. Loving Kate's important, and we have all the time in the world.'

* * * * *

FLIRTING WITH THE
DOC OF HER DREAMS

BY
JANICE LYNN

First published in Great Britain 2014
by Mills & Boon, an imprint of Harlequin (UK) Limited,
Eton House, 18-24 Paradise Road, Richmond, Surrey, TW9 1SR

© 2014 Janice Lynn

ISBN: 978-0-263-90787-2

Printed and bound in Spain
by Blackprint CPI, Barcelona

Dear Reader

Some time back I reconnected with a friend who met a man online, fell in love with him before she'd ever met him in person, and is now happily married to him with two kids. Since then I've been thinking about how technology has changed the way people find each other in this crazy, busy world we live in, and how individual love stories begin in so many ways. My friend met her man online, felt a spark, and quickly began texting that led to sexting, and their in-person relationship developed from there. The sexting someone you'd never met intrigued me, because of the trust that would have to be involved before I'd ever risk doing that.

Much like myself, Nurse Beth Taylor can't imagine ever sexting or sending risqué photographs of herself. Actually, she can't even imagine anyone in her life who would send her a sext. So when she gets a late-night photo of some washboard abs she's convinced it's her best friend pulling a prank on her. How is she to know when she texts back that she's actually texting her fantasy guy?

If Dr Eli Randolph's ex-girlfriend was as perfect for him as everyone kept telling him, why wasn't he able to take that last step with her? *He* had to be the problem. Only when he sends an accidental text never meant to be sent—and to the wrong woman at that—he finds himself quickly caught up in an excitement he hasn't felt in for ever. Texting isn't enough. Eli wants the real thing. Only how does he recover a relationship that started with a text meant for another woman?

I hope you enjoy Eli and Beth's story as much as I enjoyed writing it. Drop me an email at Janice@janicelynn.net to share your thoughts about their romance, about how our cyber world has changed romance, or just to say hello.

Happy reading!

Janice

Dedication

To Michael. Thanks for making me believe in
happily ever after when I'd forgotten how.
I love you.

Recent titles by Janice Lynn:

THE ER'S NEWEST DAD
NYC ANGELS: HEIRESS'S BABY SCANDAL*
CHALLENGING THE NURSE'S RULES
FLIRTING WITH THE SOCIETY DOCTOR
DOCTOR'S DAMSEL IN DISTRESS
THE NURSE WHO SAVED CHRISTMAS
OFFICER, SURGEON…GENTLEMAN!
DR DI ANGELO'S BABY BOMBSHELL

*NYC Angels

**These books are also available in eBook format
from www.millsandboon.co.uk**

*Janice won The National Readers' Choice Award
for her first book*
THE DOCTOR'S PREGNANCY BOMBSHELL

**Praise for
Janice Lynn:**

'Fun, witty and sexy…
A heartfelt, sensual and compelling read.'
—*Goodreads Review* on
NYC ANGELS: HEIRESS'S BABY SCANDAL

'A sweet and beautiful romance
that will steal your heart.'
—*HarlequinJunkie.com* on
NYC ANGELS: HEIRESS'S BABY SCANDAL

CHAPTER ONE

ROLLING OVER IN bed and grabbing her cellular phone off the nightstand, sleepy-eyed nurse Beth Taylor squinted at the lit screen.

Who'd be texting her at...? She registered the time at just before midnight and winced. She'd just pulled two twelve-hour ICU shifts that had each been more along the line of sixteen hours. Exhausted, she'd hit the sack minutes after getting home.

The last thing she'd been expecting had been to be awakened by a text message. The phone number wasn't one she recognized. If this was some sales advertisement she was going to scream.

Fighting a yawn, and her vision blurred with sleep, she touched the screen, opening the message.

Hello. If that was for sale, sign her up.

All traces of sleep vanishing, she stared at the text. More aptly at the photo burning her screen.

Burning her eyes into flaming orbs.

Wow.

She glanced at the number again and racked her brain, trying to figure out who the number belonged to.

Not one she knew.

Neither were those abs any she'd ever had the pleasure of setting eyes on in person. Ha, not even close. She only wished some hot guy would send her a picture like that. Sadly, hot or not, this was the closest she'd gotten to a bare male body outside the hospital—and that so didn't count—since her break-up with Barry almost a year ago.

Okay, so the truth was she didn't want some random hot guy to sext her, neither did she want her ex to sext her, text her, or anything else. It was one scorching hot man in particular she wanted paying her attention. Unfortunately, he already had an equally hot girlfriend and didn't know Beth existed. Still, Dr. Eli Randolph was her fantasy guy, had been from the first time she'd seen him smile the day she'd started at Cravenwood Hospital a few months ago.

She wasn't quite sure what it was about him that had hooked her so intently. Yes, he was total eye candy, but it was something beyond his looks, something deeper, something about the glimmer in his eyes, the sincerity in his laugh, the kindness with which he dealt with his patients and coworkers, and, yes, the warmth of his smile. She really liked the man's smile. Then there was the outer packaging to all that inner wonderfulness that just made her knees weak. Eli was the whole package.

He was also someone else's.

She would never step across that boundary. She'd been on the opposite side of that coin and it wasn't a fun place to be. Never would she do that to someone.

Still, a girl was allowed a secret fantasy or two, right? Especially when that girl was as beat as she currently was. Perhaps she was so tired she was hallucinating the entire sext thing.

Maybe one of her friends was playing a joke on her.

A light bulb went off in her head. Sighing, she looked at the photo again. Yeah, that was a very realistic scenario now that she thought of it.

She'd pulled a prank on Emily earlier that week and her best friend had promised retribution. Hadn't Emily mentioned a new phone application a while back where one could have their number appear as someone else's?

Better to just ignore Emily than to encourage her. No telling what her roommate from college would do if given a little slack. Beth had learned that long before she'd moved to be near her friend when she'd wanted to make a fresh start far away from Barry and his new fiancée.

Stop sexting me, you perv.

Beth set her phone back on her night stand, punched her pillow, and prayed those sexted abs made an appearance in her dreams. At least in her dreams she should have a fabulous sex life, right?

At any rate, Emily couldn't accuse her of showing how desperate she actually was. Her life, particularly her love life, was boring, boring, boring. Her best friend knew that and kept encouraging her to quit letting a man who didn't know she existed hold up her love life. Problem was, no real-life man measured up to her fantasy guy.

Emily also frequently voiced that Beth might have subconsciously become fascinated by someone out of her reach so she didn't have to move on beyond what had happened with Barry so she wouldn't get hurt again. Wrong. She was so over that jerk who'd screwed her over. She knew not all men went back to their old girlfriends. Anyone who met Dr. Eli Randolph would know exactly why she'd become fascinated by him. It didn't have a thing to do with her old hang-ups. The man was mega-hot and brilliant to boot.

Still, she really should take Emily's advice and get a life outside work. Maybe she would go out with that guy from Administration who'd asked her to dinner a few times. She closed her eyes, saw a flash of blue eyes, curly brown hair, and a smile that took her breath away—all of which did not belong to the admin guy, but instead to a certain fantasy doctor.

Now wide awake, she rolled over in bed, picked up her phone and decided she might as well tell her friend she was onto her.

Leaning back against the leather sofa he'd sunk onto, Dr. Eli Randolph wondered just how low he'd gone.

Grimacing, he stared at the reply to his idiotic accidental text message.

Obviously not as low as he was going to go.

He raked his fingers over his tired eyes and shook his head in frustration.

He should have known better than to have taken that picture, much less considered sending it to his ex-girlfriend...or whomever he'd sent the bare-bellied photo to.

He'd been erasing Cassidy's phone number one digit at a time, retyping it, time and again, wondering what was wrong with him that he couldn't be happy with such an ideal-for-him woman, that her unexpected sext message and photo hadn't provoked any of the right feelings inside him when logically it should have. She was a beautiful woman. What was wrong with him? Berating himself for not being able to love her the way he should, he'd hit a random number, realized what he'd done and gone to erase it, but had accidentally hit send instead.

He'd sent an inappropriate photo to a complete stranger whose phone number was one number off his perfect ex-girlfriend's.

Perfect.

There went that word again. Tonight the word nauseated him.

Everyone was always telling him how lucky he was, how he had the perfect girlfriend, how he and Cassidy were the perfect couple, how he had the perfect life. Perfect. Perfect Cassidy. He'd dumped her a couple of weeks ago because of…he didn't know why, just that he had told her they should start seeing other people.

Truth was Cassidy was the perfect woman. He'd spent three years of his life with her and had imagined he'd grow old with the pretty blonde hospitalist. Yet recently, when she'd started hinting about a ring, questioning why they hadn't taken that next step, something had held him back. For lack of a better explanation, he'd told her they lacked physical passion. Tonight, she'd sexted him in ways that should put physical passion into any relationship. He'd wanted to feel something, but hadn't. Knowing the problem lay within him and not within perfect Cassidy, he'd toyed with the idea of sexting back, to try to make himself feel something, anything. What was the worst thing that could happen?

He frowned at his cellular phone. What indeed?

Never in his life had he snapped pictures of his own body. But, nevertheless, he'd raised his shirt, flexed his abdominal muscles, snapped a picture, and let the thing sit unsent on his phone for over an hour. The sickening feeling in his belly had held him back, just as the feeling had held him back from giving in to Cassidy's desire that he propose. No amount of sexting or wishing was going to make him want to marry Cassidy.

There was something wrong with him that he wanted more than a perfect woman, that he couldn't be content with the idea of Cassidy as his wife and the mother of his children, that he couldn't see himself waking up next to her for the next fifty-plus years. He hadn't lied when he'd told her they lacked physical passion. He just didn't feel a spark. Hadn't in so long he couldn't recall if there ever had been a spark or if she'd so ideally matched his criteria of what he wanted in a woman that he'd just imagined electricity between them.

Thank God he'd had enough sense to only snap his midsection. No face and nothing below the waist. The worst thing that could happen was he could be reported for harassment and his picture could be a social media blunder sensation, right?

His phone buzzed again. Wincing, he opened the text that no doubt would blast him for his depravity. Deservedly so. Maybe he should just apologize and admit to having sent the message by accident.

By the way, I know this is you, Emily. What did you do? Download that application to make your number appear as someone else's? I'm so onto you. No worries. You didn't interrupt anything in this girl's bedroom except sleep.

Whoever had gotten his text thought he was someone else. That was fortunate. He should let it go at that, not say or do anything more. So why was he texting back? Boredom? Curiosity? Insanity?

What would you like me to have interrupted?

Feeling an even bigger fool than when he'd realized he'd sent the message and to the wrong number, he wondered at the force within him that had directed his fingers to reply. He really was messed up in the head, perhaps just from fatigue, but he definitely wasn't thinking straight. He closed his eyes and waited for about thirty seconds before his phone buzzed.

Ha. As if you don't already know the answer to that.

Remind me.

Dr. Eli Randolph tied to my bed and at the mercy of my tongue.

Eli's jaw dropped. His brows rose. He stared at the number. He wasn't tired any more. He was curious. Who had he sexted? Why was he typing out another message, because this had to be some kind of joke.

What would you do to Dr. Randolph with your tongue?

He'd started typing "me" and had to change it to "Dr. Randolph."

The same thing every other living breathing woman wants to do to that man with her tongue.

Eli doubted that most women would even give him the time of day much less have tongue fantasies about him, especially if they knew there was something wrong with him emotionally. Okay, so he was a decent guy—minus the wayward random sext message and lack of ability to take that final step in a relationship—he enjoyed exercise and sports to where he stayed in decent shape, worked hard to where he had financial security, and he lived a good life. All of which had inspired Cassidy to want to shop for rings, but no tongue fantasies for either of them. Lord, how long had it been since he'd even let his mind fantasize about a woman? Any woman? To just close his eyes and think about sex?

With Cassidy, he'd thought about how compatible they were, how well they got along, how they could have the perfect life together, how she'd pass along her good genes to his children, but he hadn't been able to take the steps that would bring all those things to fruition. Just as he hadn't thought about sex.

He was a man. He should have been thinking about sex at least occasionally. What was wrong with him?

Tell me.

Because, crazy as it was, he wanted to know. He wanted to think about sex, to feel normal, rather than somehow lacking for not being able to commit to an amazing woman like Cassidy.

Lick every pore on his scrumptious body until he screams my name in ecstasy.

Eli swallowed. This was crazy. He was crazy. He was thinking about sex now.

What name would that be?

You're a little slow here, Em. He'd be screaming my name.

Which didn't tell him anything. He stared at his phone screen and tried to figure out how to reply. Before he could decide his phone buzzed again.

The woman he needs to dump his perfect girlfriend for and whisk me away for a wild weekend of really hot S-E-X. Our bodies slick with sweat and gliding against each other. His mouth on me. My mouth on him. That's what you should have interrupted. Not that I'd have answered your text had I been doing any of those things.

Eli gulped. He was not a guy who got off on this kind of thing. He was sure of it.

Dr. Randolph doesn't have a girlfriend, he typed. They were no longer a couple even if she had sent him the unexpected sext message. He'd thought she was okay with their break-up, but maybe he'd been wrong. Regardless, he wouldn't be changing his mind. That he couldn't respond to her sext message, that he had sent his fumbled attempt to a stranger, that he was more stimulated by a text conversation with that stranger than his ex-girlfriend spoke volumes.

Which was crazy. For all he knew, he could be texting with an eighty-year-old granny. Or a man.

Now, there was a buzz killer of a thought.

No, the texter had implied she was female when she'd said it was the same thing every woman wanted and when she'd said "this girl's bedroom." He was texting with a female. A female around his age. He was sure of it.

Dr. Randolph and Dr. Qualls broke up? When? Why haven't you told me this? What kind of best friend are you?

He should put his phone down and not text any more. He wasn't a man who texted with women he didn't know. Totally not cool and not his style. He'd broken things off with his perfect girlfriend and needed to figure out what was wrong with him, not become some weirdo who texted with strangers.

Or not with a stranger. This was someone who knew him and Cassidy. Who?

A couple of weeks ago, he responded. So maybe he was a weirdo who texted with strange women.

Em, if this is your idea of a joke, I'm going to kill you.

Why would this Em person joke about him and Cassidy having broken up?

Are you sure? I hadn't heard that and you know how everyone at the hospital gossips.

He doubted many people knew about them having broken up. Not that he cared who knew, but he hadn't advertised the fact around the hospital. His private life wasn't his coworkers' business. He doubted Cassidy had told many people either.

Positive.

They'd stay broken up. He'd truly believed Cassidy to be the woman he'd spend his life with. Maybe he just hadn't been ready for marriage; maybe when the time was right, his expectations wouldn't be so impossible. Maybe.

They're still friends.

Picture me rolling my eyes, Em. She was clearly in love with him. If they're still friendly it's because she hopes they'll get back together.

Was that why she'd sexted him tonight? Because she'd hoped to spark physical passion and for them to get back together? Deep down, Eli knew the reasons he hadn't proposed to Cassidy went much deeper than their lack of physical passion. Something more than sex had been missing. Which was why he knew there was a problem with him. Cassidy was his best friend, a beautiful woman, brilliant, good-hearted, and he'd broken up with her because when it came to the rest of his life, he wanted more. He was insane.

Was it also insane that he wished he could picture the texter rolling her eyes? That he'd like some visual image to go with their conversation? He had friends who'd dated via meeting someone on social media. He'd thought them nuts, but maybe there was something to the anonymity of it all that let a person step outside their normal shells. Certainly, he'd never imagined himself being intrigued by a stranger saying she wanted to tie him to a bed and lick him. But he was.

If she's smart she'll win him back.

Eli shook his head at his phone. Not going to happen. Ever. Until tonight he honestly hadn't thought Cassidy wanted to win him back. She'd accepted his ending things as if she'd already come to the same conclusion.

How would you win him back?

Hell-o! I'd never have lost him to begin with, came the immediate response.

Eli laughed, liking the texter's spunk. Yeah, he wished he had a visual to go with the messages.

I'd have him tied to my bed and at my mercy, remember?

How could I forget?

Eli closed his eyes and tried to imagine being tied to a bed. He'd never done that. Never given up control during sex, or to a woman, not that there had been that many. There hadn't.

I guess you have heard me mention my obsession with Dr. Randolph a time or two, huh, Em? Sorry.

Obsession? With him? Who was he texting with? Was it someone who had recognized his number and was having fun at his expense?

Em. Emily. He racked his brain. The only Emilys he knew were Emily Jacobs, a bright dyed red-haired registered nurse who worked in the hospital emergency department most of the time, but occasionally filled in at ICU, and the Emily from high school who had sat behind him in chemistry, but he hadn't seen her in years. Then again, Cravenwood was a decent-sized college town. There were probably hundreds of Emilys in the middle Tennessee area. But this one was privy to hospital gossip. Were there other Emilys at Cravenwood Hospital?

Game's up, Em. You've had your fun. We both know the perfect couple are still in hotness bliss.

Eli winced at the texter's use of the word perfect.

Maybe you're right and I just need to forget him, the texter continued, and Eli felt her frustration in each word.

I can't believe you chose tonight to do this. You know I just pulled two sixteen-hour shifts thanks to Leah being out sick.

Leah being out sick. Whoever this was definitely worked at the hospital with him. Bells rang in Eli's head.

Leah Windham?

She's the only Leah in ICU. You've had your fun. We've both got to be at the hospital early in the morning. Go kiss your hunky boyfriend and let me sleep. Goodnight, Emily.

Goodnight.

Whoever she was.

"This isn't funny," Beth insisted, grabbing an apple from the lunch line and wishing she could squeeze it like a stress ball. "'Fess up. You were just telling me about that phone app that makes your number appear as someone else's last week. I know it was you last night."

Following closely behind her in the hospital cafeteria lunch line, her best friend snickered. "I wish it had been, but I'm telling you, it wasn't me."

Emily had insisted the same thing earlier in the day when she had called the ICU regarding a patient and Beth had asked about the messages. She still wasn't convinced her friend hadn't sent the texts. The body build was wrong for the photo to have been a posed shot of Eddie, but Emily could have easily found the picture online. It was just the kind of thing jokester Emily would do. No doubt her friend would play the prank out a bit longer.

"You should show me the text messages," Emily said as they sat down at a table in the hospital cafeteria. Not that either of them would be able to stay there long. Beth was surprised her friend had been able to sneak away from the emergency department at all. As a nurse, one never knew if you'd actually get a lunch break or not.

"You should confess that you sent the messages."

Emily shook her head. "Wasn't me, I promise." Her friend waggled her perfectly waxed brows and crossed her heart. "Hope you didn't say anything incriminating."

"You know exactly what I said and about whom."

Her friend's eyes widened. "You revealed your crush on Dr. Randolph—" her friend mouthed the name rather than speaking it out loud in case someone t overheard "—to the mystery texter? As in, you gave a name?"

The absolute shock on Emily's heart-shaped face had Beth's stomach spasming. Despite the local theater her friend often volunteered at she wasn't that good an actress, was she?

Trying to pretend she wasn't freaking out inside, Beth took a bite of her apple, chewed slowly, let loose an inner scream of denial, then shrugged. "I don't want to discuss this any more."

"I do." Emily's eyes glowed with excitement. "I want to know who you were texting with, because Eddie seriously had me otherwise occupied last night."

Trying to squash her doubts and thoughts of what her best friend claimed to have been doing instead, Beth shrugged. "Then I guess we'll never know, will we?"

Lord, she hoped her friend was teasing, that Emily had been the texter, as she'd been so positive about the night before when she'd been too tired to think clearly. Good ole Emily. Always pulling her leg and trying to push her out of her comfortable protective shell.

"Sure we will."

Beth cut her gaze to her best friend. "How?"

"Hello." Emily snapped her fingers in front of Beth's face. "You're smarter than that."

Realization dawned and Beth's jaw dropped. "Uh-uh. No way am I calling that number."

Emily held out her hand. "Fine. I will. Give me your phone."

"No way." Beth's gut clenched into tight knots. "If I wasn't texting with you, then I prefer not knowing who now knows my biggest secret. How humiliating?!"

Emily didn't look impressed by Beth's inner misery. "So what if someone knows you think Dr. Randolph is the cat's meow? The man is hot. It's a fact."

Beth couldn't stop her blush.

"Plus, if what you said is true and he and Dr. Qualls have broken up, then he's fair game now." Emily waggled her perfectly plucked brows. "If you ask me, you should tell him you think he's one fine specimen of a man."

Beth went into sensory overload and mental shutdown any time the man was near. The last thing she should do was tell him how fine she thought he was. She shook her head. "I don't know that they've broken up. Plus, even if they have broken up, they'll probably just get back together."

"Ask him, and you can't judge every man by what Barry did."

Beth shook her head harder, faster, as if that made her response more negative and would jar Barry Neal from her mind forever.

"You have a serious problem, you know."

Beth knew.

"You let a stupid ex influence how you view all men, influence how you dress and act, and then, when you finally start getting over him, you fall crazy in lust with a man you avoid at all costs. I've never seen feet move as fast as yours any time he comes near." Emily gave a disappointed sigh. "I really think this whole Eli thing is just another way for you to avoid getting back into the dating saddle."

"Maybe." But she really didn't think so because she'd like to be back in the dating saddle. As far as the way she dressed and acted went, Emily was referring to her college days. One couldn't wear streaks of blue in one's hair, a nose ring, and colorful Hello Kitty T-shirts and retro make-up forever. The changes in her had nothing to do with Barry having crushed her heart and spirit. She'd grown up, had a more mature look, that was all.

"You're crazy," Emily accused.

If she'd revealed her silly schoolgirl crush on Dr. Randolph to some stranger then she couldn't argue with her friend's assessment of her mental state. She was crazy.

Crazy about a man who didn't know she existed.

Whether to distract himself of his failure with Cassidy or for some other insane reason, Eli had thought of little other than the previous night's text messages. He'd even gone so far as to try to track down who the number belonged to via the internet but had been unsuccessful as the number wasn't a public one.

He couldn't seem to put the messages from his head.

Especially at moments like the present one.

Moments he was at the hospital and searching every face as if somehow he'd figure out who the texter was by the look on her face. What did he expect? That the truth would be stamped across her forehead like a scarlet letter?

Most likely, whoever the texter was, she worked in ICU since she'd had to work late to cover for Leah Windham. She was also probably a nurse. Which made sense since she was friends with Emily Jacobs.

With a little patience and a leading conversation to find out who'd worked late the night before, he'd have this figured out before the day ended.

Usually he rivaled Job on the patience score, but today he just felt antsy. He wanted to know whom he'd been texting. Why it was so imperative, he wasn't sure—he just needed to know.

He'd actually considered asking Emily which one of her friends was obsessed with him, but figured the woman would tell him where he could go rather than give him a name.

"Dr. Randolph?" A pleasant female in her mid-fifties caught him just as he'd been heading for the elevator. "A patient is being admitted to 303 with a pulmonary embolism and you've been consulted on her," the charge nurse told him. "She's not on the floor yet, but should be within a half hour."

"Thanks, Ruth." Glancing at his watch, he figured he should grab something to eat while still at the hospital. Then hopefully the new admission would be on the floor and he'd do the consult prior to heading back to his office to start his afternoon appointments.

Maybe, just maybe, while in the ICU, he'd get a glimpse of whoever he'd been texting with the night before, because, whoever she was, his interest was piqued.

CHAPTER TWO

"Don't look now, but guess who just walked into the cafeteria."

Before her friend had said a word, Beth knew exactly who had walked into the cafeteria where she and Emily were eating their lunch. Her Dr. Eli Randolph radar had started bleeping. Big time. Bleep. Bleep. Bleep. Which sounded ridiculous but all her senses seemed to be tuned into the man. Whenever he came around, she was just… bleeping aware.

Which made her palms sweat, her tongue thick, and her feet antsy.

Which had led to her asking her superior to please avoid assigning her to Dr. Randolph's patients. Nurse Rogers might have thought her request odd, but without too many questions and an empathetic look she'd said she would do her best. She couldn't avoid doing so altogether, of course, but for the most part she had attempted to accommodate Beth's request and the few times she'd had to, Beth had avoided him during rounds.

"What if he is single now?" Emily asked, not willing to let go of their subject. "What are you going to do about him?"

Beth grimaced. "I never should have told you that I find him attractive."

"You more than find him attractive. I've known you since college, have seen you through your two major relationships, and knew you way before Barry messed up your head and your sense of style. I would have known."

Ugh at the reminder of her ex. She couldn't care less about Barry, but her stupidity still stung. She could point out that it wasn't her head Barry had messed up. It had been her heart, but what was one organ compared to another? Either way, she'd gotten over the cheater the hard way.

"I see how you look at that man so it's not as if you could hide how you feel from me," Emily pointed out, her gaze raking over Eli as if sizing him up. "I could point out that you never lit up like this around the doofus who left you for his ex and that Barry wasn't even fit to tie Eli's dirty ole tennis shoes."

No, she hadn't lit up around Barry. Just as well as he'd done the un-decent thing of sleeping with his ex while still living with Beth. Men.

"My question is, are you going to act on that attraction? Tell him you think he's hot?"

Emily's question snapped Beth back to the present and she frowned at her friend.

"Don't be ridiculous and quit staring at him," she ordered, but was unable to stop herself from doing the same. What was it about Eli that got to her so? Besides the fact that he was brilliant, breathtaking, and had the most amazing smile of any man ever, that was. "I've worked with him for months, and I seriously doubt he even knows my name. Why would I make a fool of myself that way?"

Why indeed?

"Because if you don't, some other smarter, braver woman will and then you'll still be pining after him from afar while he becomes someone else's boyfriend because you were too chicken to go after the man of your dreams."

Ouch. Emily didn't mince her words.

"From afar is good." At least from afar she could still breathe. But Eli with another woman...okay, so that thought made every organ in her body twist up like a wrung dishrag. Still, it wasn't as if she wasn't used to him having a girlfriend. He had from the moment she'd met him and felt whatever that instant crazy fluttering in her chest had been. Not that he'd felt it. He hadn't. Not that he'd noticed. He hadn't. So why should the fact that he might no longer have a girlfriend matter? She obviously hadn't made an impression.

Plus she'd had a relationship with a man who'd had a perfect ex and ultimately he'd gone back to the woman he'd invested so much time in. No thanks on a heartbreak repeat.

"From afar sucks," Emily needlessly pointed out. "Admit it."

Okay, she admitted it. To herself at any rate. Emily was right. From afar did suck. Not making an impression on a man you couldn't quit thinking about sucked. Being told that dating you had made your ex realize his ex hadn't really been that bad after all? That sucked a big one too.

"If you don't at least let him know that you're interested, I'll know that you really are using him as a shield from jumping back into the dating world."

"That's not what I'm doing. The man is wonderful. You've admitted as much yourself."

"True, so prove it."

Prove it? What did her friend want her to do? March up and tell him she wanted to lick him from head to toe? That she thought about him way too much morning, noon, and night?

"Look." Her stomach clenching into a tight knot, Beth gestured toward where Eli stood. He wasn't alone. A gorgeous blonde bombshell with kind blue eyes and an almost always present smile had joined him. "Dr. Qualls is smiling at him like crazy." And touching his arm quite possessively. Ugh. Not that Beth had any right to feel the green flowing through her veins.

She'd already resigned herself that Eli and Cassidy would marry and for the rest of her life she'd watch them from afar, wondering, What if? Emily was right. From afar did suck, but there were some things that were just wrong. Going after another woman's man was one of them, especially when that woman was someone as nice as Dr. Qualls. At least she hadn't liked Barry's ex. Not that she'd known her well, but Cassidy Qualls seemed to be a class act inside and out. "I don't think they've broken up."

Eyeing the couple, Emily waved her fork. "Actually, I think your sexter was right. I think they have. Look."

Beth forced her gaze back toward the couple. Dr. Qualls still stood there, but she was no longer smiling. A pensive, unsure expression on her lovely face, she was watching Eli walk away and sit down at a table. By himself.

Oh, wow. Could he possibly be single? She hadn't dared dream it possible. Well, she had dared, but hadn't believed that her weird texter could have been right.

"I think you should go and talk to him."

What? The man's girlfriend—ex-girlfriend?—was standing ten feet from him. His nice ex-girlfriend whom Beth admired and thought a great hospitalist and often thought that if she had to pick someone to be like, she'd pick Cassidy Qualls. The woman had it all. But had she perhaps lost the one thing Beth envied her?

"No way. What would I say?" She took a drink, her gaze darting back and forth between Eli and Cassidy, looking for a clue to the truth. They weren't behaving normally, that was for sure. Probably a lovers' spat that they'd soon recover from.

"Hello." Emily mimicked Beth's voice and mannerisms. "My name is Beth Taylor and I want to have your children."

Water spewed from Beth's mouth and she gasped at her best friend. "I do not!"

"Sure you do but, okay, let me try again," Emily cleared her throat and started over, still doing a fairly decent impression of Beth's voice. "My name is Beth Taylor. I'd like to rip your clothes off with my teeth and have you for breakfast, lunch, and dinner on a regular basis." Emily fluttered her eyelashes. "Be forewarned, I'm a girl with a hearty appetite."

True, but not words Beth could see spilling from her mouth during a conversation with him. Words in general had difficulty spilling from her mouth when she spoke to Eli, which was yet another reason why she avoided him.

She glanced toward where he sat alone at a rectangular table for six. He had on blue scrubs that were a little darker than the shade of his eyes. His slightly curly brown hair was rumpled, as if he'd run his fingers through it more often than usual today. Another doctor, a cardiologist, came over and must have asked if he could join him. Nodding, Eli smiled at the man and Beth's heart thump-thump-thumped.

Crazy how something as simple as his smile caused her body to react so profoundly. She'd probably go into cardiac arrest and need the services of that cardiologist if Eli ever aimed one of those smiles directly at her. That would be her luck. He'd walk by, smile politely, and she'd fall over. Kaput. At least she'd die knowing that if he was that close he'd perform mouth to mouth and that would be the last thing she felt against her lips. Hmm, might be worth meeting her maker a little sooner.

"I see you aren't denying that one," Emily pointed out with an all-too-smug grin.

Her friend was right. She wanted to gobble Eli up and go back for seconds. And thirds. And... Beth sighed. "At least that diet sounds like one I could stick to," she conceded with a slight shrug.

Emily laughed. "Regardless of your reasons for being interested in Dr. Randolph, if he's single you really should let him know you're interested. Not every man is Barry, whom I personally never thought good enough for you anyway, nor did he ever rev your juices the way Dr. Randolph does."

No one had ever affected her the way Eli did. Just thinking about him made her heart pound and her body clench with excited flutters. If by some grace of God they did date, but then Eli told her that dating her made him realize how wonderful Cassidy was, at least she would understand that. The woman was the total package—looks, brains, heart.

"Dr. Randolph is a good man," Emily continued between waves of her fork. "A hot man. You'll regret it always if you don't at least try. Go for it."

"That doesn't mean Dr. Randolph would be interested in me." His tastes obviously ran to quite the opposite of her. Tall, blonde, perfect.

"Why wouldn't he be? You're smart, pretty, fun, kind, a little quirky at times, but, hey, no one is perfect…except me." Emily grinned.

"That's a given." She half smiled at her friend's exception and didn't point out that she'd just labeled Cassidy as perfect as well.

"You know you want him."

From the moment she'd first seen him. Never had she felt such a crazy intense attraction. Not for any of her few high-school and college boyfriends, or for Barry, whom she'd thought she'd marry. Emily was right. From the beginning there had been something different about Eli and quite frankly that terrified her.

"As I've pointed out, that doesn't mean he'd want me in return. He's never even noticed me."

Emily failed to look impressed by Beth's argument. "I'm not quite sure how he could have since you go into hibernation any time he comes onto the ICU floor, but hello!" Emily snapped her fingers in front of Beth's face. "The man has had a girlfriend. One he has been in a relationship with for a long time. He's a good guy, not one who has a wandering eye while in a relationship. It's a good quality that he hasn't noticed you up to this point. Now that he's single, you need to shake your tail feathers and make sure he does notice."

She wasn't much for shaking tail feathers these days, wouldn't even know where to start. "He may not even be single."

"He is."

"You don't know that for sure. Just because he isn't sitting with Dr. Qualls doesn't mean they've broken up. Besides, even if they have broken up, who's to say they won't get back together?"

"Wherein lies the real problem," Emily accused, then narrowed her gaze and pursed her lips. "Chicken."

Beth winced. Was she letting the past keep her from even going after what she wanted in the present? Probably. She bit the inside of her lower lip. Fantasizing about a man she considered beyond her reach had been one thing. Actually acting on that fantasy if he'd become single, well, that was another thing altogether. She'd resigned herself that Eli would never be available, that he'd always just be the man who fascinated her from afar. She'd fully expected him to marry Dr. Qualls and have beautiful children with the gifted doctor. Odds were that even if they had broken up, that's still what would happen. Beth knew the score.

But if he were single right now, at this moment...

If he was single, then what if he'd be interested in her?

Even if for a short while, even if he later told her that she didn't measure up when compared to Cassidy, she wanted that shot.

Question was, what was she willing to do, to risk, to make that shot happen?

Had he been too harsh with Cassidy? Eli hoped not. He didn't want to be unkind to her. At the same time, they needed to start having more space between them. Perhaps that was wrong as last night she'd sent him sext messages and he'd briefly considered sending her one back. Much better to cut the ties for a while. She'd just claimed to have been drunk the night before, but Cassidy never drank more than a single glass of wine. Had she just been embarrassed that he'd not returned her message? If only she knew the truth.

Regardless, they were meant to be friends, not lovers. To pretend otherwise for a single second longer would be cruel to a woman he liked and respected. That was what made this all so difficult. He didn't want to lose Cassidy's friendship.

Ending their relationship had meant more than admitting there was something wrong with him that he couldn't commit to spending the rest of his life with such an amazing woman, but it also meant damaging his relationship with his best friend.

"What's up with you and Wonder Woman?" Dr. Andrew Morgan said as he joined Eli.

Eli took a deep breath, then exhaled. He preferred his personal business to be private, but he supposed it was unrealistic that his colleagues wouldn't question what had happened. "You mean Cassidy."

He supposed she was a wonder woman of sorts. There was little she couldn't do and do well. She was a great catch. He was the fool who couldn't take that next step with her because he wanted more. More of what he wasn't sure, but if Cassidy had been his soul mate surely he wouldn't have found himself backtracking when she'd hinted she wanted a ring.

"Yes, I mean Cassidy," Andrew said, as if Eli wasn't in his right mind or he'd have known exactly to whom he referred. "You two having an argument?"

He shook his head. "We decided to go our separate ways."

"She dump you?"

Eli struggled with how to answer. He didn't want to say anything that might hurt Cassidy.

"We've decided to just be friends."

"How could you possibly just be friends with a woman like Cassidy?"

Eli looked a little closer at his colleague, noting the heightened color in the man's cheeks, the rapid pulse at his throat, and the strong set to his jaw. Interesting.

"Because that's how we feel about each other. Friendly. It's all we should have ever been." Even as he said the words out loud, the truth echoed through him.

"Sure took you long enough to figure that out."

"Tell me about it," Eli snorted, wondering why it had taken so long. "Then again, like you said, Cassidy is a wonderful woman." His family had loved her. His mother had repeatedly told him how Cassidy was everything she'd ever hoped for in a daughter-in-law. To say she'd been disappointed at his news was the understatement of the year. "A man hesitates to let her go even when he knows it isn't going to happen between them."

Andrew nodded as if he understood, but Eli could tell he obviously didn't. His mother hadn't either. For that matter, he himself didn't understand why he hadn't been content with Cassidy.

"You should ask her out." Andrew obviously felt a passion for her that Eli couldn't, no matter how much he'd wanted to.

Andrew's eyes widened, then he glanced away rapidly. "I couldn't."

"Why not? She's single. You're single. Go for it."

The man regarded him suspiciously. "You really wouldn't care?"

Eli shook his head. "I'd be happy for you if things worked out. She's a great woman and deserves a man to treat her so. I plan to date and imagine she will too. Ask her."

Andrew toyed with his fork. "Maybe I will."

It struck Eli that he should feel remorse or jealousy or some sense of loss that a woman he'd invested years with might be moving on with another man, perhaps this man. He didn't feel any of those things. Just relief that he was no longer tied to Cassidy, which again made him wonder if something was wrong with him, if he'd set his expectations so high that even a woman who was perfect for him on paper couldn't meet them.

"You should," he repeated. "A woman like her isn't likely to stay single long."

The flash of panic in Andrew's eyes said it all. He had a thing for Cassidy, but had obviously held it at bay in respect for her relationship with Eli.

That was when Emily Jacobs caught Eli's eye.

Emily Jacobs. As in the person his texter had thought he was the night before. Was the woman sitting across the cafeteria table from her his mysterious texter?

Dark hair, light colored eyes, although he couldn't make out their exact blue-green color, creamy complexion with a spattering of freckles across her face. Naturally pretty. Somewhat familiar.

She worked in ICU. He recalled seeing her there, although usually only glimpses here and there. Odd really when he thought about it. He was in the ICU a lot. How come his path rarely crossed this woman's—Beth something—in the ICU?

Unless she purposely avoided him.

Why would she do that?

Unless she was the texter and because of her attraction to him she'd purposely steered clear.

It was a possibility. One he wanted to put to the test.

"Excuse me," he said to the man lost in his thoughts sitting across from him, and pulled out his cellular phone. He opened his text messages from the night before and glanced at the number. Was it hers? Beth's from ICU? Logic said it was, but he wanted proof, to know for sure. He hit the telephone icon button that would dial her number and watched her closely.

When she set her fork down on her plate and reached into her scrub pocket to pull out her phone, answering without looking at the number, Eli smiled.

Bingo.

His smile widened. Although he didn't quite understand, an excitement filled him that he hadn't felt in years…maybe ever.

Maybe he wasn't ready to settle down with Cassidy, maybe there was something wrong with him that was holding him back, but at the moment, he wasn't going to worry about those things. For now he was going to quit stressing about the future and his expectations, his parents' expectations, the fact he'd chosen to become single rather than marry the "perfect" woman. He was going to enjoy life, to have fun, and not take everything so seriously. Something he'd just realized that he'd forgotten to do over the past few years.

"Hello?" Beth answered, expecting to hear her nurse supervisor's voice telling her that they needed her back on the floor. Rarely did she make it through a full lunch without an interruption from a patient or one of her coworkers, which was why she usually just ate in the ICU break room. Today she'd wanted to pick Emily's brain.

Instead of Ruth telling her to come back to ICU, she heard a resounding click.

Pulling the phone away from her ear, she looked at the number.

Aiiiiggghhhhh!

"What?" Emily asked, making Beth wonder if she'd just screamed out loud or if it was the way all the blood in her body had drained that had clued her friend in that something was wrong.

"It's…" Her voice choked up.

"Come on," her friend encouraged. "Spit it out. You look like you just got news your best friend died and I know that didn't happen because I'm sitting right here."

Beth closed her eyes then held the phone out toward her friend so she could see the screen.

"What? It's clicked off. Tell me."

"It was the number."

"The number?"

"The number." She put great emphasis on her words.

"The number you thought was me?"

Wondering if one could hyperventilate to death in a hospital cafeteria, Beth nodded and struggled to get air into her vice-gripped lungs.

"What did they say?"

"Nothing."

"Nothing?" Emily looked bamfoozled.

Beth shook her head, feeling a bit bamfoozled herself. *Breathe, Beth, breathe.*

"Then why did whoever it was call you?"

She shrugged, took a deep breath, then another. "Maybe they're going to harass me."

"About what? You didn't do anything wrong."

"Nothing wrong per se, but...I might have mentioned wanting to tie up and lick a certain doctor all over."

Emily's eyes widened and then she burst out laughing. "You didn't?"

Beth grimaced at her friend's mirth and at her own foolishness. "I told you that I revealed my fascination with the man."

"That isn't the same thing as saying you want to tie up the man and for your tongue to get up close and personal with his personables."

Her friend had a point. Unfortunately.

"What else did you say?"

Beth gave a pained look. "I don't remember exactly. Something about wanting our bodies slick with sweat and gliding together."

"Oh, baby." Emily's eyes danced with delight. "I wish I had been pulling your leg and sending those messages. Sounds like some hot reading and you know I love a steamy read."

Feeling a fool, Beth nodded. "I was tired and you'd promised retribution. If I'd been thinking clearly I'd never have sent those messages."

"Like I said before, so what that you did. So what that someone knows you think Dr. Randolph's hot. What does it matter in the grand scheme of life?"

"I don't want him to find out."

"Hello." Emily snapped her fingers in front of her face again. "We've already had this conversation. You do want him to find out that you're interested in him. You need to let him know. Up close and personal." Emily waggled her brows, then added mischievously, "With your tongue. And his personables."

Fighting the panicky feeling still welling within her, Beth rolled her eyes. "You really aren't my best friend, you know. You're just some freak with great hair I tolerate because we work together."

Patting her pulled up dyed bright red locks, which matched her personality much more than any natural shade could, Emily leaned back in her chair and grinned. "You love me and we both know it."

"Sad, but true."

"Just as we both know I'm not going to let you sit on your butt while your dream man is single and needs consoling."

Beth's eyes widened. "You wouldn't."

"I would." Emily's eyes sparkled with mischief. "You make a move or Dr. Randolph and I will be having a very interesting conversation."

"You wouldn't," she repeated.

"Wanna bet on that?"

No, she didn't, because if Emily believed she was doing what was best for Beth she wouldn't hesitate to spill the beans to Eli.

Which meant that she would have to make a move herself. Otherwise there was no telling what her friend would say to him.

Taking a deep breath, she glanced toward his table. Her gaze collided with his. The air caught in her lungs and threatened to burst them.

He was looking straight at her!

He didn't look away when their eyes met.

Instead, he grinned.

Grinned.

At her.

That's when she noticed what he held in his hand.

His cellphone.

CHAPTER THREE

"Hello, Beth."

Where was that cardiologist? Beth needed him. Pronto. Her heart was going to stop any moment. She was sure of it.

Dr. Eli Randolph was smiling at her, had just said her name.

He knew her name?

He'd said her name!

For no good reason except to speak to her. Had he ever done so before?

No. Never. She wasn't even sure that he'd ever looked directly at her before lunch today. Definitely, they'd never locked eyes. He was looking now and, try as she might for fear of what he might see, she couldn't break their eye contact.

A light shone in his twinkling blue gaze that she'd never seen before. She couldn't quite label what she saw, but she couldn't deny that a definite interest shone there.

Had whoever she'd texted with the night before revealed her secrets to Eli? Recalling his smile in the cafeteria, the phone in his hand, Beth swallowed. Had she texted with Eli the night before? Was that even possible? If so, was he toying with her because of the things she'd admitted while thinking she was talking to Emily? Or by some miracle was Eli actually interested in her? Had he intentionally texted her the night before and, dimwit that she was, she'd revealed her secret fantasies to him, not realizing who she was texting with?

Why would he have texted her? Not just texted, but sent a photo? Not really a risqué photo, but hot all the same. Nope. Her texter couldn't have been Eli. Probably the guy from Administration had snagged her cellphone number from her employee records and when she'd stuck her foot in her mouth, he'd realized he didn't stand a chance and had told Eli about her comments. A much more likely scenario.

So what was he doing now?

Tongue lassoed around her vocal cords to where speech was impossible, she blinked at him. Why was he still here? He never hung around the nurses' station, making idle chit-chat. Never that she knew of, at any rate. Until today. She'd steered clear as long as she could, checking and rechecking her patients. Each time she'd exited a room, he'd still been leaning up against the counter, making small talk with the unit secretary and two nurses standing there.

The infuriating man had hung around in the ICU as if he had nowhere else to go. Surely he had an office full of patients waiting to see him? *Why are you still here?* she'd wanted to scream. *Leave.*

But he hadn't. Instead, he smiled down at her as if he knew her every secret.

He might.

"Beth?" he prompted, when she didn't respond to his greeting.

"Drink of water," she choked out past her bound-up vocal cords by way of explanation and took off down the hallway. She could feel his eyes on her, knew her colleagues had seen the interplay between them and also watched her scurry down the hallway as if competing for a gold medal.

Eli probably thought she was weird. Her colleagues probably thought she was weird.

She *was* weird.

The man of her dreams had gone out of his way to say something to her and she'd taken flight.

Why? She'd never been a tongue-tied ninny around men, but with Eli her brain shut down. Her body, on the other hand, went into hyperdrive, every sense more acute, making her feel more aware, more alive.

Too bad she couldn't just act cool and suave around him, let him know she thought he was the cat's meow.

More like the lion's roar.

Beth crawled into her bed, exhausted from the fifteen-hour day she'd put in at the hospital yet wide awake.

No question as to why her eyes were bright and she was feeling bushy-tailed. Or as to why her brain was auditioning for the Indy 500 and gunning for pole position.

Eli.

First, in the cafeteria, smiling at her.

Then in the ICU, when he'd spoken directly to her for the first time ever.

She'd run away.

She closed her eyes and shook her head back and forth on her pillow, disgusted at herself. What was wrong with her? She'd dated before and never been so uncool around guys.

Then again, she hadn't ever looked at any of the men she'd known and immediately wanted to get naked either. Eli Randolph made her clothes want to come off. No wonder she'd run. If she'd stuck around, she might have been arrested for indecent exposure.

Her phone buzzed on the night stand. Although not completely surprised by the noise, she jerked in her bed and grabbed for her phone.

A text.

Before she looked she knew who it would be from. The number.

But who was the person behind the number?

From the point she'd seen the phone in Eli's hand in the cafeteria, she'd asked herself, What if? What if Dr. Eli Randolph had sent her a photo because he was interested in her? He was single, had apparently been single for a couple of weeks. It was possible. Highly unlikely, but possible.

Her phone may have just buzzed with a text from Eli.

Could it be true? Her heart raced just at the remote possibility. She clutched the phone tighter in her suddenly clammy palms and read the short message.

You awake?

No, she responded, because it was the first thing that popped into her mind.

Guess you're dreaming, then.

Something like that.

I thought about you a lot today.

Shame on you.

I like that.

What?

That you make me laugh.

You should see me naked.

Had to be Eli, because there she went, trying to get rid of her clothes again.

Yes, I should.

Ha-ha. That really would make you laugh.

Doubtful, but you do make me smile. Want to know what else you make me do?

Wonder why she ran away when he said something to her? Assuming that she really was texting with Eli?

I'm all ears.

You make me really need to hear more about the things you'd do to Dr. Randolph if he were tied to your bed.

Because she was talking to Dr. Randolph? Somehow, she believed she was. The thought made her giddy happy and terrified and embarrassed all at once.

You perv.

You know you want to tell me.

Ha. That's what u think. I never should have said those things to begin with.

Why? Because you don't really want to stroke your tongue over Dr. Randolph's entire body?

Was she talking to Eli? Was he asking her outright if she wanted him? Maybe it was better that she didn't know a hundred percent. Much easier to be forthright when she might just be talking to a stranger whose path she'd never cross in real life.

I never should have told u. I thought u were someone else.

Emily?

Yes, my friend Emily.

What does your friend Emily say about you wanting to lick Dr. Randolph?

Oh, she's all for it and says I should start slurping immediately now that he's single and all. You were right on that, btw. Word spread like wildfire around the hospital this afternoon. How is it u knew he and Dr. Qualls had broken up before anyone else?

Was it because he was Dr. Randolph?

A little birdie told me.

Right. I have a little birdie in the middle of my hand that tells people who wake me up where they can go.

There you go making me laugh again.

I wasn't trying to be funny.

Which makes it all the better.

If u say so.

I do. Sorry if I woke you, but now that we've established that you are indeed awake, tell me what you're wearing.

Beth rolled her eyes at her phone.

Really? That is so cliché.

Then give me a cliché answer.

In the glow of her cellular phone Beth glanced under the bed covers at the old Nashville Predators T-shirt and the silky panties she wore. The panties were passable as sexy, maybe. The well-worn hockey T-shirt—ha, not by any stretch of the imagination.

A teddy and garters. Four-inch heels too. Customary sleepwear, you know.

Of course. Very cliché, but great visual.

Implying that he could visualize her. Of course he could visualize her. Whether it was Eli or some random guy, he'd sexted her specifically.

What are u wearing?

Who says I'm wearing anything at all.

Beth gulped. Okay, so it wasn't an image of some random guy she was picturing. Just as always, her fantasy consisted of only one man. Eli in the buff, as the owner of that magnificent abdomen and chest from the photo.

Would be a shame to cover up those abs. That picture really u?

Would it matter if it wasn't?

Depends.

On?

Your sparkly personality. That is why I'm texting with u after all.

Oh? I thought it was because you had a thing for pervs.

Beth smiled at his quick comeback.

Well, there is that.

You owe me.

I owe u nothing.

Sure you do.

What, please tell, do I owe u?

A picture.

She laughed. Not that he could hear her. But she laughed at the absolute absurdity of her sending him, whoever him was, a photo of herself. If it was Eli she was texting with, the last thing she'd want to do was scare him away with a selfie.

I wouldn't hold my breath if I was u.

If I did would you resuscitate me?

Give you a little mouth-to-mouth?

Hadn't she just that very day been thinking of Eli giving her mouth-to-mouth? If this was him, there really was some weird connection between them.

For starters

You implying it would take more than my mouth on yours to resuscitate you? Are u like old and decrepit or something? They make little blue pills for that u know.

I'm old enough to know what I want. Are you saying that your mouth on mine is all it would take to get me... resuscitated?

Ha, Beth thought, she was no siren and her experience wasn't that she drove men wild with her kisses, but this was anonymous—sort of—texting. She could say whatever she wanted. She could be a sex goddess. A sext goddess. If this was Eli for real, well, at least while texting from the privacy of her own bed she wasn't tongue-tied, breathless, or running away from him. She kind of liked the freedom their sexting gave her.

One stroke of my tongue across your lips and you'd go up in flames, Old Man.

Eli gulped. A real honest-to-God gulp. He was pretty close to going up in flames just at reading Beth's text.

It had been all he could do at the hospital to keep from pulling her aside and commenting on their conversation the night before. He'd thought about doing so a hundred times. He'd wanted to. He'd wanted to ask her to dinner with him, to sit and talk and get to know her. Maybe do a little shopping for tying-to-the-bed rope afterwards.

Maybe if she hadn't turned a pretty shade of pink and refused to say a full sentence to him, he would have at least issued the dinner invite. But she'd purposely avoided him. He was a hundred percent positive she'd stayed away from the nurses' station as long as she could. Was that why he barely knew her despite the fact she'd worked at the hospital for several months? He had a vague memory of her starting four or five months previously. Of seeing her in the ICU, but it hadn't really registered that he'd only seen her from a distance. Until today. Today he'd realized that it was a rare occasion that he'd directly had interaction with her regarding a patient.

His phone buzzed and he realized he hadn't yet responded to Beth's text. What would she say if he told her that her text, thoughts of her, had his entire body hard? That texting with her was the most fun, the most excitement he'd had in months? There might be something wrong with him that he hadn't been able to commit to Cassidy, but even beyond that, there had been something wrong with him that he'd fallen into a horrible life rut, forgotten how to have fun, and hadn't even realized it.

You fall asleep on me? she asked.

I wish.

Crazy, but he did wish that. Not until after he'd done a lot of other things with her but, yes, then he would like to fall asleep on Beth Taylor.

You saying I'm so boring u would doze off?

Zzzzzzzz

I think I'm insulted.

Don't be. I'm teasing you. You know exactly what I meant when I said I wish.

What else do u wish?

That you'd pay up.

Pay up?

Don't play dumb. You know a picture is worth a thousand words.

Depends on the picture.

True, but if that picture was of you it would be worth more than all of Webster's words.

A dictionary doesn't have enough words to convince me to send a picture. Better luck next time u sext some random babe.

Eli laughed. He loved her witty comments.

I didn't text some random babe. I texted you, Beth.

I'm a babe?

Definitely. Just not random.

You intentionally texted me?

He felt a bolt of guilt. Technically, he hadn't intentionally texted her the picture. Exactly what did one say to that? He wasn't into deception, but trying to explain how he'd texted her that photo didn't even make sense to him. How could he make it make sense to someone else?

I got lucky last night.

Got lucky? Lucky would have been if I'd sent u that picture you requested.

Exactly. Quit teasing me and pay up.

But teasing u is so much fun.

He smiled and wondered if she was smiling too. He was positive that she was. He tried to picture her, lying in her bed, phone in hand, smile on her face, typing her responses to him. She wouldn't be wearing the outfit she'd described, of course, but probably some sensible pajama bottoms and top. Somehow that thought turned him on every bit as much as the other.

If you're not going to send me a picture, the least you could do is talk dirty to me.

Okay, but just remember, you asked for it.

Even before the rapid succession of texts started arriving he guessed what she was going to do and his smile grew bigger with each message.

Mud.
Sloppy.
Grungy.
Sweaty.

Better stop, he warned. You're turning me on.

Well, don't ever say I'm not a woman who doesn't give a man what he asks for.

Remind me to be more specific next time I ask for you to give me something.

Hey, I talked dirty to u.

Maybe I should have asked you to tell me more about tying Dr. Randolph to the bed.

You did ask that. You liked that, didn't u?

I'm not the kind of guy who is into that kind of thing, normally, but you've planted a seed that keeps growing in my mind.

I think you're referring to what's growing in your pants.

There you go talking dirty again.

Just giving u more of what u want.

I want you.

You don't even know me.

True. He didn't. Yet he felt as if he did. Which had to just be lust and perhaps rebound from his break-up with Cassidy. Maybe even his mind's way of distracting him from the reality that there was something wrong with a man who couldn't love Cassidy.

I'd like to know you. Everything about you.

As he hit send, he meant every word. He did want to know everything about Beth Taylor. For a lot of different reasons. Everything about her felt fresh, new, exciting, fun.

He would know everything about her. Soon.

Beth stared at the phone and wondered at herself. Was she insane? Part of her felt insane. She was texting with someone she didn't know. Eli? Maybe. Probably.

Deep in her gut she believed it was him. Her Eli radar had started bleeping.

Yet the not knowing a hundred percent seemed to have freed her from the anxiety that overtook her when he was near. While texting she could be fun and flirty and pretend she was a sexy siren whom he should fall down and worship, rather than a woman whose ex left her self-confidence and heart in tatters.

Ask and u shall receive.

I asked for a picture.

Ask something else and perhaps u shall receive, she clarified, thinking that maybe this texting thing was just what she needed. Maybe Barry had messed with her head more than she gave him credit for. Maybe she no longer felt safe in a relationship. Maybe from the safety of texting, she could rebuild her confidence in her femininity.

Favorite color?

Red. Boring question, btw.

I'm not bored. Not in the slightest. Actually, I'm so

stimulated my neurons are probably in shock. I am now seeing you in a red garter and heels, btw. HOT!

You say the sweetest things.

Although she teased him, his comment flattered her. Her neurons, and a lot of other body parts, were pleased and shocked, too.

Favorite sexual position?

Yep, shocked neurons were firing away in her little brain. Fire. Fire. Fire. So how did a good girl who wanted to be bad with the right man answer that question?

Still working on figuring that one out. There's so many to choose from.

I could help you with that, you know.

There u go wanting to get lucky again.

Exactly. Okay, let's try another question. Top or Bottom?

Top. She wasn't really sure, but it was the first answer that popped into her mind so she went with it.

Leather or lace?

Depends on my mood.

Whipped cream or chocolate syrup?

Since when can a girl not have both?

Lights on or off?

On.

Because if she were ever with Eli she'd want to see him, to commit every minuscule detail about him to memory. This was a fantasy so she didn't have to acknowledge that having the lights on also meant he could see her much less than perfect body. Hadn't Barry made a point of letting her know that she was too curvy? That she wasn't tall enough, wasn't pretty enough, wasn't smart enough? Screw Barry. Ha. That's what his ex had done. In *her* bed. Ugh. She closed her eyes, took a deep breath, and filled her mind with Eli. Just Eli. The tension in her neck and shoulders eased.

Fast or slow?

Shall I repeat myself and say, Since when can a girl not have both?

Touché.

That some subtle Freudian way of you trying to tell me you want to touch me? she teased, determined to stay relaxed, to enjoy the playfulness of their texts.

Nothing subtle about me wanting to touch you. I want to touch you, Beth. All over.

She gulped.

All over?

Oh, yes. When I touch you, am I going to hear a soft satisfied sigh or a mind-blowing scream?

Either option sounded pretty darned good to her and had her skin tingling. Depends, she texted. How good are u?

Never had any complaints. Are you as turned on as I am?

How turned on are u?

Throbbingly so.

Poor baby. Need me to kiss and make u all better?

Pretty sure your mouth anywhere near me is only going to make my ache worse.

Hurt so good?

With all capital Os.

YOu bragging?

Just making a prOmise.

Of really big Orgasms?

Till yOu can't see straight.

Cause my eyes will be rOlled back?

NO, I want yOu lOOking intO my eyes when yOu Orgasm, Beth. I want tO watch yOur pleasure.

Beth's skin tingled. Her breath came fast. Her heart raced. She swallowed the lump that had formed in her throat. She was totally turned on by reading text messages. She was crazy.

That's a lot of Os. I'd like that.

Yes, yOu wOuld.

Was this Eli? Panic hit her, making her throat tighten up again. She was sexting. And wasn't even a hundred percent sure who she was sexting with. After the incident in the cafeteria and then him saying hi to her at the ICU nurses' station she believed she was texting with Eli, but what if she wasn't?
What if she was?
What about Dr. Qualls? Would they really not get back together? Could she really risk having another man walk away from her for his ex?

Sorry, but I need to go.

Tired?

Not the adjective I'd use to describe myself at the moment.

Hungry?

I'm not answering that.

It's okay, Beth. I'm hungry for you, too. Starved.

Her entire body tensed. She was hungry. Powerfully so. Needfully so. She wanted Eli, had wanted him for months.

Dream of me feeding that hunger.

I only dream of one man.

Dr. Randolph?

She didn't answer. She couldn't answer. She was so foolish. All of this was foolish. Just because she was texting in the privacy of her own home, in her darkened bedroom, with no one around to see or know, that didn't mean no one knew. Someone knew.

It's okay, Beth. I guarantee you that tonight Dr. Randolph will only dream of one woman.

She waited, somehow knowing her phone would buzz again even before she read the next message.

You.

CHAPTER FOUR

SEVENTY-TWO-YEAR-OLD Claudia Merritt watched Beth with sharp old eyes. No doubt now that the woman was conscious and feeling stronger, more able to breathe without the aid of a machine, she was tired of the ventilator tube that ran down her throat and prevented her from talking. She was vastly improved so perhaps Dr. Randolph would start weaning her off the ventilator.

Dr. Randolph. Her texter hadn't directly said that he was her fantasy man.

But he was her fantasy man.

Neither of them had specifically acknowledged his identity. Beth wasn't sure if that was a protective reflex on her part or if it was that she was afraid of asking because she was afraid of an answer either way.

How was it that this morning her patient load consisted of his respiratory patients? That had never happened before. When she'd asked her supervisor about it, Ruth had just shrugged and given a noncommittal answer that had raised more questions than given answers.

Although her patient couldn't speak with the ventilator in place, Beth chatted to the woman she was checking, then recorded her stats into the computer system. She was just finishing in the room when Eli entered, looking more tempting than chocolate-dipped sin.

Just as it always did when she looked at him, her breath caught and her pulse pounded as if trying to burst free from her body.

His gaze met hers and he grinned.

Hello, heart attack. Because her heart had just stopped in her chest, leaving her feeling light-headed and giddy. Quick! Someone find that cardiologist. These days she needed him on speed dial.

She tried to respond, but was just as unable to talk as her ventilator patient. Embarrassed, hot-cheeked, and short of breath, she went to rush past him, to get out of Dodge as quickly as possible.

"Wait." He grabbed her arm, his touch gentle but causing shocks waves that must have registered around the world.

Eli was touching her! For the first time ever, his skin connected with hers. Total body meltdown.

"Stay," he said, so low she barely caught the word.

She forced her gaze upwards, stared into sparkly blue eyes that she'd swear saw into her very soul. His fingers stroked over her skin, slow, sensual, completely blocked from the eyes of their patient. Her skin goose-bumped, her core melted, her knees weakened, her brain couldn't quite comprehend that Eli was touching her.

His hot gaze searched hers and visions of their bodies doing wild and amazing things together flashed through her mind. She wanted to push him up against the wall and mash her body against his while kissing him like crazy. She wanted to rip off his clothes and kiss his throat, his chest, his flat stomach, to run her hands over all of him then hold on tight while he rocked her world.

Heat flashed in his eyes and she wondered if he could read her thoughts. If he knew how much she wanted him this very second. Every second. Always. Because she couldn't think of a time when she wouldn't want this man.

He'd texted her the night before. Had told her he'd dream of her. Hello, second heart attack!

"Don't go. I'm removing the ventilator and would like you in the room in case I need anything."

Had they been texting she'd have made some crack about knowing what he needed, but the thought only caused her face to burn all the hotter. Yowsers, the man affected her in a crazy way.

Because what she wanted him to remove was her clothes, his clothes. She wanted him to need her. To want her the way she wanted him. But whatever the heat in his eyes had been, he had gotten it under control and his attention had moved elsewhere.

Which reminded her that she needed to do the same. They were at work, the hospital, taking care of the sick, and there was a patient in the room with her. Beth so wasn't into spectator sex. Or getting fired. Focus—that's what she needed. Focus. On her patients and not on their very handsome, very sexy doctor.

He examined his patient then, while chatting to Ms. Merritt, he pulled out the ventilator tube that ran from her mouth down her throat and into her lungs. The woman's hand automatically went to her throat and she coughed.

"I put in an order for a BiPAP machine for Ms. Merritt before I came in. Will you check on the status as I do want her on BiPAP to help maintain her breathing status."

Her gaze colliding with his, she nodded. His eyes were magic, she thought. Had to be because their blue depths had her mesmerized, under his spell. They twinkled with secret messages just for her and her body zinged back its replies just as surely as if words were being exchanged. His lips curved into a smile that said he knew exactly what was happening beneath her clothes and he liked being responsible for that awareness.

"Oh, you're here." A harried-looking woman in her fifties entered the room and practically cheered when she saw Eli.

Eli and Beth didn't jump apart because they hadn't been standing that close, but the woman's interruption had the same effect as if they had. Beth could tell he wanted to say something to her, but wouldn't with others present. Just as well because she suspected her tongue had gone mute from the absolute steam of his smile.

Eli had noticed her. They'd texted the night before. He'd just touched her. Angels were playing harps somewhere off in the distance. She was sure of it.

"I was hoping to get to talk to one of Mother's doctors about her progress." Ms. Merritt's daughter's gaze went to what Eli held and she smiled. "Thank goodness that thing is out. It's really bothered her, not being able to say anything to us during the short time we get to visit with her." The woman frowned, not pausing long enough for Eli to respond and making Beth wonder if their patient would get in a word edgewise even without the ventilator tube.

"Is there anything you can do about that?" the woman continued. "The short visiting hours in ICU, that is. Thirty minutes twice a day is just not enough time with Mother when she's like this."

An older-appearing man, who was likely the woman's husband, met Beth's gaze and just gave a slight sigh as if he was used to his wife monopolizing the conversations.

When the respiratory therapist arrived to place the woman on her BiPAP machine, her daughter was still talking a mile a minute, occupying Eli's attention. Beth checked with her patient to be sure she didn't need anything then hurried from the room while Eli was trapped in the room with Claudia's talkative daughter.

If not for how her body and brain were frazzled at her encounter with Eli she could almost smile at Eli fielding the woman's rapid-fire questions, all with patience and

kindness that far surpassed that of many of the doctors
Beth worked with. She'd spent quite a bit of time on the
phone with the woman earlier in the day, giving her an update on her mother, and knew how trying the lady could
be. Eli spoke to her with respect and real concern over his
patient. Beth liked that.

Okay, so she liked everything about the man. Which
was the problem.

She pushed Claudia's room door closed behind her and
leaned against it. Shutting her eyes, she took a deep breath.
She sweated. Literally, she could feel the clamminess of
her skin. What was wrong with her that just being near Eli,
just having him speak to her, made her sweat?

Eli had done more than speak to her. He'd touched her.

For the first time ever his body had touched hers. Intentionally, his skin had pressed against hers. Sure, it had
only been a brief touch, but her body still zinged from the
flesh-to-flesh contact.

She ran her finger over the spot, took a deep breath at
the memory of his skin against hers, of his finger stroking over her. She could only imagine what her body would
do if he ever really touched her, if there was lots of flesh-
to-flesh contact.

Later that night Beth opened her eyes and glanced at where
she'd set her cellular phone within reach of the bathtub. In
hopes of a text? She'd gotten plenty enough today but none
from her mystery sexter. Neither had she seen said mystery texter again after leaving Mrs. Merritt's ICU room.
Because if she'd had any doubts that Eli was her mystery
texter, his grin, the way he'd looked at her, touched her
today had completely resolved them.

Eli had been sexting with her the past two nights. Odd
really as she wouldn't have guessed him as a sexter, but,
then, hadn't she been right there, sexting him back? And

she'd never have thought herself capable of that either. Sexual attraction did crazy things to a person.

Would he send her hot messages again tonight?

Was it crazy that she kept checking her phone every few minutes despite the fact that she knew it hadn't made a sound? She was right here beside her phone so it wasn't as if she'd somehow missed the ding and vibration of an incoming message. But that didn't stop her from hitting the button to light the screen up just in case. No little text message icon.

Yep, she'd gone crazy.

When she'd gotten home a little while ago she'd stripped and slid into a hot, steamy, bubble-filled tub, determined to soak away the day's stresses. Still, she'd kept her phone close. Ever since her encounter with Eli she'd been on edge, wondering if she'd hear from him. Wondering if perhaps he'd track her down at the hospital and talk to her in person. Or maybe he'd text her and admit to his identity and tell her he wanted to see her in person.

But nothing. Not a single text or call. Maybe her phone wasn't working properly? Drying her pruny–from-the-water fingers with an unused washcloth, she reached for the offending silent contraption from the chair she'd pulled over near the tub so she could light up the screen yet again. Nothing. Urgh.

Maybe she should send a message to Emily just to be sure there wasn't a program malfunction. Maybe there was a cellular tower down somewhere and that's why—

Buzzzzz.

Almost dropping the vibrating phone into her bath water, Beth jerked, causing water to slosh up over her water-wrinkled skin. Her breath caught. Could it be? She hated the nervous anticipation welling within her at the possibility that the text might be from Eli. Probably just Emily or one of her own brothers, checking on her to be sure she was still alive since she hadn't talked to her siblings in several days.

Nervous, she opened the text, telling herself it wasn't him so she wouldn't be disappointed if it wasn't, yet all the while praying it was, because she would be disappointed if it wasn't.

The second her eyes lit on the number, a tightness she hadn't acknowledged eased in her chest and she let out a long, relieved sigh.

You asleep?

I can sleep when I'm old, she responded with her pruny finger.

Oh, really? Doing something fun and fabulous while awake, then?

Beth wanted to laugh. If she answered honestly she'd have to say, "Not in years." But this was some fun game she and Eli were playing and that freed her to be and do whatever she pleased. He freed some hidden-away part of her that she hadn't known existed, a part of her she had to admit she liked because he left her feeling wanted, desirable. Something that she hadn't felt since walking in on Barry with his ex.

Don't you wish you knew? she teased, moving her leg in the tub and enjoying the way the water slid over her suddenly sensitized skin. Despite the water's warm temperature, her skin prickled into goose-bumps and she wished it was his fingers gliding over her skin.

Yes, I do. Tell me, came his instant reply.

Tell u what?

What you're up to

About five foot five inches.

Smartie.

Smart women intimidate you?

Nope. I'm a guy who appreciates a smart chick.

She knew that about him. Hadn't he been dating one of the most brilliant women she knew for the majority of the time she'd known him? Didn't she expect him to eventually go back to that woman? Nope, she so wasn't going there. This was just fun between her and Eli. She wouldn't let possible future doom ruin her present.

What else do u appreciate? she asked, to take her mind off of his ex. This was fun, a fantasy. She didn't have to let reality intrude. Soon enough it would. For now, she was going to enjoy whatever this was between them because he was all she seemed able to think about. Amazingly he seemed to be thinking about her, too.

A woman who knows what she wants.

You just say that because u know YOU are what I want.

Doesn't matter how much a woman wants a man if he doesn't want her in return.

Beth stared at her phone. Just what was he saying? Doubt filled her.

Do u want me in return?

What do you think, Beth?

She sloshed her toes around in the tub, letting the luke-warm water run over her skin, but even if she dunked her head under the water, it wouldn't wash away her old hang-ups.

I think u like that I want u.

She hoped that he wasn't just using her to pass the time until he and Cassidy kissed and made up. Urgh, she was letting the future into her head again. Not good.

What's not to like about that? You're a smart, witty, beautiful, sexy woman who makes me smile.

His words echoed Emily's from the day before, making her acknowledge that she hadn't really believed her friend, hadn't really believed any of those things about herself. Not since…ugh, Barry. Perhaps there had been more truth in Emily's accusations than she had wanted to admit. She'd thought that because she wasn't pining to have the jerk back she was over him, but perhaps that didn't mean he hadn't left jagged scars in her very being. Scars she hadn't seen until Eli's texts.

Truth was, Eli made her feel sexy. Sexier than she'd ever felt. Which was crazy. How could a text conversation make her feel desirable? And smile? Because she was smiling like a grinning idiot.

Good answer, she praised his comment.

An honest answer, he replied. Are you at home?

With what I'm wearing, I'd better be at home.

Okay, you got me, came his immediate response, just as she'd anticipated. What are you wearing?

She wanted to get him.

Who says I'm wearing anything at all?

She tossed his line from the night before back out at him.

You make it HARD on a man to concentrate.

Who? Me?

Yes, you. Tell me why you're not wearing clothes. That how you do your household chores?

Beth snorted.

Right, because that's how women choose to do their housework. In the buff.

Sounds like a good idea to me. There should be a rule somewhere that says all housework should be done nude.

You're such a guy. Hate to burst your bubble, but I'm not bobbing around my house nude with a feather duster in my hands. I'm in the tub.

Would like to burst your bubbles so I could see everything in that tub with nothing to impede my view. Rub-a-dub-dub. You and me in that tub.

She glanced down at the water. When she'd first sunk into the tub, bubbles had floated on top of the water. Now she'd been in the water long enough that only a few stragglers remained. If Eli were there, would he be behind her, with her body cradled between his legs, her back resting against his chest, his arms around her while he washed her breasts with tender, loving care? Or would he be facing her? Sure, her tub wasn't that big, but this was a fantasy and in her fantasy they'd have room for all sorts of rub-a-dub-dubbing.

Be my eyes for me, Beth. Tell me what I'd see if I was there.

Beth studied her body and grimaced. Somehow she didn't think her waterlogged wrinkly skin was what he had in mind, or that an accurate description would turn him on. She wanted him turned on, as turned on as he made her.

Better yet, show me.

Shaking her head, Beth stared at the phone. She'd give him points for persistence, but no way was she shooting him a permanent image of her nudity. Not happening. If she looked like the Nordic Track girl, sure, she might consider flexing into a few sultry poses, but no fitness equipment sponsor would be knocking on her door for a photo shoot any time soon. Then an idea hit. She'd show Eli all right. She posed then snapped a photo and hit send.

Smiling in a silly way on the inside, she waited for his response, knowing she wouldn't have to wait long.

Hot! I think I just developed a foot fetish.

She laughed out loud, loving how he made her feel.

I like the glimmer of moisture on your skin, makes me

want to glide my hands over you. I bet under the right circumstances you glisten all over.

Beth gulped. Okay, he'd taken her silly picture of her feet propped up on the water spout and he'd come back with something that stimulated all her senses.

Glimmer. Glide. Glisten. Ur good with G words.

Great with G words, he corrected.
Pure genius, she praised. Grand, even, she added, sending another text before he could reply.

Hey, it was my G word turn, but I always say Ladies first.

Such a Gentleman! You were too slow. Something you should know about me, I have no patience.

Gimme…

I'll slip lower in my bath and wait…impatiently.

Glimpse, he finished.
Gasp, she sent back.

Grab.

Goose-bumps.

Because her skin prickled with excitement that had nothing to do with her bubble bath.

Give.

Grinning.

Because she couldn't wipe the smile off her face. He made her feel giddy deep inside. From the inside out.

Gratification.

Generous.

Gaze.

Gymnastic, she teased, imagining her body contorted around his. Wrapping herself around him would motivate all her inner yoga moves.

Grind.

Gallant.

Groove.

Graceful.

Groan.

Glad.

The thought of him imagining them together, of him reacting, groaning from the sheer thought of it, made her glad indeed. Made her want to groan with pleasure, too.

Growing, he told her.

Gyrating.

Beth closed her eyes, moved slowly in the water, letting the water caress her skin.

Is this supposed to be turning me on? If so, good job.

How could a silly letter game set her imagination to running so wild? It was as if he was whispering each word into her ear, as if his hands stroked over her bare, wet body, as if he was there, sharing each word with her.

Grudge

Grudge? Okay, that one threw her momentarily out of her fantasy haze and she glared at her phone as if the device could explain for him.

Really? Grudge?

You never heard of a grudge...um...match? used to vent anger between a couple?

Match? Um, yeah, I know exactly what u mean and, okay, although I don't want to vent anger with u, I'll give u grudge.

She sent the text, then realized how he could read the message and went on to clarify.

Um, well u know what I mean when I say I'll give u grudge.

Although at the moment he had her so turned on she'd give him grudge any way he wanted grudge.

Golden grudge gift.

Glorious, she sent back, because he made her feel glorious, her body, her mind, her spirit.

Guided tour?

Greedy.

She doubted she'd ever feel comfortable enough to sext a photo. Not just because she didn't want a photo of herself out in cyberspace but also because to send that showed a level of trust that she wasn't sure she'd ever feel again. *Thank you, Barry, for screwing up my faith in men and myself.* But sexting with Eli was fun and sexy and appealed to her on levels she didn't even begin to understand.

Greek? Sorry I'm running out of Gs, not into Greek.

She laughed at his text.

Greek? As in it's all Greek to u? ;)

Have I ever told you that you make me smile? Or am I supposed to say "g"rin?

Good one.

He made her smile, too. So much so that her face hurt from her mouth curving so high.

Gush.

Gooey.

Globes.

Gotcha goodies.

Groan. Give greater glimpse?

"Not going to happen," she said out loud, although there wasn't anyone to hear her.

She shivered. Her bath water had gone cold some time ago. Not that she'd noticed. Her skin was on fire. Her whole body burned with desire. Their sext game had turned her on way more than she'd have dreamed possible. She'd lost her mind and was on the verge of losing her will power he had her aching so for physical release.

Stepping out of the tub, she wrapped herself in an over-sized towel and stared in the mirror, wondering what Eli would see if she did snap a photo and send to him. Would he look at her hair clipped high on her head and see sexy tendrils or a tangled mess? Would he look into her desire-filled eyes and be captured by their intensity for him or would he see desperation, a woman who hadn't been able to hang onto her live-in boyfriend because she hadn't been good enough?

And her body? She wasn't some pin-up girl by any means. Just an average woman with an average body. A little too much jiggle here, not enough there. That kind of thing. Nothing horrible about her looks, but definitely nothing spectacular either. What would Eli think if she dropped her towel and sent him a photo? Not that she would, but if she did, what would his reaction be? Would he be as turned on as she was at their texting, at the photo of his abs that she'd caught herself looking at a hundred times because she couldn't bring herself to delete it, wondering if that was really him and knowing it was? Or would her phone suddenly go silent except for the chirping of lonely crickets? Would he find her "too curvy", too?

Going? Going? Gone?

Not gone. Had to get out of tub. Was turning into a prune. Drying off now.

I'm jealous of your towel. How 'bout that guided tour?

Jealous of her towel? Wow, he was good, Beth thought and dropped said towel to the floor. She stared closer at her body in the mirror. There would be no photographed guided tour. Only silly women who risked having their pictures shared with others or, worse, shared on the internet would send a "guided tour" photo. She might not be the brightest girl in the world, but she wasn't stupid.

At least, not too often.

Waiting… he sent, when she didn't immediately respond. Not wanting to turn their play into a serious talk, such as *You're going to be waiting forever, bub, if you think you're going to get a photographic tour of my body because I don't trust any man that much,* Beth sent him a teasing text instead.

What? U want more? I sent u a pic of my fabulous Passion Berry red toenails. What more could any man possibly want?

She picked the towel back up and ran the cotton material briskly over her skin, drying her moisture-slick body the best she could and trying not to think about Eli's comment about being jealous of her towel, of wondering what it would feel like if it were his hands caressing her flesh. The man sure knew exactly what to say to set her imagination afire, which wasn't helping the whole trying-to-dry-off situation.

Graffenburg? Is that a town in Germany?

Huh? Where had his question come from?

Well, is that a town or not?

I don't know. Never heard of it. Geography is not my thing.

Look it up sometime.

No time like the present. Beth pulled up the search engine on her smart phone and typed in the word. Oh, my. Oh, my, oh, my, oh, my. She should have known that one. Or maybe based on her past sexual experiences, maybe she shouldn't have. Because although she had no complaints, she couldn't honestly say Barry had ever visited that particular German town…er…spot. Maybe he'd needed that guided tour Eli had mentioned.

Okay, so maybe I am into geography after all. You are so good for my education, Old Man.

Not that she shouldn't have known that one. She was a nurse and had studied female anatomy.

Nothing like hands-on training. You should let me show you.

Aww, are u offering to lend a helpful hand? How sweet of u.

Grateful?

I already sent you a picture of my toes.

Toes? You have toes?

She laughed at his reply, slid on an oversized Tennessee Titans T-shirt and a pair of silky panties, then crawled between her sheets.

Talented toes.

She wiggled them beneath her cotton sheets as if demonstrating.

I'll even show u my talented toes someday. Oh wait! Already did. Well, my toes, but not their talents. ;)

Lips?

Sooooo talented.

Not that she thought they were, but if her lips ever got the opportunity to touch Eli she was positive they'd take on a mind of their own and achieve things she'd never done before. The right inspiration could do that to a set of lips. She was positive.

I'm daydreaming again.

Again?

I've been daydreaming about you for the past few days. You have to know that. I want to kiss you, Beth. Touch you. To get to know you, all of you. For real. Texting isn't enough.

Beth's insides tingled, melted, grew hungry with anticipation of touching Eli's body for real. She closed her eyes and recalled how electricity had zapped her at his touch at the hospital earlier that day. She wanted that. All over.

I can't imagine kissing u. Well, I can and do, but just seems too good to be true that someday my lips will touch u.

They will. Soon.

Promise?

Oh, yeah.

Beth sighed. Once upon a time she'd never fathomed that she'd actually kiss Eli. Now? Knowing what he tasted like, what his lips felt like against hers seemed a distinct possibility and something she craved so strongly that she hated to think of the lengths she'd go to make that possibility into a reality.

You have to work tomorrow?

Not tomorrow. I finally have a day off work. Yay! J

So I won't see you tomorrow? That's not good. I will miss you.

Close your eyes and dream of me.

I can guarantee that when my eyes close, I'll be dreaming of you. For that matter, my eyes are wide open and I'm dreaming of you.

That's good.

Beth smiled. She knew exactly what he meant. She was doing exactly that, too.

Is it?

I think so. Don't u?

Yes, Beth, I think it's very good. And on that note I'm going to say goodnight, because I do have to work in just a few hours.

Beth glanced at the time on her phone. Wow. They'd texted into the wee hours.

Night... she texted back. Wondering if she should acknowledge him by using his name. For some reason she didn't want to, wanted to keep their seemingly safe little anonymous-on-his-part game going for a while longer. Silly of her, she was sure, but nothing about any of this was logical, so what did it matter, really?

Sweet dreams.

CHAPTER FIVE

"So, HE'S NOT admitted that it's him?" Emily wrinkled up her nose and not because of the smell of their favorite local coffee shop. Bennie's smelled fabulous as always with various coffee blends and pastries that would tempt an anorexic over to the other side.

As she poked the last bit of her muffin into her mouth, Beth acknowledged that she didn't require nearly that much temptation.

She'd been ecstatic when she'd called Emily and asked her to meet for a late breakfast and her friend, also off work for the day, had agreed. Sometimes a girl just needed to see her best friend first thing in the morning. Especially a morning after sexting into the wee hours with her fantasy guy.

"Not in so many words, but it is him." Mindlessly, Beth picked up her keys, toyed with them, clicked her keyless entry, and listened for the resounding beep, letting her know her car was indeed locked.

"I'm confused." Emily's perfectly drawn-on brows made a V. "Why wouldn't he just tell you it was him?"

Her horn beeped again and Beth glanced out the window at her car, not realizing she'd hit the button again. Setting her keys down on the sleek tabletop so she'd quit fiddling with them, she shrugged. "It's hard to explain, but I do understand."

It was the same reason she hadn't asked him or called him by his name.

"He told you he'd miss seeing you today?"

Smiling, Beth nodded.

"I'm still confused. If he's missing seeing you, why didn't he make plans to see you?"

Her smile faded. Yeah, while lying in her bed, thinking over their conversation, she'd wondered that too. Why hadn't he asked her to dinner or for a bed-tying session?

Then again, maybe he didn't want to rush things.

Which didn't quite fit since he'd started their relationship with a photo of his bare abs. An anonymous sext message. Although perhaps he hadn't meant it to be anonymous until she'd mentioned wanting to tie him to the bed.

"I don't know why he didn't ask to see me." Ugh. She sounded depressed and dejected when in reality she was far from it. Emotionally, she was turning cartwheels of joy that Eli had texted her. A simple little thing really but when that text was from *the* guy, well, getting a text was huge. Enormous. Gigantic. Big times infinity.

"That's an easy fix. Ask him."

"Ask him why he didn't make plans to see me or ask him to make plans with me tonight?"

"Either. Both."

There went panic skyrocketing her blood pressure and heart rate again. Beth picked up her keys, realized what she'd done and forced herself to set them back on the table. "No, I don't think so."

Emily regarded her, no doubt taking in the heightened color in her blazing cheeks and how Beth wouldn't meet her gaze. "Why not?"

"It doesn't feel right."

"You've sexted with the man the past few nights and

yet you don't feel right asking him to make plans with you?" Emily scowled and clicked her nails on the table-top. "I don't like that."

"There's no rush. It's only been a few days."

Emily sighed. "I guess you're right, but I'm surprised at how understanding you're being about this. I'm not sure I would be. Why isn't he making a move?"

Beth was positive her friend wouldn't be patient. But every gut instinct said not to push Eli, that he would make his move when he was ready. "He's worth the wait."

"Without a doubt." Emily took a sip of her frozen mocha latte. "Do you think he'll text you tonight?"

Knowing her cheeks were flaming again, Beth gave a secretive little smile. "I know he will."

Emily's brow arched high. "My my, aren't we smug?"

Face flaming, Beth laughed. "Not smug, it's just that I know he will." She felt another vibration in her pocket and smiled. "Actually, he texted me first thing this morning."

Both of Emily's brows shot up. "Excuse me, but why are you only now telling me that? Morning texts up the game. Lots of people do and say things late at night, but a morning message, that's more serious." Her friend leaned across the table. "What did he say?"

Beth wasn't sure if she bought Emily's logic, but she'd had similar thoughts, that somehow getting texts from him in the light of day held more significance than texts sent under the cloak of night. "I am only now telling you because we were working up to that point in the conversation and I was telling you things in chronological order. We just got to this morning."

"And?"

Beth's insides practically glowed at recall of the happiness she'd experienced at reading his message. "He said, 'Good morning, Beautiful.'"

His simple text had made her feel beautiful, not too curvy at all.

"Sweet, but generic." Emily tapped her fingernail against her coffee cup. "I want more. What else did he say?"

So much for her inner glow. Emily's comment punched a hole right through Beth's giddiness. "He asked if I'd dreamed of him."

"Did you?"

From the moment she'd closed her eyes. In vivid color and detail. "What do you think?"

"That by your blush you had a very busy night. Tell me all."

Beth put her hand over her mouth to smother a nervous smile. "I'm not quite sure if I told you my dreams that you wouldn't think I was giving TMI."

Emily's eyes widened and she clapped her hands together. "And?"

"We've been texting back and forth all day. Just getting to know each other kinds of things with a lot of suggestive comments thrown in. He has amazing wit."

"Oh, this is good. Very good."

"Maybe." Beth took a sip of her frappucino, liking the sweet mocha flavor. "Like you said, he hasn't asked me out or anything. He's just texted with me in private. He may not have any plans to ever do more than that."

"I'm not sure why he hasn't asked you out yet, but it sounds as if he's going to. You need to be prepared." Emily's facial expression turned thoughtful then took on the aura of a drill sergeant. One that had Beth sitting a little straighter in her chair. "How old is the underwear you're wearing?"

"What?" Beth gawked at her friend, grateful she'd already swallowed her frappucino or else she might have spewed it all over her friend.

Emily leaned forward and stage-whispered, "Seriously, how old is the underwear you're wearing?"

Knowing that her face had to be as red as the cherry topping on the cheesecake in the dessert display case across from their table, Beth racked her brains. "I don't know. Two years maybe."

"Well." Emily's smile was lethal. "I know how we're spending the rest of the day. We're going shopping."

Beth packed away the last of her new purchases, wondering if she was a fool to have spent so much on such tiny scraps of silk and lace. She'd always been more into practical underwear than whimsical. There hadn't been anything practical about her afternoon purchases. Ha, there hadn't been much of anything at all about her purchases period. Just expensive little triangles and strips of material.

Then again, Emily was right. If she and Eli did have a real-life encounter, did she want to be wearing old boring panties? Dream Guy Eli meet Granny Panty Beth? Not hardly.

Her phone buzzed. She grinned and forced herself to wait a full two minutes before opening the message. Couldn't have him thinking she was desperately awaiting his next text—even if she had been.

ICU wasn't the same without you there today.

Why's that?

I kept looking for you.

You knew I wasn't working today.

Didn't stop me from wanting to see you.

Emily's words played through her head. If he wanted to see her, why hadn't he made any effort to do so? Which left her stuck for a response. She had no claims on him, just as he had no claims on her. All they'd done was text with each other, fun, light, sexy texts. That might be all they ever had.

Do anything exciting today? he asked, apparently not wanting to wait on a response.

That's none of your business.

What if I want to make it my business?

Beth's breath caught. Her imagination went wild.

Do you?

His response wasn't immediate and she stared at her silent phone. Hello? Did he? Or was he just toying with her until something better came along? Or, worse, until he went back to his ex? Her heart throbbed in her throat and her pulse jittered through her body.

It's complicated, and I admittedly have some issues I have to work through, but, yes, Beth, I want you to be my business. I feel as if you already are.

She let out her pent-up breath. Complicated because of Cassidy? Issues that involved still having feelings for his ex? She wondered but didn't ask because perhaps there were some conversations that shouldn't take place via text messaging.

Are you okay with that?

His question seemed a no-brainer. On the surface. Deep beneath, where her emotions lay vulnerable, might be a different story. Could she bear being hurt again the way Barry had hurt her?

Are u okay with that? she countered.

Love your quick wit.

Just wait until u experience the rest of me. You'll be hooked.

She hoped, but was afraid to be overly optimistic outside their safe text conversation. Eli was telling her upfront that he had issues he had to work through. She'd been burned before. Barry had talked about marriage, she'd believed in him, and look where that had gotten her.

In case you haven't noticed, I already am.

Feeling as if she were freefalling emotionally, Beth shoved away her doubts. How could she not? Curling up on her sofa, she keyed in a response.

Tell me more.

You want the gory details?

She smiled.

I'm female, aren't I?

Most assuredly. Let's see. Female, that's a good place to start. Fantastically female.

Fun, she countered, because in spite of all her concerns, Eli was fun. Texting with him was fun. If she could ever get over how nervous he made her feel in real life, she bet being with him in person would be fun, too. Very fun.

Flexible?

Fortunately.

She'd always enjoyed yoga, went to Zumba several times a week, and loved sports. Working up a sweat made her feel good the way nothing else did.

Flicking?

Beth stared at the word on her screen. Flicking? As in his tongue flicking? His finger flicking? She closed her eyes, imagined his hands running over her body, his mouth kissing every nook and cranny, his tongue tracing, teasing her, flicking.

Oh, my! Her pelvic muscles squeezed at the thought of Eli's tongue delving her most sensitive spot. She squirmed on the sofa, wanting to rock her hips to the imaginary tempo playing in her head.

Her phone buzzed in her hand, the vibration rocketing pleasure through her already sensitized body, sending a fresh wave of shivers over her.

She read his text.

Firm.

Good to know she wasn't the only one whose body was reacting to their messages. Too bad they weren't doing W because she had a few w words that aptly described her body. Wet. Wild. Willing.

Fabulous, she answered, sticking with the letter they'd been using.

Fondle.

Frequently.

Because the more he fondled her, touched her, the better. The sooner the better. She wanted him.

Flattery.

Finger.

Forceful.

Frantic.

Frenzy.

Feed.

Feel.

Full.

Feverish.

Their texts shot back and forth so fast Beth could barely keep track of who'd last texted. Her breath came just as quickly. Her heart beat just as rapidly. Her whole body tuned into her phone screen, to the words Eli sent, to the unusual foreplay setting her imagination alight.

Fiery feline

His messages made her feel that way, like a seductress, like she was beautiful and he wanted her more than anything.

Meow.

He certainly had her insides purring, wanting stroked.

That was an M. I WANT AN F.

Beth bit the inside of her lower lip, struggled with the intense need washing over her, with the reality that Eli wanted her every bit as much as she wanted him. Well, not as much, but he did want her and that was a heady sensation.

I just bet you do, she countered.

Frustrated

Yes, so was she. Horribly so. But she kept her message light, teasing.

FAKING. *grin*

Frigid?

She laughed at his fast comeback.

Fortunately not.

Flirt.

Floating.

Feet.

Fetish.

Flavor.

Flying.

Fragrant.

Fellatio. Hey, if u get to use a German town, I get to use an Italian one, she teased, amazed at herself, at their conversation, at how in sync she felt with him as they zinged messages back and forth, stimulating each other higher and higher with each F word.

Get that map, he told her.

I already Googled it. You any good at geography? Hope u didn't Flunk it, she challenged.

You'd know if I had. Fulfilled. Have I done that one yet?

No, u haven't, but I'm waiting.

She was waiting, her entire body was on edge of something big, of a huge meltdown that he had taken her to the precipice of, had her yearning for the next level that would send her into a cataclysmic pleasure overload.

See—it's contagious.

What is?

I want an F.

I think I have a bad case, she admitted, her hands running over her arms, sending tingles through her body and settling at the apex of her thighs. She repositioned herself, sliding her legs beneath her on the sofa, liking the pressure against her bottom. Is there a cure?

It's an ongoing treatment.

Frustrated—have I done that one yet?

She sent him his own words back, wanting him so much her body ached with need, so much she ached for release.

Finish, I'll help you.

Beth gulped, staring at her phone, wondering if she was reading right.

Help me?

Finger flicking fluidly.

Yes, she was reading correctly. Oh, my. Could she? No. That would be too much, would make her too vulnerable to him, would set her up for ridicule as Barry had done more than once regarding her sensuality.

Ugh on the thoughts of Barry. He was not allowed in her head. Not tonight. Not ever.

Beth? Follow my lead. Finger flicking fluidly.

Eli repeated his text.

She sucked her lower lip between her teeth. Closed her eyes, concentrated on Eli, on how he made her feel when he smiled, when he'd said her name for the first time, when he'd touched her in Mrs. Merritt's room, on how good she'd felt when he'd called her beautiful. She imagined how good she'd feel if Eli were there, complimenting her in person, touching her body with purpose. All her thoughts on Eli, she gave in to the demands of her body.

You are good at this.

Feeling fuller, firmer.

Beth gulped at the image his message put in her head, at how her body instantly responded to that image.

You have my Full attention, that's For sure. I want you.

I'm right here.

Too far away.

Breathing on your neck. Hands on your hipbones…

I woke up this morning dreaming. You were holding my hands above my head with me stretched out beneath you. Lots of those g words were happening. Gliding. Gyrating. German towns.

Sweat dripping off my brow…

And u were kissing me. Deep, hard kisses.

Deep and hard?

DEEP and HARD.

With her last text, Beth closed her eyes and let her body burst into a prism of colors, all bright, all glorious, all Eli's doing.

Fantastic finale finding fulfillment?

No way was she going to tell him that he'd just given her the best orgasm of her life without him even being present, without him even having touched her. No way.

Only he *had* been present, encouraging her the entire way. The man got inside her head and did amazing things to her body, made her feel free, sexy.

She could only imagine what it would be like if he had really been there, had really been touching her.

Then again, maybe it was all in her head. Maybe because he was her dream guy, the guy she'd fantasized about for months, maybe that's why she'd just seen stars and had had a major body meltdown. Maybe if he'd really been there it wouldn't have been anything spectacular, because maybe she wouldn't have been able to relax, to have gotten Barry's words out of her head.

Maybe.

But as her eyelids became heavier and heavier she couldn't quite convince herself of that.

Fulfilled? he asked again.

Fatigued.

Sorry. Guess I've kept you up late again tonight and tomorrow you do have to work.

I didn't tell you that I had to work tomorrow.

I checked the schedule today. Night, Beth. Sweet dreams.

Beth was pretty sure she'd been dreaming for the past several days. Sure felt that way.

If that were the case, no one wake her up, please.

At his office, Eli flew through his morning patients with gusto.

"What's up with you this morning?" his nurse asked him. She'd been giving him an odd look all morning, but hadn't said anything while they'd been seeing patients.

"What do you mean?" Not that he didn't know. He felt more alive than he had in years. No doubt that bled through into everything he did.

"You're always pretty even keeled, but today you have an unusually good mood and can't seem to quit smiling. Plus, I heard you whistling in your office earlier. It's not as if the whole office doesn't know about you and Dr. Qualls falling out a few weeks ago. Did y'all kiss and make up?"

He had been whistling, hadn't he? Eli shook his head. "That isn't going to happen."

Eyeing him curiously, his nurse arched her brow. "Is there someone new on the scene? I can't imagine anyone more perfect than Dr. Qualls, so this new woman must really be something to have you smiling that way."

Eli fought flinching at "perfect".

"We'll leave it at life is good." That's all he was saying, because he wasn't ready to share his personal life. Not where Beth was concerned.

As crazy as it was considering he'd yet to have a single date with the woman he couldn't stop thinking about, life was good. Especially now that he was leaving the office, headed across the breezeway that connected the multi-specialty office complex to the hospital, and would soon see Beth.

Had she been as blown away as he'd been by their texting the night before? As shocked? He hardly recognized himself because he sure hadn't done anything like that before.

Not even as a silly teenaged boy had he behaved so... horny. He didn't know another word for how she made him feel. Beth did something to him. Freed his mind and burned his insides with physical need.

Crazy and not the basis for a long-term relationship, but wow on the here and now. Maybe an affair with a hot-blooded woman like Beth was just what he needed to help him figure out what it was he really wanted out of life, to help him figure out where he'd gone wrong, why he couldn't love a woman everyone told him was perfect for him. Or maybe spending time with Beth would just be fun and free him to rediscover who he was, then he could worry about his failures and his future.

He checked on all six of his current admissions, including the two assigned to Beth, but she was nowhere in sight. Had she gone back to hiding from him? Eli looked up and down the ICU hallway for the woman who had occupied his every free thought for the past few days.

There. He caught a blur of blue scrubs and brown ponytail disappearing into a patient room.

His lips curved upward at just the glimpse of her. The woman made his insides feel... He searched for the right word. Better? Lighter? Excited? Turned on?

He lingered in the hallway, passing the time by asking the charge nurse about a patient. But his brain was focused on the room where Beth was, waiting for her to come out, wondering if she'd been as affected by their sexting as he'd been.

"There's no one in that room, you know," Nurse Rogers told him, eyeing him curiously.

"Huh?" Because he'd seen Beth go in and doubted she'd slipped out without his noticing. He'd definitely have noticed.

Nurse Rogers shrugged. "Not a patient, I mean. The patient who was in the room was transferred to the regular medical floor. The tech was busy and Beth volunteered to prepare the room for another patient."

"Oh." Eli glanced toward the room, then back at the nurse. "Why are you telling me?"

"Because you're about as subtle as a ton of bricks."

He grinned at the nurse manager because he really couldn't deny the woman's assumption and she seemed to approve of his interest in Beth. To deny it would just be insulting the woman's intelligence. A ton of bricks had nothing on him.

"That smooth, eh?"

Smiling back, she nodded. "My first clue was when you asked me to assign her to your patients a couple of days ago. As many as possible. Smooth as silk."

Okay, so that hadn't been real subtle of him, but he'd wanted the opportunity to get to know Beth beyond their texting, to interact with her in person. With how she'd scurried away any time he'd been near, he hadn't been sure if she'd give him that opportunity. Fortunately, Beth's supervisor seemed to approve of his interest and hadn't been above co-operating. "A dead giveaway, eh?"

She shrugged. "About as much as when just a few days after she started working at Cravenwood she asked me to please not assign her to your patients."

Eli winced. That explained a lot and raised even more questions. Beth hadn't wanted to be assigned to his patients? "Did she give a reason?"

She shook her head. "She didn't have to."

Eli arched a brow, but rather than elaborate she just shook her head again.

"If you want details, you'll have to ask her yourself."

Right. Not that he didn't know the answer after texting with Beth. She'd felt an instant attraction to him. Lucky him. Only he'd been taken so she'd avoided him as if he'd had leprosy. How could he have been so blind?

"No time like the present," he quipped, grinning at the woman he was grateful to have on his side. "Is it okay if I occupy one of your nurses for a few minutes, Ruth?"

"I'd already told her I'd cover anything that came up on her patients while she was in the room, so no problem." She narrowed her eyes, although her smile somewhat killed the warning in her gaze. "Keep it at just a few minutes, though."

"Point taken."

Eli went to the vacated ICU room, stood in the doorway and watched Beth move efficiently about the room. Just looking at her took his breath away. How had he not noticed her in the past? She was beautiful and sexy without even trying. But way beyond the surface, she heated his blood, made him burn from the inside out, made his insides feel alive and raging with fire that needed to go up in flames with her.

When he'd touched her arm two days ago, she'd seared him to the core, turned him inside out. He wanted her more than he recalled ever wanting anyone, anything. So much so he ached with need that went far beyond satisfying a physical need.

She glanced up, acknowledged that she knew he was there but kept about her business of stripping the bed sheets.

"You don't look surprised to see me."

Without glancing toward him, she shrugged and rolled the sheets up.

"You know, this seems a little silly considering you've worked here for several months, but I'm not sure we've ever been properly introduced. I'm Dr. Eli Randolph." The man of your fantasies, he wanted to add, but she already knew that. She'd been the one to tell him, to spark his imagination, to tell him in explicit detail what she'd like to do to his body. Over and over. Sweat broke out on his brow just at the thought.

He also fought adding that she had rapidly become the woman of his fantasies. She'd brought his imagination to life, brought him to life as if he'd been walking around zombiefied.

Beth looked up again, this time a frown marring her lovely face. But she didn't speak. Not a single word and Eli fought against shuffling his feet.

"I'd like to take you out to dinner after work tonight." Or away for the first weekend they could manage to escape the hospital. Both. He wanted everything with her and the sooner the better. He'd have asked her the night before but he'd been on call and hadn't wanted to possibly have to run out on their first date.

She stopped to stare at him, but still didn't say anything. He didn't like her silence, couldn't quite understand why she didn't say anything when his insides were bursting with nervous excitement that they were so near, that her delectable body was within reach, and yet really so far away because, despite their texted touches, he had no right to touch her in person. Which irked him and made him determined to change that as quickly as possible.

"We can go anywhere you like." It had been a long time since he'd asked a woman out on a date for the first time. Years. But he didn't recall ever feeling as if he needed to convince a woman to say yes. In the past, women had always chased him.

Nothing about Beth was typical. Everything was fresh, new, and unique to her.

Still, she just stared silently at him, as if waiting for him to say some magic phrase that would trigger an affirmative from her. He'd chant "Abracadabra" or "Hocus pocus" or whatever he needed to say to get this woman under his spell. Then again, according to her texts she was already under his spell, so she should be nodding her head or leaping into his arms or something, right?

Under different circumstances, the leaping into his arms would work nicely for him. Since they were at the hospital, he'd settle for a simple "yes".

"Beth? Say something. Anything, just so long as it's not no, because I don't think I could stand it if you said no to seeing me."

"I can't." She glanced at him then rapidly looked away. "You make it difficult for me to talk."

At first he'd thought she'd meant she couldn't see him, then he'd realized she meant to talk. He heaved a sigh of relief. "Because?"

"You know."

Just like that, he did know. Actually, he felt foolish for not realizing from the moment he'd walked into the room and she'd failed to do more than acknowledge him. He grinned. She wanted him and that made her nervous, tongue-tied, shy. She really, really wanted him and it was a heady sensation to be the recipient of her desire. An honor. He really was a lucky man.

All he had to do to know that was to look into Beth's eyes, to see the emotion that shined there this very second. She wanted him to the point of flustering him and giving him thoughts of pushing her up against the hospital room wall and kissing her until neither of them could breathe, could speak, and to hell with whoever saw or gossiped.

"If it'll convince you to say yes to going to dinner with me tonight, you don't have to say a thing."

Her brows veed in pseudo confusion.

"We'll just text each other," he clarified with a waggle of his brows. "Just so long as I actually get to spend time with you, it doesn't matter. Just think, if you say yes, I could even snap my own pictures."

Her cheeks blazed red, but her eyes came alive, and she arched a brow. "From across the dinner table?"

"I'm flexible."

"I thought that was my line." She took a deep breath that sounded just shy of a gasp. Had she startled herself with her quip?

"Last night it was. I'm anxiously waiting for you to demonstrate." He grinned, liking the in-person glimpse of the fiery passion and fun that always laced her text messages. As much as how he affected her flattered him, he didn't want her so nervous she couldn't be herself. Herself was who he wanted to get to know better. Much better. "You get off work at seven?"

The beginnings of a smile on her face, she shook her head. "I'm supposed to, but it's unlikely to happen. I'm a nurse, remember?"

"I remember everything about you."

Her cheeks tinged pink again. "You don't know me. Not really."

"I'm trying to correct that, but you aren't co-operating," he pointed out, liking the low laugh that spilt from her full lips.

"I'm not a yes kind of girl."

He moved closer, so where only a few inches separated them, stared down into her beautiful face, wondering yet again how he could have seen her without really seeing her for the past few months. Everything about her stimulated him. "That make you a no kind of girl?"

Her lips twitched. "No."

He laughed, liking the rumbling feel in his chest. He'd laughed more the past few days than he recalled laughing in years. Her silly little texts had lifted his insides. Lifted his outsides, too. "I'll be on my best behavior. I promise."

Her smile drooped slightly and she swallowed. "You know how I feel about you."

"I'd thought so, but your lack of the right enthusiastic answer is starting to make me have my doubts," he teased. He did know. He could see the excitement in her eyes, could feel the sizzling anticipation in the air between them. He could also see the fear in her eyes. Had she been hurt in the past and was afraid he was going to do the same? "I know we've texted like crazy. You make me crazy with wanting you. But tonight doesn't have to be anything more than just dinner and actually being able to see you in person rather than just in my head."

He knew she was going to go with him. He could see it on her face. He also understood her hesitancy.

"I promise I won't pressure you for anything beyond your company, Beth. Just text me your address when you clock out and I'll pick you up at your place, okay? We'll talk. Or text," he added with a grin.

Taking another deep breath, she nodded. "I'd like that."

So would he. More than he would have dreamed possible. He wanted to touch her, to pull her into his arms and hug her. She was so close. So close he could smell the soft, sweet scent of her. Not floral or overpowering, just a faint spicy sweetness. But to touch her would lead to much more because he longed to kiss her…among other things. They were at work. He didn't want to make her work life any more stressful than it had to be. He'd probably already been in the room alone with her too long.

"I'll see you tonight, Beth."

"Eli?"

He turned at the door, waited for her to say more, hoping she wasn't changing her mind.

"For the record, I can't make you the same promise as the one you just made me."

His heart thudded to a stop and restarted with a jolt. "That's okay, Beth. I'm a big boy and I'm really good under pressure."

"A girl can hope."

His gaze met hers, saw the flicker of desire burning there, and he instantly went hard. Which was a problem, considering their location. He fought crossing the room, knowing when he touched Beth he was likely to lose control completely. He wanted her so much. At the hospital wasn't the right time or place for their next touch, their first kiss.

"Text me," he said, then left while he still could.

Tonight was time enough for living out fantasies.

CHAPTER SIX

AMAZINGLY, BETH DIDN'T have to pull overtime. Had Eli somehow convinced everyone to show up for their shift and for there to be no new admissions right before shift change for once? Because clocking out at just a little past seven was a rarity and had only happened a few times since she'd started at Cravenwood.

All through shift change and giving report she'd expected something to happen to delay her leaving the hospital. Nothing had.

She exhaled a long breath and texted Eli her address and instructions to pick her up at eight. That gave her time to get home, jump in the shower, shave, moisturize and perfume herself just in case, stress over what she'd wear, then nervously wait for his arrival.

What would she wear? Would nothing at all be too obvious as to what she'd rather have than dinner? Then again, she did have all those new sexy undies Emily had convinced her to buy. Would she wear red or go with black?

Just as she got into her car, her cellular phone rang. She half expected it to be Eli, canceling. Part of her still didn't believe he could possibly feel the same about her, that none of this could be real, and that soon enough he'd reunite with Cassidy.

It was Emily.

"Need me to pinch you again?" her best friend greeted her.

At the reminder, she rubbed her upper arm, then started her car and pulled out of the hospital parking garage. "I still have the bruises from where you did earlier today."

"Well, you told me to pinch you because you had to be dreaming," Emily reminded her with a giggle, then sighed. "Oh, Beth, I'm so excited for you that he asked you out and even more so that you said yes! This is wonderful."

"It's just dinner."

Emily made a clicking sound over the phone line. "You texted the man that you wanted to tie him to your bed and lick him from head to toe. It's not just dinner."

"I never should have told you that. I didn't know it was him when I said that, and you're making me nervous."

"No, I'm not. You were nervous before I called. You're a nervous kind of girl when it comes to that man. Since you never were in college, I blame the fiasco with Barry, but we aren't going to talk about the douche bag tonight because he is history. I called to calm you down."

"True and it's not working." She braked at a traffic light, wondering at how long the drive home seemed tonight. "Try harder."

"Beth, relax. The worst that can happen is that you realize that y'all have nothing in common, he's horrible in the sack, and you go your separate ways. You're no worse off than you were a week ago."

All true, but Beth's nerves didn't feel soothed at all.

"Actually," Emily continued, "you're better off because then you'll know rather than spend your entire life wondering if he was the one and you missed out on your chance. Plus, being with Eli will definitely put to rest any lingering thoughts of Barry. That's a big plus."

Crazy nervousness or not, her friend made way too much sense. "I guess you're right."

"Of course, I'm right."

"I don't sleep around. Ever. You know that." But she had already admitted to herself that she wanted sex with Eli. She'd admitted as much to him even. The sooner the better, so why was she whining? Nerves? Or was it just that she wanted reassurance from her best friend?

"You're not a virgin," Emily reminded her, as if she'd thought that was what Beth meant.

"This feels different." She'd been in college when she'd had sex for the first time. When she'd returned to the dorm room, Emily had taken one look at her face and known something had changed. Then there had been Barry. Barry, whom she'd lived with for several months before he'd realized he was still in love with his former girlfriend, but had forgotten to mention this until Beth had walked in on them in the apartment she and Barry had shared. After which he'd pointed out all her shortcomings and thanked her for making him realize that his ex-girlfriend really was the woman for him. Gag at the memory. Gag at the sharpness that gripped her chest.

"Randy was a decent guy you were never that crazy about but who made studying more fun," Emily pointed out about Beth's college boyfriend of more than a year and who had been her first lover. "Barry was an idiot who never deserved you. I never liked him. We've discussed this."

They had. At length during the conversations they'd had leading up to Emily convincing Beth to apply for a job at Cravenwood.

"But Eli is a man," Emily continued over the phone line. "A man with needs. If he wants you, count your blessings and go for it."

Go for it. It's basically what she'd already decided. To go for it. With Eli. But maybe she'd needed to hear Emily confirm what she knew because she just didn't trust her own instincts any more.

Unlike how her best friend described Beth's college flame or how she'd felt about Barry, she was crazy about Eli and had been from the first moment she'd laid eyes on him and that fabulous smile of his.

Today, he'd flashed that smile at her.

Tonight, he'd do much more than that with his mouth because one way or another she'd know what Eli's mouth felt like against hers, what he tasted of, before the morning sun rose. Deep inside she knew that to be true.

Oh, wow. Tonight she'd kiss Eli. Possibly much more than that.

How lucky could a girl get?

Then again, she'd never been that lucky.

"What if he gets back together with Dr. Qualls?" Was she whiny or what? she thought as she slowed for another traffic light. But this was her best friend so she was allowed a little whine, surely?

"Quit worrying about what might happen in the future and enjoy what is happening right now. Whether for a night or a lifetime, your fantasy guy wants you. That's pretty spectacular when you think about it."

"I can't seem to think about anything else."

"Understandable, but, Beth, you need to remember something else, too, that you seem to have forgotten over the past year."

The traffic light changed and she pressed her foot against the gas pedal, grateful she was almost home. "What's that?"

"Dr. Randolph is a very lucky guy to be your fantasy man. Never forget that or underestimate what a great woman you are. That's pretty spectacular for him too. Don't dare think otherwise."

* * *

Because she changed outfits three times, a very unspectacular-feeling Beth wasn't ready when her doorbell rang at about ten minutes till eight.

Her skirt was down about her high heels and she'd been about to kick the black stretchy material across her closet in lieu of trying on yet another that might possibly make her hips look a little less curvy and a lot more svelte. Oh, crap!

Well, that solved what she was going to wear. She yanked the stretchy material back up over her hips and smoothed out any wrinkles her indecisive garment changing had caused. Telling herself that tonight was no big deal, just a first date—with her dream man!—and that there was no reason for her to feel as if she was going to pass out, she headed toward the front of her house.

He was lucky to be her fantasy man. It was spectacular for him that she wanted him. Emily had said so. Calm. Cool. Collected. That was her. No big deal.

When she opened the door, all pretense of any of those C words vanished. Her eyes widened in surprise. Not at the gorgeous freshly showered man standing there in khakis and a blue polo that matched his eyes, she'd been expecting him and the jolt to her senses looking at him always caused, the hello, let me rip your clothes off you with my teeth, please, reaction that always hit her when she saw him. What he held in his hands was what had her jaw dropping and her yet again thinking someone should pinch her.

She rubbed her already sore arm, thinking that might do the trick but, no, he still stood in her doorway, looking like a dream come true, holding a bouquet of colorful fresh flowers.

"You look amazing," he said, his eyes raking over her body in obvious appreciation.

He made her feel amazing, as if she'd made the perfect wardrobe choice. Then again, so had he. His shirt pulled just right across his shoulders, his chest, and just beneath the material lay those fantastic abs, the image of which was permanently burned into her mind from an inches-big photo on her phone.

Her gaze went to his and she tried to hold it there because, seriously, she was in danger of ripping off his clothes, to run her fingers over those abs and memorize every ripple of flesh, to try out some of the things they'd texted, all the things they'd texted. The man made her ache. "You didn't have to bring me flowers."

His gaze smoldering, as if he knew what she was thinking and perhaps was thinking of telling her to go right ahead, Eli grinned. "I know I didn't have to. I wanted to. You're a beautiful woman and I want to show you that I know how fortunate I am to be here with you."

There went Emily being right yet again.

Eli handed Beth the bouquet of multicolored blooms and their fingers brushed against each other. The feel of his skin against hers fried her brain and a few other choice body parts felt the sizzle. What was it about him that over-loaded her senses so?

She raked her gaze away from his baby blues, over the strong, handsome planes of his face, the fullness of those masculine lips, the width of his broad shoulders, the powerful thickness of his chest tapering down to a narrow waist. There she had to stop because the flames shooting out from her cheeks just wouldn't allow any further inspection. Needless to say, just looking at him answered exactly what it was about him that overloaded her senses. Everything. Every single thing about Eli made every single cell inside her body take notice.

So that made everything she was feeling just physical, right? That was the right label for all the emotions swirling inside her? Lust. Pure and simple animalistic, instinctual lust. That's what this had been about from the moment she'd first seen him and every moment since. Lust. Yet that didn't feel accurate. Not by a long way, because surely lust alone couldn't be this overpowering?

"Thank you." She took the flowers, wondered at the moisture stinging her eyes, then turned away from him so he wouldn't see how touched she was at his gesture, how aroused she was at her visual perusal of his attributes, how confused she was by knowing deep inside that lust didn't begin to cover the emotions she felt for this wonderfully unique man. "I'll just go put them in some water."

Because she really needed to escape so she could drag in oxygen for her poor deprived brain.

Once in the kitchen, she took a deep breath, dug through her cabinets in search of a vase and finally settled for a large glass jar when she didn't find anything more appropriate. Just how long had it been since someone had given her flowers? Actually, other than dance corsages and a couple of arrangements after her tonsillectomy at fifteen, she'd never gotten flowers. Randy had been a poor college student like herself but she doubted giving flowers had been his kind of thing anyway. Barry had never bothered with flowers. Why should he when he hadn't ever really loved her despite him having told her so many times?

Telling herself not to read anything into Eli's gesture and not to do anything to his body that would get her arrested, she arranged the flowers in the jar and wondered at the man in her living room.

"I like your home. It suits you."

Not in her living room. In her kitchen.

She spun toward him, startled that her Eli radar hadn't gone to bleep. Then again, her entire circuitry was pretty much shot by the fact he stood in her house. Who would have ever dreamed Eli would be in her house? In her kitchen? That he would have been the first man to bring her flowers? That she'd see attraction glimmering in his eyes? He wanted her. Whether it was just because of their sexting or if it was something more, Eli was attracted to her. He'd let her know in an unexpected way, but he had let her know. Maybe she was old-fashioned, behind the times, and sexting was just as good a way to show interest as any these modern days. Who knew?

Definitely, in Eli's case, sexting had worked. But only because she'd already been crazy about him, otherwise she'd probably have been creeped out.

She gulped and glanced away from the intensity of his eyes. She stared at his feet, liking the soft leather no doubt Italian shoes he wore with his khakis and pullover. She'd bet he looked even better without them. She closed her eyes, imagining him naked, in her kitchen. Would she have him tied to a barstool or would she be the one bound and at his gentle mercy?

Gentle. G word. All kinds of other G words popped into her head and she sank her teeth into her lower lip in frustration. Frustration. An F word. Which brought her to other F words. Which, combined with the way he was looking at her, made her knees want to buckle.

What was wrong with her? She'd had an ordinary sex life, good but nothing spectacular and definitely nothing kinky, with either of the men in her life. She'd never even thought of anything out of the ordinary until Eli. Did that mean passion hadn't ever been inspired within her?

Eli sure inspired passion. All her creative juices flowed. Flowed. Another F word. She groaned, then grimaced.

"Beth?"

"Thank you," she rushed out, realizing she hadn't acknowledged his presence in her small but homey kitchen, hadn't acknowledged his compliment. She'd not done anything except get hung up on two letters of the alphabet.

Did he feel as awkward as she did? How could she feel awkward when she'd texted with him into the wee morning hours, telling him her deepest fantasies? All of which featured him?

Or maybe because she'd shared so many of her private thoughts with him was why she felt so crazy?

"You're welcome." Those shoes and the hunky body attached moved close to her.

She looked up into blue, blue eyes. Blue. A B word. See, her brain could focus on letters besides G and F. B. Beautiful. Bold. Bite. Bite? Oh, yeah, she wanted to sink her teeth into him.

Blushing, she refocused on what he was saying.

"Before we go to eat, there's something I need to do. Something I believe we both need me to do."

His fingers went into her hair, caressed her nape, giving her time to protest should she so desire, because she knew what he was about to do. Eli was going to kiss her. Her heart pounded against her ribcage, threatening to burst free. The man she had dreamed of kissing her so many times was actually going to put his mouth against hers of his own free will. Miracles happened every day.

"This." His mouth covered hers and her miracle happened.

She wasn't sure what she'd expected. Maybe it was completely normal to have fireworks explode inside you when the man of your dreams kissed you for the first time. A whole Fourth of July show was going off inside her body. One humdinger of a show. Wowzers.

His lips brushed against hers, soft, warm, and experimental, yet masterful. "You taste good."

A sound escaped her lips, but she wasn't sure if it was intelligible or not. All her brain power focused on how his mouth touched hers, on how his touch grew hungrier, more and more demanding, on how her hands had found their way into his hair. Soft. So very soft.

But not his body.

His body was rock hard.

And mashed up against hers. Hot and heavy and moving against her in ways that boiled her blood.

He felt amazing.

Better than anything she'd ever imagined and she'd imagined lots.

Her heels not giving her the steadiness she needed to keep from ending up an ooey-gooey puddle on the floor, she leaned into him, aligned her body just so against his. Her arms wrapped around him, touching, committing every sinew to memory, every ripple of his muscles, the texture of his skin, the intense heat radiating from his every pore.

She savored the feel of him, the smell, the taste, the intensity of him. This was Eli.

She was kissing Eli.

Her Eli.

She wanted him so much.

She could barely breathe, could barely hear above the pounding of her pulse, the thundering of her heart that echoed his name over and over.

"You feel good," he whispered into her neck, kissing her there, breathing in her scent and pulling her even closer. "So good I can't believe how good you feel, that I am finally kissing you."

Ha, wasn't that her line? She'd been the one waiting for months and months.

"It's only been a few days since you texted me for the first time," she pointed out between kisses, between his hands running over her body, between her hands stroking over his body.

"Seems a long time to go without touching you."

To prove his point, he tugged her shirt loose from her skirt and cupped her breast through her bra. "I don't mean to go so fast, or to put that pressure on you that I promised I wouldn't, but I need to touch you, Beth. Tell me to stop if that isn't what you want."

She knew all about that need because she felt it too. A deep need that wouldn't abate with just a few light kisses or even the passionate ones that followed. She wanted him, felt as if she'd always wanted him, that every moment of her life had been bringing her to this moment, to him.

Following his lead, her fingers found their way beneath his polo and skimmed across his abs. He sucked in his breath, causing the muscles between her fingers to tighten. Her own muscles contracted, clenching in response to him. That photo had been him. Wow.

"This is crazy. You have me on edge," he said, sounding as if he'd been exercising intensely or was one of their pulmonary patients.

His so-real reaction to her touch empowered her, freed her nervousness to tease him much as she did when they texted, to slide her fingers beneath his waistband. "On the edge of what? Tell me, Eli. I want you to tell me. Better yet, show me."

He shivered and she marveled at how he responded to her touch, to her words. No one had ever reacted to her touch as if it were the most wondrous thing they'd ever felt. Eli did.

In the past, sex had been good. Nothing to shout out to the heavens about, but she'd enjoyed it well enough to understand what all the hoopla was about. Or so she'd thought. She hadn't understood anything, hadn't felt anything, hadn't known this intense craving, this intense pleasure.

Just touching Eli made her want to sing and shout. To Snoopydance around her apartment and squee with delight that her fingers had actually touched his beautiful belly, that she knew the pleasure of his lips against hers.

"Beth, you have me wound so tight. All I've thought about is touching you, of having you touch me. I feel like a schoolboy about to lose his mind at the slightest touch."

"Your mind?" she breathed against his throat, pressing kisses to the beat there, inhaling the musky scent of him.

"Something like that."

"The slightest touch?" Having worked his pants loose, she traced her finger over the hard ridge beneath his cotton briefs.

"Be-eth." Her name came out as two syllables. His abdomen contracted and his hands found her hips, pulled her to him and ground their bodies against each other while he kissed her mouth. Hard. Passionately. Desperately.

Really? Was this happening? her brain questioned. Was she really touching him and him acting as if she were the sex goddess she'd pretended to be during their text conversations?

Did dreams ever really come this true or had she bumped her head and was hallucinating some fantasy world where an ordinary girl got the guy of her dreams?

CHAPTER SEVEN

ELI MUST BE dreaming. He had to be. Beth had him quivering like a schoolboy. Unbelievable. The way fire had leapt through his veins at her kiss, at her touch, was unbelievable. Never had he experienced such heat.

Never had he wanted a woman as much as he wanted this one.

She was so beautiful, so responsive to his every touch, every kiss. Her body clung to his and he couldn't get hers close enough. He wanted inside her, but his brain warned him to take it slow, that he shouldn't rush this, that he hadn't figured out his head, his future, any of those things, and that acting on pure instinct might land him in trouble. His body wanted more, faster, and was obviously in control.

He pushed her skirt up her thighs, bunching the clingy material at her waist as he lifted her onto the kitchen countertop. Not taking his eyes off the glorious vision of her high heels, gorgeous long legs, and sexy little black panties, he finished undoing his pants to where they slid to his ankles from the weight of his pockets.

"You're beautiful."

"You make me feel that way."

"You should always feel that way because you are absolutely breathtaking." His gaze locked with hers because he wanted to watch her pleasure; he pushed her panties aside and slid his fingers inside the warm, moist apex of Beth's body.

Heaven.

She clutched his shoulders and cried out his name.

The look in her eyes, the unrestrained sound of his name on her lips undid him, pushed him beyond reason, not that he hadn't been close to slipping already. Using his fingers and mouth, he brought her to climax, donned a condom, then slipped inside her.

Tight. Hot. Wet. Amazing.

He'd wanted something more, passion, to feel alive.

He'd found it and a lot more.

He'd found a woman who stimulated his brain and his body with her quick wit and her sexual appeal, a woman who freed him to do and feel more. A woman who made him smile.

He really was a lucky man.

Too bad that in all Beth's many fantasies she'd never followed through to what happened after the mind-blowing sex between Eli and her. Perhaps then she'd have some clue as to what she was supposed to say or do at this very moment.

She didn't.

Oh, she could point out that she'd sighed in pleasure and screamed in orgasmic ecstasy. Or that nothing about their coming together had been slow. They'd gone desperately fast and furious.

And lots of other F words.

Thank goodness he'd at least had enough wits about him to put on a condom. She wasn't sure she'd have had the mental capacity to remember one had he not taken care of it. She'd been that lost in emotion.

Then again, he probably had more experience with this kind of thing than she did.

Her forehead rested on his slick-with-sweat shoulder. When had they removed his shirt? Had he done so or her? She vaguely remembered clawing at the material, at wanting to sink her fingers into his shoulders, while he...

She closed her eyes and bit back a sigh.

While he'd taken her to another world.

No way had what she'd just experienced been a mere earthly experience. Oh, no. He'd sent her right into orbit and onto some other plane, some other existence, where pleasure dominated one's every sense.

But now that she'd fallen back to earth and their urgency was spent? Now that reality had set in that this was a man she worked with and she'd just had sex with him on her kitchen countertop without them even having removed their clothes other than his shirt?

They'd never even been out on a date.

She winced, mentally shaking her head at her lack of restraint. Eli's reaction to her slightest movement, to her slightest touch had given her a heady high. She had been on fire. He had been on fire. Together they'd burned her house down. Now came the ashes of their spent lust and she was mortified at how wantonly she'd behaved. She'd not even known she was capable of such complete and total release.

"Did that really just happen?" Eli's question echoed her thoughts exactly.

She nodded without lifting her head from his shoulder. She couldn't bear to look at him just in case he already felt regret. Or what if he'd found her enthusiasm a bit too much? What if he'd found her as lacking as Barry had?

As if sensing her uncertainty, he grabbed her arms and gently pushed her back, forcing her body to separate from his just far enough that he could see her face.

She wanted to close her eyes, but couldn't. The intensity in his gaze wouldn't let her.

"For the record and just so you know, you're my fantasy, Beth Taylor."

Sure she'd just dreamed everything about this evening, she blinked. "Ditto."

"What just happened..." He raked his fingers through his hair then met her eyes with his intense blue ones and grinned. "That's never happened to me, Beth. Not ever."

"Doing it on a kitchen countertop?" she asked, trying to make light of what he was saying, because she was already crazy about the man. She didn't need him giving her other ideas. She didn't need him being so wonderfully sweet in addition to being a genius on the kitchen countertop.

"That," he agreed, although the gleam in his eyes said that he could have had dozens of kitchen countertop endeavors had he so chosen. "But more than that. The having to have you."

"Oh." She wasn't sure what to say, what to admit. More than anything, she didn't want him to think she went around doing this all the time. "Me, too."

"You've never done it on a kitchen countertop before?" He grinned at her. "Must have been beginner's luck, then, because you totally owned it. You're amazing, Beth."

His praise pleased her, made her feel less self-aware of the reality of their situation and more like a heroine in a fairy-tale come true. "I just followed your lead."

"Honey, you weren't following a thing. It was all I could do to keep up with you. You set one helluva pace and refused to let me bring us down a single notch."

She had been a bit frantic with her touches, with her demands of his body. "Sorry if I was too intense. I wanted you. I feel as if we've been in foreplay for days."

"We have." Smiling, he touched her face, cupped her jaw. "Don't apologize. You were amazing. Just right.

Perfect. If you couldn't tell, I wanted you too and wasn't complaining. Quite the opposite. I'm sorry if I was too rough."

With that, he leaned forward and pressed the softest of kisses to her mouth. One that was so gentle that she almost cried from the sheer tenderness.

Her gaze met his and they stared at each other in wonder.

"Do you feel that too?"

She nodded, knowing he meant the instant heat that his kiss had brought, the instant shifting of his body against hers, the instant coming alive within her body.

"Lady, if we're ever going to actually go to dinner, you'd best tell me to stop kissing you. I really didn't mean for us to do this." He grinned then shrugged. "Well, not until after we'd gone to eat, at any rate."

Food schmood. She could eat any time. Being taken to other worlds by the man of her dreams? That might be a once-in-a-lifetime moment. She wouldn't waste a single second of her time with him on mere mortal food when his body offered ambrosia.

"What if I don't want you to stop kissing me?" What if she didn't want him to ever stop kissing her? Scary thought and one that worried her because really how did one ever move on beyond one's dream guy? What if he woke up in the morning and regretted everything? What if he realized he still wanted Dr. Qualls? He'd told her it was complicated, that he had issues he had to work through. Beth fought back a burst of panic, reminded herself of Emily's words. Eli was here, with her. At this moment he wanted her, was smiling at her, was getting turned on again because of her. For now, that was enough.

"I don't want food, Eli. I want you. Over and over."

The blue of his eyes darkened and it appeared as if he was going to say one thing but then changed his mind. His gaze liquid fire, he shifted his body against hers. His amazingly aroused-again body. "Then show me the way to your bedroom so I can properly make love to you this time."

"If what we just did was improper, then forget proper and just make me scream again."

"Scream?"

"In my head I was screaming."

Leaning down and drugging her with a lingering kiss first, he grinned. "No worries. By the time I am through loving that delectable body of yours you're going to have lost your voice from having screamed my name in pleasure so many times. In your head or otherwise."

Hugging his waist with her thighs and digging her heels into his butt, she sighed. "Promises. Promises. You're all talk and no action."

Eyes twinkling, he moved against her. "Let me remind you just how action-packed I am."

Manny Evans had worked in a factory that produced glass for more than twenty years. Despite rules and regulations to prevent such things from happening, years of improper protective equipment had left his lungs a scarred mess capable of only poor oxygen exchange.

Manny had been on the lung transplant list for more than a year and if one didn't come available soon, he would slowly suffocate to death.

Due to his condition, he was a frequent flyer in the ICU. Beth had seen his name on the roster several times, had heard the other nurses talk about how much they adored him, but she had never actually been assigned to his care in the past. No doubt due to her request not to be assigned to Eli's patients.

She hadn't said a word to her nurse manager, but obviously Eli had said something because now she seemed to be making up for lost time with almost exclusively being assigned Eli's patients.

She hadn't seen him yet today, but expected him to stop by the hospital any time to round on Mr. Evans and his other seven ICU admissions. What would she say when she saw him?

Hello, Eli, thank you for the greatest sex of my life?

The truth, but not exactly appropriate conversation for work.

Not that Beth knew what was appropriate conversation for their morning after.

She and Eli had talked. A lot, actually. While lying in her bed after falling back to earth from whatever celestial place he'd lifted her to, they'd talked about all kinds of things.

Like how much he liked it when she raked her fingernails lightly over his back, causing his flesh to goosebump.

Like how he was a bit stunned at his short recovery time between lovemaking sessions. She'd admitted to being a bit stunned and a whole lot impressed by that ability, too. He'd attributed it to her inspiration.

Like how when he kissed her belly her nipples puckered into hard pebbles and strained toward him, wanting his attention too.

Like how much he liked how her body clung to his as they orgasmed together, which they'd done more than once despite the fact Beth had never before experienced that dual sensation.

Like a hundred other things that had seemed so important at the time but in the light of day left her wondering exactly how things stood between them. Were they a couple? Or had she just been a one-night stand?

Or a piece on the side while he waited for Cassidy to realize she'd made a mistake to let him go?

Any woman who let Eli go was making a mistake. A huge one.

Which made her wonder exactly what had happened between him and Cassidy. No one seemed to know or if they did they weren't saying. Beth wasn't asking. Other than Emily and maybe her nurse manager, no one knew something was happening between her and Eli. At least, not that she knew of. Had Eli told anyone? She didn't think so because if he had, someone would have commented, wouldn't they?

If he had, was he using her to make Cassidy jealous the way Barry had used her to make his ex jealous?

She closed her eyes and prayed not. Fate wouldn't be that cruel, would it? Eli hadn't faked wanting her, hadn't faked what they'd done, but that really was just physical.

Not that she wanted more.

Only she did want more.

Much more.

Which was a problem because who knew what Eli wanted?

"Are you new?" Manny asked in his winded way, snapping Beth back to where she was. At work. In a patient room. Checking an intravenous line. She'd been taking care of her patient totally on autopilot without the personal interaction she believed to be so important in a person's recovery and hospital experience. What was wrong with her?

Not that she didn't know. She'd been distracted from the moment she'd gotten that first text message from Eli.

"Fairly new. I've been working at Cravenwood for a few months now and have been a registered nurse for a few years." She gave him her brightest smile. "I've just never been lucky enough to be assigned to take care of you, but no worries, the other nurses warned me what a charmer you are."

They had. Manny was a favorite on the floor.

"You were lost in thought."

"Sorry." She was. She didn't like it that Eli affected her job performance. Even during the worst of times following her break-up with Barry she hadn't let her personal problems intrude during patient care, just her personal life and self-esteem. Her fascination with Eli had influenced her workplace from the moment she'd first seen him and realized he was off limits. Avoiding him had kept her sane. "You have my complete and undivided attention now."

"Manny was just teasing ya." He gave her a crooked grin. "A man?"

She winced. Was she that obvious? "What makes you think that?"

"When a woman looks that lost in thought…" he paused, took a couple of breaths "…it always involves a man." He gave her another mischievous grin. "We're a troublesome breed."

Beth gave him a small, knowing smile. "You said that. Not me."

"I call 'em as I see 'em. Men are nothing but trouble. Only thing worse than a man…" he paused again to catch his breath, waited to finish his sentence until she met his gaze "…is a woman."

Beth laughed. "You're probably right. I bet you were a ladykiller in your day."

"I'm still a ladykiller," he breathily corrected her with a twinkle in his dark eyes.

Smiling, Beth nodded her agreement. "That you are."

"Are you flirting with the nurses again, Manny?" Eli asked, coming into the ICU room and shaking his patient's hand. "I've warned you about that."

"Every chance I get, Doc." Manny held onto Eli's hand much longer than necessary and Beth noticed that Eli didn't pull away, just let the man hold on. Beth's gaze soaked up everything about Eli. The sparkle in his eyes when he glanced at her, the smile on his perfect mouth, the broadness of his shoulders, the thickness of his chest. She'd laid her head against that chest, listened to the beat of his heart while he'd dozed in her bed.

Here he was acting all normal when her insides screamed in recognition of his body, recalling the magic he wrought within her with the stroke of his fingertip. How could he just look so normal when she felt so all to pieces at his nearness?

"How 'bout you, Doc?" their patient continued. "You still chasing that purty blonde doctor or has she finally given up on outrunning ya?"

Beth's insides plummeted. She did not want to hear this conversation. Not today. Not ever.

She punched a button on Manny's IV machine that reset the flow rate, entered the data, and went to the computer to quickly document what she'd done so she could escape. She did all this without looking directly at Eli again, because if she did, no way could she hide all the emotions welling inside her body. Not the good, the bad, or the ugly green ones.

There was still that part of her reminding her that only hours before she'd had this beautiful man's undivided attention and it had been glorious. As in she'd really like to announce to the world that he was hers.

Only he wasn't.

And she couldn't. Because somehow she was involved with Eli in a relationship that no one knew about yet. Did he plan to keep their involvement a secret? If so, what did that say about her? Not that she meant anything to him. Other than a good-time distraction.

Was he just killing time with her until he went back to Cassidy, until he settled down with his ex, just as Barry had done?

"Actually, Dr. Qualls and I aren't seeing each other any more."

Beth's breath caught and she waited. Had she been wrong? Was he going to tell Manny there was a new woman in his life and it just so happened she was in the room?

Silly how much she craved Eli's acknowledgement. She didn't need validation for what they'd done the night before, yet she needed exactly that. She longed to know where his mind was, what his thoughts were about what had happened between them, what it all meant. She needed to know that all the crazy emotions running through her mind and heart this morning hadn't been ill founded.

She needed to know that she shouldn't worry about him going back to his ex-girlfriend, that he really wasn't like Barry.

"But that doesn't mean you get to start chasing her in addition to my nurses. Hands off. She's way too good for the likes of men like me and you." Eli's tone was teasing as he slid his stethoscope from around his neck, completely oblivious that he'd just poked a hole in Beth's balloon of hope.

Was that how Eli saw Cassidy? As being too good for him?

"Ha, who says she'd be running if it was Manny doing the chasing?" the old man teased, having to stop to take a breath twice in between his boastful words.

Eli laughed. "Lord help the female population once you get that lung transplant."

Manny gave another crooked grin. "'Cause they aren't going to be able to resist this devilishly handsome bloke once he gets his wind back."

"Something like that," Eli agreed, shaking his head while he checked his patient. "What do you think, Beth?"

Having just logged off the computer system and preparing to make her escape so she could analyze his comment about Cassidy being too good for him and what that meant exactly, Beth refused to look at Eli but forced a smile onto her face for her patient's benefit. "I think I need to check my other patients before Manny decides to prove just how much chasing he can do now. Bye, boys."

CHAPTER EIGHT

You avoided me at the hospital.

Eli stared at his phone, waiting for a reply, not getting one, hating the sick feeling inside him that Beth wasn't answering him. He sighed.

I'm sorry if I said something wrong today.

Still no response. Obviously he'd said or done something very wrong. He'd racked his brain, playing over every nuance of the night before, of the early morning hours when he'd forced himself from her bed so they could grab a few hours' sleep before their shifts. He hadn't been smooth, that was for sure, but he'd needed her in ways he couldn't explain and sure didn't understand.

His insides had lit up when he'd entered Manny's room and seen her there. He'd wanted to take her into his arms and kiss her until she'd been as breathless as Manny.

But they hadn't really discussed how they'd handle their relationship at work and there were a lot of things they needed to talk about. Like how crazy he was about her.

While he'd been checking Manny, he'd struggled to keep his eyes off her. She was so pretty. So full of life. So exactly what he ached for this very moment.

Which had him feeling out of sorts.
And desperate. And even more confused.

Beth, talk to me.

No.

Well, at least that's something.

I don't feel like talking tonight.

Because of what happened last night?

What happened last night?

Good question and one Eli wasn't sure of the answer to. At least not the full answer. Just as he wasn't sure what had happened today. When he'd left her apartment during the early morning hours, he'd left her with a smile on her sleepy face. Then again, perhaps he'd deserved her silence for discussing Cassidy in Manny's room. As a mutual patient of his and Cassidy's, Manny knew them both and liked to tease them about each other. He'd been doing so for years. Manny had meant no harm. He himself had meant no harm. He'd simply told the man that he and Cassidy were no longer seeing each other. Was that what had upset Beth?

We made love.

He answered her question, thinking perhaps she needed reassurance. Probably only an idiot even mentioned his ex around a woman on the day after they'd had sex for the first time, but he hadn't really been the one to bring up the subject of Cassidy. And, really, he hadn't said anything out of line. At least, he didn't think so.

Had sex, she countered.

Eli took a deep breath.

If that's what you want to call it.

Is that what u want to call it?

He stared at his phone screen, ran his fingers through his hair, and sighed in frustration.

What do you want me to say, Beth?

I'm not sure.

At least she was texting with him now. It was a start. Maybe he'd been in a relationship for so long that he'd forgotten all the insecurities that came at a relationship's beginning.

You're feeling uncertain about what happened between us?

He wasn't surprised by her reply.

I guess so.

As in you regret what happened between us?

Long moments passed before his phone beeped with her answer.

Do u regret what happened between us?

Was she seriously going to answer every question he asked with a question of her own? Eli sighed again, realized that a lot of his frustrations currently came from his own insecurities, the ones that had slammed him when Beth had avoided him at the hospital, when she'd ignored his text messages. When all he'd wanted to do was take her into his arms, he hadn't liked not having any contact with her at all.

No, Beth, I don't regret our making love...

He deleted *making love* and typed *having sex*. She could call it whatever she liked. Whatever it had been wasn't like anything he'd ever experienced before.

But if you're having second thoughts about last night, maybe we shouldn't have moved so fast.

He already knew that. He'd treated her like a one-night stand. Only she wasn't. She was... He wasn't sure, just that he wanted her in his life and not just in a physical way so he shouldn't have started their relationship out that way.

I take the blame for last night, Beth. I promised you I wouldn't push you, but then I kissed you and... There's no excuse other than that I moved too fast.

I'm not sure it could be any other way between us except fast.

She had a point. He hadn't meant his kiss to send them both over the edge. But it had. From the first touch of his mouth against hers he'd been a goner, needing more than he would have imagined possible. How could he have known a kiss meant to set their nerves at ease would instead cause a nuclear reaction?

Are you saying I have no self-control?

Maybe I'm saying where u are concerned I'm the one with a lack of self-control.

For whatever it's worth, I don't regret last night, Beth. Far from it. Last night was amazing. You were amazing. We were amazing.

I agree.

Then you aren't upset with me?

Not that he didn't know she was. Hadn't she disappeared after she'd exited Manny's room? Hadn't she refused to answer any of his text messages up to just a few minutes ago?

Only with myself.

With herself? Eli didn't understand. Not her response or the way he could feel the sadness behind her words, the way he felt as if he'd move heaven and earth if it was within his power to get rid of that sadness.

I don't want you upset with you, with me, or with anyone. I want to make you smile.

You do.

You're sure?

Yes.

Can I see you tonight?

Was asking that pressing his luck? Apparently so, because she shot him down.

Not tonight.

Tomorrow night?

Ask me tomorrow.

Can I call you?

Not tonight.

What can I do?

Text me.

He sighed. He wanted to see her, to touch her, to hold her close. Obviously, she hadn't been as affected by what they'd shared. Maybe he was too tame a guy for as an exciting woman as she was. Maybe he hadn't lived up to her fantasy-guy expectations. Maybe he should have let her tie him to the bed and lick him all over. Or maybe he should have kept his hands to himself and taken her to dinner as planned.

Tell me what happened today in Manny's room.

I'd rather not.

Why?

Because there are some things I prefer not to talk about.

If we are going to have a relationship, we may have to talk about those things.

Are we going to have a relationship?

Eli swiped his fingers through his hair.

I thought we already were.

I like you, Eli. You already know that. I still can't quite get around the idea that you might like me back.

I do like you, Beth. A lot. How could you possibly think otherwise?

Curled beneath a blanket on her sofa, Beth stared at her phone. What was she doing? Eli must think her an emotional mess. She *was* an emotional mess. An emotional mess that needed him.

How could she explain how he made her feel? How Barry had destroyed her self-image? How she was terrified of getting hurt?

She wished she could make her insecurities disappear completely. Then again, she was only human. Female human. He'd been discussing his ex-girlfriend being off limits with another man. Surely that allowed her a little green-eyed leeway?

How could she not be a little green-eyed when Eli hadn't volunteered to tell Manny that, no, he wasn't chasing the beautiful blonde doctor because he was busy chasing short dumpy Beth? When, as far as she knew, he hadn't told anyone? Okay, so apparently he had talked to her nurse manager to have her patient load shifted to include his patients but, really, what was that in the grand scheme of things?

Despite whatever jealousy and uncertainty she'd felt,

his persistence in texting her since the incident soothed something within her. So why hadn't she let him come over? Because she was afraid he'd leave her for Cassidy, the way Barry had left her for his ex? Because hearing Eli discuss Cassidy had brought home her biggest fear and she'd gone into defensive mode?

Beth, talk to me.

He probably thought she'd gone back into silent mode.

I'm sorry, Eli. This is difficult for me.

Talking to me?

You already know that my vocal cords refuse to co-operate when I'm near you, but that's not what I meant.

You didn't have trouble talking to me last night.

No, she hadn't. She'd amazed herself at how vocal she'd been with him, telling him what she wanted, what she liked, how her body felt when he touched her. Never had she felt so free, so completely in sync with someone. So why couldn't she just tell him her fears?

That was different. That was physical. Sharing my emotions is harder.

She realized that sounded as if she devalued what had happened between them and she quickly clarified.

I've only been with two men, Eli. My first was a boyfriend in college. The second was a man I'd planned to marry.

Tell me about him.

Barry?

She so didn't want to tell Eli about Barry. What good could come from telling your fantasy guy that a man who wasn't worthy of shining his shoes had found you lacking?

He's the man you planned to marry?

Yes. I'm not sure what you want me to tell you.

Whatever you want to tell me about him. Tell me why he's no longer in your life so I can be sure not to make the same mistakes he made.

She took a deep breath and went with the bare facts. Literally.

He had sex with his ex-girlfriend in my bed.

Eli stared at his phone. Hell. No wonder Beth had clammed up when he'd talked about Cassidy.

I'd never do that to you, Beth.

I'd never give you the chance to.

Eli frowned, trying to decipher what she meant. That she'd never let a man get that close to her again? That she was some crazy stalker chick who would go psycho on him if he tried to get back with Cassidy? Instinctively, he knew Beth would never hurt anyone, regardless of how that person might have hurt her. Which meant that she'd erected walls to protect her heart.

I can't believe I just told you that.

I'm glad you did.

Why?

It helps me to understand you better.

I'm not sure that's a good thing. I'm a mess.

Just because you had your heart trampled on doesn't make you a mess, Beth. It just means you cared and your Barry was an idiot.

Just thinking about the man, about him having hurt Beth, made Eli want to track the guy down and return the favor but in a more physically painful kind of way.

That's what Emily says, but that I believed in him, that I let him hurt me, makes me feel like I was the idiot.

I'm sorry you hurt, Beth, but I'm not sorry that he's not in your life any more. Actually, I'm grateful for what he did because his mistakes brought you to me, didn't they?

Her moving to Cravenwood had been the direct result of her ex's treachery. Her being single, available to be a part of his life, was a direct result of that treachery. He'd never choose for Beth to hurt, but he could only be grateful that the idiot she'd lived with hadn't been man enough to hold onto her.

Yes. It all happened about a year ago. When Barry got engaged around six months ago, I let Emily convince me to move here. I just needed to get away and start over somewhere I didn't have to constantly see him.

Because she couldn't bear to see the man she loved with someone else? The thought of her caring for another man, anyone other than him, didn't sit well.

Are you still in love with him? Eli asked, not sure if he wanted to know the answer, wondering why the muscles around his ribcage contracted to the point he could barely breathe.

No. I'd never have had sex with you if I was in love with another man. That isn't who I am.

Great answer.

He pulled in a deep breath, slowly blew it out, wondered what was happening to him that he was so caught up in a woman he'd known for such a short time.

The truth. How is it this started about your ex and ended up being about my ex?

I suspect it's because your ex influences how you view my ex.

Probably.

Cassidy is no threat to you.

She's smart, beautiful—perfect, really.

Perfect. He closed his eyes.

I thought so once upon a time.

You said she was too good for you today.

Had that been what had upset Beth?

She is.

Not through my eyes.

Thanks, but she really is a much better person than me all the way around.

Did you end things or did she?

I did.

Why?

How did he explain what he didn't fully understand himself? That although, yes, Cassidy was perfect, she wasn't perfect for him.

I wanted my relationship to work with Cassidy. She's a wonderful woman. My parents adore her, but ultimately I just didn't want the same things she wanted.

Which were?

Marriage. Kids.

You don't want marriage or kids?

Suddenly he couldn't breathe again.

I do want those things, but no matter how much I tried

to see myself growing old with Cassidy, I couldn't envision it.

If someone as amazing as Dr. Qualls couldn't inspire you to envision marriage and kids, perhaps you really aren't looking to settle down yet.

Perhaps not.

He admitted that, although he knew that had Cassidy been the right woman he wouldn't have hesitated to propose.

At least, he didn't think so. Wasn't that what he'd been struggling with on the night he'd first texted Beth? That he couldn't be content with a perfect woman and that there must be something wrong with him? That Cassidy was the best woman he'd ever known and yet she hadn't been enough. What did that say about him?

What are we, Eli?

I'm not sure.

I can't sleep with you if you're going to be seeing other women.

I'm not seeing other women and have no plans to.

Plans change.

If my plans change, I'll tell you.

I'd want you to.

Beth, I won't sleep with another woman while you and I are seeing each other.

He couldn't even fathom wanting another woman. Couldn't fathom not having Beth in his life. Crazy since Cassidy had been in his life years and yet he knew he'd miss Beth in ways he didn't miss Cassidy.

All I can think about is you.

I know the feeling. I wake up thinking about you and go to sleep thinking about you.

And in between?

I'm thinking about you.

I like that.

It scares me.

Scared him, too, because he didn't understand it. Was he going through some kind of mid-life crisis? Some kind of rebound to his break-up with Cassidy?

Don't be afraid of me, Beth.

Don't hurt me.

I'll do my best not to.

He would. Crazy, but he felt protective of Beth, as if he wanted to fight her dragons and be the hero who saved her time and again.

Don't hurt me either.

He wasn't sure where the plea had come from, but it

was a plea, a heartfelt one, which made him wonder why he felt so vulnerable to Beth.

Ha. As if I could.

You might.

How insane he'd felt when she'd shut him out this afternoon gave testimony to the power she already held over him.

I won't. It'll be you who ends our relationship.

You can't know that.

Sure I do. You ended your relationship with Dr. Qualls. I don't fool myself that u won't do the same with me.

You aren't Cassidy.

Exactly. I'm not perfect.

Beth, from my perspective, that's a good thing.

I can't see how.

Because you aren't looking through my eyes.

Then you must be blind.

He smiled.

There goes that sharp wit I adore.

So u say.

Can I see you tomorrow, Beth?

Depends. You working?

I am.

Then you'll no doubt see me.

No doubt I will. Night, Beth. Think about me.

No doubt I will. Night, Eli.

CHAPTER NINE

BETH ASSISTED THE respiratory therapist to fasten a pulmonary vest onto her chronic obstructive pulmonary disease patient who'd been admitted the day before with pneumonia. She adjusted the settings to provide a gentle but effective pounding against the patient's back to break up mucus in his diseased lungs.

No doubt Mr. Gunn would be transferred to the medical floor later that day if his vitals continued to improve as they'd done throughout the night.

No wonder, with Eli as his doctor.

Nope, she so wasn't going to let her mind go to Eli while she was at work. Still, her face flamed as her mind went exactly to Eli. To their texting the night before. She couldn't believe she'd opened up to him, told him about Barry, that she'd essentially admitted to him that she knew he'd eventually hurt her. He'd texted all the right things back, of course. Then again, Barry had always said the right things to her. He'd claimed to love her right up until she'd walked in on him with his ex.

Eli didn't claim love. Surprisingly, their messages hadn't gone physical the night before. She'd expected them, to, really, because wasn't that what their relationship was based on? Sex?

Perhaps, but perhaps there was more. Then again, Dr.

Qualls hadn't inspired him to want more, so why did she think she had a chance of him wanting more with her?

But rather than worry about that, she'd take one day at a time, enjoy that for now Eli wanted her and, regardless, tomorrow would take care of itself. Living one day at a time was all one could really do anyway. One could make all the plans in the world but could only carry out those plans in the actual moment.

"This thing is a torture device, you know?" her patient commented, causing Beth's gaze to lift to his as she adjusted the vest's strap.

"I know," she agreed.

"Figure it's me who should look like I was taking a beating, not you," her breathy patient mused, eyeing her curiously. "But I'd bet money you had a more tortured look on your face than was on mine."

"Probably so. Maybe we don't have your settings high enough," she teased, giving the older man a pointed look then glancing toward the therapist. "What do you think? Should we crank him up a few levels?"

The therapist laughed and nodded her agreement.

With a grin on his wrinkled face their patient nodded his understanding. "I see how it is. You two pretty ladies ganging up on a poor, defenseless man while he's down on his luck."

"I'm sure you do see exactly how it is," Beth agreed, patting his hand in feigned commiseration. "Now, you settle down and do your therapy."

"I'll see you a little later, Mr. Gunn," the therapist promised, waving goodbye to them both and then leaving the room.

After a few minutes during which Beth was on the computer, logging in his vitals and her nurse's note, he sighed. "Not much therapy when I just have to sit here, letting this contraption beat the crap out of me."

"Mucus," she corrected, giving him a teasing wink and signing off the electronic chart. "Mucus is what it's supposed to beat out of you. Not the other."

"I'll keep that in mind," he said, his laughter leading to a coughing spell. When he had difficulty clearing his airways and his oxygen saturation dropped to the low eighties, Beth grabbed a suction kit and aided him with the removal of the mucus, thinking that if his numbers didn't rise significantly, she'd be calling the respiratory therapist back into the room.

She glanced at his oximetry readings and was glad to see his oxygen level had risen to eighty-nine percent. Not great and not where she wanted his numbers to be running, but, unfortunately, not far from his baseline either.

"Hey, Mr. Gunn, Beth," Eli greeted him on entering the room, hoping the pounding of the man's pulmonary vest drowned out the thudding of his heart at seeing Beth.

When her gaze met his and she smiled, full-blown smiled with it reaching her blue-green eyes, everything in him came to a screeching halt, including the thud of his heartbeat.

"Am I glad to see you," she greeted him, and all her body language screamed it was true. "Mr. Gunn here decided to cough up a lung just a bit ago."

Hmm, was her joy at seeing him just professional? No. Her gaze searched his, spoke volumes, told him she really was glad to see him, that perhaps she'd missed him as much the night before as he'd missed her.

"Ain't my fault if this contraption done pulverized my insides." Mr. Gunn went into a coughing spell to emphasize his point.

Eli shot a quick wink at Beth as he moved to Mr. Gunn's side. "I came in here to listen to your lungs, but I can hear the junk still in there and I'm not going to remove the vest since you've just started the treatment. I'll come back by when you've finished and have a listen then." He turned to Beth, who hadn't left Mr. Gunn's side. "Go ahead and give him another round of Solu-Medrol via IV and have the therapist give another nebulizer treatment."

Beth verified the steroid dosage for the intravenous infusion and which inhaled medication Eli wanted given in the nebulizer. He nodded then turned back to his patient while Beth put his orders into the man's electronic medical record.

"We'll have you breathing easier soon," Eli assured his patient.

"I hope so, Doc."

He moved so he could see the computer screen where Beth entered the medication request to be sent to the pharmacy. He was so close he could practically feel her body heat. Whether it was his imagination or reality, her light fresh fragrance filled his nostrils, making him want to inhale deeply, making him want to close his eyes and just remember.

She turned, coming within inches of his body, and glanced up at him. "Excuse me, Dr. Randolph."

Her lips twitched and his entire body throbbed to feel that flutter against his mouth. He wanted her. Pure and simple, he wanted Beth.

His mind filled with the night he'd spent in her arms. In her kitchen. In her bed. It wasn't enough. Not nearly enough. He wanted more.

"Go out with me tonight."

"Dr. Randolph?" Her eyes widened, obviously shocked that he'd asked her in their patient's room.

Yesterday she'd gotten upset that he hadn't acknowledged her role in his life. That wouldn't be the case today.

"You heard me."

She glanced behind him at their patient, who was eyeing them curiously and making no pretense otherwise. "I'm not sure this is an appropriate time for you to be asking me that."

"Sure it is. There's no time like the present, right, Mr. Gunn?"

"Right." The man cackled, obviously enjoying being privy to their conversation. "Would be mighty embarrassing for the doc for you to shoot him down in front of one of his patients."

Eli nodded in commiseration with the man's observation. "Mighty embarrassing. Might be impossible to recover."

Beth rolled her eyes and shook her finger playfully at Mr. Gunn. "You're supposed to be on my side."

"Nah," the man disagreed. "We men have to stick together."

Beth laughed. "I should have known."

"Is that a yes?"

Meeting his gaze, her lips curved upwards and he knew that, despite her scolding, he'd done the right thing. "What do you think?"

"That you are going to text me when you get off work?"

Her smile widened and she nodded.

He watched her leave the room, liking the slight sway of her curvy hips, liking the warmth emanating through him at her smile, at the knowledge that tonight he wouldn't have to text her from his lonely bedroom. Tonight he'd be with Beth and even if all he did was hold her hand, just being with her would be enough. If more than that happened, well, okay, he'd be honest, if they were alone together, more than that would likely happen. His body went a little crazy around Beth.

But it was a good crazy.

"What a woman," he told the older man lying in the hospital bed.

"I thought you were dating some fancy doctor."

"I used to."

"Not any more?"

"Obviously not."

"That one there reminds me of my Lucy. A real fire-cracker. Not that she knows it. But some lucky man is going to light her fuse and get to see one heck of a show."

"Sounds scary."

The older man gave a so-what look. "Relationships aren't for the faint of heart."

Eli laughed and patted the man's vest-covered shoulder. "Isn't that the truth?"

"I'm sorry we couldn't leave earlier," Beth apologized two weeks later for what had to be the twentieth time since they'd climbed into Eli's car. Despite having worked all day, excitement flowed through her veins at their plans.

Eli glanced toward her, the glow of the luxury car's instrument panel lighting up his handsome face. "Not a problem. I knew we'd have to wait to leave until you got off your shift."

"I seriously wouldn't have minded if you'd just picked me up from the hospital so we could have left directly from there." She'd wondered why he hadn't since it would have saved them about thirty minutes.

"Your car would have sat at the hospital all weekend if I had. We're not in that much of a rush."

Had he worried about people gossiping? Or was it more about Cassidy possibly hearing that he'd gone out of town with her?

Since she'd opened up to Eli about Barry, Beth had forced thoughts of the doctor from her mind, had carried on at the hospital as if nothing was different when she worked next to the woman, had pretended that she wasn't worried that dating her wasn't going to make Eli realize that he'd had the perfect woman for him already. She'd mostly succeeded. She wouldn't start failing now. Not at the beginning of their weekend away together.

A weekend away with Eli. Wasn't that what she'd sort of requested on the first night they'd texted? Wow, but that seemed so long ago. Trying to recall a time when her world hadn't revolved around Eli seemed impossible.

"Speak for yourself," she replied to his comment about them not being in a rush.

He glanced her way again and laughed. "I hope you're not disappointed. It's just a small cabin in Gatlinburg."

Didn't he realize a weekend away with him was a fantasy come true? That he was what she was excited most about? But she was excited about their trip, too.

"I've not been to Gatlinburg since I was a small girl and my family went there. It was one of the few vacations we went on." It was a good three hours away from home, but he'd asked her to go away with him for the weekend and she sure wasn't going to say no.

"Tell me about your family," he encouraged, pulling onto I-40 to head east toward the Smoky Mountains.

Beth did. She told him about her brothers, her parents, about family get-togethers, and the pranks they pulled on each other. She told him about different childhood memories, high-school memories, about meeting Emily in her freshman year of college and how they'd become fast friends. She even told him a little more about her relationship with Barry. The abbreviated version, of course, but she told him. Amazing what one could reveal during a three-hour-plus car drive.

"So this guy you lived with, the one who cheated on you, he's engaged to be married now?"

Beth nodded then realized his eyes were on the road as they zoomed through the late-night Knoxville traffic, which consisted mostly of eighteen-wheeler trucks, and then said, "For all I know, they're already married. I haven't kept up with him since I moved to Cravenwood. What about you? Any serious relationships prior to Dr. Qualls?"

"A few that stand out from high school and undergraduate, but none that lasted more than a year until Cassidy."

Cassidy. Beth's insides pinched involuntarily. They hadn't discussed his ex nearly as much as they had hers. She didn't want to talk about Cassidy, yet she did. Part of her needed to know how he felt about the beautiful doctor, what about her had made him believe they didn't have a future together? She sucked in a deep breath and went for it. "How did you meet her?"

"Mutual friends during medical school," he answered, sounding casual, as if her question, his answer were no big deal. "We kept being at the same social functions, the same study groups, and frequently we'd be the odd man and woman out. I suppose it's natural that we migrated toward each other."

She digested that. "So it wasn't love at first sight?"

He laughed. "Not by any stretch of the imagination. More mutual admiration and respect for each other. Everyone kept telling us we were perfect for each other and meant to be together and then we just were."

"She's very beautiful." Why she pushed she wasn't sure, maybe just to see his reaction to talking about Cassidy. Regardless, she didn't want to fight with him, not on their weekend away together, so if he didn't respond, she'd just let the topic go.

"Yes, she is a beautiful woman, and so are you. I'm a lucky man."

"Thank you," Beth told him, staring out the front windshield with her hands in her lap. She wasn't quite sure what to say beyond that. She didn't want to be jealous, didn't want to think about his ex-girlfriend, yet the woman popped into her mind way too often. As a defense mechanism or because of some real sense of impending doom?

"She and I aren't going to get back together, Beth."

Had he read her mind?

"After you telling me about your ex, I understand why you would be cautious, but you have nothing to worry about on that score. Cassidy is my friend now. Nothing more."

"Okay," she answered, because, really, what else could she say? She hoped he was right. "I'm sorry. I really don't have a right to ask you about her."

He glanced toward her, frowned. "Surely you don't believe that?"

She bit her lower lip.

"Beth, we've been having sex for the past two weeks. We're going away for the weekend. You have a right to ask me about things that concern you. I expect you to. I want you to."

She reached across the car console and touched his thigh. Not a sexual touch, just one of comfort and care, although that tingle of awareness was always there. "Thank you."

"For?"

"Being in my life."

He placed his hand over hers, gave her a reassuring squeeze, then lifted her hand to his lips, and kissed her fingers. "No, Beth, thank you for being in mine. Like I said, I'm a lucky guy."

The cabin turned out to be even better than it had looked online when Eli had reserved it. He'd paid more since it had been a last-minute reservation and they were in the middle of fall leaf season, but the look on Beth's face had been well worth the expense.

A weekend alone with Beth when he could fall asleep

next to her, wake up next to her, and spend two whole days with her without worrying about anything beyond the two of them. He couldn't think of anywhere else in the world he'd rather be.

"Eli, this is marvelous!" She spun around in the rustic living room that was open to the kitchen and dining area. Bear carvings and photos were scattered around the room and there was even a fake bearskin rug on the floor.

Visions of Beth, naked and arching into his touch while laid out on that rug, filled his mind. Instantly, his pants tightened.

He wanted her. He always wanted her. Couldn't look at her without getting turned on. He at least needed to unpack the groceries they'd stopped and bought in Sevierville prior to stripping Beth naked. Maybe, just maybe, he could hold out that long. Maybe.

When he didn't respond to her comment, her gaze followed his and she grinned. "I know what you're thinking, Eli Randolph."

"And I should be ashamed of my dirty thoughts?" he asked, moving to her and taking her in his arms, looking down into her smiling face and thinking he really was the luckiest guy in the world.

Especially when she shook her head.

"Nope." Her smile served as a flame, lighting fires all along his nerve endings. "I like what you're thinking. It's what I'm thinking too."

"You are?" He swallowed the lump forming in his throat and decided the groceries could wait. The night air was just brisk enough they wouldn't quickly ruin.

Beth nodded, rubbing her body against his, hardening him to epic proportions. "I can't wait to see the bedroom. You think there's a fireplace in there, too?"

"Let's go find out." With that he scooped her into his arms and carried her through the small cabin toward what he hoped was the bedroom, because either way it was the room where he was going to strip off Beth's clothes and kiss her all over.

Waking in Eli's arms was a new experience for Beth. Sure, he spent most every night in her bed for the past two weeks, but he'd always left before dawn. Today they had nowhere they had to be other than with each other. It was a marvelous sensation to wake up, realize he was next to her, his arm draped over her body possessively. She liked it.

So much so she hated to let on that she was awake because it would mean leaving the warm comfort of their bed. Slowly, she lifted her eyelids to welcome the day and soak in the vision of Eli next to her.

"Good morning, beautiful."

Beautiful wasn't the right adjective to describe her first thing in the morning, but Eli looked at her as if she really was beautiful so she didn't argue. Instead, she glowed on the inside over his words, the same words he'd texted her every morning the past two weeks. He might not have been there when she had woken up, but he had texting her first thing down to an exact science.

Apparently, he'd been awake for some time and had been watching her sleep. Great. She hoped she hadn't snored, snorted, or made some other more embarrassing body noise.

"You should have woken me."

He shook his head. "No way. I've been enjoying the view."

She rolled her eyes. "If you had woken me we could have been outside, enjoying the view for real."

"The view will still be there when we do finally make it outdoors and nothing out there could ever compete with you."

Warmth spread through Beth. "You sound like it might be a while before we make it outdoors."

He reached out, touched her face, stroking his fingers over her cheeks and starting fires all through her body at his gentle touch. "Just a guess."

She turned to where her lips brushed his fingertips and she kissed them. "I'd say more of an educated assumption."

"I try not to make assumptions where beautiful women in my bed are concerned."

"Have that problem often?"

He shook his head. "Not as often as you might think."

"I'm glad. I want to be the only woman in your bed."

"You are the only woman in my bed."

She didn't clarify that she meant forever. To do that would mean actually acknowledging that fact herself and she wasn't ready to do that. Besides, he probably already knew. After all, he was her fantasy guy.

Much later, they cooked breakfast together, laughing, talking, playing, and touching frequently while they moved about the kitchen.

When they'd eaten the scrumptious omelets, Eli helped clear their dishes, a bit amazed at how in sync they were, at how efficiently they worked together. Then again, he should have known. Weren't their bodies amazing together? Why should he have expected this to be any different?

"What would you like to do today?"

"Just so long as I'm with you, I'm good." The smile on her face said it was true. Just being with him made her happy. Which made him happy. Because just being with her made him happy, too.

He didn't feel the need to entertain her, to make sure she wasn't bored. Just being together was enough. He liked that a lot.

Her smile was contagious and spread to his face.

"That's way too easy," he mused.

She wrapped her arms around his neck and smiled up at him. "That doesn't make it any less true."

He agreed. Lots of things felt easy with Beth. Being himself, not feeling any pressure to be more than who he was, just going with the moment and feeling. He wrapped his arms around her waist, smiled down into her lovely face, thinking he'd have to make it a priority to kiss each and every one of the light freckles that dotted her nose. Never had he felt so giddy on the inside. Or so absolutely turned on by a woman.

"I'm crazy about you, Beth. I hope you know that."

He wouldn't have thought it possible, but her smile broadened. "Thank you, Eli. I hope you know that I'm crazy about you, too."

"Uh-oh."

"What?" she asked, her eyes filling with feigned concern because she could obviously feel exactly what his problem was.

"I just realized something."

"What?" She moved against him, her body brushing against what he'd realized.

"I no longer want to go anywhere except back to bed."

Her lips twitched. "That's odd. That's exactly where I was hoping to go first." She stood on tiptoe and pressed a light kiss to his lips. "And second." Another kiss. "And third…"

Eventually they left the cabin. Eli drove them out of their mountain alcove to downtown Gatlinburg. They parked the car in a paid parking lot so they could walk along the quaint shops. They went through several gift shops.

"Have you been in the aquarium?" he asked when they

stood outside the large building, trying to decide what to do next.

"No, we never made it here when I came with my family." She gave him a puppy dog eye look. "I always wanted to go."

"Come on." He tugged on her hand and, laughing, they headed up the winding deckway to the entrance, where he bought tickets.

They went through the aquarium, marveled over the shark tank they traveled under on a conveyor belt, and then petted sting rays.

When they finished, hand in hand they resumed their walk along the strip, stopping to peer in one shop or another and occasionally going inside. Currently, they stood inside a candy shop, watching taffy be made.

"I remember watching this when I came here with my family," Beth mused, her eyes glued in fascination at the machine pulling the taffy. "My parents bought us a box and my brothers ate almost all of it before we'd even made it back to the car. They'd make silly faces with the taffy stuck to their teeth."

Unwrapping a sample piece of taffy, Eli's eyes were glued on her, in just as much fascination, he was sure. Her eyes were joy lit and her smile was genuine.

So was his. He couldn't recall feeling as at peace as he did when he was with Beth. Which was crazy because he was also in a constant state of need when he was around her, which wasn't peaceful in the slightest.

"What?" she asked, catching him staring.

"Nothing," he told her, leaning forward and kissing the tip of her nose. "Just you."

"What about me?"

"Everything, Beth. Everything about you." He popped the candy into his mouth.

"Is that a good thing?"

Taffy stuck between and on his teeth, he grinned. "Oh, yeah."

Laughing out loud, she smiled back at him. Pink taffy clung to her teeth. Her eyes twinkled. "O?"

"Woman, you are insatiable," he accused, linking his hand with hers and attempting to clean the candy from his teeth with his tongue.

"Only where you're concerned," she admitted.

"Good answer."

"Honest answer," she said, squeezing his hand. "I've never felt the way you make me feel, Eli."

His heart swelled. "I know just what you mean. I feel the same." He lifted her hand to his mouth, kissed her then tugged her toward him. "Come on. Let's go find something to eat then we'll go back to the cabin."

"And you accuse me of being insatiable."

Beth stared at herself in the bathroom mirror. She wasn't sure the red lace outfit she wore exactly fitted with the rustic décor of the cabin, but it's what she'd packed. She and Emily had gone for another shopping trip this week after Eli had asked her to go away for the weekend and Beth had had one specific goal in mind. To find the red outfit and heels she'd described to Eli during one of their first texting sessions. She'd known immediately when she'd seen the lacy get-up that she'd be buying it.

So why was she standing in front of the mirror, freshly showered, shaved, moisturized and ready to go find her man, yet procrastinating?

Last night, this morning, all day had been wonderful. No doubt tonight would be wonderful, too. Tomorrow they'd wake up together, cook breakfast together again, pack up their belongings, do the touristy thing— he'd promised to take her to one of the photo booths and take a cowboy/saloon-girl shot with her—then drive home. Then what?

Then what did she want to be then what? She didn't even know.

She shouldn't feel as if her very being was tied up in Eli. Yet she did.

She wouldn't think about what that meant, wouldn't label the emotions she felt for him. Instead, she'd go into the other room and surprise him with her outfit. Then she'd show him everything in her heart, even if she wasn't ready to say the words out loud.

Eli aimed the remote control at the flat screen and flipped through the channels until he found a recap of the day's football games. He enjoyed sports, but couldn't focus on the numbers and plays flashing across the screen.

All he could think about was the woman in the cabin with him. They'd had a great day. A wonderful day that would always stand out as special in his mind.

Everything about her felt right. Her smile, the way she looked at him, the way she kissed him, the way her hand fitted so perfectly with his, the way she made him laugh.

He wanted this when they got back to Cravenwood.

Although he certainly hadn't been trying to keep his developing relationship with Beth a secret, he hadn't advertised it either, and he knew why.

He didn't want Cassidy hurt that he'd so quickly moved into another relationship. He hadn't intended to find someone else so quickly, hadn't even been looking when he'd accidentally texted Beth, but now that he'd found her, he wasn't going to let go. He wanted her with him all the time, and for the first time ever was considering asking a woman to move in with him. His mother would hate the idea, would not be receptive to anyone who wasn't Cassidy, but with time she'd come to the same conclusions he had.

Maybe he'd take Beth to meet his parents the next time they were both off work together and after that, he'd see about asking her to move in with him. Not just to have her in his bed every night but for the waking time he was home, too. He enjoyed her company, enjoyed her sharp wit and fast comebacks, enjoyed how she stimulated his mind as much as she did his body.

Speaking of stimulation, where was she?

"Hey, baby, hurry up and maybe we can get another game of checkers in. Maybe I'll let you win again," he called, getting antsy that he'd been away from her for so long when he knew she was so close.

"I'm game if you are," came her voice from right behind him, "but we both know you didn't let me win, Old Man. I won fair and square. All three games."

Startled that she was behind him, Eli turned. His jaw dropped. He whistled. "Wow."

Striking a pose that was meant to be silly but had his pulse quickening, Beth smiled.

"I've died and gone to heaven."

"Not yet." She batted her eyelashes in mock innocence, just about doing him in. "But you might think so in about twenty minutes."

Eli stood from the recliner, soaked in the lovely vision of her, letting his gaze travel from the upsweep of her hair, several damp tendrils hanging loose, the desire in her made-up eyes, the soft pout to her full lips, the smooth curve of her neck and shoulders, the fullness of her breasts beneath the red lace, the narrowing of her waist and flare of her rounded hips, her shapely legs that looked long in her red stilettos.

He'd never seen her in shoes like these, in anything other than sensible tennis shoes, actually. He whistled again.

"Have I ever mentioned to you that I have a foot fetish?"

She glanced down at her feet, lifting one high heel off the floor as if examining it, then met his gaze. "Really? A foot fetish? Who knew?"

He clicked off the television, dropped the remote, and reached for her. "It's a rather new thing for me but powerful. I think I should show you."

"Actually, I planned to show you."

Eli arched his brow. "Show me?"

She nodded and twirled something he had just noticed in her hand. "Take off your clothes."

Not quite sure where she was going with this but having a pretty good idea, he pulled his shirt over his head, tossed it onto the floor and put himself into Beth's hands, figuratively and literally.

CHAPTER TEN

"HEY, ELI. YOU have a sec?"

"Sure thing." Eli stopped on his way to the ICU and waited for Andrew to catch up with him. A few more minutes before seeing Beth wasn't going to kill him. Maybe. He'd not seen her since he'd dropped her off at her house the night before. It had been late and as much as he hadn't wanted to leave, he'd gone home so they could both get some rest before starting their work week. Every second without her seemed like an eternity. Crazy to think that just a few weeks ago he hadn't known her.

"You headed to ICU?"

Eli nodded. As fast as he could get there. A beautiful brunette he was crazy about was there and he needed to reassure himself that she was real.

"Me, too." Andrew fell into step with him. "So, how's it going?"

Eli wondered if his colleague realized how weird his voice sounded. How weird his question was.

"It's good," he answered, guessing the real reason for Andrew wanting a minute with him. "You?"

"Good." Andrew punched a code into the locked double door that separated the office complex from the private breezeway that led into the hospital. "I took Cassidy out this weekend."

This was good. Very good. "Oh?"

"That okay with you?"

"More than okay. I think it's great," he answered honestly. He wanted Cassidy to be happy, to find someone who could appreciate her the way he appreciated Beth, although he couldn't imagine any man appreciating another woman that much. "She's a wonderful person."

Andrew's expression was pensive. "You haven't changed your mind about getting back together with her, then?"

Eli frowned at his colleague. "Definitely not. We're friends, nothing more."

But rather than look relieved, Andrew sighed. "Guess that rules out that theory."

"What theory is that?"

"She told me that we could only be friends so I figured maybe you were reconsidering."

"We've not discussed how she feels about dating right now so I'm not sure where her head is on that subject. Maybe she just wants to go slow." He hoped that was it, because Andrew was a nice guy who seemed to really care for his friend.

Andrew shrugged. "Maybe. Or maybe she is really in love with you and thinks with time she'll win you back. Knowing her, she will."

Cassidy didn't want him back. Since she'd sexted him, she'd also admitted that perhaps he was right that they'd fallen into their relationship and needed to explore options. She'd asked him what it was that had made him realize she wasn't the perfect woman for him. He hadn't been able to come up with a good answer because he didn't know why he hadn't been able to fall for the perfect woman. Why hadn't he been able to commit to a woman who complemented his life so well?

And what about Beth? He was planning to ask her to move in with him, but if he hadn't been able to commit to Cassidy, what made him think he'd be able to commit to Beth?

"That what you think is going to happen?" Andrew prompted, when Eli became lost in his own thoughts rather than responding.

"I'm sorry that things didn't work out between the two of you," he began, because he really was.

"Me, too, but I'm not going to chase a woman who's in love with another man." Andrew stopped in the hallway, just shy of the ICU nurses' station. "I'm not sure what happened between the two of you, but I just thought you should know that she's still in love with you, because you'd be a fool not to go back to her."

Eli grimaced. Cassidy wasn't any more in love with him than he'd been in love with her. Yes, they did love each other, but not that way. That had been the problem. They hadn't been in love with each other. They hadn't pushed each other's emotions to the limits, not like he and Beth did. Whereas Cassidy had been calm and secure, life had made Beth a flight risk and insecure. And being with her made him question everything he'd once thought he'd wanted. What he and Beth shared was the best relationship he'd ever been in. Also the scariest.

Suddenly she was right in front of him and his heart thudded to a thunderous beat.

She stared directly into his eyes, but the happiness that had shined in their depths had faded to cloudy and unsure and he knew exactly why.

Wishing she hadn't spotted Eli, hadn't been so excited to see him that she'd immediately headed his way just to say hi, Beth choked back the emotion welling within her. She was not going to overreact as she had the day in Manny's room. Things were good between her and Eli, had been since that day, had been wonderful this past weekend. In many ways her relationship with Eli was perfect.

Except *she* wasn't perfect.

Except she'd just overheard his cardiologist friend advising him to go back to his ex, who was perfect.

And he wasn't saying no. How was she supposed to feel about that?

Beth's stomach churned, threatening to upchuck the grilled chicken salad she'd scarfed down at lunch.

"Hi, Beth," Eli acknowledged her, his eyes begging her not to react to what she'd heard, which stabbed a very vulnerable spot inside her chest.

"How are my patients today?" he continued, as if Beth hadn't heard what Dr. Morgan had just said. Did he think her deaf? Or just dumb?

Why wasn't he telling his friend that he didn't want to go back to Cassidy? That he was happy with his new girlfriend? Why wasn't he taking her into his arms and reassuring her that history was not going to repeat itself?

Sure, they weren't advertising that they were seeing each other outside the hospital, but perhaps more people were catching on to something going on between them than she'd thought because a couple of the other nurses had commented on her seeing more than her fair share of Eli's patients since he'd become single. Another had commented on how she must have had one heck of a weekend because she practically glowed this morning.

She wasn't glowing now. She was trying to not want to strangle him for refusing to acknowledge that she had a place in his life, outside the hospital. Why wasn't he? For that matter, why hadn't she let on to anyone at the hospital that she and Eli were an item? Was she afraid of jinxing their relationship by telling someone? Or was she trying to save face for if/when he realized Cassidy was the woman for him and he went back to her?

"Sorry, Dr. Randolph." She emphasized his formal name. "I didn't mean to interrupt you and Dr. Morgan."

"Not a problem. Andrew and I were finished, I believe?" He looked at the other man for confirmation then back at Beth. She could see the concern in his eyes, knew he knew she wasn't happy. Surely he didn't have to question what about.

"Oh, yeah, sure thing," Dr. Morgan told him, not even looking at Beth but focusing on Eli. "Good luck and I hope you realize what a lucky man you are to have Cassidy waiting in the wings when you get your act together."

To give him credit, Eli winced.

Beth hoped she hadn't, but suspected that if all she had done was wince she'd consider trying out for Emily's next theatrical production. In reality, she felt as if the cardiologist had delivered a blow to her chest.

Was that what Eli was doing?

What would she do if Eli left her? Losing Barry to his ex had hurt and she'd never felt about him the way she felt about Eli. How would she recover from such a loss?

"Excuse me," she managed despite the spasms rocking her chest, despite the moisture stinging her eyes. Without another glance, she left the two men near the nurses' station. She went into a patient room, grateful her patient was asleep, and checked telemetry. Anything to be doing something with her shaky hands.

Could she recover if Eli left her? Sure, she'd go through life's motions, but would her heart ever be whole again?

"Beth?"

She turned, gave him a weak smile. "Hi."

"Hi," he said back, looking relieved and a bit cautious.

What had he expected? For her to spear him with an IV pole? "I'm sorry you had to hear that."

"Because it's true?" she asked, amazed at how calm her voice sounded when her insides shook.

"Cassidy isn't waiting for me. She and I are finished as more than friends. I've told you that."

He had told her. Several times. Granted, she had heard that before, but she couldn't judge Eli by Barry's sins. Yet history did have a tendency to repeat itself. She fought to keep walls from going up, but she felt so vulnerable that doing so was difficult.

"Why didn't it work with Cassidy? She seems so perfect. What if you realize that someday?"

He shrugged. "I don't know and Cassidy is as close to perfect as they come. I already know that and I don't want her. I want you." He glanced toward the sleeping patient, ran his fingers through his hair. "This is a conversation we should save for later, don't you think?"

He was right, of course. They were at work.

"That's fine."

"Which is what my mother used to always say to my father when he'd upset her and she refused to talk about it, but would make him pay dearly for it later."

She lifted her gaze to his, her breath catching as it always did when she looked at him, amazed that even for a brief period of time he wanted her.

"I'm not refusing to talk," she clarified. "I do think we need to talk about this."

Studying her, he nodded. "You're right. Good. We'll talk tonight."

"As for the other, I've never made you pay for anything. I've given you all I have to give and not asked for anything in return."

Eli's face contorted with confusion. "What is that supposed to mean?"

She glanced at their patient, who was still breathing evenly via the oxygen nasal cannula. "Like you said, we'll talk later."

Punching in her code to get into the medicine cart, Beth tried not to stare at the ethereal beauty of the blonde woman chatting with a resident a few yards away from the nurses' station. Cassidy smiled, touched her upswept hair, and pointed out something on the computer tablet the resident was showing her.

Was she waiting for Eli? It made sense. That they'd been together for so long, that he'd want one last wild ride prior to settling down for the rest of his life. It's what men did, right?

Emily waved her hand in front of Beth's face. "Hello. Anybody home in there?"

Absently, Beth nodded. Emily didn't routinely work in the ICU, but her friend was picking up an extra shift to cover for Leah, who was missing more work than attending these days.

"Um, am I imagining things or are you not smiling any more? Is everything okay with Dr. Do Me All Night? Or should I say Dr. Do You All Night?" Emily teased, nudging Beth's arm to try to get her to smile. When Beth didn't, Emily moved in front of her, blocking her view of Eli's ex. "Okay, tell me what's up before you stare a hole in Dr. Qualls's head. This morning you were walking on clouds, telling me you'd had the best weekend of your life, showing me goofy pictures of you and Dr. Wild Wild West, now you look on the verge of crying…or murdering someone."

"She wants him back," Beth mused, imagining the scenario. Maybe when they talked tonight he'd tell her as much, that ultimately he'd go back to Cassidy, that she,

Beth, was good enough for a weekend romp but long term he'd chose to go back to the good doctor.

"So what? What sane woman wouldn't want him back?" Emily countered, as if Beth hadn't just told her something earth-shattering. Any moment Beth expected her to fake a yawn.

Eyes suddenly stinging, Beth felt rising panic in her throat, panic she couldn't control. "He thinks she's perfect and he's going to go back to her."

Emily frowned. "Has he told you that? After spending all weekend with you, he told you that he thinks she's perfect and he's going to go back to her? When? This morning?"

"He did say she was perfect, but he hasn't said he was going to go back to her. But I know he's going to."

Pinching the bridge of her nose, Emily shook her head. "Why would he do that when you two are getting along so fabulously? And why did he tell you she was perfect?"

Beth gestured in the direction where Cassidy stood with the resident. "I'm not her and I said she was perfect and he agreed with me."

Emily shook her head. "Thank goodness, and why would you say she was perfect? Obviously she isn't perfect for Eli."

Confused, Beth blinked at her friend.

"She had her chance and things didn't work out. You're the woman in his life now. Be grateful and quit looking for problems that aren't there. You are in his life and I'm grateful for that. I want you happy and have been worried that it's taken you so long to date someone else."

"Eli and I aren't really dating. We have sex together, but that's it. You know that." Beth closed the medicine cart and electronically signed off that she'd removed her patient's next medication dosage.

"You went away with him for the weekend, you have

sex with him, call it what you will, but you are dating the man." Emily logged into the computerized medication cart and removed the medication for her patient as well. She closed the drawer, electronically signed that she had removed the medication, then gave Beth a thoughtful look. "You're happier than I've ever known you to be and at the same time you're scared to believe in that happiness because you don't have any real faith in his feelings for you. What does Eli say when you ask him to define your relationship?"

"He doesn't say anything because I don't ask him."

Emily rolled her eyes. "Beth, you have told the man your every fantasy. You've experienced quite a few of those fantasies with him. You just spend the entire weekend with him. Surely you can ask him to define the terms of your relationship."

"But…"

But she didn't feel as if she could. Which was ridiculous.

Emily was right. If she could get naked with the man, she should be able to carry on a conversation with him.

Actually, she could. After they'd had sex they'd had brilliant conversations. This weekend they'd had brilliant conversations about so many things.

About everything but what was happening between them.

Well, that wasn't exactly true. They did talk about sex.

About how in tune their bodies were. About how each time they were together they brought the other higher and higher. Physically they seemed to be able to discuss anything, their wants, desires, needs, what pleased them most. How they talked to each other, how comfortable she felt telling him where she wanted to be touched and how amazed Beth, but when she was with him she felt completely in sync with him, completely comfortable. Unless she let her brain start working.

Once that pesky organ kicked in, she questioned her bliss.

After all, if Eli had any real intentions toward her, even of dating her, he'd have taken her to dinner rather than feeding her at her house each night. He'd have wanted the world to know that they were dating, that she was no longer available, because, hello, with the way it was that guy from Administration had still been asking her out even. She had gently told him no, not interested, but if people actually knew she and Eli were an item she wouldn't have had to do anything. Every man would have known they didn't stand a chance when compared to Eli. Dr. Morgan wouldn't have been telling Eli to go back to his ex in front of her.

But, for whatever reason, Eli was content with the status quo.

Pure and simple, he wanted sex from her. No strings attached.

She wanted sex from him, too. Had initially believed that anything with Eli was so much more than she'd ever believed even a possibility and she'd be content with whatever he'd give her.

Only she wasn't. She wanted more. Was that why she hadn't made a big deal of their relationship at work? Because she wanted more, knew ultimately he didn't, and as long as no one else knew, she wouldn't have to see their pitying looks when things ended? There was only one way she could think of to protect herself.

"Uh-oh. I'm not liking that expression."

Beth took a deep breath and gave her best friend a tight smile. "I can't see Eli any more."

Emily's eyes widened, but her friend only waited for her to say more.

"But I may not be able to not see him."

"What's that supposed to mean? If seeing Cassidy is what triggered this current line of thought, you're being ridiculous. This is your Barry hang-ups coming to surface. Eli is not Barry. You need to talk to him, tell him how you feel."

Yes, she supposed she did. That she would. Tonight. When they talked.

Eli pulled off his scrub mask and cap, left the operating room, and headed straight for the ICU.

He'd been tied up in the OR all afternoon, doing bronchoscopies, and he'd not seen Beth since she'd overheard Andrew talking about Cassidy and their exchange in the sleeping patient's room. He was finished with work for the day but wanted to see Beth before leaving the hospital. He'd do so under the guise of checking on a patient but, really, he just needed to see her. There had been a worrisome light in her eyes that concerned him, made him wonder what was going on in that sharp brain of hers.

He hadn't known quite what to expect when he'd seen her standing there, watched her expression transform from one of happiness to uncertainty. He'd watched her walls go up, had felt himself being shut out.

They did need to talk. Tonight.

He needed to explain about Cassidy. Only how did he explain what he didn't really understand himself? Everything with Cassidy had been so easy and that hadn't worked. Everything with Beth felt so out of control, so intense. What was it about easy that hadn't worked for him that he'd choose this craziness of needing Beth so much?

He paused, took a deep breath. Quite frankly, his choices didn't make logical sense.

"Code Blue, Room 312," he heard someone call down the ICU hallway, then realized it was Beth.

He was almost there, but took off at a jog as Beth rushed a crash cart into the patient room. Just as he entered the room, another nurse followed him inside to record the code.

He paused only a millisecond when he saw who else was in the room. Cassidy leaned over the bed, compressing the patient's chest.

Beth opened the crash cart, gave an injection of epinephrine at Cassidy's order, then prepared the defibrillator.

"Here, let me." Eli took over for Cassidy on the compressions, because he well knew how exhausting doing CPR on a person was. Until one had actually performed the procedure it was difficult to comprehend just how much effort was required. "You do the air bag."

"Thank God, it's you!" Cassidy exclaimed, stepping up to the head of the bed and squeezing the air bag to deliver another breath to the flatlined patient. Eli recognized the older lady as one he'd seen a couple of times after she'd been transferred to a local nursing facility and Cassidy had requested he consult on her care.

Eli shot her a reassuring look and focused on compressing the woman's chest while Beth put on the defibrillator pads. Beth hadn't acknowledged his presence in the room at all, had just stayed safely tucked behind those walls she'd erected earlier.

"Ready?" he asked her, not liking being completely ignored regardless of the situation.

Not looking his way, Beth nodded and called, "All clear."

Eli and Cassidy stepped back from the patient and Beth pressed the button that would deliver the jolt of electricity to the patient's heart. Nothing. No heartbeat. No gasp of breath.

Eli started compressions again while the defibrillator reset itself.

Cassidy gave a squeeze to deliver air. "We have to save her, Eli. She's such a sweet little lady."

"I know." He gave her a look of commiseration. Cassidy always took losing a patient hard, always felt that she was somehow responsible, when, regardless of anything any medical professional did, eventually nature was always going to take its course.

Her compassion for her patients was one of the things that made Cassidy such a good doctor but was also one of the reasons why she stressed so much and gave so much of herself to medicine. Maybe that's why they'd never had any sparks. Because Cassidy's real passion was medicine and he'd only been in her life because he fit so well into that.

Staying in rhythm with his compressions, he shot a glance her way, admired the doctor she was, the woman she was, and understood how he'd been in a relationship with her for so long, understood how he'd wanted his relationship with her to be more than it had been.

But he also knew he'd never settle for what they'd had. Not ever again.

Beth focused on what she did, on getting the defibrillator reset to deliver another shock to their patient, but she wasn't blind. Or deaf. She'd have had to be to miss the emotions between Eli and Cassidy. Perhaps Dr. Morgan had been right. Perhaps Cassidy was waiting for Eli to sew his wild oats and return to her to settle down.

Perhaps that's exactly what he was doing.

She was the wild oats he was sewing.

She glanced toward him, seeking some reassurance that she wasn't, but caught him staring at Cassidy with something akin to awe.

Another one of those blows to her chest hit, but she forced herself to focus on their patient. A woman was dying, was technically already dead. They all needed to focus. Their patient took precedence over Eli Randolph and his perfect blonde beauty.

"There's no one I'd rather have at my side during a code," Cassidy said to Eli.

La-la-la, Beth chanted in her head, not wanting to eavesdrop on this particular conversation. Not wanting to be in this room. Why had she had to choose nursing as a profession? Surely she could have done something less demanding? Something less likely to put her in a room with the man she was crazy about working alongside his ex-girlfriend?

"You remember that code we worked together during residency at Vanderbilt?"

Beth's ears must have heard her thought because her brain couldn't interpret Eli's muffled reply. Good, she didn't want to know if he remembered spending time during residency with the woman beside him. It was bad enough that she'd had to see that look, that admiration and emotion on his face when he'd looked at his ex.

"All clear," she called, grateful the machine had reset. It seemed to take forever, when actually only a few seconds had passed.

Eli and Cassidy stepped clear of the patient. The woman's body gave a jerk, then nothing. No breath. No pulse. No anything.

They continued to work on the patient, trying to revive the woman, but to no avail. Finally, when all hope was gone and had been for some time, Eli called the code.

"No, Eli, don't do it," Cassidy pleaded, squeezing the air bag to deliver another breath to affirm her position. Her big blue eyes implored him to not stop. "We have to keep trying. For her family's sake."

"She's gone, Cass. There's nothing we can do." His voice was gentle, full of comfort.

His use of the shortened name jolted Beth's heart as surely as the defibrillator had shaken their patient.

Losing a patient always hit Beth hard. She'd only worked a few codes, all of which had left her in emotional turmoil. Currently, she wasn't sure if it was the code or the couple making her feel as if her legs might give out from beneath her.

Once Eli called the code, the intensity in the room faded. All except the intensity of the emotions twirling through Beth's brain and that clung to the air so heavily it weighed her down to where even moving felt impossible.

The recorder placed her hand on Cassidy's arm. "I'm sorry, Dr. Qualls. You did everything you could. You and Dr. Randolph make a good team."

Hello, Beth thought. What was she? Chopped liver? She'd been a part of the code team too. Was she totally invisible or what?

But the recorder was right.

Looking at Eli, how perfectly handsome he was, and at the watery-eyed beauty next to him, Beth had to admit they made a great couple.

They looked so perfect together, so yin and yang. Eli might believe he wouldn't go back to Cassidy, but how could he not go back to her?

"Sorry," Cassidy sniffed, wiping at her face with the side of her hand. "I'm being silly, aren't I?"

Eli gave her a compassionate smile. "I've always said you had too big a heart."

"Yeah, you have always said that." Cassidy's gaze lifted to his and she gave a weak self-derisive smile. "Better hope I don't decide to take up drinking again tonight. You might get another crazy text."

Eli shot a nervous glance toward where Beth was restoring the crash cart. Her job. That's all she was doing. Nothing more. She wasn't eavesdropping. She wasn't feeling like a fifth wheel. She wasn't wondering what kind of crazy text Cassidy had sent him.

"Oops, sorry, Beth," Cassidy apologized, following Eli's gaze. "I forgot you were in here."

Beth didn't say anything. What could she say? Apparently she was chopped liver, totally invisible, and all too quickly forgotten. Or maybe chopped liver wasn't right. Maybe wild oats was a more apt description.

"This guy has a way of making a woman forget a lot of things." Cassidy patted his biceps. "Will you go with me to talk to the family? I could use the moral support."

Beth bit the inside of her lip. Awkward—that's all she could think. This situation was totally awkward and she just wanted out of there.

"You know I will," Eli told her, then his gaze met Beth's and what she saw scared her. His expression was guarded, as if he didn't want her to know his thoughts, his emotions.

If she wasn't careful she was going to have her heart broken.

Beth had sworn that she and Eli were going to talk and not have sex when he arrived at her house that night. So how was it that their food sat untouched somewhere between her front door and her bedroom and they lay naked, breathing hard, in her bed?

Was she just feeling desperate for one last time, one last touch, one last memory because she knew what she had to do? That she needed to walk away before he did?

Lying in his arms, she traced her fingertips over Eli's chest, liking the smoothness of his skin, the slight roughness of hair that grew there, the muscles that rippled just beneath the surface of his skin. Quite simply, she liked everything about him and was addicted to him as surely as if she were a druggie. He was her high, always leaving her needing one more fix, one more kiss, one more touch.

Maybe Emily was right and she just needed to talk to tell him what was running through her mind. Maybe her past hang-ups really did play tricks on her and she was angsting for nothing. Maybe. Maybe not.

Because although Eli had acted just as desperate for her physically, he had been distracted from the moment he'd walked into her house.

"What are we?" She couldn't believe the question had slipped out of her mouth quite so easily.

"We are pretty spectacular." As if to prove his point, he bent and kissed the bend of her elbow, then blew hot breath onto the slightly moist skin.

Her goose-bumps got goose-bumps. But she wasn't going to be sidetracked. Something was definitely on his mind other than her tonight and earlier he'd been all googly-eyed over his ex-girlfriend right after his friend had been encouraging him to go back to her. Was he thinking himself a fool for being with the wrong woman?

"Sexually, yes, we are." She couldn't deny how spectacular they were. "But what are we beyond sex?"

"What do you mean, what are we beyond sex?" He looked genuinely confused. "Don't you know?"

Beth sat up in her bed, fluffed her pillow behind her back and met his gaze head on. "Actually, I don't, but I'd like you to tell me, please, because I'd like to." She hesitated, pulled the covers up over her body, suddenly not wanting him to see her body, not wanting to feel vulnerable to him.

Unfortunately, the sheets were so tangled at their feet that she barely covered her legs, much less anything vital, and, really, her body wasn't what was most vulnerable to the man studying her.

Giving up on the sheets, she crossed her arms over her bare breasts, because, really, how seriously could he take her when her nipples were still all quivery from his touch? "Am I your wild oats?"

"What? Where did that come from?" Eyes wide, he sat up and went from looking semi-amused to shocked.

"You heard me."

"Of course you're not."

"Then what am I?"

"I've told you what you are."

Beth frowned. "When have you told me what I am? Because I pay close attention to every word that leaves your mouth, to everything you do. I don't recall you ever telling me what I am to you."

"Then you've not been paying close enough attention, Beth." He took her hand into his, lifted it to his mouth and pressed a kiss to her palm. "You're mine."

Involuntarily, she shivered then jerked her hand free, because right now was not the time to be reacting physically.

"You're the woman I wake up thinking about, that I think about all day long, that I go to sleep thinking about." He laced their fingers, held her hand firmly within his. "You, Beth. No one else."

She couldn't help herself. "Not Cassidy?" Beth felt his flinch and the effect was like a bucket of ice water dumped over the warmth of his previous words.

"I don't think of Cassidy when you and I are together. Surely you don't believe I could think of anyone but you when we are together?"

When they were together. Was there significance in his repeating that?

"But you do think about her?"

"Yes," he admitted, and Beth's breath gushed from her lungs in a painful whoosh. "But not like you're obviously taking my answer."

"How am I supposed to take your answer when you say that sometimes you think about your ex-girlfriend?"

His jaw worked back and forth as if he was agitated. "The way it was intended."

"Which was?"

"You asked me if I ever think about Cassidy. She was the most important person in my life for the past few years," he pointed out, sounding way too logical. "Of course I think about her. I care about her."

He wasn't denying his feelings for his ex the way Barry had. Eli was flat out admitting that he still cared for Cassidy. Great. She scrambled to get out of the bed. "Maybe you should be in her bed and not in mine."

He grabbed her just as she was standing, wrapped his arms around her waist and pulled her back down to the bed. She scuffled with him, but only half-heartedly because she didn't want to walk away from him. Not really. She also didn't want him to see the tears forming in her eyes so she closed them.

With care not to hurt her, he pushed her back onto the bed, covered her with his body to where Beth couldn't have gone anywhere had she really wanted to.

When long moments passed without him saying anything more, she opened her eyes, met his gaze. His very blue, very intense gaze that was staring straight into her soul, or so it sure seemed.

"You're not paying close enough attention again."

Beth swallowed, knowing he was going to continue without her having to say more.

"Cassidy was the most important person, as in past tense."

Hope welled in Beth's stomach, but she'd been down this road before, had walked that mile, and suffered the road rash to her heart before the kill had come.

Why stick around for the axe to fall?

"She isn't any more. Right now, in the present tense, you are the most important person in my life, Beth. You."

Oh, sweetness. She wanted to believe him, to believe in him, but her doubts ran deep. She'd been burned before and knew better than to play with fire. Eli was fire. "Because of sex?"

He gave a light snort. "Sex with you is amazing, but I think there's more to you and me than just sex. Don't you feel the connection between us?"

Beth closed her eyes, unable to take the intensity of his gaze a moment longer.

"Tell me you feel this." He put her hand on his chest.

His heart beat strongly against her palm. She bit the inside of her lip. Prayed for strength. She opened her eyes and glared. "You're saying all the right things, but the reality is that you're not doing any of the right things."

That seemed to throw him. "I didn't hear you complaining earlier that I wasn't doing the right things."

Of course he'd misunderstood her. She pushed against his chest and he let her dislodge him, rolling to beside her in the bed. Propping the pillow behind his back, he sat up and raked his fingers through his hair.

She scooted up in the bed, too, because she didn't like him towering over her. "Say what you will, but I saw you with Dr. Qualls today."

His brows veed. He raked his fingers through his hair again and shook his head. "This lack of trust in me is really starting to get old."

His voice sounded angry, offended.

"If you're getting back together with your ex-girlfriend I have a right to know."

He took a deep breath then exhaled slowly. When his gaze met hers his eyes were cold, colder than she'd ever seen or thought possible. "If I was getting back together with my ex-girlfriend, I wouldn't be here. You think I'd be in bed with you while considering getting back together with another woman? You really think that little of me?"

He made it sound impossible, but she knew better. Men did get back together with women from their past. Men lied. To her. She knew that first hand. Hadn't she and Barry had a similar conversation once? Near the end? Right before he'd dumped her to go back to his ex? Right after he'd slept with his ex in the bed he'd shared with *her*? Hadn't he accused her of being crazy? That, of course, he still cared about his ex because of their history together, that he wanted them to still be friends, but that he loved Beth now, and she needed to quit overreacting?

Yes, she'd heard all this before.

Except that Eli hadn't professed words of love. Not that those words had mattered to Barry. They hadn't. Wouldn't it be better to end everything now rather than live in constant fear of him leaving?

"Obviously you don't believe anything I say, because I have repeatedly told you that I'm not getting back together with Cassidy."

She wanted to believe him. She wanted to trust that he wouldn't break her heart.

She wanted him to be in love with her and no one else.

Oh, God. She wanted him to be in love with her.

She took a deep breath, met his gaze, and went on the offensive. "What am I supposed to think when you looked so torn when you were looking at her?"

What indeed? Eli wondered, trying to squelch his anger that Beth would think so little of him. "Let's just set the story straight here one last time and I do mean one last time because I am not going to keep rehashing this." He gave her a pointed look. "I'm not getting back together with Cassidy. Ever."

Leaning back against the bed's headboard, Beth seemed to be digesting his words. She closed her eyes, took another deep breath as if she fought hyperventilating and asked, "Do you love her, Eli?"

"Sure I do."

Beth's gasp warned he'd said the wrong thing. Her rapid scoot away from him confirmed his bad move. He was trying to be honest, to tell her everything, but she was as prickly as a porcupine and words were failing him.

"Beth." He grabbed her wrist, pulled her back when she tried to scramble off the bed. "Let me elaborate. I love her, but I am not nor have I ever been in love with Cassidy. I wanted to be, but it just never happened."

"I don't understand." Which was clear by the lost look on her face. "You wanted to be in love with her?"

"Sure I did. She's a wonderful woman who fits perfectly with what I want in a woman and wife someday."

"Oh." She didn't sound thrilled with his explanation, and with the way he was fumbling around with words he couldn't blame her.

"At least I thought she was. I was wrong. We didn't have a physical connection."

"Oh," she repeated, not sounding any happier with his clarification. "I guess that's where I come in."

Eli sighed in frustration. "We're more than just a physical connection, Beth. You know that."

If she did, she ignored him, focusing on his previous comment instead. "If Dr. Qualls fits perfectly what you want in a woman and wife, what does that make me exactly? I'm not sure how to label our relationship."

"You want me to label us?" He scratched his head. Hadn't he been asking himself exactly what Beth was to him since the night they'd first made love? She amazed him, stole his breath, left him wanting more and more. Quite simply, he couldn't get enough of her.

"First, let me clarify, that I thought Cassidy was the

perfect woman for me once upon a time, that on paper I guess she still is, but in reality…"

Beth sat stiffly next to him, staring straight ahead as if afraid to even look at him. "In reality?"

If their conversation wasn't so serious, Eli might laugh at how haughty her expression was, at how she held her body so rigid. When she'd questioned him about Cassidy, he'd gotten just as prickly as she was. He wanted Beth to believe in him unconditionally, and it irked that she had so little faith in him. But none of that changed the truth.

"In reality, she isn't you."

Beth swallowed again, still didn't look at him. "And that matters because?"

"I want you."

"Yes, I know. We have physical sparks." She made her words sound like something dirty. "So you want me until the attraction burns out?"

He supposed, in some ways, what she said was true. That he did want her until the attraction burned out, but he couldn't imagine a time of not wanting her. Not when every touch just left him longing to touch her again, when holding her left him wanting to hold her even closer.

"What if the attraction doesn't wear itself out, Beth? What if it never burns out?"

"Physical attraction always does." She sucked in a deep breath, scooted further away from him, and reached for the tangled sheet at their feet. "So I'm your sex partner until you tire of me?"

Stinging at her confidence that their chemistry would fizzle out, he shrugged. "Or until you tire of me."

Which felt like a much more likely scenario because he couldn't fathom ever getting his fill of her. Yet she seemed convinced that they were doomed from the start.

"So our relationship is solely about sex?"

"You know that isn't true."

"How do I know that? No one at the hospital even knows we've been seeing each other."

"What is it you'd have me to do? Have a T-shirt printed proclaiming that I can't get enough of you? Perhaps I should have two printed so you can wear one as well?"

She glanced at him with narrowed eyes. "Don't be a smart aleck."

"Don't not believe me when I tell you I'm not your ex."

"Don't expect me to believe you when I saw how you looked at your ex, at how perfect you two were together." She took a deep breath and looked him straight in the eyes. "Plus, what did she mean when she said that about drinking and sending you a crazy text?"

There it was. What Eli had been struggling with from the moment Cassidy had mentioned it. He needed to set the story straight with Beth. He needed to tell her the truth about the night he'd first texted her. All evening that thought had distracted him.

"She drank more than she should have and she texted me," he began.

Beth's lips twisted. "What did she text you?"

Eli winced. He hated this, felt as if he was betraying Cassidy by telling what had happened, but making things right with Beth was more important. "She sent me a sext."

Beth gasped. "When?"

"The night I first texted you."

"The night..." Beth's eyes widened, filled with confusion. "Cassidy sexted you and you sexted me?"

"Something like that." Part of him said to leave it at that, not to elaborate, but he didn't want secrets between him and Beth. "I took the photo to send to her."

Beth's lips parted, she shook her head and she scooted away from him, partially hanging off the bed.

"I didn't send it to her, Beth. I was erasing her number and hit another number and send by accident."

"My text was an accident? You hit my number and sent to me by mistake?"

Oh, yeah, Beth was a flight risk and she was ready to take off any moment.

"Your text was the best thing that's ever happened to me."

"I can't believe this. From the beginning, it's all been a lie."

"Nothing has been a lie, Beth."

"Sure it has. You never even meant to text me. I'm a mistake."

He couldn't deny it. "I was a fool not to have noticed you before our texting."

"This is all just sexual."

"It's not."

"Then what is it, Eli? Because that's sure what it feels like from where I'm sitting," she accused. "You're using me for one last fling before settling into your perfect happily-ever-after. Great, y'all go be perfect together."

"I'm not and that's not what I want."

"Right." Her word dripped with acid. "I'm not stupid."

Eli raked his fingers through his hair. "If you really don't believe me, if you really believe she and I are perfect together, then I should leave." He wasn't sure where the claim came from, but when Beth just shrugged her shoulders as if it didn't matter one way or the other if he stayed or went, Eli reached for his pants.

"Go ahead and leave. It's what you're destined to do. Maybe you could sext her on your way home."

"You really should get that chip off your shoulder, Beth. Until you do, you aren't going to trust anyone and that lack of trust is going to make you one lonely woman."

"Ha," she scoffed, covering herself completely with the sheet. "Blame it on me that you're leaving. We both know it was only a matter of time before you went back to Cassidy. I'm just an accident."

Eli put on his shoes and looked around the room. His shirt must be somewhere on the way to the front door. Good. That's where he was headed.

When he reached her bedroom door, he paused. "You're not an accident, Beth. You were fate. My fate. I'm in love with you, but without trust there's really not a reason for me to stay."

The walls shrouding her didn't budge. "I didn't hear anyone ask you to stay."

Wincing, Eli turned, walked away from Beth and didn't look back. Time enough for regrets later.

"He said what?" Emily screeched, smacking her forehead like she could have had a V8.

"You heard me." Because Beth wasn't repeating herself. Not again. She'd been repeating herself over and over in her head and she didn't want to hear the words again. Not in her head. Not in her heart. Certainly, not out loud.

"You need to tell him you're sorry. Beg him to forgive you. Whatever you have to do, just make things right with him."

Beth stared at her best friend, not sure she'd heard her correctly. "Huh?"

"You single-handedly chopped your relationship with Eli to smithereens because you were too scared to believe in it." Emily slapped her hands against the tabletop. "Fix it."

"No."

Emily's drawn-on brows veed deeply. "Why not?"

"Because some things can't be fixed."

"Some things can. Fix this. Before it's too late, make this right."

"What are you so concerned about? There are more men in the sea."

"Seriously?" Emily shook her head with disappointment. "You're sure about that? Because I'm pretty sure where you are concerned, there aren't."

Beth winced. "Don't say that."

"What? That you had your fantasy guy eating out of your hand, literally I might add, and you blew it. He told you he loved you and you shot him down."

Wincing, Beth crossed her arms. "Why are you taking his side?"

"Because he's right. You are so paranoid that he's going to do the same thing Barry did that you pushed him away."

"Hello, it's not as if we've been seeing each other that long. Just a couple of weeks. How could he have loved me? Besides, ultimately, he did do what Barry did, didn't he?"

Gossip had it that Eli and Cassidy were together again. That their working the code together must have ignited old feelings, because they'd been seen together repeatedly. Just like ole times, Beth had overheard one nurse say.

Gag. Just three days after he'd walked out of Beth's house he was already back together with Cassidy. So much for his claims of love.

"Yeah, after you giftwrapped him and sent him back to her. Beth, you've got to deal with what Barry did, let it go, and move on with your life without the past shadowing the present and future. Now. Fix this while there is still hope because of course Eli could really love you. Time doesn't dictate emotion. Love happens. Sometimes immediately. Sometimes gradually." Emily rolled her eyes with great frustration. "How you couldn't realize that when you're madly in love with the man yourself is beyond me."

"I'm not in love with him."

Emily snorted. "Sure you're not."

"I'm not. I…" Beth hesitated, her words tearing at her

heart, but she forced them out all the same. "He was my fantasy guy, Emily. Nothing more."

"Keep telling yourself that if you need to, but I'm not buying it and neither is your heart."

Beth lay in bed, thinking over her conversation with Emily. Had she pushed Eli into Cassidy's arms? Probably. Definitely.

Lord, she missed him.

With the clarity of hindsight she knew pride had gotten in her way, as had the past and fear.

She hadn't wanted him to leave. She'd wanted to beg him to stay, to love her, to stay forever, to somehow convince her that she was the one for him. But she hadn't said any of those things.

Because she hadn't trusted him to stay.

Because she hadn't believed in his feelings for her.

Because she'd known he was going to go back to Cassidy so she'd not let him behind her walls.

Only he had gotten behind her walls all the same.

Her insides ached without him.

Her heart ached without him.

Because she loved him.

He'd said he loved her. She'd let him leave, practically forced him to.

Idiot! she told herself. How could she have just let him walk way when in doing so he'd carried her heart with him?

She picked up her phone, opened it, clicked on the text message icon. She took a deep breath then clicked the screen off button. What could she say? That she'd changed her mind? That she wanted him back? That she loved him and needed him and was lost without him?

Would he believe her?

No, probably not. She needed to show him. To show him those things. To prove to him that she trusted him.

But how?

She knew, of course. The answer was obvious and one she'd sworn she'd never do.

Love made one do a lot of things one thought one would never do.

Like don a naughty red nightie and take a risqué selfie.

Eli smiled weakly at the woman sitting across the restaurant table from him.

"I'll make a deal with you," she offered. "I'll agree to go out with Andrew again if you will call Beth."

"Wouldn't do any good."

"You think she'd say no? It's obvious she misses you. I see how she looks at you at the hospital, how she looks at me. She's crazy about you and hates me with a passion."

Eli had done his best to avoid seeing Beth. Not an easy feat since Nurse Rogers was still assigning his patients to Beth. Fortunately, Beth had a lot of past experience in avoiding him and their paths had barely crossed. "She might say yes, but it doesn't matter. She doesn't trust me and we'd just end up right back at this same place."

He and Cassidy had talked so much the past few days. He'd needed his friend after leaving Beth's house, had gone to her and spilt the truth about everything. She'd listened, scolded him for not being straightforward with her from the beginning, and then told him he needed to win Beth back because he was obviously in love with her.

He loved Beth.

But love without trust was useless.

He wanted what his parents had, what he'd believed he could have with Beth, but she was so scarred from her relationship with Barry that she didn't know how to trust. No relationship could survive without it.

So he needed to teach her how to trust.

Because he was miserable without her.

But how? How did one teach trust? Wasn't it either one of those things that was inherently there or not there?

"You're doing it again," Cassidy pointed out, taking a sip of her wine.

"What's that?"

"Thinking about her."

"I'm always thinking about her."

"So call her."

"I can't. It's going to take more than a call to convince her to let me inside those walls around her heart."

"Then give her more. Woo her. Earn her trust. If she's the woman for you, prove it to her."

Eli stared at his ex-girlfriend then shrugged. "She is the woman for me. I just don't know how to convince her of that."

Cassidy took a sip of her wine then shrugged. "I'd say that's pretty obvious. Earn her trust, Eli."

It hadn't been a good morning in the ICU. A patient had died just before shift change and that had set the tone for the day. Leah had called in sick again and Nurse Rogers hadn't found a replacement. Beth and the other nurses there had pulled heavier than normal loads, but had made it work. Fortunately they'd had a couple of transfers to a step-down unit and things had almost eerily calmed down in the ICU. Beth only had about another thirty minutes left before her shift change and she was ready to call it a day.

Only she wasn't.

Because she'd not done what she'd toyed with doing the previous night and all day. Her phone burned a hole in her pocket even now, reminding her that she'd not sent her peace offering to Eli. Peace offering? No, her message was more a token of trust.

She had the message typed, had the photo attached. All she had to do was hit send and it would leave her phone. But she'd hesitated. What if she'd waited too long, what if she'd pushed him too far away? What if he was happily back with Cassidy? What if he laughed at her message?

Beth finished checking her comatose patient, logged in the information, then paused in the doorway.

Sending a photo of herself was a scary prospect under any circumstances, was risking making a fool of herself, but to send it when she wasn't even seeing the guy any more? That was pure craziness, right? Or a show of the utmost trust in him that she knew he'd never intentionally hurt her, that she knew her photo was safe in his care, that, although she was scared and had messed up, ultimately she did trust him and he just needed to be patient with her because having a man in her life worthy of trust was all new to her.

Love came with risks. But to shove love away for fear of those risks was just stupid and that's what she'd done.

She'd had something special with Eli and she'd ruined the most precious thing she'd even known. She might not be able to save their relationship, might be a fool for what she was about to do, but she was going to take action all the same.

Because she loved Eli and would fight for him.

She would show him that, despite her fears, she did trust him.

Beth hit send and held her breath as her first real sext photo left her phone.

No turning back now.

Eli would know that her photo wasn't meant to be sexual, although it was. He'd know that it was her showing him she trusted him, that she'd give him that power over her heart, and she trusted him to wield that power with gentle hands and a protective spirit.

She'd thrown out her token of trust. The rest was up to him.

Now she'd wait.

Hopefully, not for the rest of her life.

She left the patient room, headed for the nurses' station, paused at what she saw.

Eli stood in the midst of several nurses and even a couple of doctors. It was an odd sight this late in the evening. Cassidy stood near Eli, laughing at something he'd said.

Had she really just sent a naughty photo of herself to him while he stood in the midst of her coworkers? Seriously? Could her timing have been any worse?

Beth's heart squeezed. Part of her felt like running, but she wouldn't.

Not ever again.

She wouldn't run from love.

Instead, she'd embrace it. Or even chase after it if need be.

She loved Eli and, despite how foolish she'd been, she wasn't going to let him make the mistake of ending up with the wrong woman for the rest of his life.

Cassidy might be perfect, but she wasn't perfect for Eli. *She* was the perfect woman for him.

Neither Cassidy nor any other woman could love him the way that she did. How could she have been so foolish not to have realized that?

Beth almost stumbled when Cassidy noticed her and nudged Eli's shoulder, causing him to turn, face her.

Beth's feet quit working and she paused in mid-step, stopping about ten feet from him.

Everyone around him stepped back as Eli stepped forward. "Beth Taylor, there's something I need to say to you."

Oh, Lord, had he been standing around everyone and opened her text? Had everyone seen her vulnerable photo and that's why they all stared at her as if they knew something she didn't?

She couldn't believe he'd do that. She didn't believe he'd done that. Even if he no longer felt the same about her, he wouldn't have shared her photo. That wasn't who he was. She knew that about him.

Warmth spread through her, knocking down the remaining walls around her heart. She trusted Eli. With her heart, her body, her life.

She stood, head high, shoulders straight, and didn't waver from looking into his blue eyes. She loved him, would do whatever it took to prove that to him, to prove to him that although she'd made mistakes, she'd learned from them and wanted to give him everything she was and would ever be.

Turning, he reached behind him, picked up a bouquet of red roses he'd had hidden behind the nurses' station desk. Handing her the flowers, he dropped to his knees and took her free hand in his. "Beth Taylor, this is quite possibly overboard, but after all we've been through, overboard seems the only way to go. Sso…" He paused, took a deep breath. "Will you be my girlfriend?"

Holding the flowers in one hand and the other shaking in his hand, Beth stared at Eli in confusion. "What?"

"I want you to be my girlfriend and for the whole world to know you're mine, that I want to date you and learn everything about you and spend my life with you. Say yes." He squeezed her hand gently, stroking his thumb over her skin. "Although if all that is too much but you're willing to agree to dinner, I'll take you anywhere you'd like to go."

"Eli?" Her forehead wrinkled. "What is this?"

"This is me asking you to be mine in front of our friends and coworkers."

Beth glanced around, caught Emily's eye and her friend

gave her a thumbs-up signal. Nurse Rogers was smiling as if she'd played cupid and Beth and Eli had been recipients of her arrow. Even Cassidy was smiling and nodding her approval.

"Seriously, I didn't expect quite this quick a response to my text."

This time it was Eli who looked confused. On cue, she heard the resounding buzz of his phone receiving a message. Her message. Beth laughed.

He hadn't gotten her text. Not yet. He'd come for her anyway.

Of course he'd come for her anyway.

Even if he had gotten her text prior to her stepping into the hallway, he'd obviously already had this planned. Obviously had missed her as much as she had missed him and had come to set their relationship right.

Tears welled in her eyes and she squeezed his hand. "I love you, Eli. I really, really love you."

His breath caught then he grinned. "I was looking for a yes, but that'll do just fine."

He stood, took her into his arms, and kissed her until they were both breathless and the sound of clapping began to register.

Glancing around at their spectators, Beth blushed. "I wasn't expecting this." She held up the flowers. "Or you."

"I'm like a bad penny, I'm always going to turn up wherever you are."

"More like my lucky penny." She smiled at him, feeling happier than she'd have believed possible just minutes before. "And I hope so, because I need you, Eli."

"The feeling is mutual, Beth." He kissed her cheek. "I've missed you."

"Okay, you two, enough mush is enough mush," Nurse Rogers interrupted. "Beth, it's slowed down and several of the night shift crew have already arrived. Why don't you go ahead, give report and clock out?"

"Thank you," Beth said, hugged Emily, who reminded her not to say or do anything she wouldn't do, and even got surprising congratulations from Cassidy.

Beth gave report, clocked out, then turned back to Eli, realized what he was about to do and grabbed for his phone. "No. Give me that."

But he'd already seen. First shock registered on his face then a smile.

"'Night, folks," was all he said, as he slipped his phone into his pocket, reached for Beth's hand and led her out of the ICU.

The minute they were alone in the elevator, he took the phone out of his pocket and waved it in front of her. "Wow."

She shrugged. "Don't ever say I'm not a girl who doesn't give her guy what he asks for." Her lips twitched. "Just maybe not always in the time frame he wants. Sometimes I'm a little slow to trust, but I do trust you, Eli. More than I ever dreamt I could trust another person."

He hugged her to him, lifting her off her feet and spinning her around the elevator. "For the record, I'm going to ask for a lot, Beth. All your love, all your trust, all you have to give. I want it all."

She arched a brow in question, liking how he'd taken her into his arms and held her close.

"I'm going to ask for you to be mine forever."

Her breath catching, she smiled.

His chest rumbling against hers, he laughed. "You are, you know."

"I know." She hugged him close, barely able to comprehend the enormity of what they were saying. "I'm going to ask for all those things from you, too, you know?"

"They're already yours, Beth. All that I am belongs to you."

Just as she'd typed "YOURS" in all capital letters beneath the photo she'd sent him, she was his, now and forever.

Just as she knew he was hers, now and forever.

* * * * *

MILLS & BOON®

Why shop at millsandboon.co.uk?

Each year, thousands of romance readers find their perfect read at millsandboon.co.uk. That's because we're passionate about bringing you the very best romantic fiction. Here are some of the advantages of shopping at www.millsandboon.co.uk:

* **Get new books first**—you'll be able to buy your favourite books one month before they hit the shops

* **Get exclusive discounts**—you'll also be able to buy our specially created monthly collections, with up to 50% off the RRP

* **Find your favourite authors**—latest news, interviews and new releases for all your favourite authors and series on our website, plus ideas for what to try next

* **Join in**—once you've bought your favourite books, don't forget to register with us to rate, review and join in the discussions

Visit **www.millsandboon.co.uk**
for all this and more today!